para||e||ines

A novel by

Ruth Marks Eglash

Black Rose Writing | Texas

ISBN: 978-1-68513-216-3
PUBLISHED BY BLACK ROSE WRITING
www.blackrosewriting.com

Printed in the United States of America
Suggested Retail Price (SRP) $22.95

Parallel Lines is printed in Garamond Premier Pro

*As a planet-friendly publisher, Black Rose Writing does its best to eliminate unnecessary waste to reduce paper usage and energy costs, while never compromising the reading experience. As a result, the final word count vs. page count may not meet common expectations.

To all young people growing up in adult conflicts.

Jerusalem Light Rail

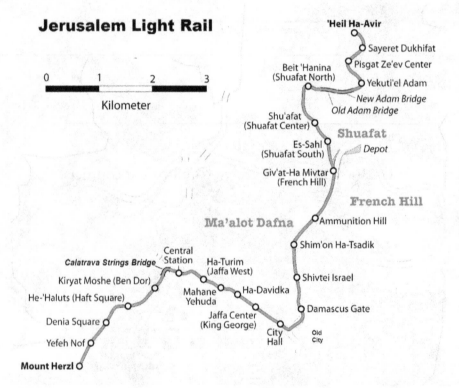

0   1   2   3

Kilometer

'Heil Ha-Avir

Sayeret Dukhifat

Pisgat Ze'ev Center

Beit 'Hanina
(Shuafat North)

Yekuti'el Adam

New Adam Bridge
Old Adam Bridge

Shu'afat
(Shuafat Center)

Shuafat

Depot

Es-Sahl
(Shuafat South)

Giv'at-Ha Mivtar
(French Hill)

French Hill

Ma'alot Dafna

Ammunition Hill

Shim'on Ha-Tsadik

Calatrava Strings Bridge

Central
Station

Ha-Turim
(Jaffa West)

Shivtei Israel

Kiryat Moshe (Ben Dor)

Mahane
Yehuda

Ha-Davidka

He-'Haluts (Haft Square)

Jaffa Center
(King George)

Damascus Gate

Denia Square

City
Hall

Old
City

Yefeh Nof

Mount Herzl

para||e||ines

TAMAR

October 2015

Tamar forced her way through the carriage searching for a place to stand. It was only six stops to her school, but the ride felt rougher in the mornings. Instead of gently easing into the day, she was jerked awake rudely and thrust headfirst into the clash of life. Or at least that's how it felt.

Elbows were sharper and bad manners were not restricted to any one of this holy city's specific tribes. All souls, regardless of their religion, culture, gender, or age, jostled their way inside the light rail's narrow carriages, and everyone was in a rush. Early risers heading to catch the first deals in the *shuk*, empty shopping trolleys in tow, went head-to-head with round-bellied and bearded men in black Borsalino hats. Scruffy laborers in faded blue jeans and tired T-shirts, who would spend their day mixing cement and laying bricks, took up places next to those smartly dressed in slacks or skirts topped with button-down shirts heading to the offices and stores that filled the city center. Backpackers, tourists, and schoolchildren, like her, crowded into an already cramped space.

As unwieldy and unruly as it was, it was also familiar. Tamar made this journey every day, her body moving rhythmically as the light rail shuttled down Sderot Haim Bar-Lev, the tree-lined boulevard that marked a clear border between the eastern and western parts of the city, between ancient stone buildings and modern high-rises. Past playgrounds and museums, history, and life.

Nineties grunge, Nirvana, blocked out much of the chaos as Tamar counted five more stops to school. In a cocoon of sharp guitar chords, Tamar barely noticed the hand that brushed against the small of her back, but then she felt it moving, slowly and downwards, reaching inside her jean shorts.

Rough, coarse skin rubbed against hers as the hand reached beyond the elastic of her underwear. Tamar tried to wriggle free, but her backpack was wedged among the bodies. She twisted and turned some more, finally freeing her bag and moving her shoulders around to greet a pockmarked face framed with dark curly hair. She could smell his minty breath. He grinned at her flirtatiously and winked a dark eye, thrusting his hand further inside her shorts.

A gasp escaped Tamar's lips, but it was not nearly loud enough above the light rail's clattering and chattering. Those not engrossed in conversation with travel companions stared zombielike into their phones, paying no mind to the sudden anguish of a teenage girl. Tamar tried to pull away from him, but her body was penned in by the mass of people.

Suddenly, the train came to a halt, and the doors slid open. Quick as lightning, Tamar stomped on his foot with her combat boot, running through a gap in the shuffling crowd. She bolted through the door, praying she landed on his foot. But didn't stop to find out.

Outside, on the platform, Tamar's head felt like it was being squeezed from all sides, and she fought to let air escape from her chest. She grabbed the low fence separating the pedestrian platform from the road, trying to steady herself, and bent her head towards her knees.

"You okay, miss?" came a gravelly voice. Tamar shrank back. It was an elderly man, shrouded in the black overcoat of the ultra-Orthodox, a dusty hat perched on his head. He scratched a scraggly gray beard with a thick hand. "You look like you're about to faint. Come, sit down, have some water."

Tamar hesitated for a second before allowing him to direct her to a nearby bench. He handed her some water and she accepted it thankfully, putting the bottle up to her lips. She felt the cool liquid flow through her body in smooth waves.

"Would you like me to call for help?" asked the man, straining his neck as if to search for someone.

Tamar shook her head. "No," she said, handing the bottle back to him. Her breath was almost back to normal. "It's okay, I'm okay." Her eyes quickly scanned the space around her. She hoped he hadn't followed her off the train.

"I have to go." Tamar told the man. She was still two stops from her school, but too on edge to wait for the next train. She wasn't sure she could get on it anyway. "*Toda*, thank you."

He nodded at her with kind brown eyes.

As she walked, Tamar tried to empty her mind, but each step brought flashes of a pockmarked face, a twisted grin, a grotesque wink. She could still feel the dirty hands, grime-covered like the pavement beneath her feet, and the dirt began to engulf her, leaving a layer of filth on her skin. Her stomach sloshed and churned.

. . .

Tamar was still shaking when she reached the school gates. Her whole body felt like it was patched together with stringy glue. One touch and she would break. From a distance, she spied her friends in their usual spot on the torn, mismatched couches outside their classroom, but instead of joining them, she turned towards the bathroom.

"Tamar, hey, we're over here. Where are you going?" Tal's wounded voice called after her.

Without turning, Tamar lifted a lead-heavy arm and pointed to the bathroom. Pushing through the white door, she made it to the porcelain bowl just in time to see a mash of bran flakes and milk fly from her mouth.

Outside, holding back her thick curls, she threw her head over the wide sink, turned on the tap, allowing a forceful stream of water to wash over her face. She let some drops enter her mouth. It was warmer than what the ultra-Orthodox man gave her, but it soothed her just the same. Gathering all her remaining strength, Tamar brushed the stray honey-brown hairs from her face and forced herself to go outside, almost crashing headfirst into Aviv and Tal.

"Tamar, *kapara*, what's wrong? Did you just throw up?" Aviv's face was filled with concern. "You want me to call someone?"

Tamar felt a hand on her shoulder and jerked back a step. "N-no, I'm fine."

"What the hell? You can't even say good morning to your friends?" Tal grinned and then turned serious. "Tam, what the... you look awful."

Tamar looked at their familiar faces and felt stinging behind her eyes. Tears threatened to burst through and never stop. Finally, she managed a deep breath, "I, I, I'm fine..."

"But you just threw up and you're super pale. Your eyes are the greenest I've ever seen them," Aviv interrupted her frantically. "Come sit down over here. Maybe she needs a cracker or something?" She ushered Tamar to the couches and pulled an energy bar from her backpack, but Tamar shook her head. The thought of putting anything in her body now made her stomach lurch.

Tamar felt Aviv's warm hand slide onto hers hand and tried to speak. "I did throw up, but I'm not sick... It's just... I was on the train and... There was a man, he... I ..." She searched for the right words. "I, you... promise me you guys won't tell anyone?"

Aviv squeezed her hand. "Go on..." She looked straight into Tamar's eyes. "Tell us... we won't tell anyone. You can trust us."

"Well, he, you know, but you promise, right?" Tamar felt safer now with a friend on either side. She waited a few seconds and then went on, "Well, he, like, he put his hand down my pants." She gulped short bursts of air, expecting tears to come, but her eyes were dry.

"Ichs! Gross!" Tal spat. Tamar felt the weight of his body next to hers. "Probably an Arab, they always do things like that to our girls. Makes me furious. We have to call the police. Can't let him get away with it!"

"No. No police, Tal, you promised..." Tamar's head felt light again.

"Fine," his voice was still hard. "But I bet he was an Arab, right?"

Tamar finally managed a long breath and closed her eyes. She tried to recall the finer details of the man. His skin was dark and so were his eyes, which now took on an evil glare in her mind. Then there was the wink. How could the mere act of closing one eye have made her feel so cheap? She felt the dirt crawl onto her skin again.

But was he an Arab? There were many Jews with this complexion, a combination of dark skin and dark eyes. Tamar couldn't tell. Why didn't she pay more attention? Why didn't she examine him more closely? But in the confusion of the moment, the rush to get as far away as possible, she didn't look hard enough and now she didn't know.

Tamar felt Tal's eyes on her, and she was deflated. Like she'd somehow let him down. "I-I … don't know, his skin was dark, so were his eyes. His hair was black and curly, very curly, but I really don't know what he was..." Tamar's voice trailed off.

"Tal! You sound like a racist!" Aviv's voice was high and piercing. "We don't know that he was Arab, and what does it matter anyway? Some guy rubbed up against me on the light rail the other day. It was an awful feeling, and I don't know and don't care if he was Arab or Jewish or whatever! No man should touch you. Hell, no one should touch you, regardless of his nationality or his religion, without permission. But Tamar, we do need to report this."

Tamar turned to her other friend in surprise. Aviv never mentioned that happening, but then again, her golden locks and wide blue eyes often drew unwanted attention.

"It's not racist, it's a fact," Tal snorted, wrinkling his nose. "I hate the way they look at our girls, especially on the train. They undress them with their eyes. They're the racist ones. Not me! They wouldn't behave like that with their girls. The problem is they don't see Jews as human beings."

"That's quite enough, Tal, I won't stand here and listen to you rant any longer. We need to help Tamar. She just went through a terrible ordeal, and she should be our focus... Tamar—" Aviv put an arm around Tamar's shoulders and this time she did not pull away. "We need to tell someone about this. Shall we call your mom? What about the police?"

"We're not calling anyone," said Tamar, feeling a heavy thud replace the lightness in her head. Her friends' words hung in the air like sparring matadors. "Listen, I just want to forget about it. I'm fine, really. Let's go. We're already late."

• • •

Tamar was still trying to erase the winking guy from her mind when she arrived in the auditorium that afternoon for practice. She had managed for most of the day, ejecting any thoughts of rough, groping hands whenever they appeared in her brain. She hoped that a few hours of singing would help fade the memory even more.

The only problem was Tal. He was still pressing her to go to the police, and each time he brought it up she felt a ball of sickness in her stomach and a film of filth on her skin. She hoped he wouldn't mention it again during band practice and was consoled by the fact that, as the vocalist, she would have her back to him for most of the next hour.

Their group, The Jerusalemites, was an eight-member set formed last year as part of the school's music elective. They would be graded based on their overall performance and how well they worked together. The final grade would then be included in their matriculation results. Tamar loved the power of singing, holding a microphone, and belting a tune. People enjoyed hearing her sing too, or at least that is what she was told, but she was still unsure if she wanted music to be part of her future, certainly not a career choice. Her bandmates, on the other hand, were sure they were destined for fame and fortune, making practice competitive at times.

"I thought we'd practice my new song today." Kobi, the band's resident songwriter, started strumming chords from a battered guitar as soon as everyone was in the auditorium.

"*Yallah*, let's hear it," said Ron, another guitarist, and their self-declared manager.

"We're ready for ya," Tal announced from behind the drum set. Tamar turned around and smiled at him and he grinned easily back. Maybe he decided to drop the whole police thing. They had been in the same class since Tamar started in the school three years prior, but only became close last year when they both joined The Jerusalemites. Over the summer, when Aviv was away with her parents for what seemed like forever, Tamar and Tal hung out almost every day. Now they were closer than ever.

"*Sababa*, cool. Is everything set up?" Kobi called up to the sound engineer and suddenly a voice filled the loudspeakers. "Let's go on three."

"*Sababa*," said Kobi, taking a quick puff of a small purple inhaler and fiddling with his phone. "Just texted you all the lyrics. It's about my brother's friend. He was killed in Gaza last year. We ready?"

As heads nodded and phones pinged, Kobi reached for his guitar and counted to three. He signaled to Leon, poised at the keyboards, to hit the first note. Leon, also in Tamar's class, was probably the most talented of The Jerusalemites, but unlike Tal and the others, he never flaunted his musical prowess. In fact, he barely spoke at all. It was as if the only way he could communicate was through his keyboard.

Leon's fingers tapped the keyboard delicately, sending a jolt of life into the echoing auditorium. Kobi joined in, brown stringy hair flopping down over his face. He nodded sharply, signaling the vocalists to begin. He sang the words with them, guiding them through his poetry.

He wanted to go, thought it'd be fun.
He needed to go. Fun with a gun.
But when he arrived and started to fight.
He saw with his eyes, nothing was right.
Oppression and blood, death, and war.
He didn't want to be there anymore.
Still, they ordered him to fight, eventually die.
In a freshly dug grave, the last place he would lie.

As the final notes ended, there was silence in the auditorium.

"We can't sing this," burst out Ron. He was in the year above Tamar and would start his military service in less than a year. "It's our duty to go into the army. Of course there are risks, people die—it's the army, not summer camp—but why scare people unnecessarily? It's too dark. I don't like it."

"That's not true, Ron," said Kobi dismissively. "We don't have to go to the army if we don't want to. We've all been brainwashed. War is immoral. We can and we should fight back against it. I plan on being a conscientious objector." He pointed to a lone black and white sticker on his guitar. "Make hummus, not war," it read.

Gaya, also from the year above, grinned and nodded, her iron-straight black hair bobbing even after her head stopped shaking. "Maybe if we didn't have an army, we wouldn't be in a perpetual state of war; maybe there would be more chance for peace?"

Tamar didn't realize they were such peaceniks. She'd just assumed that most of her peers felt like Ron, simply accepting that all eighteen-year-old Israelis were drafted into the army. With very few exceptions, it was a natural progression after graduating from high school. Besides, what choice did they have?

Tal suddenly rose from behind the drums and threw down his sticks. "You can't make peace with those Arabs; they want to kill us. They don't want us here; they want to drive us into the sea."

Tamar studied Tal for a second wondering why she never noticed how wide his shoulders were.

"We all need to do the army. There's no choice," his voice cut into her thoughts and suddenly Tamar was hyper-aware of where she was and Tal's words. "The Arabs want us out of here; they want us dead or in the sea. If there was no army, none of us would even be here. Remember Trumpeldor's words? 'It's good to die for your country.'"

There was silence again as each of Tamar's bandmates readied their response. Most people in her school were patriotic, even while they also tried to understand the plight of the Arabs and promote peace—some a little too much. Last year, after a geography trip to East Jerusalem and an emotional meeting with Arab students their age, some of the kids staged a protest. They blocked the entrance to the school with banners decrying the occupation and racism. When a member of the Knesset came to talk to them, they refused to let him pass through the school gates.

Tamar usually stayed far away from politics—she didn't understand much of it—but in that instant, Tal's words filled her soul. What was it he said earlier? *They don't see us as human beings.*

"He's right. Our country needs us," Tamar's voice was shaky at first, but then an image of a winking eye rudely arrived in her head, and she started shaking. "Our enemies are ruthless and many, and this song undermines that. I don't think..."

The last words of her sentence were swallowed by a rush of angry words now flying across the auditorium. Kobi and Gaya chanted peace slogans and lobbed accusations of racism, fascism, and a few other 'isms' at Ron, Tal, and Tamar. Tal and Ron furiously argued back in nationalistic tones. Leon and the others remained silent, dumbstruck at the force of the fight now unfolding around them.

Tamar took a step back and was gripped with an overwhelming urge to flee from the auditorium, just like she did from the light rail train that morning. She looked from Kobi and Gaya's rolling eyes to Ron and Tal's snarling lips. For a brief second, Tamar's eyes locked with Tal's—they were ocean blue—then, without another word, she grabbed her bag and bolted out the door.

NOUR

It was only by accident that Nour noticed the time. She was in the fitting room, trying on a whole new ensemble, when she accidentally tipped the rickety stall where her schoolbag was slung, causing her phone to slide out. Retrieving it with a bony hand, Nour scanned the digital display. It revealed she was late. Very late.

"Damn it," she cursed, shoving the phone back into her bag.

It wasn't her fault, Nour reasoned. There was magic in Mamilla. It flowed all around her like electrical currents. That explained how time escaped whenever she was shopping here. The fairy lights strung up over the street twinkled even during daylight, placing a spell on her. She was blinded by the gold hues cast by the sun, hitting the smooth, wide stones. Even the mannequins, draped in the latest fashions, whispered to her, luring her into store after store. Tops, dresses, pants, bags, hats caught her eye at every turn. There was no way to escape the power here.

"A few more minutes," Nour pleaded with herself in the mirror. "There's time and then I'll run, I promise."

She smoothed down her long black hair and studied herself coyly. The jeans she picked were an unusual chocolate brown. They skimmed her slim hips, making her legs look longer, slender, and the high-collared shirt, set with brightly colored fall leaves of yellow, orange, and matching brown, reached to the middle of her thigh. Exactly how she liked it. She pulled the whole design together with a mustard-colored jacket that nipped at the waist and then flared out stylishly, stopping just a little shorter than the shirt hem.

"Very smart, Miss Asa'ad," Nour mouthed, looking into her dark eyes. She posed for a few more seconds, checking the ensemble from every angle, debating with herself if there really was an excuse to buy all these new clothes. Probably not, she frowned at her reflection. The school year had just started; no big events were coming up. It wasn't even Eid. Besides, nothing was on sale. That made even less sense to buy, but sometimes it delighted her to simply try. It inspired her own designs. Reluctantly, Nour pulled off the ensemble, redressing in the ugly red and white checkered tunic of her school uniform.

"*Shukran*, maybe another time." Nour handed the re-hanged clothes to a scarf-clad shop assistant, admiring the sharp black strokes of kohl around her sparkling green eyes. Maybe she would return before the season was out and buy it. She could use the money she got from tutoring.

For now, though, she needed to hustle. Nour welcomed the cool breeze of the powerful air conditioning wafting out of the shops, as she stepped up her pace in the direction of the Old City. She willed herself not to look into the bewitching shop windows. Break the spell, she told herself. Mama needed her.

Mama asked her to pick up spices from the *suq* and come home as soon as possible after school. She wasn't even supposed to be in Mamilla, let alone trying on new outfits.

. . .

Nour entered the Old City through *Bab el-Khalil* and opted for the most direct route through the Christian and Armenian quarters to Abu's Spice Store. She walked this way a million times past tacky souvenir stores and overpriced falafel and juice stands. This time, though, the primary thoroughfare was packed. She forgot it was the Jewish High Holy Days and the Christian Feast of Tabernacles.

Cursing her own tardiness, Nour stepped off the main passage into one of the side alleyways—it would save time. If she kept walking down the hill, the labyrinth of lanes would deliver her to the Muslim Quarter, somewhere deep in the *suq* and near where she needed to be.

Nour saw the rowdy group of boys before they saw her. Religious Jews with long white tangled strings swinging at their hips, oversized skull caps perched on their heads. Wispy curls of hair snaked down the sides of their faces. She counted six of them. They were talking loudly.

She saw boys like these a million times and tried to have as little to do with them as possible. Usually, it was easy—they didn't want much to do with her either, but just as she was about to pass, she heard one of them shout, "*Aravia.*"

They obviously identified her as an Arab by her school uniform. It was hard not to notice the ugly gingham, though Nour didn't dwell on the point for long, as within seconds, the boys fanned out in a line, blocking her path through the narrow walkway.

"Where d'you think you're going?" came a menacing voice.

The others sniggered. Was she supposed to answer? Nour didn't think so and besides, her words were suddenly stuck, like oversized packages, in her throat.

"Oh, she doesn't speak! Is she mute? Or maybe she doesn't understand Hebrew?" One of the boys moved in close. He stared Nour directly in the eyes. She wondered if he could see her fear or hear the thump, thump of her heart, which threatened to burst out through her ears.

"*Ya sharmuta,*" he suddenly screamed, wet particles splattering across her face, but she made no move to wipe them away. "Bet you understand that." He motioned to the others, and she smelled their sweat as they moved in around her.

"*Lo, bevakasha,*" Nour tried in Hebrew, but her voice was a whisper. "Please, I don't want any trouble."

"Filthy Arabs." She heard a voice behind her. "This is our city. Go back to Saudi Arabia."

"Get out of here, *Aravia zona,*" came another. "*Am Yisrael Chai*, the nation of Israel lives!"

Nour closed her eyes and began mumbling all the words she could remember from the prayer for protection under her breath.

She heard someone spit on the ground. Then suddenly clammy hands, fleshy and thick, grabbed around the front of her neck, forcing Nour to cry out in a splutter. The fingers pushed in tighter, deeper, threatening to stop any air from getting in or getting out. She willed herself to fight back, but when she tried to move her arms, they were frozen at her sides. Instead, Nour focused on keeping her legs strong and stopping the blackness from taking over her mind.

. . .

Nour heard a different voice. Loud and deep, it came booming down the lane. "Leave her alone, get out of here, filthy scum, pussies, what are you doing? Fighting a girl! Come here and fight me."

It took her a few seconds to realize the fat hands were no longer there and then, unwittingly, she drew a rush of air into her crying lungs. Daringly, she opened her eyes to see the Jewish boys scuttling away, turning the corner in the same direction they came from.

"She started it, dirty *Aravia, sharmuta*..." one of the boys turned and shouted before disappearing.

Then she heard the voice again. It was strong and powerful, accompanied by heavy, booted footsteps. "Hey! Cowards! Come back here. I'll get you. You can run, but you can't hide from me. We've got cameras everywhere!"

Nour turned to see who the voice belonged to and froze again when she saw it was an Israeli soldier, dressed in the deep green uniform she knew only to fear. Still shaking from the assault, Nour felt her knees buckle slightly, and she shrank back against the wall as he swept by her.

"*Shu ismekk?*" came another voice, this one was softer and speaking in Arabic. "What's your name?"

Nour turned again. Another soldier, but this time, inside the rough green fatigues, was a female. She didn't look much older than Nour herself.

"Nour Asa'ad," the words scratched at her throat, and she cast her gaze downwards, examining her now scuffed shoes. A soldier was a soldier. It didn't matter that it was a she.

"*Shvi*, sit, take some water, Nour," the soldier said slowly, reverting to Hebrew and gesturing to a low wall nearby. "Do you speak Hebrew?"

Nour nodded, her head still bent. Yes, she spoke Hebrew, but no, she didn't want to sit, and she didn't want water. She wouldn't take anything from a soldier. But the soldier insisted, holding out her army-issued water bottle. Nour took it reluctantly, taking short sips that stung each time she swallowed. Stiffly, she handed the bottle back to the soldier and wiped her mouth with the back of her hand, feeling tainted.

"Shapira, come in. Did you get them? Copy." The soldier cocked her head as she spoke into a small receiver hanging from the loops on the shoulder of her uniform. The device crackled for a few seconds before the same voice Nour heard previously, heavy and out-of-breath it filled the static. "Not yet, but I know who they are. I've seen them before. They're real troublemakers, copy."

"Good. Remember the cameras, we'll find them. Out." The girl soldier pressed the button on the radio again and this time a different voice answered. "Read, Golan, listening."

"Copy, in pursuit of six *dosim*, real troublemakers. Me and Shapira saw them trying to strangle an *Aravia*," the soldier told the voice on the other end. "It was in the Christian Quarter, near the Latin Church, but they're coming your way. Over."

"Control, Golan here, you sure? Sure, the Arab girl is not a *mehabelet*—,"

The girl soldier cut him off. "She doesn't look like a terrorist, and it certainly seemed like they were attacking her. Shapira will get them. He'll bring them to you... you just might need to provide some backup. Out."

Nour lifted her head slightly, studying the soldier from the corner of her eye. She'd seen female soldiers before. Sometimes they were even more heartless than the men, but this one seemed different. Her eyes were a soft brown, her skin a dark olive, much darker than Nour's own. She could be an Arab, thought Nour, if not for the green helmet that crowned her head and the garb. Even in the ugly uniform, though, this soldier was attractive. Nour supposed Israeli soldiers were allowed to be pretty, but it didn't excuse the ugliness of their behavior.

At least she appeared to have understood what happened—that Nour was only walking by when the Jewish boys started with her and only because she was Arab, Palestinian. What of the commander, or whoever it was who answered the radio? He thought she was a terrorist! The pounding around Nour's neck threatened to explode through her entire body.

The soldiers were stationed in the Old City to maintain law and order, but Nour didn't think their mandate extended to her. Palestinians had few rights in *al-Quds* and were arrested or humiliated for less. She saw it happen many times—soldiers stopping and harassing her people, forcing them to stand for hours on the side of the road, taking their ID cards, and their phones for no good reason.

"I was only walking, on my way to the *suq*—" Nour tried to clarify that she was the victim, but she was cut off in mid-sentence as the radio crackled to life again.

"Come in. I've got two of them. I'm taking them in now, over."

The girl soldier reached for the walkie-talkie, bringing the metal receiver up to her lips. "Nice going, Shapira. Take them to headquarters. We'll find the rest later. Copy."

"What about the *Aravia*? Over." The voice on the other end asked.

"I'm talking to her now. Out." She gave Nour a small smile.

"Sure, you're okay?" The soldier turned to Nour again, clipping the radio to her belt. "You look pale and you're shaking. Those shits. We saw what they did to you, don't worry. Maybe you should see a doctor? Do you want me to call someone to take you to the hospital?"

Nour shook her head slowly, although her throat still screamed. Why was this soldier being so kind? Maybe it was a trick to get her to confess. She felt eyes studying her and realized she needed to answer.

"*Ani beseder*," Nour responded shakily in Hebrew. All she wanted was to get away from there. Far away. She didn't care how nice this soldier was being to her. "I'm fine, I-I-I need to go home," she added decisively.

"Well, let me walk with you, make sure you're alright," the soldier replied immediately.

Nour was about to protest. How would it look for her to be walking with a soldier? But then, she certainly didn't want to bump into those Jewish boys again and didn't trust the crackly voice of the commander to not free her attackers. This girl was a soldier, but she was still the lesser of two evils.

"Do you live in the Old City?" the soldier asked in an easy tone, as if they just met at a party.

"N... no... Shuafat, the neighborhood," Nour answered. The words came out stiffly.

"I know it. I was there two summers ago when there were riots after that... Arab boy was murdered." She mumbled the last part.

Nour nodded. She knew the boy; his name was Muhammad. He had been her neighbor. The steps where the three Jewish extremists grabbed him from were right by her house. She had passed them a million times. She shivered picturing Muhammad's doe eyes and soft face—he was only sixteen, the age she was now, when those Jewish men drove him to the forest, covered him in gasoline, and set him on fire. He was still alive as the flames licked his body and consumed him. Every time she thought about what happened that summer, Nour tasted the bitterness of burned ash.

After the murder, all the boys, and some men in her neighborhood, took to the streets to protest. The police told them to go home, but that made people even angrier. The police tried to disperse the crowds and then there were clashes. People were so upset; they smashed the light rail stop near her house with hammers and set it on fire. The stop used to have a digital screen with details of the next train, but they broke that too. It still wasn't fixed a whole year later.

She really shouldn't be walking with an Israeli soldier. What was she thinking? Mama and Baba would be nervous that she was even speaking to one. Her friends would be outraged, and her brother, Abdulrahman, would be even worse. Muhammad's murder incensed him. Her other brothers were too young to understand what was going on, but Abdulrahman went out and joined the protestors. He nearly got arrested. Now, since starting university, he was even more hot-headed about the occupation. He was angry all the time and said awful things about Jews.

"They're not all bad," she heard Baba reasoning with him. "You need to learn to judge people for who they are, not what they are, and don't be fooled by outer appearances. It's the inner light that counts."

Nour liked Baba's words. She felt the same way, observing how, inside every community, every tribe, there were good and bad people. Sometimes it wasn't immediately obvious. Sometimes it was.

She decided that was how she would view this girl soldier.

"Where do you live?" Nour asked her new companion, decompressing her lungs and finally releasing her shoulders.

"I'm from Tel Aviv, but I've lived in Jerusalem for the past few years. I miss seeing the sea every morning, even though there is something very special about Jerusalem." The soldier turned to her and smiled. "I think this is where you wanted to go. Nice meeting you, Nour Asa'ad."

Nour looked at the soldier and tried to reach into her heart for words to thank her. Then she felt guilty. Could she say "thank you" to an occupation soldier? Instead, she just gave her an awkward smile before turning into the market.

RIVKI

It was mid-afternoon by the time Rivki left the hospital with her mother. Heat, like blasts from a hairdryer, greeted her as she passed through the great glass doors and began trudging up the hill toward the light rail stop. She trailed her mother's determined strides and tried to shrug off the sun's unforgiving rays as they beat on her back.

Small beads of sweat trickled down slyly behind the high neck of her polyester blouse and wet patches began forming under her arms, as her skin tried to breathe beneath long sleeves that clung to her skinny wrists. Rivki's legs were also covered and, in the intense heat, her nylon stockings, despite being the thinnest she could find, started to itch. All she wanted to do was stop and scratch, scratch, scratch. She hated being in the sun for too long. She also hated that every inch of her body, bar face, and hands, was completely covered up.

Suddenly, Rivki was overcome with the urge to rip it all off. Peel back the layers. Discard every excess piece of clothing. Expose her skin in a vain attempt to find some cool air. She imagined standing naked, under cold flowing water. She needed a break from the heat. From the sun. From her life. From this sickness that kept pulling her back to the hospital week after week. Everything was dragging her down. Or that's how it felt.

"Do you mind walking a little faster, Rivka? We're very late." Her mother's voice was soft, but tinged with impatience. She stopped a few meters ahead and turned, beckoning her with a thick hand. They must be really late because her mother had used her full name—Rivka.

Her Ima didn't own a phone and wore no watch to check the time, but Rivki had noticed the clock above the hospital reception area before they left, which read 3:33 p.m. She always paid attention to freaky numbers like that. Now, she guessed it was a little past 4 p.m. Dovi and Shimshon finished school in less than an hour and they still needed to collect Batsheva from Mrs. Cohen, the neighbor who watched her little sister on hospital days.

Rivki tried to quicken her pace, pulling up briefly alongside her mother, before the older woman snapped around and marched on. Rivki sighed, chasing after Ima's hefty frame. She moved surprisingly fast for such a large woman. Couldn't she slow down, just a little? Didn't she know it was hard for her to keep up after a day in the hospital? That she was exhausted? But instead of chiding her mother or trying to reason with her, Rivki called out in a dutiful voice, "Don't worry, Ima, I'll help you with everything when we get home."

She was forgiving of her mother's toughness. Taking Rivki to the hospital once a week was a strain on all of them, but especially for Ima. She already had so much to do. Batsheva was still only a baby, really, and her brothers, though not so young anymore, were rowdy and immature. Spending a day at the hospital with Rivki was an extra chore that Ima didn't need.

Rivki knew she burdened the entire family by being sick, though no one ever said it. She started feeling unwell months ago, before the *Yamim Tovim*, before school ended for the summer even. True, she was better these days, but the doctor still insisted she visit him once a week. Have her vitals checked, make sure the diseased tissue in her body hadn't grown or spread, like the tendrils of a noxious weed.

Once a week didn't sound like a lot, but the days she needed to be in the hospital upset everyone's routine, including her own. She was forced to miss school and Ima was taken away from her duties at home. And although Rivki wanted to help Ima as much as she could when they returned after a long day in the hospital, all she wanted to do was curl up in her bed and sleep.

· · ·

As they reached the light rail stop, Ima pulled her under the metal shade. "It'll be cooler here," she informed Rivki, dabbing her forehead and the back of her neck with a tattered tissue. "It's hard to believe it's almost *Cheshvan*, it's still so hot out. Sorry for rushing, but we're going to be so very late, and Mrs. Cohen asked me to pick Batsheva up a little earlier today." Ima wrinkled her nose. "Are you okay, Rivkale?"

"*Baruch Ha-Shem*, thank G-d, better now I'm out of the sun." Rivki breathed, though she felt anything but better. It *was* hot, considering it was October. She forced herself closer under the shade, her heart beating as her rising body temperature threatened to fry her brain. The sizzling metal tracks, two straight, parallel lines glimmering in the scorching sun, seemed as impatient as she was to greet the train.

"Is Mordechai coming tonight?" she asked Ima, trying to think about something other than the heat.

Ima nodded stiffly, her lips spreading into a tight frown. "He always comes on Tuesdays, doesn't he?"

Rivki knew Ima disapproved of her daughter-in-law leaving her son dinnerless one night a week. She didn't even like it that Zehava went out to work for just a few hours every day. Ima believed women were chosen to guide their husbands and children and serve as central pillars in their families while remaining elusive to the outside world.

"Women are like crown jewels. They're not meant to be put on display in store windows," Rivki heard Ima complaining to Abba one night. "And what sort of wife leaves a husband alone, so he's forced to return to his mother for food?"

Abba nodded in sympathy with his wife. "That's true, Goldie, but unfortunately, now that today's students of Torah can no longer afford to live without an income, their wives must support them. It's not like when we started out. Apartments cost much more these days and the government no longer helps young people undertake G-d's work. My students receive a pittance, barely enough to put food on the table."

A teacher at the nearby Kollel, Abba knew firsthand what went on with young married men dedicated to Torah study. He saw his students struggling financially and stressing over their futures. It was his job to make sure they did not drop out, and that they stayed focused on learning G-d's teachings without worry.

"There's no choice these days but for women to go out to work, in honorable jobs, of course, until they start a family," he said, patting Ima's shoulder affectionately. "At least we get to see Mordechai once a week. We shouldn't complain."

Ima grudgingly agreed. She enjoyed it when Mordechai came home, proud as she was of her *ben ha-cham*. The same was not true of Yosef, Rivki's other older brother. A year younger than Mordechai, his visits were rarer because he lived outside Jerusalem, where rents were cheaper. He and his wife, Ruthy, returned only on special occasions.

"What are you making for dinner?" Rivki studied the weathered lines on Ima's face. She wondered if each groove represented one of her seven children and tried to discern if one line was deeper than the others.

"I've already prepared some beef stew with potatoes and barley, but we'll need to stop at the store for some bread," Ima informed her, tapping a worn black shoe on the scalding sidewalk. "I hope you'll have an appetite tonight, Rivkale. The doctor said we need to work on rebuilding your strength."

Rivki wasn't sure she could eat. Her taste for food vanished the day she got sick and was yet to return, but she nodded and smiled weakly at her mother. She liked being alone with Ima, where they could talk even about the simplest of matters without interruption from her siblings.

A family like theirs—an Ima, an Abba, seven children, plus those who joined via marriage—wasn't unusual in Ma'alot Dafna, the tightly woven community where they lived in Jerusalem. The neighborhood's towering apartment blocks were packed so tightly together, Rivki saw them as a metaphor for the oversized and multiple families that filled them.

Compared with other families, they weren't even that many. There were bigger broods in Ma'alot Dafna. Much bigger ones. Sometimes, Rivki imagined what it would be like to have ten, twelve, fourteen, even sixteen siblings. She also wondered what it would be like to just have one or two. Or none at all. To have an adoring Ima and doting Abba to shine a spotlight just on her.

Her family might be one of the smaller ones, but sometimes, in their tiny apartment, Rivki wished for solitude—a place of her own that was peaceful and calm and quiet. Though she told no one she felt that way. Not even Esti.

Three years her senior, Esti was her best friend and confidant. Their bond formed, not only in waking hours but also while asleep in the bed they shared under star stickers that they proudly hung on the ceiling so long ago that Rivki barely remembered doing it. Under the glow of those artificial stars, the sisters whispered to each other late into the night, the dark like a force field around their secret words. They told each other everything— almost.

· · ·

It felt like hours before the train finally arrived and even as Rivki settled herself beside Ima, the snakelike carriages appeared to be moving at a much slower pace than usual. Why did the world always slow down when one was in a rush?

Crossing over the Bridge of Strings, its white chords majestically reaching up to the cloudless blue sky, Rivki held her breath for the buzzing life of the city's center. It was so different from Ma'alot Dafna and she loved the way different groups of people morphed from the modestly dressed ultra-Orthodox, heads and torsos fastidiously covered, to the secular, *freiers*, their bare arms popping out from tank tops, their legs sprouting from under miniskirts.

She was no longer shocked seeing the abundance of bare skin on display or by the physical closeness between men and women. Rather, it evoked a surreptitious fascination with an unexplored world that held the secrets of possibility far beyond her own life.

The first time they traveled to the hospital, Ima explained to her that even men, sans hats and beards, were Jews too. Jews, but sinners who had grown up with no proper knowledge.

"The Talmud calls them *tinokot shenishbu,* or babies who were held captive by non-Jews and therefore they could not have a Torah education," Ima informed her matter-of-factly. "They're sinners, but they still belong to us."

Rivki thought she heard a teacher discussing the term once at school. It sounded like an odd concept to her, and she imagined the *freiers* she saw as babies, separated from their parents, lost, and crying, until a stranger, a *goy*, found them and held them captive so they forgot all about their Jewish roots. She almost felt sorry for these *tinokot*.

She thought about that conversation, trying to remember who initiated it, her or Ima, nervous about her daughter being exposed to this new and dangerous world. Rivki knew she'd asked Ima about the Arabs, who dressed more like her people.

"They're *goyim*," Ima told her resolutely. "They believe in G-d, but call him *Allah*. There's no connection between us and them. They've lost their way from Him, too."

Now, as the light rail trudged along Jaffa Road, Rivki subtly shifted her eyes, drinking in the bustling thoroughfare that brought these tribes together like the twisted threads of a colorful tapestry—smatterings of her own people passed through the throngs of *freiers* that Ima so clearly disdained and past the Arabs she flippantly dismissed.

Rivki knew she was supposed to let this other world glide by her like a fuzzy dream, but she loved studying the people. She also enjoyed looking in the shop windows, seeing form-fitting blue jeans, a material she never even touched, and admiring the pretty dresses with their delicate flowers.

Immediately, she felt guilty for giving attention to such frivolity, especially because Ima sat beside her, muttering *Tehillim* from a worn-out prayer book. It was something Rivki was warned against, not only by Ima but by the rabbis, too. They said venturing into the outside world too often was dangerous, as it heightened the risk of being corrupted, becoming immodest. But Rivki couldn't help looking, studying, drinking in the views from Jaffa Road and Ben-Yehuda Street, from the Zion Square and Kikar Safra, all the while fighting the urge to go out and join this exciting world.

She wondered if she wasn't already corrupted with bad thoughts creeping into her head like tiptoeing shadows. It wasn't just about milling around the center of the city or even ripping off her clothes on hot, sweltering days. On these hospital days, she also imagined what it would be like to try on a pair of jeans, her knobby knees poking through rugged tears, or to wear a sweet summer dress that would allow the air to kiss her bare legs.

Then she worried G-d would punish her for thinking this way. Maybe he already had. Maybe that was why she got sick.

. . .

That night, after Mordechai ate, then left for evening study, as the rest of the house fell silent, Rivki raised the issue of G-d's punishment with Esti. They were lying side by side in matching nightshirts, leggings keeping them modest from ankle to waist. A single beam of moonlight shone through the window, lighting the plastic stars that glowed above their heads.

"Of course not! He's not punishing you." Esti turned to face her younger sister. Her rosy lips were just about visible in the dusky light.

But Rivki persisted. "Maybe I should close my eyes on the light rail? Maybe that's why Ima buries her nose in a book of prayers, to block out the secular world?"

Esti was patient. She always was. "We're true believers, Rivi, but we have to accept that there's a whole world around us that is not. We can't shut ourselves off from it completely, even though I'm sure Ima would like us to. I plan to work once I get married, and I'll have to talk to people who are different from us, so it's important we recognize they exist," she said.

Rivki studied her sister's outline. "Where did you find those ideas?"

"Abba," Esti responded without hesitation. "He asked me what I planned to do once I got married. He understands the reality of life. He's seen too many students struggling to support their families. He knows *Ha-Shem* doesn't want His people to live that way."

"What will you do?" Rivki was genuinely curious now. She knew a wedding for her sister would happen soon. There were already whisperings of matches and dating.

"I'm going to work with computers, in an office," Esti answered her proudly. "I'll wear a nice suit and a *sheitel* like Zehava does."

"And what about your husband? Aren't you worried... I mean about who it will be... who you'll marry?" Rivki's heart pumped in time with her words.

"Of course! It's so scary! What if he thinks I'm ugly or fat? Or worse, what if he's ugly?" Esti asked, stifling a giggle.

"Esti," Rivki's next question felt like a tidal wave that she could not stop. "And what about me? Will I.... I mean... my sickness? Will it hurt your prospects?"

"Rivi, Rivkale, what are you talking about? What you have is not life-threatening, and the medication seems to be helping. Besides, Ima already said there are some good, smart suitors lined up for me, so either they'll understand, or they won't. Whatever is meant to be will be. It's in His hands." Esti stroked Rivki's shoulder with a comforting hand.

Rivki searched inside her head for a smart way to respond, but the day, her thoughts, the conversation suddenly threatened to swallow her up.

"Yes," she answered forlornly. "You're right, Esti. *Layla tov.*"

TAMAR

Tamar stood beside the school gates for a few seconds, the fresh air tickling her shoulders, and she wished she'd brought a jacket or something to cover up. The thought of cramming herself inside the train again with all those strangers made her stomach flip. What if she saw him, the winking guy, again? She wasn't sure if her legs would even agree to carry her to the train stop.

Then she remembered that her dad sometimes held work meetings in the city center, or maybe he was already on his way home and could swing by and pick her up. She checked her phone; it was only 5 p.m., but worth a try. She hit his number.

"Dad, where are you? Not in town, by any chance?"

"Hey, princess, how was your day? Mine was fine, thank you so much for asking."

"Sorry, Dad." Tamar felt equal measures of fear and guilt rising in her, but then added begrudgingly, "How are you? How was your day?"

"I'm fine, Tamari. The day is splendid." He deliberately stretched out the word splendid. "I'm afraid I'm in Tel Aviv today, honey. I won't be back until late. What do you need?"

"Oh." She sighed, fear gripping her again. "Nothing. It's fine."

"What's wrong, Tamar? A bad grade? A fight with Aviv?" he teased. "What teenage dramas do you have going on today?"

"No, no fights. We're all good. I'm just not feeling so good and thought you might pick me up, but never mind. I'll jump on the light rail." She bit her lip as she said goodbye.

Walking to the light rail stop, Tamar scanned her phone, clicking on a message from Aviv: *Still think maybe you shld tell someone what happened to U. What about ur parents or Dori?*

Tamar sighed. How could she tell them? Even just asking her dad for a ride home, he thought she was being a drama queen. And her mom, well, she might just blame Tamar for what happened. She was always complaining about the way she dressed, saying her shorts were too short, telling her to cover up while she was "gallivanting around Jerusalem."

"It is a holy city, after all, and there are so many people that don't like seeing young girls walking around half-undressed," Tamar's mom had chided her more than once. No, she couldn't tell her parents about those rough hands touching her on the train.

She could call Dori, but what use would that be? Her sister was busy living a bohemian life in Tel Aviv. She didn't have time for Tamar's complaints about someone touching her. Besides, she wasn't sure she could find the words to tell her what had happened. No. All she wanted was to be at home, curled up in her bed, watching *Grey's Anatomy* or stupid, mind-numbing clips on YouTube.

Reaching Jaffa Road, the beating heart of the modern city, Tamar eyed the people milling along the bustling thoroughfare. If she was to cross paths again with him, it would likely be here. She was so busy scanning the crowds for curly hair; she jumped when a large hand landed on her shoulder.

"Don't touch me." Tamar spun round, sure it was him.

"What? Tamar! It's me," exclaimed a tall, slender boy with dark spiked hair and smooth caramel skin. Tamar took a few seconds to register the familiar face. It was Ami, a boy from her class.

"You on your way home?" He looked at her unsure, confusion hovering in his eyes. "I thought we could ride together?"

"Oh, erm, sure," said Tamar, feeling a flood of relief.

Ami was one of the few people who lived in the same direction as her on the light rail. Not in her neighborhood, French Hill, but a few stops beyond. Sometimes they ran into each other in the morning and would walk the short distance from the light rail stop to school together.

"Great. How was your day?" He fell into step beside her.

"Fine, but I had to escape from the auditorium just now because a big fight broke out about doing army service," said Tamar, misery still swirling inside her over what felt like one of the worst days of her life. "We're supposed to be making music, but there was nothing harmonious about what happened just now. How can so few people have so many different opinions?"

Ami laughed, his entire face becoming one big infectious grin before turning serious. "Guess going to the army makes people nervous." He shrugged. "I don't have to do it, but I'm thinking of volunteering anyway. It's supposed to be the people's army, isn't it? So, I think everyone who lives here should be represented in some format."

It was then Tamar remembered Ami was an Arab. He didn't have to serve in the army. Lucky him. But she wondered if that put him in the enemy or friend category that her friends found so easy to define. She didn't know. All she could hear was Tal's voice— "They don't see us as human beings." Who were the "they" he was referring to? The winking guy, if he really was an Arab? Israel's enemies, those who wanted to destroy the Jewish state? Ami?

Ami's real name was Amin, but no one called him that. They had been together in elementary school too, and she didn't remember anyone making a big deal about him not being Jewish back then. He certainly didn't seem to care, dressing up for Purim or celebrating other Jewish holidays with them. Physically, he blended in too. From the way he dressed to how he spoke, you wouldn't know that he was any different. But did he really fit?

They were on the train now and sat down together on a double seat. Tamar's stomach felt slick with sickness. She glanced around the long carriage, studying the other passengers to make sure there was no pockmarked face. She let out a sigh, relieved that Ami was with her.

"Hey, Tamar, I like hanging out... with you," Ami broke into her thoughts. "Maybe we could meet up sometime... you know... properly?"

Tamar pulled her head to the side and considered him. Her stomach fluttered again, but this time in a good way. Was Ami asking for a *keta*? Was this how a relationship started? She liked the way his eyes glistened slightly in the receding sunlight, and how his whole face crinkled into a smile. But he was an Arab, one she knew almost her whole life, but still an Arab. Like the winking guy. Maybe. Did she want a *keta* with him? She turned away from him, searching for the right answer.

"I'd better go." She stood, noticing they were at Givat Hamivtar, her stop. Then, gripped by a bolt of boldness, she added, "Sure, text me if you like."

NOUR

Nour made up some excuses about staying late at school to help her teacher decorate the classroom, and Mama did not question her. She was just happy to receive the small plastic bags filled with spices. She undid each knot carefully, unleashing rich aromas into her already fragrant kitchen.

"Well, *habibti*, thank you for going," Mama said gently. She was so concentrated on her food preparation that she didn't notice Nour's flushed face or the receding red blotches decorating her throat.

"Happy I could help," said Nour. The throbbing around her neck was fainter now, and the familiar spicy zest that filled her nostrils made her feel safe. She watched, mesmerized, as Mama stirred her steaming pots, her frizzy black locks springing out wildly in all directions. Mama was an enchanter casting magical spells on their food.

People said Nour looked exactly like Mama. They shared the same ebony eyes, but Nour spent hours taming her own thick mane with a mix of sprays and flat irons, forcing it to hang sleekly down her back. She was still undecided if she wanted to cover her head with a hijab like Mama did when she went out, and was grateful that her parents did not pressure her like some of her friends' parents did. Mama said the hijab was a personal choice and maybe when she was older and wiser, she would change her mind and embrace the tradition.

"Go freshen up now, *binti*. The food will be ready in about thirty minutes," said Mama, finally looking up at her with dark, bewitching eyes.

In her bedroom, Nour locked the door before carefully peeling back the collar on her tunic. She fingered the ugly marks on either side of her throat. They were already turning purple, and it hurt to swallow. Gently, she lathered her neck in skin-colored concealer and searched her neatly folded closet for something to cover it all up.

She would not tell her parents what had happened because they would certainly overreact. She hated upsetting or worrying them unnecessarily. She was fine now. She was alive, and she didn't want to explain what she was doing in the Christian Quarter, either. That would mean coming clean about her trips to Mamilla, which she undertook a little more than she should.

Her parents, especially Baba, thought going to the mall—when she should be studying or helping others study—was a frivolous waste of her time. He didn't understand that her visits were more than just browsing or buying something new to wear. Being in the stores, among the racks of clothing, smelling their newness, sizing up their fabrics, examining textures, colors, and craftsmanship, made her happy. It inspired her and provided an escape.

Not that her life was heavy on stress, but studying both the Palestinian curriculum and the Israeli one meant reams of schoolwork and double exams. On top of that, as the only daughter, she needed to help Mama around the house and constantly supervise her brothers. If there was time to spare, she usually ended up tutoring her neighbor's children in math and English. Going to Mamilla helped her let off steam. Nour read somewhere about retail therapy. It was a concept that made complete sense to her.

Downstairs, Nour helped Mama lay the table and set out the food for Baba and the boys. Abdulrahman would not be home in time, so there was no need to lay a place for him, Mama said. He seemed to stay later and later at school these days, Nour noticed, blaming the odious Qalandia checkpoint for his late return.

"Ya Nouri, how was your day? Any word on the biology test?" Baba asked, as soon as they were seated around the big table, with Mama's magical delights presented like prizes on delicate china dishes.

"No results yet, Baba. We only took the test yesterday." Nour fingered her throat unwittingly, glad for once that her father was so obsessed with her education. "There's so much going on. We have a test in Hebrew and a paper due in Arabic literature."

"Well, I am proud of you, Nouri." Baba beamed at her. "I know it seems like hard work, taking both sets of exams, but it will give you more options in the future... *Tawjihi* is your entry ticket into Arab schools, and with the *Bagrut*, you can study at an Israeli university if you want to. Who knows? Maybe you'll end up going to Hebrew University like me. Maybe you'll even become a pharmacist, like your Baba?"

Nour nodded stiffly, lips zipped. She heard this from Baba a million times and, each time he said it, she felt like her own dreams were being trampled on. Each time, she avoided his big yellow-brown expectant eyes, afraid of extinguishing their light with her counter aspirations.

When Abdulrahman said he wanted to study engineering, the angry voices and door slamming went on for days. Nour didn't have the heart to tell Baba that she also had no intention of studying pharmacy—or anything to do with science—for that matter. Her heart was set on studying fashion and design.

She tried to talk to him before about becoming a fashion designer, but he dismissed her with a flick of his hand. "It's not a distinguished career, Nouri, you know that. Being a pharmacist is much more respectable."

"But, Baba, my teacher says I have a tal..." Nour started, trying desperately to make him see she was an artist, a creator, a designer. She was holding one of the small embroidered dresses she'd sewn. It was black with a line of red *tatreez* decorating its center.

But he refused to look at her or listen to even one word, his usually level voice rising in tone. "Enough nonsense, Nouri. Do you want to be like Setty, living in a tiny shack on a hillside, sewing all day?"

Nour glanced uneasily at Mama. Setty was her mother. It was true that her grandmother's house was small and her village, in a deep echoing valley at the end of a winding, bumpy road, seemed forgotten by the world, but Setty's dressmaking skills inspired her. Setty could effortlessly convert scraps of material into art, her tiny *tatreez* cross-stitching capturing their history as Palestinians, their tradition as Arabs. The bumpy embroidered threads— silk on wool, linen, cotton—sent a thrill through Nour's fingers each time she touched it. She felt proud to don one of Setty's *thobe* dresses, in black or white, inlaid with rich, colorful diamonds.

The summer she turned eight, Nour spent an entire week with Setty. Aunt Heba. Mama's sister was visiting from America with her daughter, Fadwa, just a few years older than Nour. Everyone wanted the two cousins to spend some time together. Neither had a sister, and it was hoped they would become good friends. But Fadwa was loud and boisterous, whereas Nour was artistic and reflective. While Nour liked to sit and watch Setty weave her delicious cross threads, Fadwa wanted to roam the stony mountains that cupped the village, acting more like a boy. Her bold actions and sharp statements sometimes left Nour shaking, but she found no way to excuse herself from Fadwa's adventures.

"What's that?" asked Fadwa one time when the two cousins ventured out in the burning midday sun. She pointed to an S-shaped shadow on the path ahead of them. She snapped a branch from nearby brambles, ran towards the shadow, and began prodding it with a jagged end.

"It's a snake! A real snake," she screamed wildly, hunching down on her heels, and stroking the scaly skin with one hand. Then, without a trace of fear, she picked up the wiry creature and wrapped it around the stick, waving it in the air like a magic wand. Fadwa, the snake charmer.

Nour took one look at the stiff tail curling out to one side and ran screaming back to Setty's house. She heard Fadwa chuckling behind her.

After that, Nour refused to go hiking with Fadwa. She stayed inside with Setty and for the first time learned to draw a thread through the eye of a needle. Setty guided Nour's small fingers across the material, pressing the needle in and out until a neat row of cross-stitches appeared like magic. Nour knew then that she had found her passion and spent hours decorating every piece of her own clothing with flowers and birds, stars, circles, and squares. By week's end, she glowed with pride as one after another of her relatives commented that she must take after Setty. She decided then that there was nothing else she wanted to do than be a proud Palestinian seamstress and create her own line of clothes.

Back at home, though, Baba made it very clear that her sewing projects were childish. He brushed aside her flowing designs and frowned at her shopping trips. It was just a disposable hobby, he said. She would grow out of it.

The dull ring of pain around her neck grew sharper as Nour tried to focus on a tale Baba was sharing from his workday. Exhaustion gripped her, and she realized the only way out was to help Mama clear away the dishes. Nour stood from the table and began collecting the empties. In the kitchen, she dipped the crusted plates into foamy soap, scrubbing away newly acquired stains and arranging them to dry on the marble counter. She scraped the leftover lamb and vegetables into plastic containers and placed them neatly in the fridge. Then she excused herself, telling her parents she needed to study.

Alone in her room, Nour fell onto her bed. Her neck still felt like it was on fire, burning and poking at her skin inside and out. Her head spun, and she fought back the tears as she pictured herself standing in that cobblestone alleyway wearing her ugly school uniform. Those Jewish boys told her to "Go back to Saudi Arabia!" What did they mean? Why would they say that? Baba went on Hajj in Saudi Arabia a few years ago, but she never left Jerusalem. This was her city. She was born here.

More than that, Baba's family always lived here, in Shuafat—or at least as long as any of them remembered. They were farmers a long time ago and lost their lands when Israel's army marched in and took them over. The war took place before even Baba was born, but his brothers remembered it and still talked about it like it was yesterday.

Nour turned her face to the wall. A dry sob, like a lump of bread, burned the sides of her throat. Why did they need to talk about what happened in the past? The war was still going on today. She should know. Nour touched her sore neck. True, there were no Israeli tanks on the streets these days, but the soldiers were still there and so were the Israelis making their lives miserable.

All around Shuafat, they were building new neighborhoods, their menacing towers filled with apartments for Jews only. Ring roads circled their neighborhood, and everyone knew that the light rail, which ran through the center of the village, was built to help Jerusalem's Jewish residents bypass the Palestinian neighborhood to reach the city center. When it was still under construction, Nour remembered hearing angry adults, even those who worked with the Jews and contributed wholly to the fabric of Israeli society, grumbling about the disruption and about how no one asked them if they even wanted a train line. Four years later, most of her relatives and friends used the light rail, but no one ever said it was good for them.

Nour rode it to and from school every day too, but until now, she did not give it much thought. Now, the throbbing around her throat moved down between her shoulder blades and she wondered if those Jewish boys, the ones who attacked, might also use it. What about other Jews who hated Arabs?

Baba always told her to make the best of a situation and not judge the majority by the bad behavior of a few. "Everyone has the potential to be good, regardless of whether they are Muslim or Jewish," Baba told her once when she asked him about the Israelis he worked with at the hospital. "People are people and at the core, we are all the same, really, just human beings with many flaws."

"But we're not like them. We're Palestinian," Nour insisted.

"Yes, but we're also human beings and that should come first," he told her patiently.

Just before turning out the light in her room, Nour tried to apply Baba's words to what happened to her. Those boys attacked her only because she was an Arab. They didn't see her as human. How was she supposed to see them—Jews, Israelis—as humans in return?

RIVKI

"Whatever is meant to be will be. It's in His hands." Esti's words were still stuck in Rivki's head a few days later as she and Ima made the now-familiar trek across the city to the hospital. She wasn't sure she could be like Esti and leave it all up to Him. She wanted to know her fate. She wanted to know where this illness, which had turned her life upside-down, would lead her. Would she follow the same path as other girls? Could she follow in Esti's footsteps? Or did she need to be ready for a different route?

Rivki scrunched up her delicate nose, freckles disappearing inside her skin, and surveyed the other passengers through ice-blue eyes. The world was clearly divided. There were the girls, like her, who went from school to marriage to motherhood. Raising a family was sacred; it brought you closer to Him. Though when Rivki saw frazzled moms, bellies blown out of shape, chasing broods around the neighborhood, she didn't know how.

On the train, Rivki admired other types of girls. She felt sure the red-lipped girls in jeans painted on like skin wouldn't let someone else choose them a husband. Though she still felt her cheeks flush when she saw those same red-lipped girls holding hands with boys as if fusing fingers was the most natural thing in the world.

Rivki wondered what it would be like to hold someone's hand. It almost happened, once. Just before she got sick. Ima sent her to the supermarket to buy some rolls and a boy, about her age, was suddenly standing beside her. They reached into the bread bin at the same time, his long limbs beating hers by a second. "*Baruch Ha-Shem.*" His words were mumbled, but his brown eyes held hers without blinking. "Rivki, right?"

Rivki dropped her gaze, words threatening to choke her. She managed a stiff nod and watched the heels of his black shoes retreat down the aisle. Rivki held her breath, waiting to see if anything bad would happen to her, but minutes later she was still there, whole and alive, grasping a single roll.

Later, at home, she tried to quieten her heart as she imagined her fingers touching his smooth hands. What would have happened if she boldly replied, "Yes, I'm Rivki. What's your name?" Would his eyes still twinkle or would the other eyes, those of her neighbors, frown at her? Would someone report her to her mother, destroying her future? Rivki sighed. It probably wouldn't matter. He was beyond her reach now, anyway. The chances of ever finding a *bashert*, her betrothed, a soulmate, were floating by like a distant cloud. She was damaged goods, regardless of what Esti said.

The first time Rivki got sick, Ima thought it was just a bad case of stomach flu and she stopped the others from getting too close. Esti was ejected from their room to the couch, as Rivki, dripping with a permanent fever, writhed alone in bed, thunderous streaks of pain pushing through her stomach.

When her fever refused to break, Ima took her to the doctor, who sent them to the hospital. There, a staff member dressed in deep green pajamas sucked the blood from her body and stuck needles into every vacant vein, draining her energy and breaking her spirit. But test after test proved inconclusive and after four days in the hospital, her fever just stopped.

"It could have been a virus, or it could be a form of irritable bowel syndrome, that we will only know going forward. In the meantime, Rivka responded well to the antibiotics and the few doses of steroids we gave her. The key now is for her to rest and stay hydrated," a goggle-eyed doctor shrugged.

A few days after stopping the antibiotics, Rivki once again felt her insides being ripped out and Ima took her back to the doctor, who sent her back to the hospital. It was now the heart of the summer vacation and Yosef's wife, Ruthy, was called in to take charge of the household. With some help from Esti and a little from Mordechai's Zehava, Ima was able to stay with Rivki as she received another round of inconclusive tests.

A specialist called Dr. Amnon was called in. Rivki watched him scowl at the end of her bed as he flicked messily through her charts. Finally, he concluded, Rivki had a disease. He called it Crohn's.

"We believe it's hereditory." He cleared his throat, looking first at Rivki and then at Ima. "Usually, it presents itself in the teenage years and, at present, there is no cure, but it can be managed with medication and a proper diet. Is there anyone in your family, Mrs. Lefkovitz, with a similar problem?"

Ima scratched her hairline below her scarf. "Not as far as I know."

"Well, it's not so important." Dr. Amnon was studying Rivki's chart again. "It's not conclusive that Crohn's is genetic, but it often presents itself multiple times in families."

Rivki dared a glance at Ima and was sure she noticed a darkness wash over her face.

Dr. Amnon continued: "I'm afraid we'll need to keep Rivki on steroids for some time, but it should enable her to return to school in September. She'll need monitoring, so for the next short while at least, weekly check-ups, and she must take care not to get stressed. Stress," he emphasized the word in a stern voice, "could cause another flare-up worse than before—then she might need surgery."

Rivki shivered. She didn't like the thought of coming to the hospital every week, but an operation scared her even more. She vowed to take the small white pills he prescribed without fail.

Back home, her sister and sisters-in-law hovered over her like bees. Ima fussed too, but more about the cost of buying her special food. Rivki brushed her complaints aside, relieved that she didn't say a word about Crohn's being hereditary. Still, Dr. Amnon's words hung in the air like bursting rain clouds, and each time someone complained of pains in their tummy Rivki felt the angry monster return, ripping up parts of her stomach.

THE RIDE

Tamar pulled a thin sweater from her backpack and threaded her arms through the tangled sleeves. The sun that warmed the day was now fading from the sky, and she could feel the early flecks of Jerusalem's winter painting her cheeks. Tapping her phone to check the time again, Tamar sighed. The light rail was now forty-five minutes late.

She twisted her head from side to side, trying to erase the stiff line between her shoulder blades. She never thought too deeply about using the light rail before those rough hands touched her, but now, everything connected to it set her on edge—especially waiting around too long. Ever since that day, the thought of bumping into him again sent short, sharp pulses thumping through her body and prickles, like a thousand tiny daggers, rising through her skin.

Jerusalem was a small city, and even the faces of strangers were familiar. The same cast of characters often cropped up in different settings, with Tamar recognizing people from her daily journey in different places on different days. The hefty border police officer who got on at Givat Hamivtar was regularly seen guarding the gates of the Old City. The Haredi lady with the oversized crooked hat worked in Strauss's Bazaar. The old guy in clogs, clutching a bright red plastic shopping basket, flicking through a crumpled newspaper, she'd spied fingering fruit in the *shuk*. Tamar never uttered a word to any of them, but they were as recognizable to her as Jerusalem's iconic landmarks.

Could the man with the curly hair find her again? What would she do if she saw him again? Smelt his minty breath on her face? Maybe Aviv was right? Telling someone, talking to someone would help. But what would they say? What could they say? That it was her own fault for dressing provocatively? That she should have shouted out or stopped him at the time? That she was a drama queen, and it wasn't such a big deal?

It still bothered her that his identity remained elusive. A constant question in her head was whether he was an Arab, though Tal convinced her more or less that he was—he seemed adamant that such a detail was very important.

"He must be," Tal commented again the next day, making sure Aviv was well out of earshot. "Think about it, Tamar, Jewish guys just don't behave like that. Do you know anyone who would do that? I certainly don't."

Tamar thought for a second. She wasn't convinced by Tal's line of argument. "I think assaults happen everywhere and it can't just be by Arab guys."

"That's true, but other places aren't the same as here," Tal answered, his eyes reaching inside her mind. "Here, a guy groping you is part of the conflict. It's part of their war against us. My *savta* always says there's no way to trust the *goyim*, even if they've been buried forty years."

"Ha, your *savta* is such a character." Tamar grinned, remembering Tal's tiny, weather-beaten grandmother, and imagining her declaring such a racist epitaph in a gravelly voice.

"She is, but she's also wise and she grew up in an Arab country, so she knows exactly how their minds work," said Tal. "Just remember, here is not like other places. Here is a war. They hate us and we hate them."

"I don't hate anyone, Tal," Tamar protested, even though she thought she might hate the guy who touched her on the train.

"You think you don't, but you do," he shot back. "Even if you've suppressed it deep down inside you, and anyway, it doesn't matter, because they hate you."

Tamar glanced around her at the increasingly agitated crowd waiting for the train. It was a typical Jerusalem mix of Jews, secular and religious, and Arabs. They didn't look like they were at war with one another. In fact, there did not seem to be much interaction at all—just lots of frustrated people waiting, like her, for the train to arrive.

Tamar's phone vibrated, and she clicked on the screen to see a message from Ami. Since their ride together, he texted her often. *Hey.* He waved with an emoji hand. *Where r u? Heard there's a hefetz hashud? R u stuck?*

She replied with an angry red emoji face. *Yep, nearly an hour!* She wrote underneath. *Ppl r annoying! They forget something on the light rail, and everyone thinks it's a bomb!*

The screen flashed again with the word *shit* followed by a sad face with a tear.

A warm rush ran through Tamar's chest but stopped short of her heart. She liked getting Ami's messages, but he was still an Arab. If Tal was right, then perhaps she shouldn't trust him?

Finally, the train arrived, and Tamar jostled her way inside, dodging the other bodies as she made for the glass partition. She planted her back firmly up against it and pushed her earphones deeper inside her ears. The sweet harmonies of Lennon and McCartney allowed her to rise above the harried passengers as she closely scanned each and every face.

· · ·

Nour shifted uneasily in her seat. She could feel the girl staring at her and kept her head low, pretending to be interested in her friend's Instagram stories. Jews in Jerusalem didn't bother hiding the fact they thought all Arabs were terrorists—she experienced that in the Old City.

More than a week had passed since the attack and the marks around her neck were gone, but a ring of unease remained, and she was still hypervigilant anytime she ventured beyond the confines of Shuafat. Nour dared to look at the staring girl. She was about her own age and didn't look violent, but then again, neither did the boys who hurt her.

The incident in the Old City made Nour realize there was no way to avoid politics. She now spent hours trying to untangle the web of conflicts linking and dividing Jerusalem's tribes, as Baba liked to call them. More and more she wondered if the core of this trouble, this hatred, stemmed only from the Israeli occupation of her people. Or was it something else? Was there an ancient curse over this holy city or just a simple disconnect?

The disconnect was everywhere. From the way each group dressed—scarves tied up or tied down? White *thobes* vs heavy black suits—to how they acted and interacted with one another. What language they spoke. Hebrew, Arabic, or even Yiddish. It was also in the food they bought in the market and ate in the city's restaurants and cafés. It was even in the way they ate them.

The duality was everywhere. Painted on street signs, weaved into logos, broadcast from loudspeakers. Just riding the light rail made the divisions crystal clear. Places she knew and loved so well in this city of her birth had different names in Hebrew to Arabic, giving them different meanings to the Jews. When the light rail arrived at *Bab el-Amud*, for example, the main entrance to the Old City, the announcer also called out in Hebrew, "*Sha'ar Shechem*." Then, as if to clarify, "Damascus Gate," in English.

The first time Nour heard these names, she felt confused, as if someone had stolen away the places she always cherished. The new names sounded weird and foreign. She couldn't even pronounce them. Now she was used to hearing the three languages—it was just another sign of how the people in this city lived together but functioned as completely separate entities. Not understanding one another. Not even trying to understand one another.

"Together apart," Nour murmured under her breath as the light rail reached Sheikh Jarrah, the neighborhood Jews renamed Shimon Hatzadik, after a Jewish High Priest they said lived here more than 2000 years ago.

"He was named as righteous because he was kind to his compatriots," Mrs. Rahman, their Hebrew teacher, who was Jewish, told them in class. "According to the Jewish scriptures, he was very kind to his fellow citizens and very involved in rebuilding the walls of the Jewish Temple that stand today in the Old City. He was a great and strong leader. It's a shame there aren't more people like him around today."

Nour wondered whether building walls really made leaders great and strong. She felt too many walls—physical and non-physical—existed here already. She detested all of them. The real walls caused daily hardship, dividing her people and her family in two; the invisible walls made people stare and hate. The rules were cast in stone, rock-solid Jerusalem stone.

But Nour didn't want to hate, even when she heard Abdulrahman and others complain about the Jews. She knew it came from frustration (caused by the walls) and from not knowing the other (like the girl staring at her).

Nour stole a glance at her again. Maybe it was just innocent curiosity derived from ignorance. Could they ever get to know one another? Could they become friends? She didn't think so. Jerusalem's walls were cursed with hatred. Even among her own people, some couldn't see beyond the hatred. Nour couldn't forget the rage-filled days after Muhammad, her neighbor, was murdered. She recalled Abdulrahman arriving home with friends, out of breath, faces covered in checkered black and white *keffiyehs*.

As they peeled off the scarves, kicked off their shoes, and changed out of T-shirts that smelled of smoke, Nour moved closer to the door that separated the kitchen from the living room and strained to decipher their hushed tones.

Nour's heartbeat slowed a second when Abdulrahman called her name, but he was only asking if she could bring them some coffee. Readily she obliged, pouring the thick bitter liquid from the copper *finjan* into tiny mugs and delivering it to the half dozen young men.

An aroma of tension mixed with that of the coffee and Nour lingered, grasping for scraps of information.

When she heard her brother's words, "We must seek revenge," Nour felt that tension like a hammer on her chest and froze again just beyond the kitchen door. She tried to quieten her breathing so she could hear what followed. One of Abdulrahman's friends said they should kidnap a Jewish child and hurt him in the way Muhammad must have hurt. Nour heard grunts of agreement, animal instinct instead of human reasoning. What difference would it make killing a Jewish kid? It wouldn't bring Muhammad back. It would just bring more Israeli police to their area, which would make people even angrier.

When his friends finally departed, Nour confronted Abdulrahman. "Are you crazy? You'll end up in jail or worse! You know the Israelis would just love to make an example of you, don't you get that?"

"But we must avenge Muhammad. Enough is enough," Abdulrahman responded in a cool voice that chilled her. "Nothing will change, Nouri, unless we fight back. The Palestinian people cannot remain weak forever."

Nour searched in her brother's face for signs of reason, but his cold words and the dregs of leftover coffee formed a wall between them. Suddenly, she saw Abdulrahman lying on the ground. A neat, round bullet hole in his forehead. Streams of blood-red crawling out from behind him. She spun on her heels and went to find Baba.

Nour could hear the raised voices from her room and buried her face deeper in her pillow. What choice did she have? Killing a Jewish child was insane. Even Muhammad's parents appealed for calm. Even they said that avenging their son's death would not bring him back.

Anger over Muhammed's murder eventually subsided but never disappeared, becoming another sad chapter in a longer story of oppression. For Abdulrahman, however, it was a spark and Nour still felt his anger, including toward her, more than a year later.

• • •

Rivki welcomed the cushioned seat as she took her place next to Ima on the light rail. They left the hospital at the usual time and, as usual, were rushing to pick up her siblings. Also, as usual, the light rail seemed sluggish when a voice announced over the speaker that there was a delay ahead and the train came to a standstill at the Central Station.

"What now?" Ima huffed, more to herself than to Rivki. "Abba will have to pick up Batsheva now and meet the boys, too."

She disappeared inside an oversized purse, fishing out a battered black cellphone. Ima squinted as she punched the numbers with her chunky fingers, before holding it up to her ear. It was Mordechai's phone and Ima only agreed to keep it because he said it was certified kosher by the council of Rabbinic sages.

"*Shalom*, Shmuel Lefkovitz please." Ima cleared her throat, eyes darting around the carriage as she waited for Abba to come to the phone. Rivki imagined a young student in a crisp white shirt, sleeves rolled up, marching the Kollel's long hallways to reach Abba's classroom, then knocking politely on the door before stepping inside and whispering in his ear that there was a phone call for him in the office. She pictured Abba ordering his students to read a passage from the Mishna or the Gemara or some other important text or accompanying Rabbinic commentary until he came back. Then Rivki saw him, kind face, soft gray beard, striding in wide-legged trousers, into the secretary's small office.

Eventually, Rivki heard her mother's voice, "Shlomo, yes, the train is stopped... at the *Tachana Merkazit*. Some sort of hold-up, they say. We'll never be back in time to get Batsheva..... Could you.... Yes.... And the boys. I hope it won't take us too much longer.... Yes, yes, she's fine.... Okay, then.... Thank you, see you soon..."

Ima pulled the phone away from her ear, pressed the large button top center, and threw it back into her bag as if holding onto it for too long would infect her with secularity or worse. "Abba will pick up Batsheva." She sighed, shaking her head like she committed the gravest of sins.

Rivki nodded stiffly, her heart pinching. She should feel bad. Ima's routine was already upset and now Abba was forced to leave work in the middle of his day, yet Rivki didn't want the day to end. She felt better now and going to the hospital, even with its smells of bleach and death, made her feel alive. The building's rich colors shone brighter than Ma'alot Dafna's blacks and grays.

The divisions that pulled in opposing directions when she rode the train did not exist in the hospital, for she knew that the curious collection of people in its hallways and waiting rooms were all there for the same reason as her: to get better. This simple fact made her senses burst, and she stored every scene, every face, every interaction and experience to reflect on later.

The other upside was that she got to skip school one day a week. Not only was it a release from the overloaded schedule, but it meant she could avoid the chatter of the girls in her class that lately made her feel deflated and lost.

Returning to school after her body failed her, everything changed. As her friends discussed predictions for their end-of-year *chutzim* exams or mulled the professional tracts they would choose, Rivki's mind was as clouded as her stomach in the first days of her first Crohn's flare-up. Nothing was clear to her anymore.

Talk of the future daunted her, especially the new hot topic—*shidduchim*. Some of her friends, like her, had older sisters that were still waiting to find suitors, but others were already preparing to meet certified matchmakers or even go on their first dates.

The stalled light rail was moving now, and Ima looked up from her tiny book of Psalms hopefully. "Maybe we won't be so late." She sighed. "Abba will only miss one of his classes."

Rivki was doubtful. True, they were past City Hall and the Old City now. There were only two more stops to go, but she could almost feel the carriage buckling under the weight of so many people.

Slowly, they pulled into Shivtei Yisrael, and Rivki watched people filing off as yet more crammed on. As they started to move again, she felt the light rail lurch. A woman standing, holding onto the hanging loops, stumbled, landing on top of Rivki.

"What happened? Why did we stop?" Rivki gasped, rubbing her shoulder where the woman landed.

"Not sure." Ima stood and strained her neck above the other passengers. "Oof, it can't be another delay. What is with the light rail today? We should just get off and walk. It would be faster."

Around them, a low hum of confusion grew louder, producing one clear, sharp voice: "The light rail will terminate here."

. . .

Tamar studied a nearby girl with shiny jet-black hair that seemed to light up the entire carriage. She wondered how people here instinctively knew who was from which tribe. Deep in thought, she jolted forward when the light rail suddenly stalled and quickly threw her arms up to stop from slamming full body into the man in front of her. Steadying her feet, Tamar felt the space between her shoulders tighten again. She pushed her headphones back into her ears and breathed deeply, allowing calming melodies to rinse away the tension. Only three more stops.

But then doors sprung open, and bodies began spilling out into the night air. The crowd lurched forward as if it was one solid mass and Tamar flattened her body back against the partition to stop from being pulled along with it.

"What is it? What's going on?" Tamar let out a cry, pulled the headphones from her ears, and let them dangle.

A soldier, rifle strung over one shoulder and oversized duffle on the other stopped beside her. "There's been a terrorist attack somewhere up ahead." He pointed a muscular arm in the direction they were headed. "The light rail is terminating here."

Tamar watched him struggle off the light rail, his bag squashing everyone around him, and she wondered what it would feel like to be crushed, fall into darkness and see only black. She wanted to follow, but there was a force field around her, protecting her body from all the other bodies, protecting her skin from sharp, rough hands.

"You alright, *motek*?" A woman brushed by her, wafting a lemony scent that reminded her of her mom. Tamar moved closer to the glass partition, wanting to disappear inside it. "Are you okay? We all need to get off here. Do you still have far to go?"

"No... no... it's okay, just to French Hill, not far, thank you," Tamar answered weakly, but the woman was already gone, lost in the mass of bodies.

Suddenly, Tamar felt foolish. He wasn't here; she knew that. She closed her eyes and tried to find some clean air before putting up her elbows and jostling through the crowd to the exit.

. . .

The light rail's sudden stop ejected Nour right out of her seat. She had to brace herself to stop from falling face-first into the lap of the person sitting opposite. When the doors opened, she was one of the first people outside.

She kept her eyes down and immediately called Baba. "I think there's been a *pigua*," she breathed in Arabic, but spliced her speech with the

Hebrew word for a terror attack. She glanced around her nervously. "We're not too far from my school."

"I guessed something happened. I heard the ambulances taking off," Baba answered. "Listen, Nouri, stay where you are and let me see which paramedics are there. I'll ask one of them to give you a ride to the hospital." He hung up.

From the number of ambulances and police cars that whizzed past her, Nour suspected something really bad had happened. She stood apart from the emerging crowd, observing the chaos, as people tried to figure out where they were and how to get home.

Nour noticed a small huddle gathering and took a curious step forward to see what was happening. A religious Jewish girl was slumped on the ground and an older woman, with wide hips and a long skirt, flapped beside her. Paramedics with bags and a stretcher arrived, pushing back those who gathered and began examining the girl with gloved fingers. Within minutes, they had her on a stretcher and were carrying her to a waiting ambulance.

Nour wondered if this might be her ride and thought about approaching the driver to ask if Baba had sent him. She glanced around to make sure no one was watching her. She knew any unusual action at such a sensitive time, and she might find herself arrested or worse. Just last week in Tel Aviv, a group of Jewish passengers on a bus wrestled a young Arab woman to the ground because they thought she was about to stab them. Nour heard about the incident in school when her friends started talking about it.

"They blame us for everything when it's their own fault," Nidal, a girl in her class with sharply plucked eyebrows and a neatly tucked hijab, stated defiantly. "If there was no occupation, there would be no attacks."

"They really do blame us for everything," concurred Yasmin, another of her classmates. "One time, I went to buy milk, and the police held me for an hour. It was only when my brother came looking for me and then went to get Mama that they let me go."

Nour's phone buzzed. It was Baba. "*Habibti,* are you okay? Do you see an ambulance near you? The driver is expecting you, but you need to be quick. He has a patient."

She looked around her again before walking up to the passenger's side and pulling open the door. Making sure the driver was who Baba said he was, she jumped inside.

. . .

Rivki felt cool liquid trickling down the sides of her face, sliding into her ears. A sharp voice, one she did not recognize, pierced the air above her, repeating her name over and over and over again.

"Rivki, *motek*, Rivki, can you hear me? Rivki?" it shrilled.

Who was that? Where was Ima?

"Ima?" Rivki tried, but her voice came out as a crackle.

"Rivkale, I'm right here, Rivkale." That was Ima's voice. "You fainted, Rivkale."

She felt her mother's warm, fleshy fingers on her forehead. Then came the shrill voice again. "She needs fluids, Mrs. Lefkovitz, and she should see a doctor."

Forcing open heavy eyelids, Rivki saw Ima and the mystery woman, both leaning over her with concern on their faces. The woman was dressed in a white doctor's coat, though Rivki knew they weren't in the hospital. She remembered leaving it.

Then she remembered being on the light rail. She remembered the sharp stop and the rush to get out. Ima grabbing her arm, pulling her, but then letting go. Shoulders wide as a truck, smashing into her, flying into darkness and no air.

Rivki tried to sit.

"Stay down, Rivkale, you need to rest. They are saying we need to go to the hospital." Ima gently pushed her back down.

"But... the light rail." Rivki's throat was dry. "Terrorist attack."

"Yes, there was a *pigua*." The paramedic's sharp voice cut a line through the air. "You were knocked down in the rush. You blacked out. Your mother says you have Crohn's, and your blood pressure is very low, so we're going to take you to the hospital, for a quick once-over, okay?"

Rivki's stomach screamed out angrily. She tried to speak, but her voice was suddenly drowned out by the deafening wail of a siren. A thick knot of nausea gathered in her stomach, an oil slick rising towards her mouth. She wanted to know about the *pigua*. She needed to know. Was anyone killed?

She knew very little about politics, only that there were Arabs who also lived on this land and resented the fact it was a Jewish country. They wanted to drive the Jews away from the land G-d promised them.

Rivki also knew that awful things happened because of people's sins. She heard one rabbi saying that Israel, a country of Jews, was now a society of sinners traversing the rules of modesty and *Shabbos*. They risked losing His protection completely. The rabbi said that if people didn't take the *mitzvoth* more seriously, then the Arabs would kill all the Jews and take away their country.

Once there was a poster pasted up by the mini market that warned them to stop behaving like *goyim* and do what G-d asked. "Stop surfing the internet, stop using smartphones," it warned in thick black letters. She didn't know anyone who used the internet or owned a smartphone, so she wasn't sure who the warning was aimed at.

As the ambulance bumped over the streets of Jerusalem, Rivki allowed herself to think about G-d. If He was the Almighty, if He was all-powerful, then how did He let these corrupting forces—internet, smartphones—be invented? He was supposed to be everywhere, all around them, even coursing through her veins like the cold fluids from the IV now attached to her arm. If He was really there, if He really cared about bad things, then why did he let them happen to people? Why would He let a terrorist hurt His people? Why did He let her get sick? Surely there was another way to make people pious, to make them care about Him?

Suddenly, the slick of nausea gathering in her stomach and making its way through her body was so large and strong that Rivki was powerless to stop it. Through her lips, it came exploding like an orange sun over the ambulance floor.

· · ·

The early evening air helped Tamar regain her strength. Realizing it might be awhile before the light rail started up again, she took a deep breath and decided to walk the rest of the way home. She was only one stop from her destination, and she figured it wouldn't take her more than ten minutes if she followed the track.

She took small sips of water from her bottle before returning it to her backpack and squaring the bag onto her shoulders. She turned to face the direction of home and started her trek. Striding along beside the parallel lines, Tamar replaced Lennon and McCartney with the clashing guitar riffs of Green Day. Californian punk rock pumped her with power and helped her forget her earlier angst.

Lost in the electric metal chords, Tamar forgot she was heading straight towards the *pigua*. Even when she reached the growing throng of people, she didn't immediately connect their presence with the reason she was now walking. Even when the scene opened up before her, it looked more like a car crash than a terrorist attack. A white sedan wrapped awkwardly around a pole, its front end splayed like a pitchfork. The driver's door was flung wide open like the person inside had fled in a hurry.

It was then Tamar spied splatters of red on the road, and her march forward slowed. Up ahead, hawkers watched a grim performance of white overalled men gathering up what looked like pieces of garbage and placing them into large plastic sacks. As she reached where the onlookers stood, Tamar's heart thumped hard when she realized they were collecting body parts. Bands of lightness gripped her knees, making Tamar wobble slightly. Her gaze was drawn to two shapes, one big, one small, covered in white sheets. Lying beside them, abandoned as if forgotten, was a crumpled pink baby blanket. Splatters of red ran across it like contrasting paint.

"Look away," Tamar willed herself. But she couldn't.

TAMAR

November 2015

When Tamar woke the next morning, sickness lined her stomach. Her head ached thinking about the fate of the crumpled pink baby blanket. Was it shoved into one of the large plastic sacks? Was it reunited with its owner? Was it keeping her warm as she waited to be lowered into the ground? Images whirled before her eyes: a car wrapped around a lamppost. A mashed baby stroller. Two bodies—one big, one small—covered in white sheets.

She checked her phone. One message from Aviv asking how she was doing. "So, so," Tamar tapped, which was answered in seconds with a hugging emoji followed by "call u later." Tal's message asked the same. There was also a note from Ami. Tamar's finger hovered over his name. What should she say to him? She saw a dead mother and baby, killed by an Arab.

She was just about to scan the news sites for more information about the attack when there was a soft knock at the door. "Yeah," Tamar answered, her voice coming out flat.

Slowly, the door opened, revealing her mom's familiar face. "Hey baby, how you doing?" she asked gently, perching herself at the end of Tamar's bed. "Wanna talk about what happened?"

Tamar shrugged, sinking deeper down into the sheets. She pressed a firm index finger into the corner of each eye, feeling the weight on her chest spread out to touch her shoulders.

Her mom put a warm hand instinctively above Tamar's heart. "Listen," she said. Her voice was soft. "I was thinking... we should have some mother-daughter time."

Tamar looked into her mom's safe green eyes, a mirror of her own. "Okay," she breathed, the glob of sickness receding from her stomach a little.

"How about sushi? We can go to the one by your school. How about I meet you there tomorrow when you finish classes?" Her mom stood up, reaching over Tamar's head to open the blinds. She raised the heavy plastic slowly, allowing the mid-morning sun to flood life into the room.

"Sure," said Tamar, the sun connecting her with the world. "That would be great."

Her mom was standing over her now. "Listen, Tamar, what you saw yesterday was awful. Not normal. We really need to talk it through. I know you're still in shock—that's why I thought it best to let you stay home today, but tomorrow, over sushi, we'll talk."

Tamar nodded affirmatively, but her mind was already racing with a million thoughts of how to avoid a discussion about feelings. If she started telling her mom how she felt right now, she might not stop and that would lead to the winking guy. She shuddered. Her family was already hysterical about her witnessing an attack after it happened. Imagine what they would say if they knew something happened to her directly?

NOUR

"Will you help me clean out the spare room today?" Mama asked Nour, who was still in pajamas and wrapped in sleep, as soon as she entered the kitchen.

"Why? What're we looking for?" She regarded her mother with a prolonged yawn.

Mama was sitting at the small Formica table, frizzy locks wild about her face, as thick pillars of steam rose from a small cup of dark coffee. The smell drew Nour to the *finjan* abandoned on the stovetop. She poured herself some coffee and sat down next to Mama.

Nour was still processing the nightmare light rail journey that ended in a terrible tragedy. What happened to her in the Old City paled compared to two people—a mother and a baby—being killed. The Jews said it was a terrorist attack, and some were now angrily protesting at that light rail station, which made her blood run cold.

The thought of emptying the spare room—the place where the Asa'ad family stored their unwanted or unneeded belongings—made her feel tired. It was not exactly what Nour wanted to be doing on a peaceful Friday morning when the house's male occupants were conveniently at the mosque. Besides, she had been hoping for some quiet time to talk to Mama about getting a sewing machine so she could bring some of her designs to life.

"I'm not looking for anything," Mama said brightly. "It's your cousin, Fadwa. She's coming to stay with us, and I thought that would be the best place to put her."

"What? When's she coming?" Nour grimaced as she sipped the bitter coffee. "W-why can't she just sleep in my room like she normally does?"

"Aunt Heba called me yesterday. Apparently, she's decided to take a year off before college and was selected for an internship at some organization that helps Palestinian kids or something. Their offices are in Sheikh Jarrah, so it's perfect. She can stay with us." Mama smiled.

Nour let her coffee cup down with a thud. "Er... for how... how long will she, er, be staying with us?"

"Not sure." Mama shrugged. "A few months, or something like that. We can call them a bit later... when we're done cleaning out the spare room... you will help me, won't you, Nouri?"

Even as Nour nodded, her mind rewound to the last time Fadwa visited. Two summers ago, she was fourteen, Fadwa sixteen. Mama and Aunt Heba took them to the Old City one Friday morning, allowing them to wander around the *suq* alone, on condition they showed up at the mosque in time for noon prayers.

It started out fine. Together, they explored the narrow passageways, filling their mouths with rubber sugar candies and freshly baked *laffa* bread. At *Bab al-Amud*, the majestic archway that led into the ancient city's Muslim Quarter, Fadwa became fascinated with the elderly, toothless women selling fresh rosemary, sage, coriander, and mint leaves. She toyed with an old *keffiyeh*-covered man, challenging him to a game of *sheshbesh* on a battered wooden board, which she ultimately lost.

Then they came across the Israeli soldiers, oversized guns slung across thick shoulders, patrolling the throbbing Friday crowd. They made Fadwa agitated and whenever they passed by, she would freeze and refuse to move. At first, Nour didn't understand what was going on. Then she noticed Fadwa making faces at the soldiers, sticking out her tongue and sticking up her fingers.

"Why do they harass us like this?" Fadwa declared in a loud voice, tossing her head about.

"They're here for everyone's safety," Nour tried to reassure her. "They're watching to make sure there's no trouble. If we don't bother them, they won't bother us." She checked her watch; it was nearly noon. She tried to assess how long it would take them to reach and enter the mosque before prayers were called. Nour moved, hoping Fadwa would follow, but then she heard a deep voice—Arabic with an American twang.

"Get out of here! This is a Muslim city, you dirty Jews," Fadwa yelled. lobbing a large blob of spit that landed on the ground a few feet in front of her.

"Fadwa!" Nour hissed, feeling a thousand eyes on her. She chanced a glance at the soldiers and heaved a sigh of relief. They were not looking at them. "What are you doing? Are you crazy? Why are you starting trouble?"

"Trouble? Who's starting trouble? I'm not starting trouble. They're starting trouble. It's them. They shouldn't be here. This is our city, our mosque. They're the ones defiling it with their filthy boots." Fadwa's voice rose an octave with each word, her face turning red.

"Fadwa, this is a holy place. Please, can't you just ignore them? We need to get inside the mosque," Nour begged, her heart thumping heavily in her chest. She eyed the soldiers again. They were still oblivious to Fadwa.

"Look, they're not allowed inside the mosque, so just follow me." Nour's throat was dry, her mouth still sugary from the gummy candies. They needed to get out of there. Just one small security check and they would be safely inside the leafy courtyard of al-Aqsa but, if Fadwa continued like this, if the soldiers suddenly noticed her, they would arrest her on the spot even though they were young girls.

Nour didn't know if making faces and spitting at soldiers was a crime, but she knew the Israelis were always watching them. There were cameras everywhere in the Old City and even if they did not arrest them then and there, what was to stop them from suddenly showing up at her house, dragging her and Fadwa out of bed in the middle of the night?

Suddenly, Nour dug her fingernails into Fadwa's arm and, even though she was a head taller and a lot wider, she managed to drag Fadwa beyond the cluster of soldiers into the safety of the compound. Furious, Nour spun around and looked her cousin straight in the eyes. "What were you thinking? Why would you want to start trouble with Israeli soldiers? Especially here!"

"Me?" Fadwa flashed back. "I was standing up for our rights. They shouldn't be here. I have more than every right to be here."

"We have a right to be here, you're right about that, but they're not stopping us from doing anything," Nour answered crisply, shaking her head.

"Their presence here is enough." Fadwa brought her face close to Nour's. "They disgust me. Don't you realize they stand there, taunting Palestinians, just to remind us they are in control? That they occupy us?"

Nour sighed. "Fadwa, I don't care about politics. I don't bother them, and they don't bother me. I just don't want to get arrested."

"You're pathetic, Nour. So weak! Always have been. You live here, in the heart of Palestine—it's your job to stand up for the rights of our people. Instead, you just accept the occupation. How can you call yourself Palestinian?" Fadwa's eyes were so full of disdain that Nour shrank back for a second. "If I lived here, and I will one day, I would fight back against what they do to our people all the time."

Nour considered her cousin. What did she know about living here? She lived a million miles away in a big house, on a wide road, in a peaceful neighborhood.

"I'm pathetic? How does fighting with soldiers help our cause? What would it do except land us in jail or worse? You don't understand the situation here. How could you, living in America? It's one thing being all militant there, but this is our reality here. Spitting at soldiers in the street, shouting at them helps no one." Nour burned as she waited for Fadwa to answer, but all she heard was the song of the *muezzin*, calling people to come to prayer.

After a few seconds, Nour gave up and, turning on her heels, she walked calmly away in search of Mama and Aunt Heba. She would show Fadwa who was weak. This was her town, her turf. She knew how to behave. Her American cousin did not.

"I hope you're not misbehaving in a holy place," Mama said when Nour finally found her. She seemed to smell the bitterness in the air. Nour shrugged, but she spied Aunt Heba pulling Fadwa off to the side.

A few minutes later, Fadwa was standing in front of her. "I'm s-sorry, Nour," she huffed. "Can we be friends again?"

In the shadow of the sacred mosque, forgiveness seemed to be the only path, especially because Nour realized she could never truly win a fight with her headstrong cousin. But even as she forgave, Fadwa's words remained like an indelible watermark on her soul. She didn't consider herself weak. Wasn't she just satisfied with her life? Or should she be doing more for her people, standing up for their rights?

RIVKI

"Whoa, your blood pressure's super low! Sure you're still alive?" the nurse gently ripped the black band off Rivki's arm and, getting little response to her joke, added hastily, "Never mind, the doctor'll be here soon. Maybe he'll adjust your meds. In the meantime, we should see if your legs still work."

The red-haired nurse pulled back a thin curtain and tucked it neatly behind a chair. Rivki assessed the tired hospital room. A small, battered cabinet with a jug of water and a stack of plastic cups arranged carefully on the top separated her bed from her roommate, who was hidden behind her own curtain. Bright morning sun spilled excitedly through a large window and Rivki's eyes lingered on the dusty green hills outside. Somewhere beyond the open door to the corridor came the low muffled sound of a radio.

Across the room was a door leading to the bathroom. Rivki sized the distance and wondered if she could make it that far. She didn't need to pee—the catheter they inserted yesterday was helping her with that—and she'd eaten no solid foods for the past two days, so she didn't need that either, but the nurse suggested brushing her teeth and washing her face.

"It'll make you feel human again," she said, humming along to the distant radio. She slid a wiry arm beneath Rivki's back. "Try moving your legs to the side of the bed first."

Rivki closed her eyes and wondered if she would ever feel human again. Yesterday, when they tried this, the slashing knives inside her stomach decided to show up. Now, she let herself fall into the nurse's firm embrace, throwing her legs over the side of the bed. She stopped, waiting for rips and sparks to fill her, but today her insides were calm. Rivki lowered her toes onto the linoleum floor, its coolness giving her strength. She put a hand on the bed for balance and felt the nurse's arm tighten around her lower back. Then she was standing, the tube between her legs pinching. The nurse grabbed the other end of the tube and brought the bag down to her side, easing the discomfort slightly, and together, like conjoined twins, they shuffled towards the bathroom.

Dr. Amnon said what happened was normal for Crohn's patients. He said the shock of events on the light rail triggered another flare-up, but Rivki didn't think what happened on the train was an excuse for her body to let her down again. As the nurse helped her back into bed, Rivki fought back against the stinging in the corners of her eyes.

TAMAR

That night, after dinner, Tamar did something unusual. She positioned herself on the couch between her parents to watch the nightly news bulletin. The news was a religion for most Israelis, including her parents. Watching it every evening was part of a routine that came after dinner and before teeth brushing.

Most nights, Tamar would vacate the family room straight after dinner, leaving her parents glued to the TV set, waiting to get an update on the country's dramatic current affairs. But tonight, she needed to see for herself what was going on. She needed to know every microscopic detail of the attack at the train stop. She wanted to understand what this conflict was between Israelis and Arabs.

Tamar held her breath as the screen flipped from a brightly lit studio to erratic images of the light rail stop near her house. A pleasant-faced reporter stood clutching a microphone, and the camera panned quickly from him to the platform. Tamar held her breath, but the crashed car and the mangled stroller and the pink baby blanket were all gone. She felt like she might have dreamed it, but then the reporter started talking about a run-over attack. A young mother and her baby were killed, he said, and the car was driven by a Palestinian man. "A *mehabel*," he informed viewers. The Palestinian man lived somewhere Tamar had never heard of, but her dad mumbled, "It's not too far, just the other side of Jerusalem."

Back in the studio, a panel of gray-haired analysts dissected the information. Run-over attacks were a trend, they remarked. If you wanted to carry out a terrorist attack, all you needed was a car, said one. Another asked if this was the start of a third Intifada, an uprising by Palestinians against Israel? Was the car a new weapon of choice to fight Israelis? A new kind of terrorism? If so, how would the authorities stop it?

Tamar's head spun as she tried to follow the arguments. There was friction between her people and the Arabs, that was for sure. She witnessed it, even experienced it now herself, but if every Arab driving in a car was going to use their vehicle as a weapon, then terrorist attacks like the one with the mother and the baby would happen every second.

From her parent's reaction though, Tamar understood they viewed the situation differently to her.

"It was so close to home." Her mom gasped. She moved her body closer to Tamar and put an arm around her shoulder. "And a baby! Awful. So sad that my baby was exposed to such a terrible thing." She let out a sob.

"Tamar, I think you need to pay closer attention to the people around you, especially on the light rail, at least until things calm down," said her dad, still glued to the screen. "Who knows what will happen next?"

NOUR

Nour thought about Fadwa as she helped Mama clear out the spare room. Together they stacked up the sacks of clothes to give to neighbors and placed old, broken furniture outside on the street for whoever might make use of it. Reluctantly, Nour parted with some of her old schoolbooks that she no longer needed.

"There, it's not so bad," said Mama after they removed the last remnants of Asa'ad history from the room. "Just need to clean the floor and it will be perfect for her."

"It's perfect." Nour concurred. Fadwa scared her, but secretly she admired her cousin's tenacity and her consistent dedication to the Palestinian cause. After her experiences in recent weeks, maybe this was a chance for her to better understand her people's struggle, thought Nour.

"Let's call Aunt Heba and see if they're ready for the big trip," said Mama, heading for the nook next to the kitchen where the family computer sat proudly on a wide oak desk. Mama and her sister spoke at least once a week, sometimes more. She clicked on the mouse and the screen sprang to life, initiating Skype's dial-up tone.

"Rania, I was just about to call you!" Nour heard her aunt's voice before her face materialized onto the screen.

"We've just finished cleaning out Fadwa's room. Nour is so excited that she's going to have a sister in the house," Mama exclaimed, her voice reaching a climactic apex that appeared whenever she spoke to her sister. "Nour's here. Is Fadwa there? I'm sure they are dying to talk."

Standing behind Mama, Nour shuffled from one foot to the other. "Hi, Aunt Heba!" She waved as her cousin's curly blond hair appeared in the background.

"Nour! Are you ready for me?" Fadwa teased in a sing-song voice.

"Always, dear cousin." Nour wiped her palms against her thighs.

"So, what's new in Jerusalem?" Fadwa asked, her dark stone eyes staring directly at the camera.

"Oh, the usual, you know." She shivered, thinking about the increase of soldiers on the light rail train. "You hear what happened the other day?"

Fadwa turned her head to the side, eyebrows knotting, lips pursed.

"There was an attack? A mother and baby were killed?" Nour checked Fadwa for a response. "Well, I was on the light rail just after it happened. Suddenly, we stopped moving, and they told us to get off. We weren't even at a platform, and everyone started panicking. It was chaos."

Fadwa's eyes rolled, and she waved a dismissive hand in the air. "Yeah, I heard about that. Of course, the Israelis immediately said it was a terrorist attack, didn't they? They killed the Palestinian guy, the one who was driving the car, before even checking what happened. How did they know it wasn't a car accident, eh?"

Nour felt a lump in her throat. Why did it always feel like Fadwa was declaring a challenge?

RIVKI

Esti came to see her on her third day in the hospital. Not that Rivki was counting—she knew from experience that hospital days gave the illusion of being much longer than regular days. She also understood that between school and helping Ima, Esti probably had little time to spare.

"Rivi!" exclaimed her sister as she breezed into the room, making her way to the bed where Rivki lay still weak and groggy. She leaned over and gave Rivki a tiny peck on each cheek. "I've been so worried about you!" she gushed, plopping herself down in the recliner beside the bed. "How are you feeling? Ima says you're still in so much pain?"

Rivki nodded, arranging a defensive hand across her lower stomach. She studied Esti in the brilliant hospital lights. She looked somehow different, brighter, luminous.

"Rivi you'll never guess!" Her words came out high and fast, and she didn't wait for Rivki's guess. "I went on a date last night! His name is Yaakov. Yaakov Aaronson. He's the son of a teacher at Abba's Kollel, so the *shadchanit* thought we would be a good match and... well, Rivki, he was amazing. We talked all night long. He's such a scholar! We're going to meet again... Maybe even next week!"

Her deep, almost black eyes glowed out of her olive skin as she waited for Rivki to respond, but it took a few seconds for the words to register. A date? Last night? Rivki turned the words over in her fuzzy head. A match? A scholar? Last night? While she was stuck in here? She pulled herself up straighter in bed. "Tha... that's amazing." Her heart felt weak now, too.

"Oh, Rivi! He was perfect. I know he's the first person I've met, but they say that when you know, you just know... I don't know, well, I do know, he was perfect." She took Rivki's pale white hand in her own and squeezed it. "He was both a *ha-cham* and a *tzadik*. If it goes well, I might even agree to get his phone number and be in touch directly with him."

Rivki forced a smile. "I'm really happy for you," she said weakly, eyes stinging as she tried to focus on Esti's follow-up words. What she wore to the date, what he wore to the date, the various topics of conversation between her and this *shidduch*, what she thought might happen next and what she wanted to happen next. Rivki barely recognized the young woman beside her. Was it really Esti? How did everything change in only three days?

An hour later, as Esti breezed out of the room much as she had entered, Rivki felt a heaviness settle on her. She closed her eyes and tried to sleep but couldn't shake the feeling that she was being left behind, trapped in this stupid dumb hospital, with a stupid dumb stomach that didn't work. When she finally drifted off, she saw Esti sitting on a winking, sparkling star.

"Esti," Rivki called. "You said we would visit the stars together, remember?"

"I know, but you never came. I waited for you, but you never came." Esti's face was lit up in the darkness, the only beam in the night sky shining on her.

"I tried to come, Esti," Rivki called back, her voice hoarse. "Can I come now?"

"We'll see." Esti shrugged. "We'll see."

TAMAR

The next day at lunch, Tamar tried to get comfortable on the hard plastic chair as a colorful array of neat fish and rice packages were set down before them.

"How are you feeling, sweetie?" her mom started and, without giving her a chance to reply, she went on, "seeing something like that can be so difficult, I know. Before you were born, I worked in a place next to the Central Station. It was during the second Intifada. There were *piguim* all the time then. Buses blowing up all over the place."

Her mom hesitated before continuing. "One morning, on my way to work, the bus in front of mine blew up. It was surreal. I think I was in denial that it happened. I remember walking past all these charred bodies to get into work and saying to myself, 'Don't look, don't look.' But it didn't matter. I could still smell it, burned bodies. I was in shock and when I got into the office, I tried to pretend to myself that nothing was out of the ordinary. Of course, it was—there's nothing normal about a bus blowing up, is there? Just like there is nothing normal about someone driving a car into a train stop. I had nightmares about it for a long time afterward. I still think about it, even now."

Tamar regarded her mom for a few seconds. She couldn't imagine experiencing something so traumatic. No wonder her mom was so concerned about her. It made more sense now. Obviously, seeing a bus filled with passengers explode like that left her traumatized. Suddenly, she felt the need to protect her mom from her own horrors at all costs.

"I can't imagine what it was like then." Tamar reached a protective hand across the table and placed it on her mom's arm. "I mean, I know about the suicide bombings—we talked about them in school. And I've seen the plaques all over town, but I didn't know about you."

"Well, there's never a right time to talk about such horrific things even though it is really important to talk them through, let them out, exhale all that badness," said her mom expertly balancing a piece of sushi between chopsticks. "Or we remain traumatized."

"I know," breathed Tamar, her throat dry. "I know, but I'm fine, I promise. I mean, I still feel sick when I think about the baby, but I promise I'll be fine. The bodies were covered in white sheets. I didn't really see anything except the crushed baby carriage."

"Do you have any questions about the *matzav*?" her mom persisted. "Violence between Israelis and Palestinians is like ocean waves. It comes and goes and it's really okay to be scared whenever there's a flare-up like this."

Tamar was scared, and she did have questions about the situation. Many questions. Why did the Arabs hate them so much? Why would a man drive his car into a train stop and kill a baby? Why would a man put his hands down her pants and touch her without her permission? Tamar felt her mom watching her and all she wanted to do right then was change the subject.

"Mom. I'm fine, really. I just feel sad for those people who were killed. Sad that this is the kind of world we live in." Tamar squeezed her mom's arm, feeling more like the adult than the child.

NOUR

Nour tapped in a search for details of what happened the day she was forced off the light rail. On the *al-Quds* news website, there was an interview with the brother of the man who was driving the car, who was identified as Abdelrahman al-Shaludi—she took note of the name because it was the same as her brother's. Family members said Shaludi had a weak heart, and that he was likely having a heart attack when he drove onto the platform by mistake.

Nour was curious to see if the Israelis knew anything about this medical ailment. She searched in Hebrew but found it only described as a terrorist attack. They reported that Shaludi was shot and killed by Israeli security forces, who chased him at the scene. She wondered how, if he was having a heart attack, he could have jumped out of the car and run away.

Now, it seemed, there were two convincing versions of the same story. She scratched her forehead in frustration that Israelis automatically thought Palestinians were terrorists, but she also couldn't imagine why anyone would intentionally drive their car into a crowd. She didn't know how a driver would even know if the people standing waiting for the train were Israelis or Palestinians? Everyone in Jerusalem used the light rail—Jew, Muslim, Christian, Israeli, Arab. Nour shivered, imagining being hit by the thick, heavy metal of a moving car.

She shifted in her seat as she read more stories, in Arabic and in Hebrew, about Shaludi. She realized it really didn't matter whether his actions were intentional or an accident—the result was the same. Both sides were upset and, in the end, people would believe the narrative that best suited them.

Her people thought it was an accident. They could not conceive that someone would purposely kill a mother and child. The Israelis said it was intentional, for nationalistic reasons, and labeled it a terrorist attack. Either way, Nour understood, situations like this—in a city divided into tribes— always sparked a chain of reactions.

A Hebrew news site shared a short video clip of Jewish protestors, holding up banners demanding all Arabs be deported from Israel. Another report said Israeli soldiers visited Shaludi's house, not too far from her own. They filled it with cement, rendering it uninhabitable—to deter other people from doing the same thing, they said.

Shaludi's death and the destruction of his house infuriated her people, a bit like when her neighbor, Muhammad, was murdered. The day Shaludi was buried, there were protests, and a boy, about Nour's age, was shot and killed by Israeli soldiers using live bullets. One of the bullets went through his chest and ended up inside the schoolbag on his back. Nour watched a news report of the boy's father holding up the bullet and pointing to the hole in his dead son's backpack.

"What good is it to go to a protest when they have guns?" he sobbed into the camera. "You'll only end up dead like Nadim. There must be another way for Palestine!"

His tears were contagious, and Nour found herself wiping her own eyes.

RIVKI

The steady stream of doctors, nurses, orderlies, and roommates that paraded through the airy room did little to lighten the weight of solitude left by Esti's visit. A heaviness pressed down on Rivki's chest even as the searing pains in her stomach began to subside. Dr. Amnon said he wanted to "observe" her for a few more days to see if the problem inside her might still need fixing, but his words barely registered. Rivki could barely see.

She knew G-d was angry with her. He was punishing her for watching the *freiers* too closely, perhaps, or for thoughts of a husband and who she wanted him to be. These thoughts left no space for frustration over Ima's frantic morning visits, which she spent hunting down clean sheets or hounding certain doctors, before rushing off to pick up Batsheva from Mrs. Cohen.

Even Abba, who arrived each evening, a small Tupperware container tucked under his arm, could not dispel the darkness that was closing in on her like a never receding night. "It's really delicious, I think you'll like it." Abba waved the box, trying to tempt her with some variety of beef or chicken. "I know your stomach hurts, Rivkale, but G-d commanded us to eat for a reason. It saves lives. It makes us strong." He peeled back the plastic lid, filling the room with an aroma that churned Rivki's stomach. She turned away, letting guilt course freely through her veins.

It was only when Zehava, Mordechai's wife, came to see her before *Shabbos*, that Rivki's spirits lifted just slightly. In an elegant suit, a cloud of fruity perfume spiking the air, Zehava always came equipped with stories that left Rivki wanting more. She welcomed her sister-in-law's frank talk over the hushed whispers that usually surrounded her.

"*Baruch Ha-Shem*, I've just come from the maternity ward—Tzila Ruchel and Chana gave birth on the same day!" Zehava exclaimed, her smooth voice crisp and clear as she seated herself beside Rivki's bed. "Tzila Ruchel was due any day, but Chana, well, we didn't expect her to give birth for at least another month! The baby came early, and he's small, but *Baruch Ha-Shem* he's healthy. Though now we are stuck, one person short at work, and Matti is stressed because he needs to find someone to fill in and guess who will be the one to train them?"

"You, of course." Rivki clapped her hands together, realizing that she still knew how to smile.

As Zehava described the peaceful newborns sleeping a few floors below, Rivki watched in awe as thick red lips moved like blowing kisses. She admired the neat tucks of Zehava's gray suit, the soft folds of a blue blouse peeking out beneath the lapels, and a sparkly pin holding the shirt in place at her throat. Zehava worked every day as a bookkeeper at an accountancy firm, sharing her office with a gaggle of other young Haredi women. One day a week, she worked late, which Rivki knew Ima did not really approve of because it meant Mordechai came home from his studies to an empty house.

Still, Rivki marveled at the freedom of being able to get dressed up in a suit every morning and put on make-up. She wondered what it would feel like to sit in an office knowing you had the power to help other people, to advise them, and decide for them.

"Tell me again about your office. How is it arranged?" Rivki guided Zehava's chatter away from baby talk.

"Oh, it's not that glamorous." Zehava waved a manicured hand through the air. "Actually, we told Matti that he needed to bring in a cleaning crew. It needs a good going over and we don't have time to do that. It's not really our job anyway."

"What exactly is your job? Please tell me, I've always wanted to know," Rivki pushed, her body lighter.

"Well, we have to fill out spreadsheets to work out people's tax returns, that sort of thing," Zehava shrugged. "It involves a lot of math. Are you good at math?"

"I'm okay, I suppose. I've missed so much school lately. I doubt I will ever be able to get a job like that." Rivki felt the heaviness return to her chest again. "I don't even know now when I'll be able to go back to school. My friends are so far ahead of me...."

Zehava looked at her pensively. "Well, maybe we can ask the hospital to give you some catch-up lessons here? Do you want me to check with the nurse? I thought I saw a classroom on my way in."

Rivki blinked as she regarded Zehava. There was an official-looking woman who came into her room on the first day. She told Ima that she was a social worker and asked if Rivki might be interested in school while in the hospital. Ima shooed the woman away, saying they would make their own arrangements.

Zehava frowned when Rivki told her about it. "It's really important for us, as women, to keep up with our studies so that we can work, even when we're married. I know some people say it's more important to learn how to keep a kosher Jewish home or how to please your future husbands, but they forget we need to support them financially too so that they can keep studying Torah." She let out a heavy breath. "If we don't learn, we won't be able to get jobs, and then we won't be able to buy food for our children."

Rivki felt like Zehava just handed her the keys to a secret door.

Then she remembered her mother.

"What about Ima?" She looked at Zehava. "I mean, I'm interested... it would be a blessing, but it will upset Ima..."

Her sister-in-law moved in close and placed an elegant hand on Rivki's thin arm. "We can keep it between us for now," she whispered. Suddenly, Rivki saw her, a top executive, managing people, convincing them to work for her, and making millions. She nodded back at Zehava, her lips curling into a smile for the second time that day.

TAMAR

At school, people were still talking about the run-over attack. Tal said he wasn't at all surprised an Arab did such a thing. "My *savta* says all Arabs have a violent streak. It's part of their culture, their religion. They don't value life and they really don't care if they kill men or women and children, as long as they kill Jews."

They were on a break between classes, sitting in a café not far from the school. Tal reminded them again that his grandmother was from Baghdad. "She grew up with the Arabs, so she understands their mentality." He tapped a finger on his forehead. "We all need to be aware of what these people are capable of."

He urged Tamar to tell them what she saw at the site of the attack, and she found it much easier to talk about what happened with Tal and Aviv than with her parents. As far as she knew, none of them had witnessed a suicide attack.

"Animals! My *savta*'s right!" exclaimed Tal, as Tamar described the smashed-up car and mangled baby carriage. "Who kills a mother and a baby? Who does that? Remember what they did last year? Killing those three boys like that? They were the same age as us! Remember? It was awful!"

Tamar's stomach flipped again, but this time the feeling was not with sickness, it was with a spark of fire. She remembered the pink blanket lying crumpled next to two dead bodies, one big and one small. Tal was right. It was awful.

"Tal, you're right," she declared, looking into his blue eyes. "How could we forget what happened to Eyal, Naftali, and Gilad?"

The three Israeli boys were on their way home from school when Hamas terrorists kidnapped them. The entire country was looking for them. Two weeks later, their bodies were found in a field, murdered. Then came the militants' rockets. Fired into Israel every night for fifty-one days. It was terrifying. Tamar would never forget lying flat on the ground, folding her arms around her head, a siren wailing above her, when one rocket reached Jerusalem.

She also remembered the protests. All the usual places near her school were filled with angry people, waving banners, blowing horns, and calling for revenge. Tamar was just thankful it was summer vacation already, and she didn't need to venture into the city center.

"Look, it was an upsetting time. How could we forget all that?" Aviv's reasoning broke into Tamar's thoughts. "But that was done by one group of people, a terrorist cell, my dad said. There are thousands of Arabs living in Israel, millions maybe. If all of them were violent, then we would be living in perpetual war. It's really only a few extremists that carry out these attacks. Last year, I was in Chicago. There are more murders there than here..."

"Why are you always trying to defend them?" Tal snorted back at her. "They ran over a mother with her baby. What's worse than that? And look what they did to Tamar! Just stop it, Aviv. No one here shares your left-wing views."

Aviv turned from Tal to Tamar, her face flushed from the sudden mention of the assault. "Tamar, you understand what I'm saying, don't you? Judge the individual, not the group," she pleaded.

Tamar sized up Aviv. Her instinct was to defend her friend, but she just wasn't buying the wishy-washy rationale anymore. Too much happened over the past few weeks and in this instance, Tal was more right. The Arabs differed totally from her people. It was a different mentality; they didn't view the world the same way as Jews. She knew about cultural norms—how every group had its own acceptable methods of behavior. Even though the Arabs lived together in the same city as them, they were different.

Tamar cleared her throat, powerless to quench the fire now burning in the pit of her stomach. "I'm sorry, Aviv, but I'm not sure anymore. Too much has happened."

Aviv's face fell. "Fine," she spat, standing so quickly that the table between them shook. She grabbed her bag from her chair, but before walking away, added stiffly, "You guys can be single-minded racists if you want, but it's not for me."

NOUR

Fadwa arrived the following week, laden with three heavy suitcases and exuding national pride. "It's *so* good to be back in *Palestine*," she declared in a loud voice as she marched towards Mama and Nour.

Nour's shoulders burned with suspicious eyes as Fadwa's high-heeled boots click-clacked across the marble floor in Tel Aviv airport's arrivals hall. She couldn't help but wonder if the spike of deadly car crashes and shootings, not only in Jerusalem but all over Palestine, were timed purposely to stoke her cousin's militancy.

Night after night, as she watched the evening news, Nour's heart tore a little more as another grieving mother wailed for a lost child. Officials decried Israel's murderous tactics, even as they praised the actions of martyrs who posted rhapsodic Facebook statements declaring their desire for *istishhadi*, martyrdom, to protect the holy mosque or the lands of Palestine or the rights of its people.

Nour was sure not everyone shuffling their feet at a checkpoint or carrying a knife in their bag wanted to murder an Israeli, even if life under occupation was harsh and restricting, but Fadwa, who immediately began monitoring the news reports along with her, emphatically disagreed.

"The occupation is no picnic." She wagged a finger at Nour. "This is a war. We are fighting for our rights and for our country. We must fight and we cannot stop until the Jews return all the lands they stole from us. If some of our people die, that's the sacrifice."

Nour couldn't really see how being dead would further their national goals, but she understood why people were so angry and frustrated lately. Since the violence started, a dark rainbow of Israeli soldiers, a colony of green, blue, and black uniforms, set up camp in Shuafat. They were everywhere. On the corner next to the pharmacy, in the open lot next to the bakery, even lurking behind her friend Yasmin's house, making the insides of Nour's stomach loosen every time she walked past. She wanted to run whenever she saw a soldier, but she willed herself to do exactly the opposite, to slow down, knowing their guns were poised for any jolty steps.

While Nour tried to be invisible, Fadwa was infuriated. The burly soldiers in Shuafat were all she could talk about.

"They watch us like we're criminals when it's they who are the criminals," she declared one evening, perching herself on the faded arm of the couch right next to where Nour and Baba watched the news. "What gives them the right to be here? They're too quick and happy to shoot anything that moves! They don't see us as human beings."

When no one answered, Fadwa pressed on. "Did you see what happened in Hebron yesterday?" she declared, addressing no one specifically. She pulled out her phone and waved it in front of Nour. "Watch this," she commanded. "Abdulrahman sent it to me."

Nour obliged, not daring to move her eyes from the screen. She watched as a shadowy figure draped in what looked like a black *abaya* stood with both hands held high in the air. A soldier stood facing the person with his gun cocked between them. There was no sound, but it was clear an exchange was taking place. Nour could see his lips moving. Then suddenly there was a flash and the tip of his rifle jerked upwards. The figure crumbled to the ground, like the body inside the dress somehow vanished.

"See? See what happened? He shot her. Her hands were up in surrender and still, he shot her! Illegal occupation army! It's an outrage!" Fadwa's face was dark like thunder. "This, this, this is why we have to fight back. She was a good religious girl, and that dog shot her for no reason. Where is the world? Where is the international outrage? No one cares about Palestinians. We have to fight this ourselves."

"I... well... I, it's awful," Nour tried to muster the same indignation as Fadwa.

"What? Are you going to make excuses for them now?" Fadwa glared at her.

"No, of course not, it, it's shocking, totally shocking," Nour muttered as a thick layer of sickness formed in the pit of her stomach. Why did there have to be so much violence? Why couldn't everyone live in peace? Who cared if someone was Israeli, Jewish, Palestinian, Arab, Muslim—surely all those things were just outside labels? What counted was what was on the inside.

She glanced at Baba, still glued to the news. Her body seemed to break in two. One part was attached to her father, who kept things simple, accepting the situation around him and making the most of what he was given. The other wanted to be instilled with the same passionate outrage as her cousin and brother, who seemed to have forged their own private language whenever discussing the stream of horrific events. They used terms and concepts that blew Nour's mind and locked her out of their world.

To her, each incident that took place seemed random, uncoordinated—the *abaya* girl in Hebron, a teenage boy shot dead in Nablus, even two cousins from her own neighborhood wrestled to the ground and arrested by the Israeli police in Jerusalem—but she overheard Abdulraman declaring to Fadwa that a revolution was underway, that her people were finally fighting back. And she heard Fadwa agreeing with him, exuding a kindred warmth that she never extended to Nour.

RIVKI

On Sunday afternoon, not long after Ima left for home, a girl with bright eyes and an even brighter smile entered Rivki's room. "I understand you might be interested in taking classes in the hospital school?" She didn't look that much older than Esti.

"Y-y-yes, I'm interested," Rivki answered, feeling gray beside this sunshiny girl. "Who told you?"

"The tall lady in the suit... let me see," the girl looked down at her notes. "Zehava Lefkovitz." She took a few steps towards Rivki's bed, tanned knees poking out from scuffed-up jeans, and placed her clipboard on the bed. "So? You're interested?"

Rivki nodded, spying Zehava's curly signature on a line that read "parent/guardian." Below her name was a list of subjects, each followed by a black box.

"Great! My name's Ariel. I'm a volunteer, a *shinshin,* with *Shnat Sherut.* I just need you to mark down which subjects you're interested in—we can help you with almost anything while you are here, so you don't fall too far behind," she said, letting the r's roll from the back of her throat to the tip of her tongue.

After a week in the hospital, Rivki could determine the religiosity of the staff by the way they spoke. The secular doctors and nurses let their words flow with more ease. Their language was less complicated than the people she knew. In her community, tongues were weighed down by ancient accents and dusty holy texts.

She also liked the array of modern Hebrew names, like Ariel, which were free from the burdens of greatness evoked by biblical names such as Rivka,

Esther, Debora or Ruthy and untainted by the legacy of ancestors called Faigy or Frayda, Gittle or Goldie.

Ariel held out a pen as though it were a blessing and Rivki took it, feeling light as she fingered her way down the list of topics. Zehava's words about women studying popped into her head and she quickly marked an x in the box next to math.

"Math, excellent." Ariel peered down. "Very important subject. My friend, Ayelet, you'll meet her soon. She'll be able to help you."

Rivki handed her back the papers and pen, a glimmer of hopefulness filling her heart for the first time in months.

"We can start now if you like," Ariel offered, holding out her arms as if she was giving Rivki a blessing.

Rivki nodded, noticing Ariel's icy blue eyes for the first time. They weren't so different from Rivki's own, but they were outlined with fierce strokes of kohl, making them pop. Rivki wondered what it would be like to be adorned with such bold make-up, to unabashedly draw attention.

"Great! Follow me." Ariel slid the pen into the breast pocket of her jacket and headed for the door.

Rivki hesitated before swinging her legs over to the side of the bed and sliding her thin feet into the warm slippers Ima brought her from home. She no longer needed a catheter, but an intravenous drip delivering what the doctors called "essential nutrients" was still hooked up to her arm. She grabbed the metal pole that held the IV bag and used it to steady herself as she followed Ariel through the busy hospital ward to a bright alcove tucked away at the far end.

It was a welcoming space. A life-sized bear in a top hat clutching a pot of honey was painted on one wall and an enormous window looked out on a carpet of treetops. Rivki plopped herself down on a scuffed plastic chair, examining cluttered shelves filled with books and board games and stuffed animals.

A girl with hair a shade or two darker than Ariel's was sitting at a nearby table with a boy about Rivki's age. Her cheeks flushed when she saw that his pajama top was unbuttoned, revealing a forest of dark hairs.

"Rivki, this is Ayelet. She works with me." Ariel pointed to the other girl. "And that is Muhammed. Guys, this is Rivki. She's going to study math with you, Ayelet."

The two smiled at her, and Rivki forced a smile back. She was sure it was forbidden to be in the same room as a half-dressed boy, even though it was clear he wasn't Jewish. She stole another glance at Muhammed, noticing that he was sitting in a wheelchair. A fluffy hospital blanket covered his lap and two fat white casts poked out where his legs should be.

"Car accident. His little brother was killed, both his parents are in critical. Such a tragedy," Ariel whispered into Rivki's ear, pulling up a chair beside her.

Rivki put a quiet hand on her lips lest something inappropriate should escape from them. There must be something in the *halacha* about sympathy and kindness outweighing the ban on being in close proximity to a male who was not a relative. Someone experiencing such tragedy needed warmth and pity, even if being near them was forbidden. She promised to herself that the next time he looked in her direction, she would give him a bigger smile.

"In the mornings, Ayelet and I teach the younger children in the ward," Ariel flicked through papers on her lap. "Mostly it's games and stories, but you're more than welcome to join if you want to. After lunch, we work one on one with older patients like you."

She pulled out a wad of papers and placed them down in front of Rivki. "A quick math test so we can assess your level and build you a program. Go through it at your own pace and answer as many questions as you can. Now..." Ariel stopped, turning to the shelf behind them and grabbing a pen from a row of large round holders. "Do you want to make a permanent time to come here every day?"

"Erm, maybe like two or something?" The plastic chair suddenly felt hard, and Rivki wondered if she might be signing her soul over to a lifetime of sin, but if Ima was gone by lunch and Abba only arrived at dinner, surely she could squeeze this lesson in the middle.

"Perfect." Ariel's sanguine smile absolved her of some guilt. "Now, take your time. Answer as many as you can. This is a test for *kita yud*. Your mother said you were sixteen? So, this should be just the right level for you, although, of course, it varies from school to school."

Rivki was just about to tell her that Zehava was not her mother, but decided to keep quiet, at least for now. As she worked through the problems, Rivki felt the rusted wheels in her brain springing back to life. It was so long since she had really learned anything. Surely that made it alright that she was deceiving Ima?

Just using her brain was deceitful in her mother's eyes. Ima thought all girls needed to know was how to be a *balaboste*, that homemaking was their greatest achievement. She was so old-fashioned. Why shouldn't girls, even Haredi ones, use their brains and achieve more than just keeping a neat home or raising children?

Rivki looked up at Ariel, who was now busy sorting through another stack of messy papers, and then at Ayelet, who was sitting shoulder to shoulder with poor Mohammad. Ima would shield her eyes from such a scene.

She turned her attention back to the test, blood pumping through her veins as she reached what she thought was the correct answer for each problem.

"How's it going?" Rivki looked up to see Ayelet hovering beside her. "Those are really hard; do you want some help?"

"*Baruch Ha-Shem*, thank G-d, that would be very kind." Rivki looked beyond her, ready to offer a warm smile to the boy in the wheelchair, but he was nowhere in sight.

TAMAR

Aviv was still not talking to Tamar a whole week later when news spread around the school of a shooting attack on Jaffa Road, just five minutes away. Tamar was with Tal on the battered couches near their classroom when roaring sirens drowned out their conversation. Tal's phone began to ping like a video game.

"What the...." Tamar jolted her head back and looked at him with wide eyes.

"A shooting," he mumbled, intent on his phone screen as he continued to scroll. "I think it's the first time they used a gun in an attack, not a knife or a car." His phone was still pinging.

"Oh shit, how many killed?" Tamar watched his fingers glide over the screen, a loose frothiness enveloped her stomach.

"Not clear yet." Tal frowned, head still bent. "The push from *Hamal* is saying several injured, some severely."

"*Hamal*?" Tamar was fascinated by the pinging, buzzing, and flashing on Tal's phone.

"Tam! Why are you so clueless? We need to get you hooked up to reality." He looked at her now, shaking his head, a playfulness in his eyes. "It's a news app. It's the only way to know what is going on."

He grabbed her phone and began tapping furiously. "Okay, that should do it," he said, handing it back to her. "Now, what are you doing tonight?"

"Not much. Band practice, then home." Tamar scanned her phone. It was already buzzing with news alerts.

"Well, how about coming to a protest? With me? My cousin's organizing it. It's outside the Knesset." He leaned towards her and put a hand on her leg. "People think this government's not doing enough to protect us from these attacks, from the Arabs. We think more needs to be done."

Tamar met Tal's blue eyes. She did not move her leg. The frothiness in her stomach gave way to something much sharper. She was angry too about what was happening. It was bubbling inside her since the day of the ramming attack at the train stop, since the day she was violated, and now a shooting. "Sure, what time?"

"Let me check." Tal swiftly turned back to his phone. "My cousin says to be there at seven, so that's perfect. We'll make some music and head over there together." He looked up, putting his chin out in a grin.

Tamar shifted slightly and cleared her throat. "Great, I'll see you later."

As she was about to stand, Tamar spied Aviv in the distance. Without thinking, she raised a hand in the air, but immediately, Aviv turned away. Tamar let her arm drop in defeat. Aviv was so stubborn. Why couldn't she understand some people held different opinions from her?

"What?" Tal asked, twisting his neck.

"Aviv," Tamar grumbled.

"Ugh, she's so closed-minded." He shook his head. "How come we're expected to respect her position, but she won't accept ours?"

"You're right, Tal. She's just being unreasonable." Tamar pinched the bridge of her nose and gave Tal a weak smile, a small hole opening in her heart where Aviv once fit.

NOUR

Abdulrahman and Fadwa appeared to be inseparable these days. When he wasn't there, she was forever tutting and checking her watch, asking Mama or Baba when he might be back. When Abdulrahman did arrive home from school, Fadwa would throw down any chore or task she was doing and rush to join him. Then they would huddle for hours, a force field of low whispers surrounding them like hot steam on a chilly day, making clear that no one else was allowed into their circle.

In a way, having her erstwhile antagonist kept so busy meant Nour could focus on her own life—her sewing, her studies—but whenever she saw their heads bent together, her bones would fill with the same dread that surrounded her during the days following the murder of Muhammed, her neighbor.

She knew from her own experiences with Fadwa that whenever her cousin was involved, things got dangerous, and two matches placed near a fire almost always caused a bigger explosion.

Unease hung in the air a few days later as she and Fadwa helped Mama prepare Friday lunch. She placed rice mixed with pine nuts and raisins into a large dish and tipped the lamb with its sweet juices on top. Fadwa heated the *khubez*, crispy, round bread, to dip into the salad mixtures and together they laid it all on the table surrounded by gold-rimmed china plates.

As soon as Baba and her three brothers trooped into the house from the mosque, everyone took their places around the crowded table, helping themselves to the mouth-watering *maqluba* or the vegetable *musakhan* or chicken *shish taouk*.

"So, Nouri, how were all your tests this week?" Baba asked her through mouthfuls of lamb and rice.

"Er... I think I did okay." She shrugged.

"How okay?" Baba held his hand out for her to pass the vegetables.

"Mmm... 98." She handed them to him.

"98? In?" He took the small plate out of her hands.

Nour shuffled in her seat and glanced around the table. Abdulrahman and Fadwa were at the far end, engrossed in their own talk. Mama was busy fussing over Adam and Khalil, who filled their plates and mouths greedily.

"Hebrew," she muttered, feeling silence envelope the room.

"*Mumtaz habibti, metzuyan,*" Baba sang in Arabic-Hebrew congratulations. "Knowing Hebrew will only help you in the future and you'll be able to work in a hospital, like me! You like studying Hebrew, don't you?"

Excited expectation was painted on her father's face, but from the corner of her eye, Nour noticed Abdulrahman and Fadwa exchange a look. She knew what they would think about her learning the language of the enemy.

"Well... I mean... it's an interesting language." She blotted them out by focusing on the soft yellow spots in Baba's eyes. "I mean, it's weird because it's a completely different language than Arabic, of course, yet it's so similar. Like related, but completely different. It's also because of Mrs. Rahman..." Nour looked at Fadwa and Abdulrahman and then added, "She's an amazing teacher."

Mrs. Rahman was the only teacher in her school who was Jewish, but she was born in Egypt and spoke Arabic like everyone else. Nour loved the idea of being able to speak two languages equally. She liked Mrs. Rahman because she never shouted or lost her patience like other teachers. She was always encouraging and told Nour she had a natural talent for languages. Mrs. Rahman was pushing Nour to learn Hebrew-Arabic translation, but she didn't feel like mentioning that now.

"That's great, Nour," her father said, mopping his plate with a thin piece of bread. "Mrs. Rahman sounds like an excellent teacher."

"Yeah, she always makes the lessons so interesting. It's not just the language. She helps us understand Judaism and Jewish customs." Nour heard a small choke at the other end of the table, but Baba made her feel energized. "Did you know that many Jews, like Mrs. Rahman, came here from Arab lands? They are Arab Jews!"

"Arab Jews! They're not Arabs, they're Israeli. They can't be both. That's a contradiction," Fadwa's voice exploded into the space between Nour and Baba.

"That's what we said, too, but Mrs. Rahman made some clever arguments." Nour looked at her cousin calmly. "She said that if Muslims and Christians can be Arabs, then why can't there be Jews? That Arab was a culture and Jewish, Muslim, and Christian were all religions."

"She sounds like a very smart woman." Baba drowned out Fadwa's attempt to respond. "Surely you've all heard of Leila Mourad? She's a famous Egyptian singer and actress. She was Jewish."

"Ohhh," Nour gushed. "I love her movies, but, Jewish? Are you sure, Baba?"

Baba gave a throaty laugh. "She kept it very quiet. She had to."

Scraping chairs cut out Baba's last words. Fadwa began collecting empty plates with clattering commotion and Abdulrahman was already stomping heavily towards the living room, a pack of cigarettes in his hand.

Baba was undeterred. "What else does Mrs. Rahman tell you?"

"She told us about an international fashion show taking place in Tel Aviv," Nour started, her father's attention raising her spirits and her confidence. "There were Jewish and Arab fashion designers displaying the clothes together—Baba, did you know that some Israeli designers, not only the Jewish ones, are popular in Ameri..."

"Again with the fashion nonsense, Nour?" his tone was suddenly sharp. "I don't understand your obsession with clothes. It's so shallow and you are such a smart girl. Did your clever teacher tell you that clothes are not what makes a person special? That it's not what decorates us on the outside that is important—it is what is on the inside."

Nour studied the food stains on her plate, the only one Fadwa left on the table. "I know," she mumbled, looking back up, searching for the softness in his eyes. She thought about Leila Mourad, glamorous in sparkling jewels and fur-lined coats and silhouette dresses of shimmering silk.

"Baba," her voice came out strong. "I also know that clothes make people happy. That a person's natural strengths are boosted if they are dressed smartly too, and I know that in our culture, clothes have a long history of giving people power and status." Nour looked over at Fadwa and Abdulrahman, who were now sitting side by side in the living room, before continuing. "My art teacher says I'm talented. She says I could use that talent to become a famous Palestinian fashion designer—"

"Nour, Nouri, we've been through this before." Now it was his turn to stand up from the table. "You're not from a village. You have a bright future in a modern world. Palestinian dressmakers are a thing of the past, from a time when women didn't have the opportunity to study like they do today. They didn't have the chance to contribute great things to the world."

With his final words, Baba marched into the kitchen. The loud thud of the door closing ripped into her heart and, not caring if Mama needed her help, Nour ran upstairs to her room. Baba supported her against Abdulrahman and Fadwa. She loved that he was unafraid to state his opinion, but sometimes Nour wanted him to be a little more flexible. Especially with her.

RIVKI

It was Esti who came to see Rivki the next morning, not Ima.

"Batsheva has a fever and Ima had to stay with her," she informed Rivki, plonking herself down on the oversized chair beside the bed.

"Oh, no! Poor Batshevaleh," said Rivki, who was sure Ima was now fretting over having another illness in the family. She muttered a quick prayer for good health under her breath.

"Don't worry, it's probably just a virus." Esti dismissed the baby's condition with a breezy wave.

"*Baruch Ha-Shem*, I hope you're right, Esti." She studied her older sister's round, symmetrical face, cheeks still flushed pink from the wind outside and lips cherry red, like she'd been sucking on some exotic fruit.

"Yeah, she always gets sick like this in the winter. She just needed a day at home with Ima." Esti raced through her words. "Rivi... guess what? Yaakov sent a message saying he wants to meet me again!" She rearranged herself in the chair. "We're going on a second date tomorrow night! I'm just so excited, Rivi! I just... I don't know... I have this weird feeling..."

More words spilled from Esti's cherry lips, but Rivki felt herself moving like the sloshing, swishing trees outside. She watched them bow and bend against the gray sky and wondered how they did not break.

"It's everything we talked about, Rivi," she heard her sister's voice rise to a crescendo. "You are happy for me, aren't you, Rivki?" She put a hand on Rivki's IV-infused arm.

"Ouch." The needle dug deeper into Rivki's veins.

"Oh, no, Rivi, I, I didn't notice..." Esti pulled back, stung.

Rivki trembled and looked at her sister. Of course she didn't notice—all Esti cared about these days was herself. Suddenly, she realized this was only her second visit since she'd arrived here *last week*. Esti was moving on with her life, while Rivki was stuck in this stupid morbid prison, in her stupid broken body, with a stupid disease raging inside.

"I'm fine," Rivki mumbled, though the sharpness of the needle still stung.

"*Baruch Ha-Shem*," Esti declared, jumping up and flinging her arms around Rivki's slender neck. She planted a cherry kiss on Rivki's cheek and finally asked, "How are you feeling?"

Rivki didn't know if she could answer that, so she just mumbled, "I'm fine."

TAMAR

Tamar's head throbbed as she threw books into her bag and trudged towards the auditorium. Band practice was usually the sweeter part of her day, but even there it seemed she was wading through a battleground. Oded, the music teacher, tried to soothe tensions after the big fight appealing to them to put aside their differences, but two weeks later Tamar still detected a chill in the air and in their music. Now, a once-cohesive unit comprised two distinctly separate factions.

"Hey, how was math?" Tal greeted her with a smile.

Tamar shrugged.

"You're not still feeling bad about Aviv, are you?" He put a warm arm around her shoulders and steered her towards the stage. "Really, Tam, she'll come around and if not, it's her problem. It's time people learned to accept the views of others."

Tamar looked around the dank auditorium doubtfully. Signs of the new alliances were everywhere. Kobi and Gaya were still outside smoking cigarettes, and Leon, who didn't even smoke, was out there with them. Ron and Noa, the other vocalist, were huddled together in the small kitchenette behind the stage, the bitter smell of muddy coffee wafting into the hall.

"I suppose it will pass." She cleared her throat and gave him a weak smile. Tamar felt the space between them disappear.

"Okay, guys." Kobi's voice, cold and detached, pierced the air. "We don't have too much time. Take your places."

Tamar broke away from Tal and watched him from the corner of her eye as he sauntered to the back of the stage, taking up his perch behind the drum set.

The agreement was to shelve Kobi's previous song and avoid any more debates or songs about politics. The focus of The Jerusalemites would be on more sanguine topics, love and heartbreak, which suited Tamar just fine, and Kobi already had another tune lined up. Tamar didn't know how he managed to churn out one song after the other.

"Are we all ready?" Kobi began tapping a simple beat on the side of his guitar. He nodded towards Noa and Tamar to join him with the words. The song's tempo was low, matching her mood, and Tamar closed her eyes, imagining the power of her vocal cords ejecting the poison that lay heavy inside her lungs.

Remains of their love blew like smoky embers.
She knew right then he could not remember.
The passion they felt when it all started,
Dissolved like ice the minute they parted.
Already, she knew he was letting her go,
"It's not you, my love. I just need to grow."
Grow, she mocked him, without me?
How can it be? How can it be?
Their souls had touched, just for a day.
She couldn't let it end this way,
Couldn't let it end this way.

Tamar let the words flow through her body like freshwater smoothing down sharp stones. How Kobi injected such depth into his poetry or found the words to describe such feelings, she didn't know. She couldn't even describe the things going on in front of her eyes these days, let alone dig down into her soul and pull out the right words to express it all.

"Well, what did you think?" Tal questioned her as the band packed up their belongings.

Tamar fumbled with the microphone, returning it to the stand. For the first time in a while, she felt light. "It's a really beautiful song," she breathed, feeling Tal's gaze on her like a spotlight. "I'm forever amazed at Kobi's talents. He has such a way with words."

"True," Tal's voice seemed to crack a little. "And it sounds even more beautiful when you're singing it. You're very talented too, Tam."

Tamar looked up at Tal, her friend and music partner. In the dim light of the dusty hall, his eyes shone bright, like the bluest skies on the sunniest days. When did he start calling her Tam?

NOUR

Loud banging woke Nour from a deep sleep. She fumbled in the darkness for her phone. 3 a.m! Who was banging on the door at 3 a.m? Then came the voices, speaking in Hebrew. What was going on?

Slipping a gray sweatshirt over her nightshirt, she sauntered out of her room to investigate. As she reached the landing, six or seven Israeli soldiers, heavy boots thumping on the stairs, pushed past her.

"Abdulrahman's room, which one?" barked one soldier. "Abdulrahman?" he growled again. The other soldiers didn't wait for her response before they started flinging open all the doors.

"That one," her voice sounded distant. She pointed and took a protective step in front of Adam and Khalil's door just as it opened. A small head peeked out. "Go back inside and stay there," she hissed, closing the door tightly and leaving her hand on the knob.

Then she heard Mama's cry. She was flying up the stairs, Baba panting behind her.

"What do you want with him? What did he do?" Mama screamed, hair covered by a hasty scarf, robe tied at her waist.

"Do you have an arrest warrant?" Baba was calmer, but Nour still heard panic.

A second later, a disheveled Abdulrahman was being dragged from his room, eyes blinking in the artificial light, mouth set in a smirk. The soldiers were now inside his room, pulling open drawers, spilling out their contents. They flipped over the still warm mattress, tipping sheets and blankets to the floor. Then they grabbed his computer from the desk, unplugging it with a jerk from the wall.

"Hey! What are you doing to him? Where are you taking him?" Mama shouted at the soldiers, trying to block their path like a wild and protective mother hen.

"Rania, Rania, stop!" Baba pulled her behind him. "Look, I'm a doctor, a scientist. I work in Hadassah Hospital." He held up his hospital ID. "There must be some sort of mistake. We've never done anything wrong. Never committed any crimes.... Who's the commanding officer? I demand to see a warrant. You can't just walk into my house like this!"

Nour stood with her back to the door of her brothers' room, as one of the soldiers waved an official-looking document in his face. "It's all in here. We have an order to arrest Abdulrahman Asa'ad."

Baba put out his hand to take the paper, but the soldier just let go and it floated to the ground like a dead leaf. Anger coursed through Nour's veins as she watched her father bend to pick it up. He looked so small and weak next to the soldiers in their dark green and gray uniforms. He stood no chance next to their rifles.

"Sir, Madam, please move out of the way. We have to take him. No one needs to get hurt," said a different soldier, the one who asked her for Abdulrahman's bedroom, urging them to stand aside.

Abdulrahman was the only person not saying anything. The defiant smirk he woke up with was still plastered on his face, but when Nour looked in his eyes, she thought she saw flecks of fear in there too. Arms pinned behind his back, he was led by two soldiers down the stairs towards the open front door. The rest of the troops stomped after them, trailed by Baba's voice as he looked up from the paper in his hand. "What did you do, Abdul? What did you do?"

"I didn't do anything, Baba." Her brother's voice trailed out into the cold night air. "This is the face of the occupation. None of us is free. We'll be free only when we fight back."

"Fight back?" Baba mumbled, more to himself. "It says here he's a member of a terrorist group—that he's been inciting violence against innocent civilians."

Nour watched her broken parents make their way back down the stairs. Mama's shoulders seemed to droop. Baba was still shaking his head. As he reached the bottom step, Nour saw the soldier who did most of the talking place a hand on her father's shoulder and then talk to him intensely. Baba kept on shaking his head.

"Your soldiers," Fadwa was suddenly behind her. "Look what they do! They come in the middle of the night and treat us like animals for no reason at all."

This time, Nour did not silence her cousin. In fact, Fadwa's anger stoked her own. Why couldn't the soldier have just handed Baba the paper properly? And why did they need to storm the house in the middle of the night? Wake everyone up with such a fright?

Then she remembered her other brothers. Nour turned and opened the door behind her. When she switched on the light, the two beds were empty, covers thrown back in haste. Nour bent down and saw two bodies curled up beneath Adam's bed.

"It's okay, the soldiers have gone. It's okay to come out now, come." Nour's heart flew to her brothers as she planted her knees on the floor. "Why don't you both get back into bed now, go back to sleep?"

"What did Abdulrahman do?" Adam asked as he crawled out from under the bed. He suddenly looked much older than his ten years. "Where are they taking him?"

Khalil came out next, rubbing his eyes. "Why did they wake us up in the middle of the night?"

Nour glanced at Fadwa standing in the doorway. She was silent for once, and Nour felt grateful. "I don't know what he did... Maybe it's all a big mistake." She wished she could give them answers, but she didn't know herself what was going on. She nudged them back into their beds, kissed each one, and, before turning out the light, added, "Don't worry about it now. Baba's taking care of it."

"I doubt Uncle Samir can sort this one out," Fadwa snorted behind Nour as they made their way down the stairs. "Once they've gotten hold of him, they'll never let him go. You'll see, dear cousin, you'll see. You've been blind to the occupation, but now, you'll see what really happens."

Fadwa's words hung heavy in the air. An image of her brother and her cousin whispering together in the living room or stepping out of

Abdulrahman's bedroom flashed through her mind. The arrest warrant said Abdulrahman was a member of a terrorist group, that he incited violence, and Nour remembered vividly her brother's angry threats when their neighbor Muhammad was murdered. But surely he wouldn't really hurt anyone?

She heard of this sort of thing happening to boys from other families, but never dreamed it would happen to her own. It must all have been a mistake, or another facet of the occupation, as Fadwa said—Israelis arresting Palestinians for no reason, taking them away in the middle of the night like animals just to make them suffer.

RIVKI

A few hours later, arm still throbbing from Esti's feckless grab, Rivki gathered up her intravenous contraption and shuffled to the end of the hall for her first math lesson. She tried to push all thoughts of her sister, and Ima, out of her mind as she reached the brightly lit classroom.

"Rivki! Welcome." Ariel's wide smile pulled her through the sliding glass doors and soft music crackling from a small radio set drew her inside further.

"Who sings this?" Rivki brushed up beside the radio, a smooth honey voice filling her ears and lifting her like a cloud.

"Oh, that's Romi Sofer." Ayelet strolled up next to her. "You've never heard of her? She's everywhere these days. They call her Romi for short. She's only sixteen and a teenybopper favorite."

"I-I like it," Rivki strained to make out the words. "It's really beautiful."

"Yes, it is really beautiful." Ariel's tanned knees were hidden behind shape-hugging black leggings today. "It's called *Tikva*, hope. So glad you came back, Rivki. Shall we get started? Ayelet?"

"Ready for an hour of numbers?" Ayelet gestured to a table already set up with some books. "Your table awaits."

Rivki held on to the closing beats of Romi's *Tikva* before sitting down. "Er... where's Mohammad today?" She suddenly remembered.

"Not feeling good," Ariel answered her. "Poor guy, he's been through so much. It's surprising he's even interested in taking lessons at all."

Rivki was disappointed she wouldn't be able to test out her new conviction.

"So, I don't see any physical cuts on you. What are you in for?" Ayelet asked her, moving a chair up close.

"Me? I-I-I've got... er... Crohn's Disease," Rivki whispered the last two words like a confession. "I've had a flare-up. The doctors don't know... er, they want to see if this medicine works before they decide to operate on me."

"Crohn's Disease?" Ayelet stretched her legs out on either side of Rivki's chair.

"Well... it's-it's—er, an inflammation... of the intestine, means I can't eat anything without it causing pain." She tried not to stare at Ayelet's boyish posture.

"Yeah, sure it sucks," Ayelet's voice was leathery. Then she let out a snort. "Not being able to eat anything, damn."

"Perfect diet for you, Ayelet." Ariel walked over to them and put a gentle hand on Rivki's shoulder. "But I'm sure it's painful, isn't it, Rivki?"

Rivki shifted slightly in her seat; Ariel's touch made her smile inside. She heard no one, not even boys, talk like Ayelet.

"Aw, Rivki, ya know I'm only teasing." The darker-haired volunteer gave her a tap on the shoulder. "It's true, I wouldn't mind losing a few kilos, but not being able to eat. Now that's tough. Well, we'll get you feeling better. Now, let's crunch some numbers."

Rivki looked down at the pages in front of her, arm throbbing from Esti and shoulder warm from Ariel. "It's not good to be too thin. Boys don't like emaciated girls—no one wants to marry someone who looks sick."

"What words of wisdom, Rivki!" Ayelet slapped the table and burst out laughing.

"Oh Rivki, you're so funny." Ariel squeezed her shoulder again.

Rivki looked questioningly from one to the other.

"You were joking, right?" Ayelet hauled in her laughter. "Who's even talking about getting married?"

"Well, my sister, Esti, she's about the same age as you." Rivki sat stiffly. "She'll probably get engaged soon."

"Wow, you people get married so young! Don't you want to see something of the world? Do something else with your lives?" Ayelet composed herself now.

"Sorry, Rivki, she's never really spoken to a Haredi girl before. My family's a little *dati*, we keep *Shabbat*, but even for us, it's different to you." Ariel reached out for another chair. "My parents encouraged my brother and me to go to the army. They'll want me to go to university too, so it'll be years before we can even think about getting married."

"You're going to the army? Both of you?" Rivki looked up from the math pages. Ima always said the army was a terrible thing, taking righteous *tzadiks* away from the holy work of G-d's army and certainly not a place for girls.

One time, she heard her mother tell Abba: "The government wants to destroy Jewish life by taking our sons out of the yeshivas and forcing them to stand side by side with secular girls that will corrupt them."

Abba, who knew a few young men that served, ventured that maybe it wasn't so bad. "Goldie, not everyone can be a scholar. It wouldn't hurt for some of our men to get a bit more worldly experience. As long as we teach them right, they'll return to us."

"Well, I will not let them take my sons, ever," Ima had snorted back at Abba.

"Of course, we're going to the army," Ariel's voice filled with pride. "As soon as we've finished up this year volunteering."

"I'm going to be a combat medic and then I'll come back here to become a doctor," Ayelet declared, all traces of laughter now dissipated.

The only word Rivki heard from Ayelet's lips was "combat." She knew that meant shooting a gun, fighting the enemy. Her eyes widened. "A girl... in combat?"

Ayelet's laughter returned, this time loud and raucous.

"I-I guess—I'm sorry. I've never had the chance to meet girls like you, either." Rivki's cheeks were hot. "I-I-I've got so many questions."

"It's fine. I've got lots of questions for you too," Ayelet's voice was softer now, and she plied Rivki with all sorts of questions about her sister's marriage plans. How long did they date before the wedding? Did they really love each other or was it only because they were considered suitable partners?

"It's a rite of passage, something we are prepared for from a young age," Rivki explained. "It's kind of like a race where no one wants to be the old maid, the last unmarried *meideleh*. We all know that if a girl is not married by the time she's twenty, or at least engaged to someone, then she'll probably have problems finding a family that will want her."

"A family?" Ariel asked, confused.

"I mean that it's usually the families that make a *shidduch* between the boy and the girl." Rivki described how her parents asked a matchmaker to arrange the meeting between Yaakov and Esti.

"You mean they didn't get to choose for themselves?" Ayelet was horrified.

"Well, they did, sort of. My parents told Esti about Yaakov and his family, and then she got to meet him to see if she liked him." Rivki's head hurt picturing her sister dressed in her finest clothes, a hint of make-up on her smooth skin, sitting opposite a black-suited and hatted stranger in the dazzling lights of a hotel lobby or busy restaurant.

Ayelet's face was a picture of shock. "But do they get to spend any time together alone, you know, before the wedding?"

"No! That would be highly inappropriate. The first time they get to be totally alone together is on their wedding night." Small pricks ran up Rivki's spine.

"That's awful! How can you marry someone you don't even know?" Ayelet folded her arms tightly. She was quiet for a few seconds and then added. "I've a friend, actually my sister's friend. She was Haredi and just up and left her family one day. I never really understood until now how she could have done that, but now you're telling me about getting married, blind like that. No wonder. She wasn't allowed to take anything with her when she left home to go live in a hostel. It was really hard for her to get a job because she wasn't properly educated, but they helped her and eventually she pulled her life together."

Rivki eyed Ayelet. She imagined how all their rules and traditions sounded from the outside. Marrying a stranger, spending the rest of your life with someone you only met a few times. She shivered thinking about Esti finally being alone with Yaakov. But leaving the Haredi world, turning your back on G-d, was the worst thing anyone could do. It was one thing never having a Torah education, a *tinok shenishbar,* but people tore at their clothes and sat shiva for relatives who stopped following the ways laid out in the Torah. How could someone just pick up and leave? Turn their back on everything they knew?

It was dark outside now and the classroom's fluorescent lights poured exhaustion over Rivki's battered body. She tried hard not to picture this place Ayelet talked about that helped her friend start a new life. She tried not to imagine the feeling of never seeing Esti or the rest of her family again.

"Listen, I've really enjoyed talking to you," Rivki smiled at the two *shinshinim,* "but I've... I'm feeling really tired."

TAMAR

Tamar fell into rhythm beside Tal as they left the school and made their way through the maze of backstreets towards the Rose Garden next to the Knesset. She had been to Israel's parliament on a school trip where they learned about democracy, the nation's institutions and how the political system worked, but this time, she felt an air of freedom that put a bounce in her step.

It was already dark by the time they reached the park, but it wasn't hard to find the protestors. "Wow, so many people here tonight, much more than usual," Tal whispered, coming in close. He sounded different, more confident. Tamar saw him waving and mouthing hellos. She wondered why he'd never mentioned going to a protest before.

They made their way through the thickening crowd, towards the Knesset's black sculpted gates, stopping beside a rowdy crew of guys, scraggly side-locks falling carelessly down from oversized knitted *kippot*. Tal pulled one of them over and introduced him as Hezi.

"Hey Tam, this is my cousin." He towered over the raggedy, malnourished shape. "Hezi," Tal cleared his throat. "This is Tamar, my friend from school. I told you about her."

Hezi nodded at her, his face straight. "Tal always told me none of his school friends were interested in joining our protests. He said everyone there was too left-wing."

"Er." Tamar looked at Tal, but he just shrugged and turned to greet another, even more disheveled dude.

"Well, we're glad you're here now, joining this important work." Hezi's eyes darted about nervously. Tamar could smell his breath as he moved in towards her. "I'll add you to our WhatsApp group so you can join us in the future. What's your number?"

The next few minutes passed quickly. Tamar heard her voice reciting her phone number and within seconds her phone began vibrating just like when Tal had added the news alerts earlier that day. She glanced at the screen and was just about to ask Hezi what work he was talking about when suddenly he seemed to be swallowed up by the ever-growing crowd.

Then the noise was overwhelming, and Tamar looked about for Tal. Where did he go? All the bodies about her appeared to be merging into one enormous mass. Then she saw him, face to face with another raggedy guy. A few solo words— "sons of bitches," "*Aravim*," "our country," "Jewish State"—drifted into her ears as she approached, putting a shy hand on his arm.

He looked up at her, blue eyes wide. "Tam! All okay?"

"Erm, y—yes, your cousin added me to his group... he said there was work, but didn't say what... do you—" but her question was drowned out by a guy with a megaphone chanting. "We won't take this anymore. No more attacks! No more *piguim*. *Nekama*!"

The crowd went wild, fists pumping the air, eyebrows furrowed as they repeated the word "revenge"— "*Nekama, nekama, nekama*." Heavy placards and large floppy canvas banners with crooked letters painted in blood-red demanded "All Arabs out," and "Death to Arabs."

Tal, standing next to her, joined in the chanting, his face contorting and blending in with the anger now engulfing them. "Death to Arabs," "All Arabs out," hateful words proclaimed in a familiar voice that blocked Tamar's vocals from leaving her throat. She pulled the edges of her jacket closer, feeling the flames of acrimony lick her and drag her into the fire.

Just then, Tamar felt her cellphone buzzing. She pulled it from her pocket. Ami. She looked up at Tal and quickly pulled the phone down to her side, where the mass of rancorous bodies hid the screen. *Hey, where r u? Why you not answering? All okay? Wanna ride home 2gether?* Tamar clicked the phone off and stuffed it back into her pocket.

"You know, you're supposed to chant at a protest." Tal's voice reverberated in her ear, making her jump. She tried to smile, lifting her hand lifelessly up in the air, words refusing to leave her lips and her phone with Ami's messages, feeling like it was burning a hole in her pocket.

A politician Tamar didn't recognize greeted the crowd, and the frenzy subsided a little. "We're doing all we can to get the government and the police to take action," he declared. Only the red of his tie stood out against the night sky. "Israelis want peace, that is all we want—to feel safe and secure in our city. We know that's impossible while they're free to roam around, so action must be taken. We have a lot of work to do."

Tamar, again, wondered what work he was talking about, and what action. Of course, the Arabs roamed around the city freely. They lived here too. She thought about Ami. What action could be taken to stop random individuals from driving their cars or going to work? She stood quietly, hand on the phone in her pocket, watching Tal excitedly join in with the renewed cheers and chants.

Eventually, the demonstration began to wind down, and the crowd thinned out. Tamar saw Hezi approaching them. "We're going to the *shuk*. You coming?" His voice was low, eyes still moving wildly.

"What do you think, Tam?" Tal looked at her expectantly. "It's still early. There's a great hot chocolate place that just opened up in the market."

She never usually stayed out this late without her parents. "I need to call my mom," she answered without looking at him. She felt Tal watching her as she tapped her mom's number and asked if she could stay out.

"I guess that's fine, but maybe Daddy will pick you up," her mom hesitated. "I'm not keen on you taking the light rail home alone so late at night."

Tamar wasn't keen about doing that either and felt relief wash over her, knowing her dad would come to get her. She followed Tal, Hezi, and his friends towards the *shuk*, now the "in" place, after the fruit stands and houseware stalls closed for the night.

They were almost there when Hezi announced he needed a pack of smokes and dipped inside the small grocery store of a brightly lit gas station. The others waited rowdily on the forecourt until he beckoned them. Tamar lingered outside as Tal and the others piled into the store.

Seconds later, she heard shouting, followed by a massive crashing sound. Tamar craned her neck to peer in through the large grimy window and let out a gasp. Hezi's friend had the shopkeeper, a long, skinny guy with dusty hair, face down on the floor. Another friend was delivering kicks with a heavy boot. The others were crowded around shouting, "Dirty Arab!"

"What the... Stop it!" Tamar's voice came out as a whimper. She looked about her wildly, breath stuck in her throat, before pulling her phone out of her pocket.

"What you doing?" A hand on her shoulder made her jump back. Then she saw it was Tal.

"Tal, tell them to stop. They must stop." Tears threatened to burst through her eyes.

"Tam, he's an Arab! He probably started it!" His hand was digging into her shoulder now.

"What? No! Look what...." Tamar choked back the tears. "They're going to kill him! We have to do something!" She glanced into the store again, crystals of broken glass were now scattered across the floor and dark tentacles of blood were flowing out from below the shopkeeper's down-turned face. She shoved Tal's hand from her shoulder and took a step away from him. "What the hell! Is this what your cousin meant by work? Is this what you mean by taking matters into your own hands? Hurting people?"

"Wait, Tam, you don't understand," his voice was gentler now, but Tamar noticed a coldness in his eyes. "They're the ones who are making our city unlivable, they're the ones who want to kill us. We have to stop them; they don't belong here. Look at him, taking a perfectly good job that belongs to a Jew."

"Hey! You punks! What are you doing?" A car screeched into the gas station. "I'm calling the police."

"Hezi!" Tal spun away from Tamar and moved towards the store. "Hezi, he's calling the police."

Tamar froze as Hezi and his friends bolted out the door right past her and up the street towards the *shuk*. Tal started following, but then turned and grabbed Tamar's wrist, dragging her behind him.

"Tal!! Stop! You're hurting me." Her feet pounded the pavement automatically.

"The police'll be here any minute. We gotta get out of here," he panted, tightening his grip. The distant wail of sirens mixed with the heavy beats thumping through her ears.

When they reached the bustling night *shuk*, Tal slowed to blend with the crowd. Only when they finally came to a standstill did he let go of her arm, a throbbing replacing where his hand had held her.

"You okay, Tam?" he breathed, coming to a complete stop.

But Tamar was silent. She couldn't think of a single thing to say to her friend. She couldn't even look into his eyes. Who was he? Was he always so heartless? How could he watch as an innocent person was being beaten, maybe even to death? How could someone you know so well, like so much, make you feel so bad?

In the distance, she spied Hezi and his friends already seated around a table in front of the hot chocolate place. Laughing, joking as if nothing had happened.

Suddenly, she wanted to be far away. Away from Hezi and his friends. Away from Tal. "I need to go home," she mumbled without looking up. She turned around and made her way to the market's exit.

NOUR

Downstairs, Mama was sitting alone at the kitchen table, head in her hands. Nour put a hand on Mama's shoulder, while Fadwa filled the *finjan* and set it on the stovetop. Why did Arabs always drink coffee in a crisis? Nour mused. But as the sharp bitter aroma filled the kitchen, it seemed to contain some magical power.

"Baba left?" Nour broke the silence. Mama nodded. "It'll be okay, you'll see. Baba will sort it out." She warned Fadwa with wide eyes. "Whatever Abdulrahman did, I'm sure it's not that bad. So, he joined Hamas? So what? He didn't kill anyone."

"He joined Hamas?" Mama sounded like she was cracking. She looked from Nour to Fadwa. "Did he join Hamas? How do you know that? What are you not telling me?"

The only sound now was the coffee bubbling confidently on the stove. Nour looked at Mama's eyes, searching and wild, her hair uncovered now, equally unfettered. She suddenly felt stupid. She didn't know why she'd mentioned Hamas. She knew nothing about them, really, and truly did not know if her brother was a member.

It was Fadwa who spoke then, her voice deeper than usual, soothing even. "So what if he's a member of Hamas? They're popular on his campus and many Palestinian students join them. They also help those in need." What she said made sense. "Anyway, it's outrageous to arrest someone for being a member of a nationalistic group, especially when Israel pretends to be a democracy."

Mama's eyes narrowed now as she considered Fadwa's words. "I guess you're right." She sighed weakly. "I can't believe Abdulrahman would do anything violent, though. That is just not him."

"Mama, why don't you go back to bed? Get some rest. You're going to need your strength." Nour could feel Mama's exhaustion. "Baba's there sorting it out. There's not much else we can do."

"But we have to tidy up... they made such a mess..."

"We'll do it all tomorrow." Nour tried to sound brave. "I'm sure everyone will help us."

"No... I need to at least make a start." She placed her now empty coffee cup in the sink and headed up the stairs.

Nour turned to Fadwa. "You know more than you are saying. He isn't just a regular Hamas member. What's he been doing, Fadwa?" Fadwa hesitated, but Nour pushed on. "I want to know. If all you say about the evil Israeli occupation is true, then I have a right to know what is going on here, too."

"Ah, so finally you are interested in fighting back," Fadwa mocked. "Finally, you realize. It's about time." She told Nour in a whisper that she had visited the university a few times. "The NGO where I work has a program on the campus and I bumped into Abdulrahman. He was handing out flyers for Hamas, but Nour, you need to understand, many students are members of the group. They have all sorts of social welfare programs that help some of the poorest students."

Nour looked at her in shock. "But Baba says they're extremists, that they don't care about their own people in Gaza. They only care about themselves."

"Well, Uncle Samir is not always right." Fadwa stated, sounding confident. "At Birzeit University, they help students who can't afford their studies and offer discounts on equipment, like schoolbooks."

"But Abdulrahman doesn't need social benefits." Nour scratched her head. "It makes no sense."

Fadwa shrugged. "Remember the kid killed last month at Qalandia? His name was Nasser? The soldiers shot him in the back? They said he was carrying a knife? Well, Nour, he was Abdulrahman's friend."

Nour ran through a list of her brother's friends in her head, but didn't recall Nasser. A friend from the university, perhaps? She also tried to remember this boy's death. So many young Palestinians were killed recently. Almost every Friday, after noon prayers, there was an incident. Maybe he was the one who left behind the poem declaring that his death was the first step to establishing the State of Palestine? She remembered thinking how sad it was that this boy, the same age as Abdulrahman, gave up his life for a country. She wondered if it would really bring any changes.

"Well, Abdulrahman was upset about Nasser," Fadwa continued, "and when Hamas asked for someone to create a Facebook page in his memory, he agreed. So, you see, he is involved in Hamas, but he is not doing anything violent. Your mother's right. Abdulrahman would never do anything like that."

RIVKI

Dr. Jalal was welcoming, but business-like when Rivki and Ima entered his tiny office on the fifth floor. He made no move to shake their hands, gesturing instead to the two chairs across from his cluttered desk. As soon as he started speaking, eyes twinkling in a round, affable face, Rivki decided she liked the stocky doctor.

After eight days in the hospital, she was adept at identifying who belonged to the various ethnic groups that populated this self-contained society. It struck her that pain and illness, as well as those treating it, did not discern between people or religion. After finally once again glimpsing Mohammad, the boy whose brother was killed in the car accident, she decided to adopt the same approach.

She knew Dr. Jalal was an Arab. Not only by his name but also by the way he rolled his r's and h's from the tip of his tongue. He told them animatedly about the procedure he assured would fix her damaged insides and make her feel well again.

"Obviously, this shows a male." He tapped a diagram tacked up on the wall behind him. "But the internal organs are the same for both genders. This is the colon or large intestine and this is the ileum or small intestine... right around... here." His finger stopped. "Is where we believe your tissue is infected and where we'll need to remove part of it."

Rivki's cheeks flushed hotly as she tried to focus on Dr. Jalal's words, but her eyes were drawn to the part dangling limply between the figure's legs. She'd never seen *that* before and she couldn't help wondering if it looked any prettier wrapped in skin. She grimaced. How would it feel coming face to face with such a thing? She thought about Esti.

Ima shifted in the seat next to her and Rivki felt her cheeks get hot again. She knew it was forbidden to look at such an image, even a drawing used for science, and immediately dropped her gaze.

"Doctor." Ima frowned, putting her hands on the table. "How much longer do you think Rivki will need to stay here? It's been more than a week already. Why has it taken so long for you to reach this conclusion? Do you even know if this will work?"

"I understand your concerns, Mrs. Lefkovitz." Dr. Jalal cleared his throat. "Sometimes it takes a while to really diagnose Crohn's and decide on the procedure, but I can assure you this is a routine resection surgery. We do it all the time." He sounded confident. "You need to think of it like a water pipe that has a hole in it. We just take out the broken part and connect the remaining sides of the pipe together. You'll see, once we've done that, Rivki will be in a lot less pain. Food will pass through her system with ease, and more importantly, she'll be able to retain essential vitamins."

"What about follow-up procedures?" Ima's voice sounded harsh in contrast to Dr. Jalal's. "Until now, we've been forced to come back to the hospital once a week. Will this cure Rivki's problem once and for..."

Ima's words floated overhead like thunder clouds. Rivki's mind was turning over fast, like the second hand on a clock. How would the doctors get inside her to patch up this hole? She glanced up again at the diagram, searching for an answer and then, with clarity, she thought: They'll need to cut through my skin.

The words escaped Rivki's mouth before she even realized she uttered them. "You're going to cut me open?" Her question burst through the tiny office, slicing Ima's sentence in half. She could feel the two adults looking at her, their mouths agape, and quickly she clamped her hand over her lips. Then she heard a tiny voice in her head, *It's your body. You have the right to speak.*

Rivki lifted her head, blind to her mother's forbidding eyes, and spoke again with more force. "You're going to cut me open?"

"Rivki!" she heard Ima implore. "I'm sure Dr. Jalal and his team know what they're doing."

But the portly doctor turned his head and looked at Rivki kindly. "Don't worry, Rivka, we have special ways of operating now. We don't need to cut you open. It'll just be a tiny incision, so we can go inside with special equipment. You won't feel a thing. I promise."

TAMAR

Tamar tried her best to avoid Tal in the days that followed the gas station attack. The image of the bloodied man lying on shattered glass made her stomach clench and curl, but the thought of even being near her friend, looking into his treacherous eyes again, threatened to send anything she put in her mouth right back up.

Stories of the attack filled news reports. Journalists paraded through the gas station, interviewing the man who called the police. Camera crews invaded the hospital, filming the battered and scuffed victim, thick white bandages mummifying everything except his eyes. Tamar watched the scenes on the nightly news bulletins, tucked up safely between her parents.

Tal texted her saying: *It's probably best we don't talk for a while. Pls delete this message... and get yourself out of Hezi's group ASAP!* And Tamar easily wiped out an entire text history of friendship. She also removed herself from Hezi's eerily dormant WhatsApp group.

Erasing the scenes of the gas station from her mind, however, was a different matter. Try as she might, Tamar found no way to excuse either her friend's actions or her own.

The lone witness, the man who called the police, described a group of young scraggly guys with *kippot* running away. He said others witnessed the attack and police appealed for them to come forward. They determined that the crime was motivated by hate.

"We would like to speak to anyone with any information," a police officer spoke directly to television cameras. "This is a very serious crime, and we know there were other people who saw what happened." He noted that a big demonstration with clear "nationalistic elements" took place nearby on the same night. He frowned when he said the gas station's security cameras were not in working order at the time of the incident.

Tamar squirmed on the couch. How lucky for Hezi and Co. How lucky for Tal. How lucky for her.

"So terrible! What's become of this city?" Tamar's mom sighed as the news anchor gave audiences at home a stern look before switching to the next story. "Stabbings and shootings nearly every day and now people taking matters into their own hands. Anarchy will be next. Maybe Dori's right, maybe it's time to move."

She put an arm around Tamar and pulled her in tight. Tamar molded herself under her mom's wing, resting her head on the soft, ample bosom. She breathed in fresh lemons. Suddenly, she wished she was five or eight or ten years old again and her mom's embrace was for a careless tumble or a scuffed knee, not for being too cowardly to speak out for something she knew was totally wrong.

Curled in the safe space between her parents, under her mom's arm, Tamar considered coming clean. She could tell them everything. They would call the police and hold her hand while she gave all the information about Hezi and his ruthless gang. Then she thought about Tal. What would she tell them about him? What could she say? She was there too and did nothing, not enough to make them stop. Tamar sank lower into the couch, her insides burning. She knew she would have to see Tal again, eventually.

NOUR

Baba arrived home around noon the next day, deep lines etched on his face and dark circles beneath his eyes. He came with a man Nour had never seen before.

"This is Mr. Asali. He's a lawyer and he'll explain everything," said Baba, taking Mama's hand, leading her and his guest into the living room where they entertained visitors. "He understands the Israeli legal system and is an expert in these kinds of cases."

Nour and Fadwa were ordered to serve food and coffee, as Baba told Mama how he tried all night to get answers about Abdulrahman's arrest. "No one would talk to me," Baba faltered. "Only in the morning, when the station sergeant arrived, he said that Abdulrahman was being charged with running a Hamas website..."

"Hamas," Mama repeated the word, as if in a trance.

"They said he was inciting violence online, that he's a member of a terrorist organization." Baba threw his hands up in the air.

"Hamas," Mama whispered again.

Baba went on. "I tried arguing with them. I told them that managing a Facebook page is not a violent crime by any stretch of the imagination, but the sergeant said it was not his place to decide what was a crime and what wasn't."

"What about Abdul? Did you see him?" Mama sounded frantic now, like she'd just realized the gravity of the situation.

"No." Baba shook his head. "But then, Mr. Asali came. He managed to get some more information, and he's going to help us."

Nour, trooping back and forth from the kitchen to deliver coffee in small glasses, sweet dates, and sugared cookies, strained to listen to Mr. Asali's assessment of her brother's situation. She relayed what she heard to Fadwa, who was dutifully roasting more coffee beans, just in case another round was needed.

"He said the Israelis are pushing back against young Palestinian activism," Nour related to her cousin on one trip.

On the next, she told her, "They're trying to trap people... want to make an example... to make others scared of doing the same thing."

"*Ayawa*," Fadwa nodded. "*Mazboot*, of course they do! It makes sense. What else?"

Nour frowned at her cousin and hushed her, putting a finger to her lips. "Shhhh, let me hear what they're saying now." Nour sidled up to the kitchen door, lingering for a few seconds. When she returned to Fadwa, she said, "He says Abdulrahman is lucky. He's a Jerusalem resident, which means his case will be heard in a regular Israeli civilian court, not in a military one." She turned back to the conversation in the living room.

"If we get the right judge, then he might get away with a warning and a fine because this is his first offense," Nour heard Mr. Asali tell her parents. "The preliminary hearing is set for tomorrow at noon. I'm hopeful we can persuade the judge to give him bail. That means he'll at least come home until the trial begins and then we'll be able to prepare properly."

After Mr. Asali left, Mama and Baba sat for a long while in the living room. They spoke in hushed tones. Nour heard her mother sobbing, Baba's gentle voice promising her it would all be fine.

RIVKI

When Rivki arrived in the hospital classroom later that day, she was relieved to see it was empty of other students. "Do you mind if we skip class today?" She sighed at Ariel and Ayelet. "They're operating on me tomorrow."

Ariel rushed over and threw her arms around Rivki. "I'll go get us some hot chocolate, shall I? We'll cheer you up—you can drink hot chocolate, right?"

Rivki blinked back tears. The hug and thought of sweet chocolate lifted her heart a little.

"I'll be right back. Ayelet, get her comfortable," Ariel ordered, before dashing from the room.

"Let's sit on the beanbags." Ayelet gestured to the colorful round bags scattered on the carpet. Her voice was softer than usual.

Rivki felt sluggish as she plopped herself down in the folds of a soft bag. She tried to dispel thoughts of the surgery from her mind.

Ariel soon returned with three steaming mugs of chocolate and Rivki took hers, grateful. Rain spat against the enormous windows and the wind howled through the bricks. Rivki wrapped her fingers tightly around the mug and sank deeper into the beanbag.

"So, what do you want to talk about?" Ayelet sipped from her mug. "Yesterday, you said you had loads to ask us?"

"Yeah, don't be shy, Rivki," Ariel encouraged her. "We've already asked you about Haredim. Now it's your turn."

Rivki studied the two girls. Blue jeans. White cotton T-shirts. Carefree. Nothing could stop them. There was no Ima monitoring their every breath. No teachers or rabbis imposing on their every thought. No siblings or neighbors tracking every move. She longed for that kind of freedom, too. The voice from earlier appeared in her head: *You can have it, just take it.* She opened her mouth, spilling the most burning questions.

"What's it like to wear pants in public?" Rivki let her words float in the air and then added, "I mean, isn't it embarrassing? The whole world can see your outline... I mean, you know, your shape." She frowned now, trying to think of how to phrase it exactly. "When you wear a skirt, you can hide that part—" she pointed to the top part of Ariel's legs— "but in pants, well... you can't."

"Ha! In all my life I've never heard..." Ariel burst out laughing. "Rivki, you're just so funny. What a question!"

Ayelet laughed too, then shrugged and said, "I think we're just used to wearing pants. It never really crossed my mind."

"Do you have boyfriends?" Rivki pushed on, suddenly unafraid.

"Well, I did, but we broke up in the summer." Ayelet scowled. "I'm over it now, though."

"My boyfriend's called Itamar." Ariel giggled. She pulled out her phone and ran a long finger over the screen. "Here, this is from last month, when we were in Greece." She held the phone up to Rivki, who moved her head in closer. Itamar was taller than Ariel and tanned. A nest of black curls rested neatly on his head. He had his arm around Ariel's narrow shoulders. They were standing very close.

"Oh, he looks nice." Rivki's mind was racing. Past jeans, past pants, past boyfriends. She eyed Ariel's phone hungrily. She knew about these phones that could hold photos and show films and connect to the Internet, but never saw one up close. They were forbidden in her community. The rabbis warning those who used them would become corrupted.

Rivki's mind flicked to the *pashkavilim* plastered on billboards throughout her neighborhood, warning against using smartphones, but she immediately dismissed the image.

Ariel's phone was shiny. Rose gold. And it dangled on the end of her outstretched arm. "Show me how it works," Rivki instructed.

"iPhones work basically like any phone, of course, but I only really use the apps, like this one," said Ariel, clicking on a small picture that looked like a camera. "Instagram."

Rivki's eyes widened as a girl identical to Ariel came to life and started talking. "That's my sister, Shani. She's in Vietnam." Ariel clicked on the next image—her doppelgänger stood before a field of deep green crops sporting a wide straw hat. In another clip, Shani declared: "Ariel, my love, miss you so much! Sending kisses and hugs!" A big pink heart popped onto the screen and burst like a bubble.

"She's been gone four months." Ariel clicked the phone shut. "She's in India now, so lucky. I can't wait to go trekking after the army."

Rivki wasn't sure what trekking was, but she did wonder what it would be like to be Ariel or Ayelet. To wear pants, to have a boyfriend, or go traveling around the world without parents or siblings or neighbors or friends watching your every move and telling you what to do. Of course, G-d could still see you, He could see you anywhere, but that was comforting, in a way.

Suddenly, there was a burning inside her. "I want to try on some jeans." She cleared her throat, eyes darting right and left before fixing on her two new friends. The other two girls laughed. Then, without saying a word, Ayelet stood up. "Come with me," she commanded. The three girls walked together to Rivki's room, and Ayelet closed the door firmly behind them.

"Pass me a pair of pajamas." She pointed to a pile of hospital clothes tightly folded on the chair and Ariel handed them to her. Then she undid the buttons on her jeans, shimmying them over her thighs, and holding them up in the air. Rivki grabbed them as if they were candy, averting her eyes from Ayelet's partial nakedness. Her cheeks burned as she dashed into the bathroom.

Inside and alone, she ran her fingers over the heavy material. The light blue threads were wound so tightly together, making the jeans feel oddly strong, safe almost, but could she really do this? Should she even do this? What would Esti say? Ima? Rivki's throat felt tight, and her head swirled ever so slightly, but then she took a big gulp and quickly slipped out of her hospital pajamas, pulling the jeans up over her knees.

"Oh my G-d!" Ariel declared when Rivki stepped back out, jeans hugging her narrow hips. "You look amazing. Doesn't she, Ayelet?"

Ayelet, now seated in the oversized chair, was silent for a second before speaking. "You look like a totally different person—wow! Wait, I have an idea."

She stood up and walked over to where Rivki stood. Pulling a red elastic hair band off her wrist, she wound Rivki's hair up into a messy bun.

"There," she said, returning to her seat.

Rivki felt cool air brush her neck and the heaviness of the bun made her head sway. She moved across the room, the thick material pressed between her legs and gripping around her thighs like two oversized hands as she walked. The absence of loose fabric swamping her tiny frame, flowing around her like a storm, made her feel weightless, like she was floating, like she was free. She plopped down on the edge of the bed, immediately crossing one bony knee over the other, like she'd seen her two friends do a thousand times. A new and lighter energy pulsed through her veins.

"So, what does it feel like to... you know... to be kissed?" She felt Ariel and Ayelet staring at her and felt like she'd entered an alternate universe.

"Well," Ariel let out a breath. "When a kiss is from the right person, a person you really like, then you feel it in the pit of your stomach. It makes your knees ache and your head spin. You feel you are the only two people on earth."

Rivki cocked her head to the side. "You know from a kiss if someone is the right person to spend the rest of your life with?" She ran through the list of conditions in her world—a scholar, a *tzadik*, someone of similar background, who was from the right type of family. Then there were all the stages of checks and dating, but never being totally alone together, the family meetings, the wedding, and only then, much, much later, a first kiss.

"Rivki, we work according to feelings and emotions." Ayelet gestured wildly in the air. "Of course, you can never tell how two people will get along ultimately, in the long term, but if it feels right, then it probably is right."

"Right." Rivki let herself down from the bed. She touched her lips, imagining soft flesh on them, and then walked lightly to the bathroom to put her own clothes back on.

TAMAR

The showdown came sooner than Tamar had expected. Stepping out of the girl's bathroom on the third floor, Tal was waiting for her. He pushed her into an empty classroom, speaking before she even realized what was happening.

"You mustn't tell anyone!" His frosty breath filled her face. "Do you understand? We'll be in just as much trouble as Hezi. They'll say we were accomplices. They might even throw us in jail! After you left, we made a pact to keep quiet, but Hezi's worried that you might rat us out. I told them you were scared, but not stupid."

Tamar searched his blue eyes for the kindness and compassion that used to make her heart thump, instead there was a wall of ice. When she finally spoke, she did not even bother hiding her disappointment. "I'm still trying to figure it all out in my head, Tal. Your cousin and his friends, they just went in and beat up that guy for no reas—"

"I don't think you fully understand...," he interrupted her hotly. "They're the ones who hurt us, not the other way around. They come into our city, take our people's jobs, and carry out terrorist attacks on innocent Jews. The government is doing nothing about it. We can't stand by and let it happen anymore."

Tal's eyes darted around the classroom before fixing her with his icy blues. "Do you know what Lehava is?"

Tamar folded her arms. "No, but I'm sure you're going to tell me."

"We're a movement of activists," Tal looked at her with conviction. "A lawyer in Jerusalem started it.... He says it's time we fight back against Arabs destroying our lives. We try to stop those who are encroaching on our territory, anyone who is trying to take over our lives and destroy our culture, like the Arab man who touched you on the light rail, or those who have the audacity to date Jewish girls! It happens, you know."

Tal cleared his throat dramatically. "Lehava is the only group that is doing anything to stop these Arabs from taking over this country. We are the only ones fighting back... After your experience, Tam, I would've thought you'd think this was a good thing. You know the police would do nothing to catch that man, the one who put his hands down your pants, even if you reported it? They get away with murder, literally!"

He looked wild as he wound down his monologue and Tamar wondered why she had never noticed this side of her friend before. Angry and militant, he looked and sounded crazed. It was true there were some awful, even deadly, terrorist attacks that happened lately. She'd seen the aftermath of one with her own eyes. And the thought of the grotesque winking guy's rough hands still made her feel like ants were crawling under her skin, but she also believed that most of the Arabs in Jerusalem just wanted to live in peace.

"Listen, Tam," Tal went on, sounding more and more alien. "I could tell you enjoyed the protest and I know you thought it made sense. You also know the government is not really paying attention—they do nothing to stop these Arabs from harming us. They've been hurting us for years, and no one does anything about it."

Tamar's stomach clenched. He was still calling her Tam. "It's true they've hurt us." She looked Tal straight in the eyes now and just hoped some sense would seep into his sewed-up mind. "Demanding that the government do more to protect its citizens from terrorist attacks is one thing, even holding a protest is totally legitimate, but beating shopkeepers to a bloody pulp just because they're Arabs? That's taking things too far, Tal, don't you think? Did you even see the guy? He's in bad shape, critical!"

Tamar pulled back, leaning her weight against one of the tables. "Honestly, I think it's just racist. I feel awful that we did nothing to help that guy. Arabs live in this city too and they have a right to work as well..."

Pinching the top of his nose, Tal cut her off roughly. "I thought you were different, at least after what happened to you on the light rail—that you would see things a bit clearer, that you would see the truth now. I guess I was wrong!"

"I am different, Tal," Tamar's voice rose too. "I see the truth. There are terrorist attacks that need to be stopped, that's true, and the government needs to do more to give us security, but I don't see how beating up random people helps anyone. It's just wrong! And please stop calling me Tam!"

"Look Tam—Tamar," his teeth were gritted together. "I don't expect you to come to any more protests, but if you dare tell anyone what happened—your parents, the police, anyone—you'll regret it."

Tamar watched as he stomped out of the classroom and slammed the door. Slumped against the table, she fought back against the sting of tears that threatened the corner of each eye. More secrets. Fewer friends.

Tamar lingered in the empty classroom. Her breath was lumpy in her throat. The silence threatened to swallow her up. In that instant, she realized all she really wanted was to talk to Aviv. Aviv, her smart, sensible friend. She would know what to do, how to deal with Tal and what to do with all this guilt about the attack. She wanted their friendship back, back to how it was before. But how could she fix things?

Tamar felt heavy as she made her way from the third floor down to the auditorium for band practice.

"Finally!" Ron frowned as she stepped into the dusky hall. "It doesn't help when people are late."

Tamar mumbled an apology and took up her place at the front of the stage. She didn't dare look back to see if Tal was behind the drum set. Singing was always a remedy for her anger and stress, but after everything that had happened, Tamar wasn't sure if she could force even a single note from her lips.

Kobi tapped the side of his guitar and synthesized pulses from Leon's piano started gently gathering speed. There were no drums, Tamar noted as she opened her mouth, smoky words exhaling the remnants of her misery. The hard beats pumped fresh blood around her body, restoring it to life and lifting her loneliness.

As she sang, lungs ejecting each lyric with force, Tamar resolved to erase Tal from her mind and her life. She would make things right with Aviv somehow, and she would also answer Ami the next time he texted. She'd ignored him for long enough. It was a fact that weighed on her almost as much as her own gutlessness.

Wrapping up the first set, Tamar spied Ohad, the teacher, sitting cross-legged on the side of the stage. "Really, really great, friends!" his thick hands clapped. "I think The Jerusalemities might finally be ready for their first public performance! What do you say? Gather round, guys, and I'll fill you in."

Setting down instruments, everyone made their way over to the teacher. Tamar still thought Tal might be behind her and took her time putting the mic back in its stand before joining her bandmates.

"First, let me tell you how much you've all improved." Ohad's eyes glowed. "There's still some work needed, of course, but really, there's such a great energy here, and Tamar, whoa, where did that power come from?"

Tamar's face flushed, and she shrugged. She was glad Tal was not there.

"Now," Ohad drew in their attention, "we have our first performance scheduled."

An excited hum filled the small area where they were standing.

"Shhh, let me tell you," he continued. "It'll take place at the hospital during the week of Hanukkah, so we have about a month to really pull things together and make the sound tight. Can someone tell Tal? Where is he, anyway?"

NOUR

The next day, Nour went with her parents to the courtroom for what Mr. Asali said was a preliminary hearing. A judge would consider arguments from a prosecutor demanding that Abdulrahman stay in jail until a formal date was set for his case. Mr. Asali would argue back that he was innocent and should be allowed to stay home until the real hearing took place, which could be in weeks or even months.

To Nour, it all sounded very confusing and she didn't understand why the process had to be so stretched out. Surely someone was innocent or guilty and the judge would see that her brother had hurt no one.

Fadwa was ordered to stay with Adam and Khalil, who seemed oblivious to all the surrounding stress. She'd made it known she wasn't thrilled about not being included, but Baba gave her little choice in the matter. He tried the same with Nour, but she couldn't bear the thought of Mama being there without her, and finally, he acquiesced.

Mr. Asali was waiting for them outside and led them into an already packed courtroom. He pointed to a row of chairs behind a low wooden fence that separated the gallery from where the lawyers and judges would sit. Nour worried that her parents—Baba in a suit and tie he usually kept for family weddings and Mama in her fanciest *thobe* and matching hijab—looked too Arab for an Israeli courtroom.

She sat down stiffly in the chair next to Mama and was immediately distracted by the noisy melee at the back of the courtroom where a throng of people clamored to set up video cameras and microphones. Did they all think her family were terrorists?

Mr. Asali leaned over the low barrier and explained that they were a mix of journalists and activists, many proponents of Palestinian justice and human rights. Nour studied the activists. Only a few of them looked like Arabs, and some even spoke Hebrew. She wondered what made someone take up a cause that was not their own.

Nour felt Mama tense up next to her as Abdulrahman, escorted by prison guards, entered the courtroom. It was less than 48 hours since they'd taken him, but he looked like a different person. His face, darker than usual, was covered in coarse stubble, and he no longer appeared scared. He looked defiant. Nour heard cameras click and the hustle and bustle reached new heights just as the judge, a small portly man with a tuft of white hair on either side of his head, entered the room.

With a sharp rap, he slammed a wooden gavel down on its dock and grumpily ordered all phones and cameras to be switched off.

"If you don't abide," he warned as he held up a shaky hand, "I will have you removed from my courtroom."

A court guard not much older than Nour marched around ordering those with cameras outside and telling others to put their phones on silent. The court was now in session.

A man in a long black robe, Nour found out to be the state prosecutor, stood and began reading off a piece of paper, sharing with the room the charges against her brother. Mama shifted beside her as the man read out a list of dates and phrases he said came from a Facebook page managed by Abdulrahman Asa'ad.

"It's called 'In memory of Nasser Hamudi,'" the prosecutor informed the judge. He handed over screenshots of the Facebook page as exhibit *aleph*, the first letter of the Hebrew alphabet.

The second piece of evidence, or as he labeled it, Exhibit *Bet*, the second letter of the alphabet, included examples of posts the prosecutor said were uploaded by Abdulrahman. He argued that the posts and images encouraged others to go out and hurt, even murder, Jews. He held up an example. Nour could just about make out the words from where she sat: "A brother for a brother," read the headline at the top of the post.

The prosecutor read out the text: *If they take our brother's blood, then we must seek the blood of their brothers. Jews must pay for killing our people. Bring me their blood.* He then held up a grotesque cartoon showing a shaded sword dripping with blood directly above the split face of a baby.

Nour sensed Mama tensing again, and her own stomach flipped. Killing a baby? Was that what the Facebook post was asking people to do? Surely Abdulrahman had not written such a thing, let alone post it? It could not be. She looked at her brother, but his face was a blank mask.

After her conversation with Fadwa on the night of his arrest, Nour had searched her brother's Facebook page, but she found no incriminating posts. She hoped it was all just a mistake. Maybe Abdulrahman handed out flyers for Hamas. He was helpful like that, but he would never join a radical group, never incite violence.

Now, listening to the accusations being leveled against him, Nour felt sharp pains digging into her stomach. Nausea threatened to eject all the food currently in her system as the judge ruled that her brother's crimes were most serious and he could not be released to house arrest. He would stay in jail.

Hearing the sharp rap of the gavel, Nour realized she could no longer remain indifferent to the occupation, but she could also never accept that killing someone would bring her people closer to having the country they so desired.

RIVKI

Beeping machines pulled Rivki from a heavy sleep and she fluttered open long blond lashes.

"Rivka, Rivkale? Finally! *Baruch Ha-Shem*, you're awake. You've been sleeping all morning." Rivki felt Ima squeezing her hand.

She tried to sit upright, but a sharp pain stabbed her lower stomach. "Ugh," she cried out, flopping back down on the bed.

"Just stay down, there's no need to get up." Ima brushed a thick hand across her forehead. "Dr. Jalal says the surgery went very well. He said the hole was smaller than they thought, and they managed to close it all up. He's hopeful this will put you in remission for a long time. You'll be out of here in a day or two, *bli neder*. Isn't that good news?"

Rivki nodded. She needed some good news.

Not long after Ima's departure, Ariel and Ayelet burst into her room, two helium balloons on long strings hovering above their heads.

"You're going to be released, maybe even tomorrow," exclaimed Ayelet, perching herself on the end of Rivki's bed. "We'll be sad to see you go, but at least you'll be back at home with your family in Mea Shearim."

"Yeah, we'll miss you, Rivki," cooed Ariel. "You don't have Facebook, do you? I want to add you as a friend." She pulled out the rose gold phone.

Rivki laughed, dull pain lines drawing across her abdomen. How would she have Facebook when she didn't even have a phone, and why did all secular people think all Haredim lived in Mea Shearim?

"What's so funny?" Ariel asked, wounded. "I just thought it would be nice to stay in touch."

Rivki looked at her. She couldn't laugh. It hurt too much. "How-how-how would I... have Facebook? I don't even have a phone!"

"Ohhhhh." Ariel started laughing, too, and Ayelet joined in. All three of them were laughing uncontrollably now.

"But what if we want to visit you in Mea Shearim for more secular-religious therapy?" Ayelet teased.

"I-I-I don't even live in Mea Shearim," Rivki cried.

"Where do you live?" Ariel scratched her head.

"Ma'alot Dafna." Rivki wiped a soft tear from her eye, drawing in deep breaths to manage her pain.

"Same, same." Ayelet brushed off the explanation and then added, with a mischievous look in her eyes, "I've got an idea...."

When all three of them recovered from their giggling fit, the two *shinshinim* helped Rivki to set up a Facebook account. Uploading all the required information, they fixed her hair in a messy bun and pinched her cheeks red before snapping a profile shot. Then they added themselves as her friends, and she accepted.

"You'll get other friends soon," Ariel assured her.

But Rivki was doubtful. No one she knew was on Facebook; it was another thing *asur,* forbidden, in her community. Worse, if anyone at school discovered it, she would surely face a reprimand or even be kicked out in shame. That did not stop her from admiring the finished product or feeling that she was finally present and accounted for in the world. She dismissed the thought that she would probably never be able to access her account once she left the hospital and memorized the username and password anyway.

Dr. Jalal came to see her the next day. "Looking so much better, Rivka." His eyes twinkled and smiled at her. "Your blood pressure and white blood cell counts are back to normal, and I hear you ate something this morning without discomfort. I think it's time to send you home." He picked up her chart and marked it with a blue pen.

"Today?" Rivki watched him shuffle around her room.

"Today," Dr. Jalal echoed.

"Really?"

"Yes, really!" He raised an eyebrow. "Anyone would think you didn't want to leave us."

Rivki blinked at him. She'd been here for ten days, though the monotony of the daily routine and the continual flow of people made it seem like so much longer. Part of her forgot about her life in Ma'alot Dafna. The cramped apartment, the spying eyes, Esti. She barely thought about her friends at school, either. Being here gave her freedom.

"N-No, of course I want to go home." She took a deep breath. "Will I have time to say goodbye to everyone?"

"Are sure you don't want to stay?" Dr. Jalal regarded her again and tousled her hair with a tender hand.

Rivki stiffened. A man's touch. But then, the voice in her head reasoned, he had operated on her, fixed her. "I just want to thank everyone who took good care of me." Her shoulders loosened.

Just then, Abba walked through the door. Hearing the news of her release, he reached out a thick hand to Dr. Jalal. "Thank you for everything, doctor. May G-d bless you."

As Rivki watched the celebration, all she could think of was that she needed to say goodbye to Ariel and Ayelet, but how would she get away from Abba now? Then that little voice again. "Facebook."

TAMAR

A biblical downpour had left a slippery sheen on the large, smooth cobblestones and Tamar was thankful she was wearing her heavy-duty Blundstones as she made her way to the light rail stop—any other footwear was treacherous in Jerusalem's winters.

She'd just reached the Zion Square and was about to turn left when she heard a deep male voice behind her. Spinning around, Tamar half expected it to be Tal but immediately her shoulders relax when she saw it was Ami.

"Heyyyy," he greeted her warmly.

"Ami, hey... I'm so sorry... I didn't..."

"Oh, it's fine." He waved a hand and led them over to the stop. "You were probably busy. I was too.... What did you think about that history test, eh?" He shook his head and sighed. "It was so hard, pretty sure I failed it... though might have been easier if I'd actually read the book."

He grinned at her mischievously, dissolving some of the guilt she felt about not answering his texts and about getting involved with Tal's sordid business.

"Yep, studying might have helped." She smiled back.

"You must be scared to travel alone now, after the *pigua*." Ami looked at her earnestly.

Tamar shivered. She pictured the two covered bodies—it seemed a long time ago now. She frowned, trying to remember the last time she saw Ami. It was definitely before the last text. She wondered if he would still be interested in talking to her if he knew she was involved in the gas station attack.

"Yes," she realized she had not yet answered him. "It still freaks me out, thinking about it."

"Well, I don't mind traveling with you... if you want.... I think my soccer practice finishes more or less the same time you're done with band practice." His voice was soft. "Even if I finish a bit earlier, I don't mind waiting.... Maybe I'll get to hear you sing one day..."

Tamar laughed. "You can come hear me anytime, Ami."

"Do we have a deal then, Tamar Rubin?"

She liked the way he said her name. "I think we do, Ami Awad."

She felt him watching her and looked up. He smiled at her, and she noticed his eyes were the color of warm chestnuts.

"So, I need your help..." Tamar hesitated before telling him about the fight with Aviv, though she held back from sharing the full reason that Aviv refused to talk to her.

"I really want to make things right, but don't know how," she finished.

"You girls are such drama queens; you always make things more complicated." He gave her a playful punch on the arm.

"Hey! What do you mean by drama queens? Like guys never fight with each other?" Tamar rolled her eyes dramatically.

"We do... we just don't drag it out forever like you do," he said, emphasizing the word "forever." "We fight, a few fists, a little blood, and it's all forgotten. Want me to arrange something like that for you and Aviv?"

"I don't think me and Aviv would have a physical fi—" Tamar glanced over at him and realized he was joking. She gave him a light jab. "Don't joke, Ami, this is serious. I don't know what to do about Aviv. I don't know if she'll forgive me."

They were standing in the middle of a packed train carriage now, their faces almost touching.

"I'm sure she will," his voice was deep and smooth. "You just need to be honest."

Tamar breathed in a mix of cologne and spices and nodded.

"So," he continued, his voice still low. "When we gonna hang out properly?"

"Aren't we already hanging out?" She opened her eyes innocently.

"That's not what I mean…" Ami scowled and stumbled. "I mean, like, outside of school… when can we meet up, not just on the train?"

"How about next week?" she answered with surprising clarity. "Damn it, I gotta go."

She gave Ami a bright smile before jumping out at her stop.

Before she even reached her front door, Tamar heard her phone ping. It was Ami. Emojis of ice cream and balloons, followed by a series of questions: *Do you want to go to the mall? Do you like ice cream? What flavor?*

She texted back. *Pistachio.*

Tamar opened the front door, a clown smile plastered on her face. She needed to tell someone. She really needed Aviv.

Fingers flying across the phone's tiny keypad, all she could think of were Ami's words: "You just need to be honest."

You're right. Tal was wrong. We do need to look at people as individuals, Tamar tapped, but immediately she deleted the words. It needed to be even more direct. *I'm sorry. Please forgive me. I miss you*; she wrote and hit send.

Within seconds, her phone pinged again. A message from Aviv. A heart, accompanied by a voice recording: "I miss you too. I forgive you."

Tamar let out a small whoop. It was funny, however much you thought you knew someone, they could always surprise you. She thought about Tal turning out to be an unforgiving, racist activist, working with a bunch of vigilantes taking justice into their own hands. Aviv, so bold and unbending, forgiving her for being a crappy friend almost as soon as she apologized. And Ami, the once short, pudgy kid, was now tall with kind chestnut eyes, taking her out for ice cream.

So much to tell u, Tamar texted Aviv again.

A second later, her phone rang.

"What?!" Aviv demanded.

Tamar told her about Ami, and within seconds, they were chattering like nothing ever happened.

"What'll I wear?" Tamar was in her bedroom now, flicking through her closet.

"I'll help you decide. Don't worry," promised Aviv. "We'll look round the shops on Jaffa Road tomorrow."

"Aviv, look, I'm so sorry about our fight. I realized Tal was wrong, and that your theory is the right one. Judge people based on their own merits. That's it." Tamar plopped down on the chair next to her desk. The words were burning in her throat; she could not keep them inside. She drummed her fingers impatiently on the desk, waiting for Aviv's response.

"I know I am right," Aviv said, vindicated.

"You are." Tamar wiped a tear of relief from her eye.

THE PROTEST

As soon as school was done, Tamar and Aviv headed to the bustling stores on Jaffa Road. Any animosity between them seemed to have dissipated—there were bigger things at stake now: they needed to find something for Tamar to wear on her date with Ami.

"Stop calling it a date... we're just going to the mall, no biggie," Tamar protested, as they dodged shopping trolleys and baby strollers, oversized bags, and suitcases.

Since setting a time and day to go get ice cream with Ami, Tamar was second-guessing herself. Perhaps she misunderstood his intention. Maybe getting ice cream wasn't anything more than just getting ice cream?

"I think it is a date." Aviv paused and looked at Tamar. "He said he wanted to hang out—properly—so there's certainly some kind of *keta* going on here. Anyway, when you gonna tell me what happened with Tal?"

Tamar brushed a hand across her forehead. She knew Aviv would want all the details eventually, but she still didn't have the words to talk about it.

"It's er.... a long story...." Tamar stopped beside a window adorned with signs boasting "the latest fashions at the lowest prices." "Not sure this is the right place to discuss it."

The reunited friends entered Fashion Stop, stepping around a towering mannequin decked out with leery leopard print leggings and a glittery tank top.

"Why!" Aviv exclaimed, brushing a hand over the glitter. "I think you'd look splendid in this..." She reached out for a pair of fake leather pants and faced Tamar with a mischievous grin. "Think it's time for our game."

Tamar snorted loudly, then clamped a hand over her mouth. "Okay, I'm ready for the challenge, are you? Ready? One, two, three... go."

Their game went like this: Each was tasked with finding an outfit for the other. The more hideous, the more mismatched, the better. They had five minutes.

For Aviv, Tamar chose some teeny purple hot pants and a silvery chain-mail asymmetrical vest.

Tamar handpicked an all-in-one polka dot print catsuit and a pair of oversized sunglasses.

"Well? What do you think?" Aviv stepped stony-faced from the changing room. "I think these hot pants are really me." She spun around in front of the mirror.

Tamar stood beside her, equally mock-serious. "It just looks absolutely fab."

Then they both cracked up, laughing until tears were coming out of their eyes, posing in various configurations and snapping selfies along the way. They ignored the frosty stare of the bottle-blond saleslady, who was sporting one of the gaudy sequined crop tops. Her ample bosoms were barely contained.

"Okay, now... let's focus. I really do need to find something." Tamar let out a deep breath, her stomach muscles still contracting. Walking out of Fashion Stop, she quickly posted two shots of her and Aviv onto Instagram, titling it, "Back in business."

A few hours later, the two girls headed back to Tamar's house on the light rail, shopping bags stuffed between them. Aviv helped her pick out a cute top emblazoned with a golden *hamsa*.

"It brings out the green in your eyes," Aviv had noted when she modeled it in the store.

"And hopefully it will bring me some luck, too." Tamar fingered the gold-printed hand. She meant it.

• • •

Nour sat on the light rail fingering the folds of a bulky carrier bag. It rustled loudly each time she shifted in her seat, reminding her that folded neatly inside was the perfect outfit—the one she dreamed about owning ever since that awful day in the Old City.

For a time, Nour didn't think she could ever go back and purchase it. Her neck itched and throbbed each time she thought about returning to Mamilla, but there were bigger things to think about now and she needed a break—a distraction from Abdulrahman's awful arrest, Mama's unbearable sobs, and Fadwa's constant search for action.

She knew Baba would not approve of her sneaking off to go shopping after school, especially because Mama was still so fragile, but walking beneath the sparkling fairy lights was therapy. Breathing in the air of the Christians' Christmas and the Jews' Hanukkah holidays next month was the only way Nour could erase the cartoon image of the split-faced baby. Over and over, Nour wondered how such a picture or a few words on social media could incite others to carry out a violent crime. Surely every Muslim knew it was wrong to take the life of another person?

"You're missing the point, dear cousin," Fadwa had sung when Nour raised the issue a few days after Abdulrahman's court hearing. "This is a justified fight," she continued, emphasizing each word. "It is a fight for the freedom of our people, a fight to end an unjust military occupation of our lands. Within that framework, we have to do everything possible to end this terrible situation."

"But killing another person?" Nour whispered. "It just makes life harder for people on all sides. It makes everyone angrier."

"Nour, life is only good if you ignore all the bad things going on around you." Fadwa placed her hands on her hips. "If you continue living in a bubble, if you ignore the bad things and don't try to solve the core of the problems, then eventually, it will catch up with you. Is that what you really want for your future?"

"No.... of course not." Nour scrunched her face as she tried to frame her argument. "But does advocating violence solve anything? The only way we can improve our situation is by educating ourselves, and in the process, learning to know and understand how the Israelis work—and allowing them to know us. Baba always says that personal connections stop hatred and that fighting back just makes it worse for everyone."

Fadwa sighed heavily and tilted her head back. "Your life here, in Jerusalem, is too good. You've been spoiled, my dear cousin. But there are others, your own people, not too far from here, who are suffering. They suffer every day. What happened with Abdulrahman happens to their sons every night. If you do not fight for them, then eventually their suffering and misery will catch up with you, too. Don't you get that?"

Nour contemplated her cousin's words as the light rail rocked and rustled her bag. Was she blind until now? She certainly saw, and experienced, quite a few unpleasant things these past few months, but it was so mixed up in her head, like colorful confetti packed into a tube. She worried that if she tried to unpack it all, it would explode.

· · ·

"We shall take a taxi," Abba declared, picking up Rivki's bags and marching to the elevators.

Rivki made to follow him and then turned, scrunching her delicate features as she tried to etch into memory details of her home for the past ten days. She felt as though she now belonged in two worlds: one here, with the doctors, nurses, and Ayelet and Ariel, of course; the other at home, in the room she shared with Esti. A lump lodged in her throat. Her sister was probably already preparing for a new life without her.

The cool air outside brushed Rivki's skin as they waited for a taxi beyond the hospital's main doors. "There's a protest." A large-bellied driver invited them inside his cab. "Ride might take longer than usual. Roads clogged up all over the city."

"*B'ezrat Ha-Shem,* we'll find a way." Abba sounded upbeat, lowering his wide-suited shoulders in through the car door, settling himself in the front seat. Rivki winced as she took up a place in the back; Dr. Jalal had said it would be tender for a little while longer. She stared out the window, watching the hospital buildings receding and being replaced with neat residential tree-lined streets and soon a wide highway. It all looked familiar, yet somehow different too, like someone had come and rearranged the world while she was imprisoned in sanitized rooms and hallways.

Her attention was drawn to the radio, which informed them, "Hundreds of Haredim from the *Peleg Yerushalmi* are protesting in Jerusalem at this time against the military draft," it crackled. "Police say several have already been arrested for disorderly conduct and three officers have been lightly wounded."

Rivki wondered what her secular friends would make of hundreds of ultra-Orthodox protesting against going into the army when they were about to be drafted. She wondered if they would recognize the nuances of her community, where some groups such as this one were far more extreme in their views than others. She regretted not explaining the differences to them.

"Abba." Rivki was suddenly gripped by the urge to understand the situation better herself, too.

"Yes, Rivkale," he answered, back still to her.

She gulped, but then heard: 'Ask, you have a right to ask.' "Well, I wanted to know why don't we... er... go to the army?"

Abba adjusted his enormous frame, turning to face her. "Do you mean you, or us?"

"I mean, well, I know girls are not suited for doing things like the army, but what about our brothers?" She scanned Abba's profile, wondering if he resented the question.

He scratched his beard below his chin. "Well," he began, as if he was about to explain the weekly Torah portion. "Until now, the rabbis said the State of Israel needed an army of righteous to pray to G-d, as much as a fighting army with tanks and guns. That was the arrangement we had with the government for a long time, but things are changing, Rivkale. There's still a fear that if our boys go to the army, they will be corrupted, exposed to all different, forbidden temptations, like serving with girls or eating non-kosher *traif*. Yet, as I've said to Ima many times, just like not every one of our sons is born with physical abilities, allowing them to be in the army or the mental control to withstand the temptations, so not every one of them is designed to be a Torah scholar, to sit all day long, studying and understanding His words. We will all need to compromise eventually."

Rivki thought for a second. "Why don't all Haredim see it like that? Who are the ones protesting?"

"Every *ha-cham* or *manhig* sees the situation differently. We need to respect that, too." Abba raised an eyebrow. "Those protesting now.... well... I'm not sure they'll ever agree to serve in the army. They think going into the army spells the end of Judaism."

Satisfied with his answer, Rivki listened to the news broadcast as it wound down and music flowed out of the speakers. The driver turned down the volume, but Rivki could still make out the soft tunes. She half expected Abba to switch it off completely, as Ima would have done, but he let it play, and then, she heard Romi Sofer's soft voice singing, *Tikva*.

> *"Tikva, don't take that away from me now."*
> *"Tikva, it's all that I have left now."*
> *Now you're gone, now you're gone*
> *Tikva that I'll be able to carry on."*

Rivki mouthed the words silently, gazing out the window at the impatient drivers honking useless horns or tapping their hands on the wheel. They were all at a standstill, just like her.

· · ·

Tamar and Aviv tumbled off the light rail. It took them a few seconds to realize what had happened—up ahead of them, blocking the train's path, was a sea of black. There were hundreds, maybe even thousands, of ultra-Orthodox men clapping, shouting, and chanting. Some sat on the ground in countless rows, while others milled about, black jackets removed, sleeves of white dress shirts peeled back to the elbows as if they meant business.

"What is going on?" Tamar looked at Aviv.

"It's a protest." Aviv shook her head. "They do this all the time, but usually by the Central Station. That's why you've never had the pleasure."

"I get it's a protest, but about what?"

"The Haredim protest about only one thing—the army." Aviv's voice was tight. "God forbid they should have to serve like everyone else. They prefer to sponge off the state, spend all their days sitting on their asses in a yeshiva, pretending to devote themselves to God, while we do all the work. It's disgusting."

A woman with two heavy shopping bags huffed by and suddenly joined Aviv's monologue. "They take their anger out on the good people of this city who do contribute to the state. People who just want to take their shopping home. Now what'll I do? I'm stuck... because of them!" She hobbled off.

"They really should do the army like we do," Tamar tutted. "I just don't get why they don't."

"Agree, it's not fair, but they're so stuck in their ways, they can't see anything else outside of themselves." She turned to Tamar. "So..." She blew out the night air. "How do we get out of here?"

Tamar shrugged. "Guess we'll have to walk through them." She glanced uneasily at the ballooning crowd. Those already sitting linked their arms in a defiant chain. Police officers on horses eyed the protestors warily and down a quiet side street. Tamar spied a different group of officers kitting themselves out with riot gear.

Cars were stuck in straight lines, impatient drivers honking useless horns or tapping their hands on the wheel. Tamar grabbed Aviv's arm as a red-faced woman pulled open her car door and marched up to a meandering group of Haredim. "Get out of the way, you lazy losers!" Her arms flailed in the air. "The army doesn't even want you! Look at you, losers! All we want to do is go home, so take your stupid protest elsewhere."

The black-hatted men, probably not too much older than Tamar and Aviv, started screaming hysterically. It took Tamar a few seconds to make out what they were saying. *"Ya prutza! Ya prutza!* You whore!" The woman's expression turned from anger to fear as she fled back to her car, two small heads bobbing up and down on the backseat.

"Oh shit!" Aviv exclaimed, as Haredi men suddenly surrounded the car, pounding heavy fists on the window.

"We need to get out of here." Tamar's heart pumped as she tried to pull Aviv away.

"Wait, we need to help her." Aviv turned to go back.

Just then, two police officers arrived, shoving one of the men down onto the hood before cuffing him and dragging him away. More officers showed up, more arms flailed, more legs kicked, and more handcuffs appeared, as more black-coated men were dragged off.

"It's really getting out of control." Tamar eyed the army of black up ahead. "Maybe we should take a side street?"

Stepping off the main boulevard, Tamar and Aviv turned down a nearby street. Tamar wasn't sure where it would take them, but it seemed to make sense, direction-wise. Surrounded by peeling apartment blocks, they ventured along the darkened, narrow street until they came face to face with about a dozen black hats.

"*Ya shiksas*," one yelled in delight, standing tall and blocking their path.

Tamar felt Aviv's body stiffen next to her as the boy stepped up close to them. Tamar smelled tobacco on his breath right before she felt a blob of phlegm oozing down her cheek. Before she even had time to wipe it away, Aviv was in front of her. "Only dogs spit like that! You apologize to my friend now! Asshole."

The boy shrank back, black suit engulfing him like a coffin. Earlier rage replaced by fear. "Sssss... sorry," was all he could muster before running off in the direction of the protest. His friends followed in pursuit.

"Hey, you okay? Here, take this." Aviv put an arm on Tamar's shoulder and handed her a tissue. "Disgusting. Every one of them. Picking on someone they think is weaker than them." She shook her head.

"Wow! Aviv!" Tamar dabbed the tissue on her face. "That was just amazing.... Is there anything you are not scared of?"

"When you stand up for what is right, it's easy." Aviv shrugged.

TAMAR

December 2015

Tamar's phone vibrated, and she pulled it from the back pocket of her jeans, sliding a finger across the screen. *Looking forward 2 seeing u 2night*. Smooth, floating words that filled her stomach with soft marshmallows. Her date with Ami, or whatever it was, was finally happening tonight.

She looked around her before replying. *Looking forward 2 seeing u 2*, she tapped, letting out a heavy breath and pressing send. She stuffed the phone back into her pocket and sauntered over to the lockers. There were still so many classes between now and then.

"There you are! I've been looking all over for you." Aviv's voice boomed above the din in the hallway. "Are you all ready? For tonight?"

Tamar greeted her friend with raised eyebrows.

"What?" Aviv hung her head innocently. "It's a simple question."

"I'm ready," Tamar puffed. "What are you doing?"

"Looking for you." Aviv gave her a friendly punch. "Come."

She pulled Tamar into an empty classroom, and they sat side by side on an ink-covered desk swinging their legs in tandem.

"It's a karmic intervention, y'know." Aviv stuck out her chin wisely.

Tamar looked blank. "What are you on about now, you old witch?"

"Well..." Aviv paused for effect. "It's almost like the universe is teaching you a lesson after, y'know, the guy groped you...." She put her hand down on top of Tamar's. "I mean, we know what he did, and it made you think all Arabs were bad, even though you weren't even sure if he was Arab at all, and then *walla*! you fall in love with an Arab boy. A kind Arab boy, one who would never... you know... do that to you."

"I'm not in love with him!" Tamar gasped, her cheeks burning. "We're just going to get ice cream, for god's sake! Can you calm down?"

Aviv giggled. "Someone's getting worked up! If it's no big deal, then why do you resemble a tomato?"

Tamar touched her face. She wasn't used to this. "Your theory about not judging an entire group of people by the actions of one person is right, I already told you that, but let's just slow down here with all the love and karmic intervention stuff."

Aviv jumped down from the table and hugged Tamar. "It'll be great! You'll see. I'd better dash or my mom will kill me. Just text me after!"

NOUR

A heavy thudding startled Nour from a deep slumber and she jumped out of bed, flapping around her room until she realized it was just the thump of heavy rain outside. Awake now, heart beating as loud as the drops against the window, Nour gave up on sleep and padded downstairs in search of coffee. The house was still unstirred even as the gray dawn light battled its way into the morning, but the comforting tang of fresh java wafted from the kitchen.

Hoping it was Baba, Nour's heart dropped slightly when she found Fadwa, up and dressed, hair coiffed, make-up crisp, standing efficiently beside the stove. A manicured hand moved in a slow circular motion over the contents of the *finjan*.

"Cousin," she greeted Nour without looking up. "You're up early too."

"Yes. The rain woke me." Nour felt a twinge between her shoulder blades and wondered if she would ever get used to having Fadwa in the house.

Her cousin glanced out the window above the sink and let out a loud sigh. "Boy, it's really coming down out there. Even in Virginia, we don't get rain like this. I didn't know it would be like this here."

Nour grabbed a small coffee cup from the shelf and set it next to her cousin's on the countertop. "That's because you usually only visit us in the summer."

"Possibly." Fadwa shrugged, still stirring the grinds. "So, you're all going to see Abdulrahman today?"

"Yes," Nour answered tightly. Why did it always feel like Fadwa was challenging her?

"Well, I hope, you'll finally get to see just how ugly this occupation really is."

Fadwa raised both eyebrows and lowered her chin, emphasizing each word as though she were admonishing a child. "It's about time." In one swift movement, she switched off the stove, hovered the small pot over the two waiting cups, and poured out the thick brown liquid, unleashing its potent aroma.

Nour silently took the coffee cup from her cousin's outstretched arm. She could probably stand Fadwa, accept some of her lectures even, if she wasn't so condescending, so relentless. Didn't she realize that sometimes people needed to arrive at their own conclusions? That no amount of badgering or prompting would get them there any faster?

"Fadwa, dear cousin," Nour tried to emulate the same complacent tone. "I see how ugly this situation is every day. I am certainly no stranger to it, having lived here my whole life." It gave her pleasure adding in such caveats. "We just have different views of how to respond, that is all."

Fadwa huffed, placing herself on one of the small metal chairs. "Yes, yes, yes." She waved a curled hand past her ear. "I know. You don't believe in violence, so you say, but there is still the option of peaceful protests, peaceful resistance to Israel's crimes and I think it is time for you, dear cousin, to explore those options too. It is not enough for you to just say you recognize the injustice—you must stand up against it too."

Nour bit down on her lip, a familiar feeling of defeat gripping her. Fadwa would never give up a fight and once again, she felt herself being drawn into her cousin's indefatigable pursuits.

"You, my dear Nour, need to come with me to a protest in Ramallah. Only then will you see what the reality is for Palestinians who live on the other side of the Apartheid wall. And only then you will see what the solution is." Fadwa stared, wide-eyed and unblinking. Her fingers tapped on the Formica table in time with the rain.

"But I'm against violence. I don't believe that is the way." Nour sounded weak.

"These are *peaceful* protests," Fadwa shot back. Her hands reached upwards slightly before flopping back down on the tabletop. "It is to show the occupation how we feel about their presence on our lands."

Nour took another sip of coffee, the caffeine finally kicking in. Maybe Fadwa was right. Maybe she would better understand her brother and her people if she went to a protest. Many questions burned inside her since her brother's awful court hearing. She wondered if Abdulrahman was really the one who posted those vile images from Facebook and if he was a member of Hamas. What were his true goals? To see a Palestinian state or to prompt another violent attack, as they said in court? Did her brother just want to kill Jews, or was there something else, something that justified so many deaths?

"Fine," Nour mumbled, regretting her acquiescence almost as soon as the words exited her mouth.

"Good! Finally!" Fadwa beamed. "I'll let you know when the next one is. Now, I'd better get going, but please say 'hi' to Abdulrahman from me. Shame this visit is only for first-degree relatives. You'll just have to tell him from me to stay strong for the *muqawama,* resistance." She held up two fingers in a victory salute before clicking out the door in totally unsuitable high heels for the torrent.

RIVKI

The first few days back home were overwhelming. Rivki missed the serenity of the hospital, where people softened their voices in deference to the sick. She was quickly reminded there were no such courtesies in the Lefkovitz household, where action was a constant theme. Whether it was Dovi and Shimshon battling over some toy or Batsheva wailing at being sent to bed or Ima clanging about in the tiny kitchen, cooking for a small army, there was always a drama brewing or concluding. Even in her bedroom, Rivki was rarely alone.

The screaming pains in her stomach were a low grumble now, and she was feeling stronger, but Dr. Jalal recommended taking some more time to recover and Rivki was in no rush to return to school. Instead, Esti brought her materials so she wouldn't fall further behind her classmates, and she was supposed to return the completed work to her teachers the following day.

Rivki tried to focus on pages of text. She tried to grip her pen and ink out answers, but the minute she was alone, the minute everyone left for their respective schools, workplaces, or chores, and the tiny apartment finally fell silent, her brain got busy. She allowed herself a steely return to the hospital, to freedom, to the warmth of her new friends.

Ariel and Ayelet had nursed her emotional needs, and now they floated on the surface of her mind. Blank spaces about the world beyond Ma'alot Dafna were filled in, but she needed more. Not a day passed where she didn't think about her Facebook page, suspended out there somewhere in cyberspace. Sometimes it was so strong, she found herself staring at the backside of the front door, willing herself to open it, and she resolved to find a way very soon to get online. In the meantime, the password she'd chosen—

RivkiLife—ran through her head like a mantra. She repeated it in the mornings when she woke and at night as she drifted off to sleep.

About a week after her return, Esti bounded into the living room, cheeks a ruddy scarlet from her blustery walk home from school, pink lips singing. "I've got some exciting news."

Rivki was trapped deep inside the sagging couch beneath the window, an array of heavy blankets keeping out the chill. She often set up camp here in the afternoons, an attempt to join the household action, even though she was unsure if she would ever feel truly part of it again.

Esti crawled in beside her, eyes sparkling, as she arranged the blankets around her body too. Two small heaters in the corners of the room vied for dominance over the acrimonious tiled floor, angrily blasting out heat in response to the howling wind outside.

Without waiting for Rivki's reaction, Esti went on: "Yaakov and I are meeting tonight. I'm so excited, Rivi! There are butterflies in my stomach." She took Rivki's hand and placed it on her stomach. "Can you feel them fluttering? This is how I should feel, right? I mean, if this date goes well, then we'll have met three times and surely that means we're at the next stage."

Hot air swirled around Rivki's head, making her voice sound foggy and distant. "I'm sure that's how you should feel," she said, coughing.

"Rivi?" Esti was watching her. "Couldn't you be a little bit more excited for me? What's wrong? Are you unwell again?"

Rivki sank deeper into the couch, the blankets, the heat, her sister beside her pressing down on her until she was nothing at all. Silence hung in the air like a question mark, and she closed her eyes. "Of course, I'm excited for you." She let out a deep breath. "I meant to say, that's amazing, Esti. Where are you meeting him?"

"The King David Hotel." Her sister sounded satisfied. "He suggested it. Now I need to find something nice to wear... Rivi, will you help me?"

Helping Esti get all prepped up, finding an outfit that would ultimately pave the way to her new life was the last thing Rivki felt like doing, but what choice did she have? "Sure," she tried to summon some enthusiasm.

"You're the best." Esti planted wet lips on her cheek. "I missed you when you were in the hospital. It wasn't the same here without you. Now come... I need your help."

Esti jumped from the couch, flinging her side of the blankets on top of Rivki, and made for their bedroom. Rivki pulled herself out from under the pile, letting the icy air cool her. Esti missed her? That was the first time she was hearing about it. If she missed her so much, then why didn't she visit more? Why was she already planning on getting married so soon and deserting her?

When she finally entered their bedroom, Esti was already dressed in a black skirt with two innocuous pleats at the back, the long hem skimming tan stockings at her ankles. A button-down sweater, pink and embroidered with a delicate bouquet on the collar, made Esti's already rosy face glow and her black eyes sparkle. "Well, what do you think?"

"Nice." Rivki pushed through the sadness that covered her like the thick blankets now strewn on the couch. If Yaakov wasn't already convinced that Esti was the one, seeing her tonight would set everything in stone.

· · ·

Rivki was still awake when Esti crept into the room later that night. She imagined her sister sitting prettily in the plush lobby of the King David Hotel, so lost in conversation that she lost track of time, of place, of her. She listened as Esti slipped out of her carefully chosen clothes and pulled on her nightshirt and pajama pants before sliding gently into bed.

"Rivi?" she whispered her breath a mix of cappuccino and mint. "You still awake?"

Rivki turned reluctantly towards her. "Nu? How was it?"

"*Baruch Ha-Shem*, Rivi. It was everything I hoped it would be. He's clever, a real *ha-cham* and a *tzadik*. He's also charming and handsome. I saw it so clearly this time." Esti laid a light hand on Rivki's shoulder, excitement pulsing from her fingers. "Listen, we'll celebrate with a *vort,* an engagement party, tomorrow night! We wanted to do it tonight, but it was getting late, so his parents will come tomorrow for a *lechaim*. I can't believe this is happening, finally, Rivi! Do you understand? I'm going to be married. I'm going to start my life."

Rivki struggled to keep her head in one piece as a million thoughts flooded her brain. What was the urgency? It was less than a month since they went on their first date. It was only the third time they'd met. How did Esti know it was right? Why were they in such a rush? Why did her own life seem to be permanently on hold? How would it end for her, Rivki?

She considered how to respond to Esti, her perfection reflecting her own imperfections so starkly. She wanted to be happy for her sister, excited, supportive, but that voice in her head whispered: *Tell her the truth, tell her how you feel.* But she couldn't. "I'm so happy for you, Esti," she muttered in the murky moonlight. "It's all you've ever dreamed of."

A few minutes later, Rivki heard her sister's breath deepen into what she imagined was a blissful sleep. She remained awake, a sharp pinch in her chest and blood pounding in her ears. She stared at their star stickers illuminating the ceiling, remembering the day Abba bought them years ago. There wasn't even a discussion about where to place them. They were so small then; they needed to balance a pillow on top of the chair to reach the ceiling. Esti held on to the makeshift stand, while Rivki, always petite, climbed up to place each star up there. Esti ordered her to lay them out in a path.

"It will guide us," she assured. "They will be our path to finding true happiness. We'll walk together."

Rivki wondered now where the stars would lead her without Esti. Would she be strong enough to make it through the wedding celebrations? What would happen to her after Esti left? What if she never found a husband, never had her own family? Would she be forced to remain indefinitely with Ima and Abba in Ma'alot Dafna?

"Don't be scared, you're strong." She heard the voice again, and this time she did not dismiss it.

TAMAR

Tamar sauntered over to band practice, praying Tal would be absent again. Since the night of the gas station attack, he was staying away, apparently out sick, though Tamar was sure it was something to do with her.

There was chaos in the hall when she arrived. Ron was shouting and visibly upset. Kobi, Gaya, and Noa were meandering around, shaking their heads. Any remnants of earlier disagreements were forgotten. Leon, standing on the side, gave her a weak smile. She smiled back. There was still no sign of Tal.

"How could they do this?" Ron huffed. "Every single one is gone!"

Tamar looked at Noa. "Music stands," she whispered. "Either moved or stolen."

"What will we do?" Tamar whispered back.

"Ron wants to cancel, but I think we can just hold the music sheets," Noa shrugged, "though I guess the guitarists don't have a spare hand. Or Leon, for that matter."

Tamar frowned. "Wait." She turned brightly to Ron. "I think there are some old ones in the set room. Let me go and check."

He nodded glumly.

The set room was really just storage space at the back of the stage where discarded boards of painted scenery and boxes of costumes from past productions lay waiting to be re-upped and reused. Tamar was sure she'd seen some old music stands hidden among the debris. She climbed over some boxes and buried her head behind some discarded stage props.

"Tamar," a deep voice made her jump. "We need to talk."

Tamar looked up to see Tal. Face pale. Eyes like ice. She wiped a clammy palm down the side of her jeans. "I think we've said everything that needs to be said," her voice cracked. She preferred it when he stayed away, though she knew they couldn't avoid each other forever.

"Well... I just wanted to say that I suppose we need to agree to disagree on some things." He sounded unconvinced. "But, Tam, we move in the same circles. We can't let things get too weird between us."

A thick silence filled the stuffy air between them.

"I suppose you're right." Tamar felt a chill wash through her.

Tal's face softened into a smile. "So, what you doing back here? Running away from Ron's fury?"

"No, I thought I saw some old stands back here." She tried to smile back. He was right. They moved in the same circles and the band needed him, but she knew they would never be friends again.

Tamar turned and began shifting some boxes. She craned her neck behind a pile of props. "There, right there, I see something." Metal glimmered in the half-light. She bent down to tug on it. "It's stuck."

"Here, let me help you." As Tal moved in beside her, a whiff of his aftershave crawled into her throat. He gave the shiny metal rod a rough yank, dislodging it from its resting place and yanking it out smoothly beside them.

Tal pulled back, placing the stand upright. "Tam, I'm glad we're friends again." He was so close now that Tamar could see coarse brown hairs on his chin, and then suddenly he reached out, brushing a hand through her hair. "I've really missed y..."

"H-h-hey," came a distant, forlorn voice. "A-a-anyone here? T-t-amar? T-t-al? Find anything usable?"

As Tal turned to see who was calling, Tamar lurched forward, squeezing past him and clambering towards the small clearing near the door. There she found Leon blinking at her.

"We've got one," Tamar informed him. She glanced over her shoulder just as Tal, face as dark as thunder, pushed past her. Leon looked at her questioningly, but said nothing.

NOUR

The jail was just outside Tel Aviv. Nour spied the cluster of high-rises lost in the clouds as Baba pulled into the big dirt lot. Nour watched Mama, wrapped in a purple and green *thobe*, climb slowly out of the car. Her body seemed to groan with every movement. What a nightmare Abdulrahman was putting them all through! She wondered if he knew. If he cared.

Nour was suddenly filled with a desire to be anywhere but here. She glanced at the darkening skyline. She was lost in one of Tel Aviv's trendy clothing stores, seizing up luscious designs, trying on new outfits. Materials of silky-smooth velvet or crispy cotton. And all tailored to perfection. Nothing left to chance. Nothing unknown.

"Come, Nouri," Baba called to her from beneath a corrugated iron shelter that creaked as the downpour started up again. He pushed Adam and Khalil out of the rain. Mama just stood getting wet, her tear-stained face as dark as the thunderous sky. Nour jumped from the car and sped towards her family, guilt for having such frivolous thoughts chasing her. At least with clothes, she thought as she shook drops from her hair, if you didn't like what you saw, you could choose something else or design it yourself.

Water was already touching her toes by the time a guard signaled from beyond the barbed wire fence and ordered them through a security check like at the airport. All their belongings, including phones, were to be placed in lockers.

"To stop people smuggling weapons," Baba whispered. Mama was silent as she stuffed her purse inside one. Her clothes were still dripping wet.

A female guard with brown curly hair directed Nour and her mother into a small room on one side, while Baba took her brothers in a different direction. It was like being in an action movie. The guard asked her and Mama to lift their arms in the air as she brushed a gloved hand all over their bodies.

Then they were directed into a large waiting area where other families gathered in private clusters. Plastic chairs with bony metal legs scraped the vinyl floor each time someone moved. Again they waited until, finally, a line of prisoners snaked inside. Guards in dark blue uniforms, guns visible on their hips, walked beside them.

The coarse stubble Nour remembered on Abdulrahman's face was now a full beard and the light brown jumpsuit, sleeves casually rolled up to reveal thick forearms, made him look much older. He hugged each one of them, slapping her other brothers with a high five before taking up the only empty chair in their group.

"How have you been, son?" Baba spoke first.

"It's prison, Baba. How do you think I've been?" Abdulrahman grinned.

Nour glanced at Mama, but her face was eerily calm.

"Is there anything you need?" Mama spoke. Her voice was chalky and low. "We are so worried about you being in here Abud and the terrible things they said you did...."

"*Shukran,* thank you, Mama, I'm fine really. Please don't worry about me. I have everything I need in here." He cleared his throat like something was stuck in there and then turned to Baba. "And thank you for putting money in my canteen..." Nour thought she saw a hint of softness in Abdulrahman's eyes. "Let's talk about something else. Why don't you all tell me how you're doing?" He reached out and tickled Khalil under the chin. Khalil giggled.

"So, *akhuti,* you still learning the language of the enemy?" Abdulrahman, lounging back so the legs of his chair rose in the air, turned to Nour.

"The studying is going well, thank you. I have exams soon." Her cheeks burned. There was so much she wanted to ask him. Did you do what they said? Did you hope it would spur others to kill? Do you believe in this violence? Questions raced through her mind like racing cars, but the words remained stuck inside.

"Suppose it's good to know the enemy's language. It's useful for the battle ahead." Then, he whispered, "*Muqawama.*"

"Do you want to stay in here forever?" Baba hissed back. "If you do, Abdulrahman, then keep talking like this and I'll tell Mr. Asali to offer his services to someone who wants to be helped!"

Abdulrahman let the two front legs of his chair plop to the floor. "Sorry." His eyes flicked to Mama, and Nour thought she saw something softer pass over his face. "But you know I feel differently than you. Our people need to take a stand. We can't be compliant any longer."

"Maybe so, son, but there are many different ways to fight back." Baba put a hand on Abdulrahman's shoulder.

Her brother said little after that, and Nour was relieved when a guard called out that their time was up. Visitors and prisoners stood almost simultaneously, chairs scraping a vociferous farewell.

RIVKI

Rivki woke to a hive of activity even more intense than most days and then it struck her like the jab of a knife—plans for Esti's *vort* to celebrate her engagement to Yaakov Aaronson were already underway. She could hear Ima clanging around in the kitchen, her sister chirping above the din. She dragged herself out of bed and sluggishly made her way to ground zero.

In the kitchen, her mother and sister appeared to defy gravity as they excitedly set out Ima's precious china plates and silver cutlery. Beside the kitchenware, they lined up ingredients for cakes, cookies, and all the other delights they intended to serve to the Aaronson family.

"Erm, is there anything I can do?" Rivki felt obliged to ask, though no one seemed to notice her arrival.

Ima stopped for a second. "You're looking quite pale again today, Rivkale. Maybe you should just go and rest, eh? Esti and I can manage. Maybe later, if you're feeling better, you can help serve the Aaronsons. Such exciting news...." She prattled on, pouring together sugar and eggs that would become the basis of her famous chocolate mousse.

Back in her room, Rivki could not switch off from the voltage of excitement now running through the apartment. Even Abba stayed home to help with the preparations, though Ima dispatched him periodically to pick up pastries, cream cakes, and other delights. Rivki didn't remember the same commotion when her brothers got married, but maybe it was because the fun activities took place in the bride's household? This time, all the spotlight was on their family—on Esti—and her sister was lapping it up. She kept poking her head around the bedroom door to give updates.

"Rivi, the chocolates have arrived," came one announcement. "Wait till you see them!"

"The mousse is Ima's best ever; you need to try it!" came another.

Each time Esti's head appeared, Rivki sank further into darkness. In the hospital, she understood Esti's neglect—accepted it was difficult for her to visit. Since she'd come home, her sister seemed to make up for it; they were together like old times. Now, Esti was acting like nothing else mattered but her and Yaakov.

The next time Esti came into their room, it was to complain about Ima. "She's so old-fashioned." Esti rolled her eyes. "She doesn't realize things have changed since she was a *kallah*. She thinks Yaakov or his parents might be put off me if the house isn't spotless. She doesn't realize they just want to meet me... and the family... to make sure there is nothing wrong with us."

Rivki blinked. Was Esti talking about her? Did they think her Crohn's might affect her chances with Yaakov? Is that why Ima had sent her away to the bedroom? To keep her hidden?

"Did you tell... does he know about... me?" Rivki cleared her throat.

Esti shrugged. "I assume the *shadchanit* mentioned it to his parents. It hasn't come up in any of our conversations."

Rivki couldn't decide if that was good or bad. If the matchmaker had told the Aaronsons and they still let their son meet Esti, that was good, right? But what did Esti mean—she didn't mention that her sister was hospitalized, suffering, to the man she wanted to marry?

A few hours later, minutes before Yaakov and his parents were set to arrive, Ima ordered her into the kitchen. "Rivkaleh, I need you to pour out the teas and make sure there is always a freshly filled plate of cookies to put out." She appeared to be reveling in her role as hostess.

Unable to shake the feeling that her family was trying to hide her away, Rivki stormed into the kitchen, nearly crashing into Esti.

"I can barely breathe," she complained to Rivki, fingering a sparkling green and black pin positioned at the neck of a crisp white blouse.

Rivki knew this was where she was meant to give Esti a big hug or dole out words of encouragement, but she needed some kind, reassuring words for herself, too. Thankfully, they were interrupted by a ringing at the door.

The Aaronsons. Esti hesitated for just a second before pushing open the kitchen door.

"Come in, come in, please." Rivki heard her father's jolly voice. She imagined him ushering these strangers towards the worn-out sofas at the far end of the living room. She sensed a stream of bodies swish past the kitchen and drew up close to the door, peeking through the crack, trying to glimpse the man who'd won her sister's heart.

When he turned to sit, Rivki drank in the tall, square-jawed young man, brown ringlets framing a handsome face. He was dressed smartly in a dark blue suit jacket that fell just above his knees, revealing matching pants and shining patent shoes. She resisted the urge to be impressed that he was wearing a new *Samet* hat, one that people usually reserve for *Shabbos*.

"Would you like something to drink, Mr. Aaronson?" Abba cleared his throat and Rivki saw him signaling Ima. She knew that was her cue to get to work and backed away from the door towards the electric urn.

Then Esti was beside her, gushing. "*Nu*? Rivi? Did you see him? He's wearing his *Shabbos* clothes, and just for a *Lechaim*. That must mean something, right? Honestly, I can't believe this is happening, that he's here... in our house. My head is spinning. It's all happened so fast. I mean, I think he's the right one for me, but what if his parents don't like me?"

"I'm sure they'll love you." Rivki felt cold as she began placing cookies on Ima's fanciest platter. "Everyone does, Esti, you know that," she continued without looking at her sister.

"Rivi?" Esti watched her with bewilderment. "What's wrong? Are you okay?"

"I'm fine, Esti," Rivki replied, words coming out as a hiss. She couldn't keep this pretense up any longer. "How can you be so sure he's the right one for you if you haven't even kissed him yet?" Esti looked at her blankly. Rivki could hear the wheels in her sister's brain turn, considering the forbidden words never before uttered in their kitchen, in their home, in their community. She couldn't resist pushing the point one step further. "Personally, I plan on kissing my *bashert* to make sure he's really the right one."

Gently, she handed the tray of cookies, cake, and neatly poured coffee and tea to Esti, fighting an urge to upend its entire contents onto the floor, before turning stiffly to close the oven door. She felt her sister's eyes lingering on her back for a second before she heard the kitchen door swing shut.

TAMAR

The weird encounter with Tal was still on her mind as she made her way to Pisgat Zeev to meet Ami. She hoped Leon hadn't gotten the wrong idea. Tamar shivered thinking about it.

As soon as she saw Ami from the window of the light rail waiting for her just outside the mall, thoughts of Tal vanished. She liked the way his eyes sparkled when he saw her and the way he kissed her gently on each cheek. He smelled good too, like powder and soap.

"The ice cream place is upstairs." He led her shyly inside.

"Why weren't you at soccer practice today?" She broke the ice once they were seated under the bright lights of Sammy's Ice Creams.

"An interview! With the army," he sounded excited. "I didn't tell anyone because I didn't want to jinx it, but it went really well."

"Wow, a *tzav rishon*?" Tamar licked her ice cream, the cold threatening to freeze her brain.

"Well, not exactly." He fixed her with his chestnut eyes as he took a bite of his own. "There's a special liaison for minorities that are interested in volunteering for the army. I met him today."

"What does your family think about you going into the army?" She did not avoid his gaze.

"Hamudi doesn't think I should do it." He continued, looking directly at her. "He says it'll make me confused, that an Arab can't fight for an army that oppresses other Arabs. I don't agree. I told him, we were brought up here, went to school here, we need to give something back. Besides, all my friends are going to do it and I want to go too."

"Well, your brother might have a point, don't you think? I mean, the army is there to protect Israel against Arabs and, if you join, you'll be fighting against those who want to kill Jews. Wouldn't it be weird having to attack another Arab coming towards you with a knife?" Tamar shifted in her seat.

"Look." He took a breath. "I'm against all violence, by anyone," Ami emphasized every word, like each held a power of its own. Then he added, "All violence."

His words made her heart cheer. Against all violence. She wondered what her ex-friend Tal might have to say about that. Thinking about the gas station made her stomach clench. Then there was the Haredi protest the other day. There were so many Jews who were bad or who did not want to help their country and here was someone who did not even have to go to the army actually wanting to.

Ami wiped his lips with a square of napkin and then stood. "Shall we walk around?"

Tamar looked from Ami to the chaotic blend of mall-goers. Young, harried parents chased boisterous kids, determined shoppers lugged new purchases. There were Arabs, ultra-Orthodox Jews, the secular, packed like an assortment of chocolates, together in one box but not touching, not mixing with one another. She wondered where she and Ami, a secular Jewish girl and an Arab boy, would fit in.

As they ebbed along with the throngs stroked by the mall's fluorescent lighting, Tamar glanced up at Ami, straight jawline, smooth aureate skin. If she was going to cut across Jerusalem's natural flow, she was glad to do it with him. When, a few minutes later, he reached for her hand, Tamar didn't resist.

"Oh look, there's Gaya..." Tamar pulled Ami into a store.

"Who?" Ami strained to see.

"Gaya... you know...." She let go of his hand. "From my band."

Ami shrugged. "Are we hiding?"

"N–no–" Tamar searched for words. "I–I–just can't deal with the questions about us, not yet."

"Well, I don't know why you care." He looked out into the mall. "Looks like your friend is keeping even more controversial company than you."

Tamar followed his gaze and saw Gaya surrounded by a group of boys she didn't recognize. She frowned at Ami. "I've never seen any of those guys before."

"They look like Arabs... from the villages." He was still watching Gaya and friends as they faded into the crowd. "God knows what she's doing with them. They're bad news. All they want is Jewish ass."

His words came out in a crude hiss, and Tamar took a step backward. "Maybe we should warn her?"

"No. No. We definitely should not," Ami's voice was softer now. "We should stay as far away as possible from them."

Just as they headed out of the store, a sharp scream pierced the air. It was coming from the far end of the mall, near the food court, and suddenly people were running in that direction.

"What is it?" Tamar grabbed Ami's arm.

"Not sure, but doesn't sound good." He frowned, trying to see. "Come on."

Drawing closer, Tamar and Ami saw a scrum of guys, oversized *kippot* and ragged side locks just like Hezi and his gang, surrounding Gaya and her friends. One man gripped Gaya's arm and was trying to pull her towards him. An Arab boy, one of those Ami said was from the villages, was yanking her back.

"Let go of me, you animals," Gaya sounded like a wounded beast. "You're hurting me..... Let go..."

Tamar didn't know which one she was shouting at, but her face was turning white as streaks of black mascara began to trail down her cheeks.

"Ami, we need to do something. They're hurting her." Tamar tugged at his arm. "We can't just leave her."

"Fine, let's go and see if your friend is all right." He marched towards the ruckus.

"Gaya, Gaya, it's me, Tamar. Are you okay?" Tamar was almost running to keep up with Ami.

Gaya looked up, and suddenly, the Arab boy who was holding onto her let go. At the same time, the Jewish man flung her aside as well, and she ended up in a heap on the floor as a wall of bodies crushed together. Tamar heard Gaya scream again, but her muffled words floated to the floor.

"Oh no!" Tamar sprinted the final few meters. "Gaya… where are you?" She searched frantically, trying to glimpse her bandmate's familiar face.

Then she felt a hand on her shoulder, and she turned to see Gaya's black-lined face.

"Tamar! Thank God." She flung her arms around Tamar's neck.

"Gaya!" Tamar pulled out of the fray. "What the hell is going on?"

"These men, they told Yousef it was illegal for him to date a Jewish girl. They told him and his friends to leave the mall…" Gaya burst into tears.

"Shhh, Gaya, don't cry. I don't think it's illegal for Jews and Arabs to date." But as soon as the words were out of her mouth, Tamar began questioning them. Was it illegal for a Jew and an Arab to date? No, it wasn't. She was sure of it. People could date whoever they wanted. Israel was a democracy.

"I don't know if I'm even Jewish." Gaya quaffed between lumpy breaths. "I live only with my dad. My mom left us when I was small. She's still in Russia…"

Tamar missed the rest of what Gaya was saying as the crowd of mostly men multiplied, expanding outwards towards them, forcing them to scatter until Tamar realized that she had lost track of Ami.

"Ami!" She frantically searched faces, fighting back images of the bloody shopkeeper in the gas station. Then she saw him, tall and strong, in the center of the melee. He was trying to raise his voice above the scuffle, arms stretched out on either side of his body, palms pressed into the chests of two strangers.

Before she could call his name again, the two men—one clearly Jewish, the other Arab—were on each other, Ami ejected to the side. Fists flying in all directions.

"Ami!" she called again, waving a hand in the air. She tried to push her way inside the mass of bodies, but then her eyes clocked a familiar face and it all clicked. One of Hezi's scraggly friends headed in her direction. Tamar quickly turned her face away, exhaling only once he stomped past her.

A hand on her shoulder made her jump. "Tamar! Thank God! I lost you!" It was Gaya. "What are you doing? You'll get hurt! We need to get out of here before the police come." She began pulling Tamar towards the exit.

"Wait!" Tamar struggled loose. "I can't. Ami."

"But the police..." Gaya shrugged, letting go. Tamar watched her bolt for the door.

Then he was at her side, panting, forehead glinting slightly. "Tamar, are you okay?" Ami breathed. "This is crazy. Who are these people getting involved in other's lives? Who said a Jewish girl can't date an Arab boy?"

"They're from Lehava." The name felt bitter on Tamar's tongue.

"Lehava?" he quizzed, wiping the beads of sweat from his brow.

"I'll tell you later. Let's get out of here." She jerked him in the direction of the exit, just as two men in uniform sped past.

Outside, both instinctively understood the need to get as far away as possible from the mall and its mayhem. Ami led her through a maze of alleyways that sliced between whitewashed apartment buildings glowing bright against the dark sky. Only when they were a safe distance did he stop, his chest puffing in and out.

"Tamar," she could see his breath in the moonlight. "You know it's not true—it's not illegal for an Arab and Jew to date each other?" He turned around to face her. His skin was gold in the glow of the streetlight. "Those guys are damn liars. You know that, right?"

"I know, Ami, it's bullshit." Her words came out quietly as indignation rushed through her pumping veins. How could her people do this? Where did all this hate come from? First the man in the gas station, now this. The Arabs were people too, they lived in this city just like the Jews did.

Ami moved in towards her, bringing his face close to hers. "Tamar, I've such strong feelings for you." He took her hand. "We've become so close, I don't want anything to come between us, especially not this."

Tamar blinked back a tear, and she could see his eyes sparkling again. She wanted to tell him about her role at the gas station. She had to. She was about to open her mouth, let the words spill out, when she felt warm lips on hers and powerful arms around her back.

NOUR

Fadwa appeared at the entrance to Nour's room a few days later. Stepping in uninvited, she shut the door tightly behind her and made herself comfortable on Nour's bed.

"Listen," she spoke in a conspiratorial tone. "There's a protest on Friday. You'll come with me, yes?" She lowered her chin towards her chest and eyed Nour from beneath bushy brows.

Nour regarded her obstinate cousin. Wasn't it bad enough that her brother got himself locked up in jail? Hanging with Fadwa might be even more dangerous. Why couldn't both of them just behave like normal people? Didn't they realize that protesting and violence only made the situation worse for everyone? Even if it always started peacefully with a Facebook post or with a non-violent protest, somehow things always seemed to escalate, spiraling out of control and descending into violence.

Just last week, a young man about the same age as Abdulrahman was shot dead by Israelis in the Old City, on one of the main shopping streets. The Israeli authorities said he had stabbed a Jewish man to death. There were reports in Hebrew saying that the dead man's wife, covered in blood and holding her baby, had run through the *suq* looking for help. Shopkeepers, one report said, turned away from her because they didn't want to be seen collaborating with Israel.

In Arabic, Nour heard just the opposite. She read how this young man was a hero for the Palestinian cause and how he was killed by the Israelis unjustly. She didn't know who was telling the truth, but she couldn't understand how anyone could kill another human being.

"Well, dear cousin?" Fadwa was watching her, head cocked to one side. There was no choice now.

"Fine." Nour frowned. "Friday it is then."

Why did it feel like she was making a deal with the devil?

RIVKI

From her perch on the couch, Rivki watched the winter sun slide from the sky, a chill filling her heart. She was trying to work through the pages of schoolwork that Esti had brought home for her, but her concentration was eclipsed by dread about tomorrow.

For more than a month, she'd avoided leaving home, but the truth was, the pains inside her were fading, just like the tiny scar left by Dr. Jalal on her stomach, and Ima's patience had run out. Tomorrow, she would return to school, to her friends, to her old life.

Rivki watched thick breaths puff from her lips. If it was cold outside, inside was like an icebox. She clicked on the small electric heater, placing her toes lavishly on the bars as they warmed up. She knew she wasn't supposed to use the radiator just for her alone—Ima said it doubled their electricity bill—but who would know? This must be how the chickens on Geula Street felt like as they roasted inside the prison of those glass ovens, knowing it would soon all be over.

She tried to imagine how it would feel pulling on that ugly pleated skirt, buttoning down that stiff blue shirt, walking through the doors of Bais Yaakov. Listening to teachers, rabbis, friends talk about a life where she no longer fit, about a life that no longer fit her.

Rivki sighed, daring herself to daydream about tight jeans gripping her thighs and rose gold phones that let the world come alive and Facebook pages that let her send messages to friends that truly cared about her. She supposed that was the lesson of Chava's temptation. Once you try it, you can't go back.

But she couldn't go forward either. She was stuck. Stuck in a gray world where all anyone cared about was getting married. Stuck in a freezing apartment that she was banned from warming. Stuck in a body that refused to function as it should.

Hearing the front door creak, Rivki quickly flipped the switch on the heater just in time to see Esti march in, followed by Dovi, Shimshon, and Batsheva. Ima was not far behind. Laden with plastic bags, she entered huffing.

"Not too cold in here yet," she remarked, heading straight for the kitchen.

Rivki buried herself down inside the blankets, watching silently as Esti helped the others peel off their puffy jackets and hang them up on the rack beside the door.

"So, how's my sister doing?" Esti plopped down on the couch beside her. "Ready for the big day tomorrow?"

"It'll be nice." Rivki's words came out in a squeak.

"It will!" Esti threw an arm around her. "You have no idea how much everyone asks after you. They'll be so excited to see you back on your feet."

Rivki tried to catch some of Esti's enthusiasm, but the chill inside her was back. "Hope so," she shivered, reaching to turn on the heater now that it was allowed.

"It'll be fine, Rivi. You'll see. I'm sure you're nervous, but really, everyone will be so thrilled to see you," Esti spoke each word with confidence. "Better than sitting up here all alone."

Rivki watched the coils on the radiator turning red, feeling Esti's eyes on her. Her stomach hurt again now, though not in the same way as her Crohn's disease. She knew her sister was just trying to be nice, trying to be the old Esti. Ever since the night of the *vort*, she was making a genuine effort, but Rivki also knew it was only temporary. Soon her sister, her roommate, her best friend, would leave her for good. She would move on without her, move in with someone new. Replace her with a complete stranger. A man.

• • •

The next morning, Rivki slipped weary arms through a starchy shirt and slugged across town in speckling rain with Esti. In through the doors of Bais Yaakov, the sisters were greeted by a cacophony of girls dressed in identical light blue shirts and dark blue pleated skirts that reached down to their ankles.

Within seconds, she was surrounded by a sea of blue and a chorus of "Rivkis." In the scrum, it was hard to decipher who was who, but then Bracha, the only one of her friends to visit her in the last few weeks, was at her side, grabbing her hand tightly and dragging her from the chaos into a classroom.

"Oh Rivki! You look so much better!" Bracha welcomed her with bright eyes.

Rivki regarded the familiar face, smooth and simple, free from worry, free from thought. She wondered why she couldn't be more like Bracha. Why couldn't she just accept the path laid out for Haredi girls? Why did she have to question her destiny? Or try to understand what it was He wanted of them, or what it was she, herself, wanted? Rivki sighed. "*Baruch Ha-Shem*," she said, unconvinced.

The rest of her classmates poured in. "Rivki! We missed you!" "Rivki, how are you feeling?" "Rivki, are you all better now?" "It must have been awful in the hospital." "So glad you're back."

All she could mutter after each salutation was the standard, "*Baruch Ha-Shem*." She kept a tight smile plastered on her face, hoping it would pass for happiness, for thankfulness to be well and healthy and back in the folds of what everyone around her believed to be the right path.

Rivki's shoulders slackened as interest turned from her to chatter about bookkeeping or computer programming or kindergarten teachers. She tried to be interested in such careers and how they would fit into life as a mother, a wife, a dutiful daughter of G-d, but suddenly she was gripped with the feeling that none of this was for her. Not the schooling. Not the office job. Not the husband or the children or the small, cold apartment that cost too much to heat. Rivki wanted more from life. She wanted more than her peers or family allowed.

A line of pain crawled through her stomach. Not Crohn's, but something else. Loneliness? Longing? It snaked up her chest, gripping her heart and pinching her head.

"Bracha." She leaned over to her friend. "I'm not feeling so good. I need to go. Get some air."

"Shall I come with you?" Bracha's eyes darted from her to the teacher now standing at the front of the classroom.

"No–no–I'll be alright." Rivki raised her hand.

"Rivka Lefkovitz. Welcome back." The teacher nodded at her.

"*Baruch Ha-Shem*.... Er... please may I be excused?" Rivki ignored the stares.

The teacher beckoned her forward, and Rivki walked, eyes fixed, to the front of the classroom. "Are you okay?" the teacher addressed her, hand raised to silence the other girls.

Rivki gestured at her stomach and winced. Seconds later, she was outside.

TAMAR

I wake up just to see you
I go to bed to wake up
I work out to be strong for you
I catch the sun's rays to be tanned for you
I tell jokes to make you laugh,
I write this poem just to see your smile.

Tamar let her head sink deeper into the feather pillows as she read the words again. Then she closed her eyes, letting that Saturday morning feeling rush through her. There was no dashing out the door today, no fighting her way through the crowds on the light rail, no yawning through classes in school.

Outside, heavy clouds threatened rain, but inside, in her bed, in her heart, Tamar was warm. Ami sent her the poem a few days ago, but each time she saw the words, a smile formed on her lips. She'd never been drunk before; the sharp bitter taste, even the smell of alcohol, made her stomach curl, but it was how she imagined the feeling.

Ami underlined the poem with a row of purple hearts, the emoji that now defined their relationship. Tamar tapped a single solitary one into her phone and pressed send. She followed the sanguine symbol with a voice recording. "Hey, call you when I get back from Tel Aviv."

A week had passed since their outing to the mall, since they held hands and their lips touched. The events that night shocked them both but had brought them closer, too, and Tamar knew that if she wanted it to work, she needed to come clean with Ami about the events at the gas station. There were forces everywhere, even among their friends, that might try to destroy what was growing between them and if word got out that she was with Tal and Hezi's mob that night, it would most certainly bring an end to the purple hearts.

Tamar sighed, pushing herself deeper beneath the covers. She tried to imagine what words she could possibly use to explain that awful night, but each time she scrolled through the events in her mind, she saw herself standing amid a mass of bodies screaming "Death to Arabs" and felt her blood turn cold.

A few days ago, she tried to confess to Aviv about the events. They were nestled side by side on her friend's bed, steaming mugs of sweet hot chocolate teasing their nostrils as fierce winds hounded and howled outside.

Tamar started with what happened at the mall the night she went with Ami.

Aviv's eyes grew wide with each sorry detail. "That's sick, really sick," she said, her voice indignant as Tamar described how Gaya was almost ripped in two. "I can't believe people are filled with so much hatred that they actually spend their time patrolling the mall for Arabs and Jews dating each other."

Then she added, "Actually, ever since that Arab boy in East Jerusalem was murdered by Jews, nothing surprises me anymore."

"I know. It's almost become acceptable." Tamar inhaled, knowing it was now or never if she wanted to relieve her conscience about the gas station, but she just couldn't string the words together.

"I wonder if it's the same in other cities or if Jerusalem is just particularly afflicted with more than its fair share of hatred?" She struggled to keep her voice steady.

"People have always fought wars in Jerusalem," Aviv responded philosophically. "I just don't understand this current war—Jew against Arab, Arab against Jew, religious against secular, secular against religious. What are all these differences anyway? Aren't all people born the same? Don't we all share the same physiology?"

"I know, you're right! The differences are only cosmetic," Tamar agreed glumly. "I mean, no one chooses where they are born, right? I didn't choose to be a secular Jew in Jerusalem. Ami didn't choose to be a Muslim Arab."

"Have you told your parents yet? About Ami?" Aviv gave her a meaningful look.

Tamar shook her head and looked away again. Sadness poked her.

"So, let me get this straight: You really, really like him, you've been friends for like a gazillion years, you're together all the time and when you're not, you guys are always texting. You barely have time for little ol' me..." She sighed, making sad eyes and then scrunched up her face. "But you can't tell your parents?"

"I want to, but I don't know how they'll react." Tamar pursed her lips. "He's my first boyfriend and I know he's one of my oldest friends, but he's an Arab. My parents might flip out."

Aviv rolled her eyes and exclaimed, "Tamar, the longer it takes for you to tell your parents, the more suspicious they'll become, and what if they find out without you telling them? What then?"

Tamar let out a breath and closed her eyes. Another thing she needed to come clean about.

· · ·

Tamar was still deciding how to bring up Ami with her parents as her dad's car wound its way out of Jerusalem. The sun was fighting to break free from dark gray rain clouds as they passed a long-abandoned Arab village now shadowed by a shiny high-rise housing project. Tamar eyed the new residents—smart fur hats and long black coats, pushing strollers and dragging their children as they walked purposely to Shabbat services. She fingered her cheek, remembering the slop of saliva on the day of the Haredi protest against army service. Were the differences only cosmetic? Or were they deeper, more ingrained? She wasn't sure, but she knew she had to lift the weight of so many secrets, so if she was really going to tell her parents about Ami, it was now or never.

"Listen, Mum, Dad, I've something to tell you," she began, a sharpness in the pit of her stomach.

"What is it, sweetie?" Her father turned down the radio.

"Er," Tamar breathed. Now or never. "You know Ami? He and I, well, we're really great friends and... we've been getting closer lately, which is funny because we've known each other for so long, since we were kids, really, and it just sort of happened." She held her breath and checked their expressions in the mirror.

"What are you saying, honey? What are you telling us?" Her mom twisted around to look at her.

"Well..." Tamar swallowed. "We're dating." The words sounded weird, foreign. "I mean, he's my boyfriend. I'm his girlfriend," she clarified, as if making things clear even for herself. Tamar watched her mom place a hand on her father's thigh, but his face remained expressionless.

Her mom, hand still on her dad's leg, broke the stuffy silence. "Yes, of course, we know Ami. He's a lovely boy. We know his family too, but you know, darling, he's not Jewish," she hesitated. "He's an Arab. And... er... Jews and Arabs going together might not... be a.... very good fit."

A stuffy silence filled the car and hung in the air even as they entered Tel Aviv. Dori was waiting for them outside her apartment building and raised an eyebrow at Tamar as she greeted their parents. Tamar shook her head and followed silently as Dori led them to her favorite cafe along the beachfront.

If Saturday was a day of prayer and soul-searching in Jerusalem, in Tel Aviv, it was a day of raucous leisure. The seaside promenade was packed with families chasing kids on bikes or picnicking on the beach trying to capture the rays of the stingy winter sun.

Dori ushered them into low plastic chairs on the lumpy sand. Tamar knew she was supposed to feel more relaxed in Tel Aviv, blow away the pressures of Jerusalem, but she felt her dad's stony eyes examining her. She should have just kept quiet about Ami.

After coffees and shared plates of fries, her parents seemed anxious to take a stroll. Dori said she and Tamar would wait for them at the cafe and ordered another round of cappuccinos. "What the hell is going on?" She turned to Tamar as soon as they were gone.

"I have a boyfriend," Tamar marveled at how words, simple words, could be so complex.

"What? Really?" A sly smile spread across her older sister's lips. "Who?"

"Remember Ami? Ami Awad? He's been in my cla—"

"Yes! I know him," Dori chuckled. "His brother Hamudi was with me! Wow! Ami! He's cute! I guess Dad didn't take it very well then?" She sighed and squeezed Tamar's shoulder. "Don't worry, he'll come round. You're his little girl. It was probably just a shock."

"Actually, don't know if either of them took it so well. Now I'm thinking I shouldn't have said anything." Tamar scanned the boardwalk to make sure their parents were still out of sight. "I'm pretty sure it's because he's an Arab."

"Nah—don't be silly," Dori stopped her.

"But it was the first thing Mom said when I told them." Tamar felt a ball of sadness in her chest.

Dori rolled her eyes. "That's so stupid! How can they even think about that? You're only sixteen and he's your first boyfriend—it's not like you're getting married. I think they are just looking for an excuse, some reason why he's no good. They'll come around, little sister, don't worry. I remember they were totally off with me when I came home with my first boyfriend."

"Really?" Tamar was doubtful.

"Yes! You don't remember?" Dori smiled at her again. "Remember Idan?"

Tamar scrunched her face, remembering a boy with thick brown curls tied back in a *cookoo*. Him and Dori giggling, eating popcorn together as they watched a movie on the couch.

"Well, the first time I brought him home, phew!" Dori brushed back her own curls. "Dad was so mad, he walked around like a robot for days. Mom was a bit better, but still a little off. Anyway, eventually, they both came around."

"H-how? How did they change their minds?" There was a lump in Tamar's throat.

Dori shrugged. "Not sure, really. I guess at some point they just accepted that I was growing up, and it was part of life."

Tamar reflected on her sister's experience. Maybe there was some hope, but she still couldn't shake the feeling that her case was different. A Jew and an Arab were just not meant to fit together in any scenario.

"It'll all be okay, Tamar." Dori moved her chair closer. "You'll see. It's hard for parents when their kids grow up suddenly."

Tamar looked at her sister, and suddenly everything fit together. If there was one person who would understand and not judge her, it was Dori. "There's something else... I want, need to tell you," she began, words and relief flying from her mouth into the sea.

. . .

"So, do you wanna tell me how it happened?" her mother asked later when they were back home in Jerusalem. Her mom sat on the swiveling computer chair in her room, regarding her with familiar green eyes. Tamar could hear her dad downstairs in the small basement. She had no clue what exactly he was doing down there, but was thankful he was out of earshot.

"Oh, y'know." Tamar blushed. "It just, well, we just started hanging out... like, y'know, it's different from when you and Dad were our age. People don't date like you did, they just start hanging out, and then they become boyfriend and girlfriend."

"I understand that. I'm surprised you even hang out these days and don't just text." She laughed at her own joke.

"Funny, Mom." Tamar rolled her eyes. "We do hang out, as well as texting. Actually, we even went to the mall for ice cream, a proper date."

Tamar hesitated a second, then told her mom about what happened there. About the vigilantes and the fight. Her mom frowned. When Tamar was done, her mom stood up from the chair and climbed into the bed, pulling Tamar close to her.

"Listen, Tamar, you're not a baby. You're old enough to have a boyfriend—even though your father might not agree—I think you are. And I know you are sensible too, but you also have to realize that there are going to be some people who are against the fact your boyfriend is not Jewish." Her mom sighed. "It's a complicated situation here. Jews everywhere have always been against marrying non-Jews. Not that I think you and Ami will get married, you're still far too young to even think about that, but in Israel, there is this added nationalist element, it's almost impossible for Jews and

Arabs to even be friends. There are always going to be people who try to stop such relationships—from both sides."

"I know, Mom, but he's one of the good ones, you know that. You know his parents, they're all for coexistence, they support the State of Israel. Ami even wants to join the army, so why can't we just be like normal teenagers?" Tamar breathed in her mom's lemony scent.

"I suppose you can, but just be careful."

Tamar felt warm lips on her forehead.

"Listen, it's late and you've got school tomorrow. We'll talk about it more, at some point, but go to sleep now."

As her mom slipped out of the room, Tamar felt a heaviness lingering in the air. Why did it all need to be so complicated? Why couldn't she just find love like other girls?

NOUR

There were hundreds of young people at the DCO checkpoint when Nour and Fadwa arrived on Friday just after noon.

"It looks like a lot now, but you wait until the prayers are done." Fadwa promised with an air of authority. She stood on tiptoes, straining her neck to search across the ever-growing mass of people milling about. The junction was wide and led to the military barrier that separated Ramallah from the rest of Palestine. "Omar said we should meet him next to the square."

"Who's Omar?" Nour wondered how her newly arrived American cousin was so informed about nationalistic protests and how she already knew so many people, but Fadwa didn't answer. She was talking rapidly into her phone.

"He said wait here." Fadwa slipped the phone into her jeans pocket. "We're very lucky with the weather today, aren't we?" She looked up at the pale sky as if assessing conditions for a stroll through the Virginia countryside.

Nour nodded without looking at Fadwa, eyes drawn instead to a group of young men sharing a uniform of faded skinny jeans and tight-fitting T-shirts. As she watched them wrap green, white, and black Palestinian flags around their heads, flashes of Abdulrahman and his friends, pumped up from the protests in Shuafat twelve months earlier, ran through her head.

"Actually, it doesn't look so good." Nour's mouth was as dry as cardboard.

Up ahead, she could make out the shapes of Israeli soldiers, a wall of green blocking their path. Behind her, the hum of voices was steadily rising, rushing towards her, willing her forwards into the fight. The flag-covered guys, eyes now visible only through narrow slits, were in full operation mode fronting the crowd as they fired up piles of big rubber tires.

"It's to confuse them." Fadwa gestured towards the soldiers, the tips of her fingers getting lost as thick smoke filled the air. The blackening sky grew even darker.

"Omarrrr." Nour caught only her cousin's rolling r's before a tall, lanky guy, his own Palestinian flag draped over his shoulders, was standing right in front of them.

"Darrrrrrling." He put a long, slender arm around Fadwa's shoulders. "Here you are!"

Fadwa stood on tiptoes, planting an eager kiss on each cheek. She then turned to Nour. "Omar! This is my cousin."

"*Salaam*, Nour, welcome. It's very good you came." He extended a hand. "We need as many as possible for this fight. I hope you are as bold as your cousin."

Nour hesitated before reaching back. She certainly didn't feel as bold as Fadwa, but suddenly, the warmth of his flesh on hers sent a zing of pride through her. She was here with her people, and they were fighting for justice. Perhaps Fadwa and Abdulrahman were right: taking action was better than just sitting idly by, pondering what was right and what was wrong, and vicariously, and by default accepting this unequal, unjust occupation.

Omar pulled two black-and-white checkered scarves from his backpack. "Wrap them around your face to protect yourselves from the smoke." He handed one to Fadwa and one to Nour.

"Or so the Israelis can't identify us." Fadwa winked knowingly at him.

Nour unraveled the large swath of material and imitated her cousin, wrapping it around her head until only her eyes were free. She tucked in the ends and did not protest when Fadwa pulled an arm through hers and the three of them marched into the billowing smoke.

Through her visor, she spied several protesters gripping used Coke bottles; eager red fire crackled at the ends of rags stuffed inside. Nour blinked. Suddenly, she was back in Shuafat again, picking her way through the smashed glass on the sidewalk, dodging the black carcasses of still smoldering cars.

"Thought this was supposed to be non-violent?" Nour coughed in Fadwa's ear.

"It is! All we have are stones. Stones and improvised weapons. They have guns, tear gas, god knows what else," Fadwa coughed back, voice rising. "We also have our determination; we have our resolve and we will never give..."

A loud explosion followed by a series of popping sounds drowned her last words and Nour's eyes began to sting.

"T-t-tear gas." Fadwa spluttered, pulling Nour back in the direction they just came from. "We need to go." She let go of her arm and grabbed her hand instead, bodies working hard to separate them.

The cracking and popping intensified and Nour tried her best to hold on to Fadwa, but before she knew it, she found herself adrift in the sea of panicked protestors. She stopped for a second, trying to find her cousin or Omar, her lanky friend, but suddenly she felt her legs rising, her body propelled forward, and she landed with a thud, footsteps continuing their stampede.

"Nour, Nour, where are you?" The voice came from far away, far above her. She tried to pull herself up, but a soaring crick sliced her right arm. Then Fadwa was at her side. "Nour! Are you hurt? We have to keep on moving." She tried to pull Nour upright.

"Ah! My arm," she muttered, hot tears filling her eyes, "hurts."

And then, powerful arms lifted her. Square shoulders and a scarf pulled her close to his chest. The man cradled her like a baby, carrying her out of the smoke and away from the furious crowd. Somewhere far behind her, Fadwa was still calling, "Wait, wait for me, Nour. Nour, wait for me, Nour," but all she could feel was a stabbing in her arm and a queasy fog racing up through her stomach towards her mouth.

"Wait, please, this young woman. I found her on the ground. She's hurt," the scarf-covered man called out to a paramedic about to close the doors of an ambulance. He opened the doors wide again, and the scarfed man bundled her inside. A whip of pain flared from her wrist up to her shoulder and the cry she gave came from deep inside her throat.

"Let me see." One of the ambulance team came out of the shadows, ushering her in a spare seat and strapping her in. He touched her arm gently, and she screamed again. "Mmm, it might be broken." He held on to the offending arm, unraveling a wide white bandage with his spare hand. "You'll need an X-ray, but we can tie it in place so it will hurt less."

Nour sucked in her breath and gritted her teeth as he taped her up, dulling the pain slightly. The paramedic suggested she hold the bad arm with her good one, so it did not move as the ambulance bounced toward the hospital. He also gave her some painkillers, which she downed eagerly.

It was then that she noticed. Large drops, like crimson paint, decorated the floor of the ambulance. A man swathed in bandages, fatter and wider than the one now encasing her arm, lay rigid on the gurney across from her. His face was almost as white as the dressing, salmon pink lips slightly apart, eyes shut tight. Nour gasped. A pool of blood spread slowly from his right shoulder to his chest.

Nour sat upright on the gurney, good arm bracing bad, trying to contend with the stabs of pain that now reached right up to her shoulder. She averted her gaze from the other passenger. The thought of being so close to someone who might soon be dead filled her with dread. She watched the other paramedic working to stem the flow of blood with a tightly twisted tourniquet and felt slithers of hope as deep, rattled breaths filled the cabin.

When her paramedic leaned in to check her pulse again, Nour couldn't resist whispering: "Wh... what happened... to him?"

"Gunshot," he whispered back, counting silently as he pinched her wrist.

Nour felt the horror of the word sink in, stomach lurching. Head spinning. This wasn't real. The Israelis used live bullets? She thought about the boys standing near her and Fadwa earlier, flags and scarves wrapped around their heads, muscular arms launching Coke bottles stuffed with burning rags. Was he one of those boys? She frowned, trying to recognize him.

The ambulance made a sharp turn, throwing Nour off balance and sending flashes of pain through her arm. A small scream escaped her lips as she tried to stop herself from falling off the gurney completely.

"You okay?" Her paramedic reached out a hand to steady her. "Don't worry about him. He's not moving because he's sedated, but he'll be alright.

The bullet only grazed his shoulder. We've treated much worse, haven't we, Tawfiq?"

Tawfiq looked up briefly and shrugged. "He's the third one we've had today."

Nour studied the injured guy more closely now, a heaviness like thick cement filling her bones. She lingered on the spot where she supposed the bullet had struck. Heavy bandages covered the area, but dried blood was everywhere—on his clothes, on the gurney, and dotted across the ambulance floor.

She studied his face, he looked around the same age as Abdulrahman. Her heart withered slightly thinking that it could very well be her brother lying half-dead in an ambulance speeding through Ramallah. Did his family know he was at a protest? Did they know yet that he got shot?

Nour wondered what made some people go out and save lives like these paramedics, while others, like Abdulrahman and the injured guy, put themselves in such danger. Her brother did his protesting online, it was true, but now he was in jail; this guy went to a protest and got shot. His life might never be the same. She blinked away tears. Why did he think he could fight a sophisticated, highly trained, and lethal army with only rocks and homemade bombs? And did he believe such actions would really bring a Palestinian state? Or drive the Israelis away? Even if he killed a few soldiers, Israel would always have more.

The ambulance made another sharp turn, but this time Nour managed to brace herself, pushing back at the pain in her arm and the ache in her heart. There was so much suffering and she wondered if it was all worth it. Here she was, in an ambulance with what might be a broken arm. He was lying there, shot.

Confronting Israeli soldiers might help diffuse anger at the occupation, but in reality, it was futile. The soldiers in their green army fatigues, were well-protected and well-armed. What could a bunch of Palestinian protesters with only rocks and burning Coke bottles do to change the situation? There must be another way.

Nour felt her phone buzzing and, pulling it out, saw it was Fadwa. A thick layer of sick formed in her throat. How could she have lied to her—

tell her it was a peaceful protest when clearly it wasn't? Didn't she realize that violence only brought more violence?

"Nour! Nour! Are you okay? I only just got a signal; my phone wasn't working. Where are you?" The connection was patchy and Fadwa sounded out of breath. Nour pictured her still running from the tear gas and bullets.

"I'm okay." Nour winced into the phone. "They think my arm is broken. I'm in an ambulance—"

"I know, I know, but where, where are they taking you?" Fadwa sounded very far away.

"I, I don't... let me check." Nour turned to her paramedic. "Excuse me, which hospital are we going to?"

"The government hospital, al-hukumi. We'll be there in just a few minutes."

"al-hukumi," Nour repeated to her cousin. "Fadwa, can you hear me? Fadwa? Can you call Baba? I can't...." The line went dead.

Nour looked at her phone. There was no signal. Tears stung in her eyes again, and she realized she would now need to tell Baba everything. What a mess!

· · ·

Fadwa arrived in the hospital before Baba. "Nour!" She ran over, leaning in for a hug.

"Don't, it hurts." Nour put out her good arm defensively.

An X-ray confirmed fractures in two places. Now she was waiting for them to smooth on a cast and give her something stronger to fight the deep lines of pain striking her from wrist to shoulder.

"Oh, Nouri, poor you! See what those Israelis do? They don't care who they—"

"No! Fadwa! Quiet... I can't hear any more from you. You promised no violence, but there was! What did you expect? The Israeli soldiers, they're trained to fight. This is what happens when you go up against an army with only rocks and bottles." The throbbing in Nour's arm was now flecked with anger. "I don't want to talk about this with you anymore. I've got a broken arm, I'm in pain. I want my parents, even though I know they're going to be furious with me."

Nour took a deep breath, then looked steadily at Fadwa. She expected her cousin to push back like usual, but thought she saw a flicker of something else. What was it? Recognition? Compassion?

Then Fadwa took her good hand and squeezed it gently. "It must really hurt, but I'm glad it was only your arm and nothing more. I called Uncle Samir. He's on his way." Her voice was softer than Nour had ever heard it. "Don't worry, I'll explain it all to him. I'll say it was my fault."

Baba's face was thunderous when he arrived at the hospital. "What were you thinking?" he bellowed across the triage when he saw them. Fadwa, perched on the end of Nour's bed, shifted uncomfortably and stood up.

"You know what?" said Baba, holding up his hand. "We'll discuss this in the car. Now, where's the doctor?"

Nour watched as Baba expertly took over the whole medical process. He was a pharmaceutical researcher, but he understood how a hospital ticked. He knew the right questions to ask the doctor and the right words to get the nurse to plaster up Nour's arm efficiently. In the middle, he dialed the number of the chief orthopedic surgeon at the Israeli hospital where he worked and ignored stares from other patients as he spoke to him in fluent Hebrew.

"He'll see you first thing Sunday." Baba hung up, satisfied. "Now, let's get you out of here." He then thanked the staff profusely, before helping Nour to the car. Fadwa trailed them like a dark cloud.

"So, who's going to tell me what happened?" Baba began once they were all seated. Nour sat beside her father while Fadwa sulked silently in the back.

"We were running... I tripped... fell on my arm," Nour mumbled, a dull ache dominating her entire left side.

"I get that, Nour. The question is, why were you running? No, no, no, don't answer that... let's not play here. What were you doing at a protest? Against Israeli soldiers? You think I don't know where you were. I do. Don't ask how. I just know. The more important question is what you were doing there? Don't you know people get killed at these protests all the time?"

Nour's heart burned with sadness as she watched Baba's knuckles turn white holding the steering wheel. She thought about the guy in the ambulance. Gunshot. She hung her head in shame. He was right now more than ever.

"Nour, what have I told you? How have I raised you? Violence in all forms is wrong. I don't know how to get this message across any clearer. I failed with Abdulrahman, but you? You? Why would you get involved in this? Don't I have enough to deal with?" His lips moved fast.

"With all due respect, Uncle—" Fadwa began.

"Fadwa, you, you... I'm even more disappointed with you." Baba cut her off. "I brought you into my house, let you stay under my roof, shared my food, my love, my warmth with you, and this is how you repay me? Taking Nour to a violent protest?"

The car filled with silence as they reached the familiar landmarks of the Qalandia checkpoint, defiant fists of Marwan Barghouti jumping out from the ugly gray of the separation wall. He was a Palestinian hero who stood up to the Israelis, but where did it get him? He had been in jail since before Nour was born. Nour's head pounded more than her arm.

At home, Mama was just as angry with them as Baba, but as usual, she made her disproval clear in other ways. First, by telling Fadwa she might be more comfortable at Setty's. "You only have a few more weeks left here," Nour heard her tell Fadwa. "Your other cousins will be happy to have you there."

If Fadwa was upset at being banished, she did not show it and Nour did not ask her either when she put her head around the door to say goodbye the next morning. If she was sorry for what happened to Nour, she did not say, but she did give Nour a kiss before Mama drove her to Setty's that afternoon.

Baba's anger at Nour remained, and she knew she needed to apologize again for being so reckless. While Mama was still at Setty's, she approached him. He was calmer now, sitting on the porch sipping gritty coffee and clutching a newspaper.

"Can we talk?" Nour approached him cautiously. "I wanted to apologize for getting into trouble. I know you think Fadwa dragged me there, but truthfully, I wanted to go for myself." She held her breath, letting the confession soak up the air around them. "I wanted to go to understand for myself our people's struggle. After Abdulrahman was arrested, after everything that's been happening, I thought it was time for me to see what our options are. Should we be fighting back? And if yes, how?"

Baba folded the newspaper into his lap and brought his eyes up to Nour's. "And?" He breathed out coffee. "What's your conclusion now... now that you have seen how some of our people react to this ongoing occupation? And what happens to them? Do you better understand? Do you have the answers?"

"Well, answers I don't have, but I do know what doesn't work, what won't work. Throwing rocks at armed soldiers does nothing but get *us* killed, does nothing but bring their wrath down further on us. There must be another way to solve this, for us to get our freedom. I just don't know what that is yet, Baba."

"Listen, Nour, you need to think harder about what you went through, what you saw at the protest. You're a smart young lady. I know you'll come to the right conclusions. Use this experience to do something positive." Baba's voice was gentle. "Even bad experiences have a silver lining sometimes."

RIVKI

If Zehava was shocked to see Rivki standing in the shadows when she opened the door to her office, she didn't show it.

"Rivki!" the older woman exclaimed. Her face was a perfect composition of colorful make-up, framed with a sparkling *sheitel*. "It's so good to see you!" She hesitated a second, then added, "Aren't you supposed to be in school?"

She ushered Rivki inside without waiting for the answer, closing the door firmly behind them. Rivki had no concrete answer for why she'd walked out of school, but she could see that Zehava needed a suitable explanation.

"I went, this morning, and it—well, it—just didn't fit," she spluttered, thick throbbing around her eyes threatened to give way to wet tears. She sighed. "I-I just didn't feel well and Ima's not home and then I remembered you worked right here, so I thought.... I thought... maybe I could come to you... y'know... until I feel well enough to go home." She looked down at her shoes.

"Of course, it was too much for you!" Zehava was like a beam of sunshine on a frozen lake. "You've been so sick, Rivki, you're not ready to go back. You need to ease back into life after everything you've been through."

Her sister-in-law guided her towards an empty desk and planted a cup of steaming tea in front of her. The office was calm, with a few other women, all around the same age as Zehava, sitting quietly behind desks, tapping away on keyboards or scribbling on complicated-looking paperwork.

Rivki studied each one of them. Could this be her one day? A working woman? She tried to imagine herself dressed smartly with her face painted and her hair just so. They all looked like they were doing something very important. She wanted to do something more important than cooking and keeping a house clean, like Ima.

"You sit there and rest." Zehava hovered beside her for a few seconds before heading back toward her desk. Rivki watched her sister-in-law sit back down behind an oversized computer monitor and realized there was a computer on the desk in front of her too. Facebook, she thought suddenly. Could she? Would she? Dare ask Zehava if she could use the computer?

"Zehava," Rivki whispered over the steam of her tea. "Zehava, sorry...." She spluttered.

"Yes, Rivki?" Zehava answered without looking up.

"Can I, do you mind if I, can I... do you think it would be possible if I could use a computer? Just for a minute? I need to check something on the internet?"

"Internet?" Zehava's eyes flicked upwards.

"Yes... yes... I need to look something up." Rivki tried to sound confident. "Is it okay?"

Her sister-in-law rose from the chair with a sly smile on her face and walked over to where Rivki was sitting. She punched a passcode into the black keyboard and the computer's monitor sprung to life. A familiar image appeared on the screen: Google. Rivki knew about the search engine, since they used it in school sometimes. Though there it was monitored, sites considered frivolous or corrupting were blocked.

As soon as Zehava marched back to her table, Rivki grabbed the mouse and clicked on the search field. She typed the letters f-a-c-e-b-o-o-k with one finger and pressed enter. She added in her password, *RivkLife*, and username and, as if by magic, saw her own face appear. She smiled at the image, remembering when her hospital friends snapped it. Where were they right now? What were they doing? She clicked the section marked "Friends," just as Ariel and Ayelet had taught her, and suddenly, their faces appeared.

She looked first at Ariel's page. It was decorated with photographs of Ariel and her friends. One of her on the beach, Rivki gasped. She was wearing next to nothing. Another showed her surrounded by a group of suntanned people. In each shot, Ariel was smiling. Ayelet's page was similarly filled with pictures of beautiful, smiling people, but also interspersed with inspirational quotes set against colorful backgrounds.

"Throughout this journey of life, we meet many people along the way. Each one has a purpose in our life. No one we meet is ever a coincidence."
— Mimi Novic

"Some beautiful paths can be discovered without getting lost."
— Erol Ozan

Rivki drank in the words. Everyone we meet has a purpose; new paths can be traveled without getting lost. These phrases were not taken from the Torah. They were not uttered by the great sages and rabbis. They were the thoughts of ordinary people and she felt them reaching deep inside her, pulling her own thoughts into a tight line.

Next, she clicked on the circle in the upper right corner and found two direct messages from her friends:

Rivki! Where are you? I miss you so much. It is not the same here without you. Ayelet and I have some new students, but we still talk about you all the time. Hope you'll get on Facebook soon and then you will see this message. Love ya, Ariel.

It was sent the day after her departure, more than a month ago, Rivki noticed with sadness. There was no follow-up message. The note from Ayelet was from a few weeks later. She said the two volunteers were finished with their work placement at the hospital and were about to start their army service. *Hope to hear from you,* she signed off with a smiley face.

Rivki glanced nervously at Zehava, but she was absorbed in her work. Quickly, she typed short replies to each one and hit send with a determined click, a jolt of energy running from her fingers to her heart.

TAMAR

The winter sun was losing a battle with some heavy rain clouds as Tamar took her usual route from home to the light rail stop. She zipped up her jacket, trying to block the chill from reaching her bones.

Usually, when she walked to meet Ami, her steps felt light, but since the conversation with her mom, it was as though someone placed heavy weights on each foot. She spied him from the top of the hill. Tall and slender, stroked by the sun's rays poking shyly through the clouds. His chestnut eyes twinkled when he saw her coming and he raised his hand in a goofy wave. Then she was in front of him, his lips brushing her cheeks, sending soft waves straight to the pit of her stomach.

"Your hands are so cold!" Ami took her hands in his. He rubbed them and blew warm air on them like a father with a shivering child.

"VIP service!" Tamar pushed her mom's voice out of her head.

"Always at your service." Ami gave her a small bow, letting go. "How was Dori?"

"Yeah, she's fine, loving Tel Aviv, of course." Suddenly, it felt right to tell Ami about the conversation with her mom. "Listen, Ami, I-I-I told my sister and my parents about us." She swallowed, trying to read his reaction, but his face was straight, unreadable.

"My mom said you were a lovely boy," Tamar started with the positive. "But she also warned me that people are not always... so... er..." she scanned the busy platform and lowered her voice. "She said that people might not like the idea of a Jewish girl and an Arab boy... you know... together."

Ami looked at her blankly, then broke into a grin. "Well, that's better than I expected." Laughter came out through his nose. "I thought you were going to say that your dad wants to kill me."

"Ami!" Tamar looked around her again. "Would be good if you took this a bit seriously..." The train arrived then, and she waited until they were inside the carriage to speak again. "Ami, I am a little worried. My mom said we need to be prepared—"

"Look, Tamar, it's not a big deal. I don't know why you're worried about it." Ami pulled her into a corner, his voice barely audible above the din of the other passengers. "I mean, I don't know who your mom is referring to, but I've been in a Jewish school all my life and there's never been a problem."

It was true that he'd been in a Jewish school all his life and that most people didn't even notice or realize that he was an Arab, but then there were people like Tal and his goonish cousin. And the people who chased Gaya and her Arab boyfriend in the mall. They didn't care if Ami was an Arab who went to school with Jews. All they saw was an Arab boy stealing a Jewish girl.

"Listen." Ami laid a gentle hand on her arm. "I wanted to play you a song. I know how much you like music, but I bet you've never listened to an Arabic pop song before. Let's see if your musical ear extends across all boundaries and cultures." He held up his earphones.

Tamar pushed the offering away. "You're not listening to me, and I've heard Arabic music before. It's all wailing and wallowing." She turned and gazed out the window, watching the frosty city come to life.

Ami placed the headphones over her ears and, before switching on the music, turned her face toward his. "Listen, Tamar, who cares what other people say or think. It's none of their business. I like you, a lot. I've always liked you. That's all that matters."

Tamar breathed in his promises, the knife in her chest easing a little. "Yeah, I suppose you're right," she sighed.

"Now, will you listen to the music? I promise you, it's different to any of the usual Arabic songs you've heard before. It's modern, but with an ancient twist. He sings about love and freedom, about human emotion, and about life. I know you won't understand the words, but because you're a musical talent, you might just get the gist from the music itself."

Tamar nodded, and Ami hit play. A male voice, deep and strong, streamed into each ear. It was soon joined by electronic beats expertly laced with simple percussion. It was not overbearing, like the wailing ancient tunes she heard wafting up from the Arab neighborhood below her house. Instead, it was smoothly mixed, like the spices and smells in the Old City's Arab market that made sense in a modern world. Tamar had no clue what he was singing about, but she appreciated the passion with which he delivered the words.

"His name is Ustaz Hamza, Mister Hamza." Ami watched her shyly. "Well? Do you like it? He's playing live in Jerusalem soon. I thought maybe we'd go see him together?"

"It's cool." She handed back the headphones, feeling guilty. Ami knew everything about her and her people, while she knew almost nothing about Muslims or Arabs—nothing about his world.

"Where's he playing?" she asked, curiosity prodding her. "Arena or First Station?"

Ami laughed. "He wouldn't play in those places." He shook his head definitively. "There's a small hall on Sultan Suleiman Street, near the Old City."

Tamar looked at him blankly. "Is it safe to go there... for Jews?"

Ami laughed again. "Don't worry, it's safe and anyway, you'll be with me! You're funny, Tamar." He leaned in towards her, planting another kiss, this time on her lips.

As he pulled away, Tamar felt her cheeks turn red. She was sure everyone was watching them.

NOUR

When Nour returned to school a few days after the protest, a big white cast covering her arm, she received a hero's welcome. Girls crowded around her, demanding to know every tiny detail. Their eyes burned with admiration.

"*Habibti*, you're so brave!" said Nidal, one of the more militant voices. "They were shooting at you, and you didn't stop. You weren't even scared."

A different girl, one that Nour barely knew, told her, "Good for you, fighting back against those ugly Zionist soldiers. Speaking out for our rights. I wish I was as brave as you, Nour."

"We're so proud of you, Nour, taking on the national cause like this," said yet another girl. "We had no idea you were such a fighter."

"*Mashallah*, thank you all for your kind words, but..." Nour began, feeling the pressure of a thousand eyes on her. "Going to a protest is not brave. In fact, it's actually pointless...." Gasps from the crowd made her pause, but then she went on. "I mean... our cause, our fight as Palestinians is noble, but throwing rocks at soldiers, protesting in front of them... when they have guns... it's a waste of life and with each person, we lose more than we gain." Nour let her words float in the air. "I've seen it with my own eyes. When they took me in the ambulance, I was with someone who was shot.... It was shocking."

She pictured the guy with the gunshot wound; she could smell his blood. What happened to him? She closed her eyes for a second, seeing the chaos of people running and screaming as shots were fired. She could taste the tear gas as it crept into her throat and stung her eyes.

Nour went on, describing the protest and her ride in the ambulance. She told the girls about the splashes of blood and the kind paramedics who treated wounded people all the time. "They told me he was the third person to be shot just that day! And for what?" Nour let out a heavy sigh. "The soldiers are still there; the occupation is still here! We Palestinians have been fighting against it for seventy years and we've gotten nowhere but shot, maimed, and killed. We need to find a different path."

This was hard. She was probably losing friends, but it was the right thing to do. Nour opened her eyes and studied the girls that remained around her. Some of their faces were now hard, lips pressed tightly together, eyes squinting. Nour could almost hear each one of them considering her words.

But her talk appeared to do little to stop the gossip grapevine, and she was still greeted as a hero at every turn. By the afternoon, she realized she needed to talk to Mrs. Rahman and make sure she heard the truth before some distorted version of her bravery reached the teacher who most detested any discussion of politics.

Nour approached her favorite teacher's table with clammy palms and an ill-prepared speech. "Mrs. Rahman, erm, could we, I, talk to you, please?"

"*Beseder*, Nour, *bevakasha*, please sit down." Mrs. Rahman gestured to the chair in front of her desk. Nour seated herself, still unsure exactly how to start the conversation. It was one thing, lecturing her peers, but telling a teacher was a different story. She breathed out in relief when Mrs. Rahman spoke first. "*Ma kara lach*, Nour? What happened?" She pointed at the cast on Nour's arm.

"I, it's broken, but it's a lot better now." Nour frowned.

Silence filled the classroom as Mrs. Rahman waited patiently for her to speak. "Do you want to tell me what happened, Nour? You don't have to, but there are a lot of stories going around about you. I, of course, believe nothing until I've checked with the original source." She gave Nour a wise look.

Nour grabbed the cue. "Me too, Mrs. Rahman. I like to check things out for myself. That's why I went to Ramallah, with my cousin, Fadwa. I wanted to see what my people go through... under the occupation, you know. I wanted to understand why my people are so upset. Why they talk or act so angry sometimes."

"Do you understand now?" Mrs. Rahman looked at her.

"No, I understand it even less." Nour whispered. "Violence doesn't solve a thing and I've been wracking my brain for another way, another solution to this situation, a way to free my people and for all of us, Arabs and Jews, Palestinians and Israelis, to live together in peace." She took a long breath and went on. "That is what we should all be striving for: peace. This pointless killing of one another just brings more dead people, more hatred. It's a cycle that will never end!"

Earlier, with her classmates, Nour felt emboldened. Now, with Mrs. Rahman, she just felt deflated. Her eyes threatened to fill as she spoke. Then, for the first time since the protest, a valve somewhere deep inside her burst open and Nour just let the tears pour out.

Mrs. Rahman came around the table and put an arm on Nour's good shoulder. "I agree with you, Nour. There's too much hatred between our people, but you are too young to be worrying yourself about all this now. You have a bright future and I know you'll do something amazing with all this compassion and empathy that you have. I just wish other people could see things the same way as you do," she said. "Listen, I have an idea that will take your mind off all this."

Mrs. Rahman told Nour she wanted to take the class on a field trip, away from the boiling pot of Jerusalem, to show them there were some places where Jews and Arabs lived in relative peace together, without too much tension or violence.

"I was in Jaffa last week. It's a different world, Nour!" Mrs. Rahman sounded excited. "I want to take the class. There's a program for Jewish and Arab women who live in the neighborhood. They call it 'In My House,' and it's an incubator type thing, bringing women from both communities together to create start-up businesses. There are some amazing projects, Nour, and they're all led by Jewish and Arab women who live side by side. I already spoke to the founders of the program, and they said they would be happy to meet with us. Tell us their story. It'll be a great opportunity for everyone to practice their Hebrew and we'll get away from all the pressures here. If there's time, we can even dip our toes in the sea! What do you say? Will you help me organize it?"

Nour cocked her head to one side. Maybe this was exactly the escape she needed right now. "Okay."

"*Yofi*, I'm so happy you agreed." Mrs. Rahman clapped her hands together. "It might take some convincing to get the other students and their parents on board. I know people are resistant to this sort of thing, but that will be your task, Nour. I'll take care of the logistics. Maybe now that you're the school hero, people will listen to you."

. . .

Nour didn't feel much like a hero, but over the next week she worked hard to convince her classmates that a trip to Jaffa, to learn about a program promoting coexistence, would be to their benefit. She used a variety of lines, depending on who she was speaking to. She told them about the importance of Jaffa in Palestinian history. She argued it was futile for Palestinians to fight with violence. She said they needed to push for change from within.

"But surely that is giving in to the occupation." Nidal was adamant that it would mean collaborating.

"Why is listening to someone else's perspective considered giving in?" Nour responded calmly at first, but then, as the debate went round in circles, her arm started aching. "I told you, Nidal, what have violence and militancy brought us? Look at Gaza. They are oppressed by Israel and by Hamas. Isn't it better that we fight from within? That we educate ourselves, that we show we can be better than all of them?" She sighed, beginning to doubt her own argument.

Nidal looked unsure but said no more, and a few days later, Nour was happy to see that she signed up.

Throughout the process, Mama and Baba rallied to support her, counseling her through the hardest days, and urging her not to give up. Though a few times, Baba said she might need to accept that not everyone would always agree with her and there might be some people who simply could not allow themselves to join such a trip.

"It's their right," Baba consoled her when two girls suddenly pulled out and another person even went so far as calling her a traitor. "Nour, you tried your best, but at the end of the day, it is up to them to make their own choices."

RIVKI

As the days rolled on, Rivki felt she was trekking down a path to darkness. Nothing of her old, pre-hospital life interested her. The strict codes and procedures she accepted without question in the past were now stifling and restrictive. The hospital gave her fresh eyes with which to see her old world, and she began to question the traditions and rules she once took for granted. Why were boys allowed so much freedom, of movement, of choice? Why were girls destined only to be married and raise a family? Why was there so much scrutiny and concern about how they behaved and what they said?

Watching Esti prepare for her wedding and her new life was the worst part. Rivki felt like she was sinking into a pit of quicksand, her mouth gagged to stop her from screaming out for help. It was clear to her now that she wanted much more than just to find a *bashert*, get married, and have some monotonous job. But how could she get off this inevitable track?

School was no solution. She'd missed so many days being sick that she was now far behind the other girls. The teachers moved her from table to table until she was paired with others who were either struggling or no longer interested in learning. Their low motivation suited Rivki fine because she found she no longer cared about what they were teaching, either.

The only good thing was that she'd now found a way to access Facebook. In the two weeks since returning to school, she visited Zehava regularly, explaining that she needed to use the computer for one project or another.

Her sister-in-law barely blinked when, two days before Esti's big wedding, Rivki showed up. "Sorry, it's so hectic at home... you don't mind, do you?" she bumbled as Zehava ushered her through the door. "Thank you! I won't be long this time, I promise. I just need to look up a few things."

"I told you, Rivki, you're always welcome here. You know how I feel about education. Studying is more important than anything, and it is essential for a young woman." For a second Rivki felt the room sway, it was deceitful, but then she heard that voice in her head: *you have no choice.* She sighed. Peeling off her oversized coat, she followed her sister-in-law to one of the free terminals and watched Zehava enter a code. The computer screen sprang to life.

"It's so peaceful here and I get much more work done," Rivki enthused, specks of guilt now just a memory. Her heart thumped as she watched Zehava return to her desk and then, making sure no one else was watching, opened up a browser and typed Facebook into the search field. She thumbed in her username and password, excitement filling her as the colorful page with its thick blue banner appeared. With only two Facebook friends, her feed was mostly filled with Ariel's photos. Rivki knew she was already in the army, and she carefully examined each new post. In one picture, Ariel was standing alone, wearing her green military fatigues. A sandy landscape that merged with her blond hair stretched far behind her into the horizon. In another photograph, Ariel was huddled with a group of other soldiers, girls and boys, large black rifles slung over their shoulders, smiles as wide and shiny as the sun.

Last time, Rivki had written to her, asking where she was exactly and what she was doing. Now, she clicked on the message button at the top of the page to see if she responded. A square popped up from the bottom of the computer screen. "I'm in a mixed-gender combat unit," Rivki read. "When we're done here, we'll be on patrol at the border with Egypt."

Mixed gender? That meant she was serving with boys and on the border with Egypt! Rivki gasped. She tried to imagine what it would be like, living and working with boys in the same way she did with girls. She shook her head. Her secular friends never ceased to amaze her.

"All okay? You find what you need?" Zehava watched her curiously from the other desk.

Rivki fumbled for the mouse, opening up a decoy tab to hide Facebook from view. "Erm, yes." She smiled brightly at her sister-in-law and watched Zehava return to her work.

She clicked Facebook open again and typed a short message back to Ariel. *What's it like serving with boys?* She hit send. She opened Ayelet's page. Also a soldier, but training to be a medic. She'd written to Rivki: *I was inspired by working in the hospital. Now I get to help soldiers in the same way. When I'm done here, I'll hopefully go study medicine.*

Ambition, thought Rivki, examining Zehava's stuffy office. Half a dozen young women, all Haredi, all married—she could tell from their *sheitels* and head coverings—sat behind identical desks, tapping on identical keyboards. Most were even dressed in a similar way. Rivki's head was heavy. Was this her future, too? Was there any way to change the trajectory? What if she wanted to do something different, something worthwhile, help people, like Ayelet?

"Maybe I should consider becoming a doctor too," she typed back to Ayelet, before x'ing out of Facebook and switching off the computer.

"I'm going home now," she informed Zehava. "See you Thursday."

"Ohhhh, I know! It's so exciting," Zehava gushed, her eyes lighting up to match the bright greens and browns of her perfectly applied eye shadow. "Esti! A *kallah*. How beautiful! Please G-d by you, Rivki!"

Rivki smiled back, but somewhere inside, a knife stabbed furiously at her heart. Was it jealousy or fear? She couldn't tell. All she knew was that the jabs were getting bigger and bigger as Esti's wedding grew closer.

TAMAR

Walking into the auditorium, Tamar was relieved to see Ohad, the music teacher, sitting on a lone chair in the middle of the hall. His presence meant there would be little free time during this practice, no option to discuss the ugly events from the mall with Gaya—not that she seemed interested in bringing it up anyway—and there would also be no time to worry about awkwardness with Tal.

"I heard you've made progress and wanted to see for myself," Ohad informed them as they rushed to set up their mics and instruments. Without waiting for the last-minute fine-tuning, he pushed on. "Are we all ready?"

Tamar was sure Tal was watching her as she stood beside Noa at the front of the stage, but she willed herself not to turn around. Instead, she opened up her mouth, breathing out smokey vocals like fire, burning away her mom's doubts about Ami and killing her final thoughts about Tal. For the first time in days, she felt normal, grounded as she lined up in tune with Noa and let the harmonies carry her high above the hall.

"Wow guys, that was excellent! You're really sounding good." Ohad beamed at them as the tempo wound down. "Let's take a short break and then get right back to it. Only a week till the gig and we need to make sure every number is perfect."

Tamar didn't follow the others outside for a smoke or enter the small kitchen for a coffee. It would be easier to avoid Tal if she hid out in the bathroom. Grabbing her bag, she wound along the narrow corridor that led to the toilets, but after a few steps, she sensed someone behind her. She spun around slowly.

"You can't ignore me forever, Tam." Tal moved towards her.

Tamar took a step back. "I'm not ignoring you," she said defensively.

"Well, it seems like you are. You barely said hello just now and you don't answer my texts." He took another step forward and grabbed her arm.

"Let go of me!" Tamar demanded.

"Why can't we be friends?" he carried on, ignoring her request. "Like we were before?"

Tamar suddenly saw smashed glass flash through her mind. Blood. A man lying on the floor. "Because we can't," she spat, shaking off his grip and charging for the girl's bathroom. Inside, she locked herself in one of the stalls and held her breath as she heard the main door creak open slightly and then swing shut.

When she cautiously emerged from the bathroom a few minutes later, the hallway was clear. Tamar exhaled and began making her way back to the auditorium until she heard someone behind her again. Damn it, she thought, and swung around to find Leon.

"Tamar—what's going on with you and Tal?" He looked at her with questioning brown eyes.

"Nothing... why do you ask?" Tamar shrank back, surprised by his directness.

"I just saw you. It looked like you were running away from—"

"Look, Leon, really, all is fine. It's nothing!" she snapped a little harsher than she meant to. "Please, just leave it."

"Okay... if you're sure." Leon shrugged and started to walk away, but then turned. "If he's hassling you, Tamar, then you really need to tell Ohad."

"No... no... it's really nothing, really." Tamar quickly calculated that telling Ohad, or even Leon for that matter, would only end in disaster. It would mean that her involvement in the gas station attack might become public, or worse, bring an end to The Jerusalemities. She couldn't risk it.

Back in the hall, Ohad ordered them to take it from the top again, but something felt off this time. Tamar tried to focus on her delivery, but her throat was tight and someone else was playing off-key.

"Stop, Tal, you're off by a beat." Ohad held up his hand. "We're going to have to start again!" His voice turned edgy now and Tamar didn't dare turn around to assess her old friend's reaction, but from the corner of her eye she could see Leon looking at her and she shuffled on her feet. She knew he was only trying to help, but if he continued to stare, the others would surely notice and the gossip would start.

As soon as Ohad permitted them to leave, Tamar grabbed her bag and fled out the door. She didn't even look back to see if Tal or Leon might be after her, but as soon as she got outside, she heard a shaky voice again. "I-I've been thinking, and I r-r-really think you need to tell someone about Tal. I saw how he grabbed you. It wasn't right."

"Look, Leon, just stay out of it. I told you it was fine. It doesn't bother me." She didn't slow down.

"I c–c–can't stay out of it, Tamar, you need to tell someone," Leon implored her. She'd never seen him so determined, and for a second she wondered if he had an ulterior motive, too. Seemed like everyone did these days. Then she discounted the thought. Leon was just trying to help, even though he wasn't.

"Please, Leon, it's really nothing. He hasn't done anything specifically. We're in a fight, that's all." She didn't know why she was defending Tal, but in that moment, it was Leon who was annoying her. She tried to move around him.

"T–t–that's irrelevant, and you know it." Leon stood his ground and continued blocking her path.

Tamar frowned, wondering at what point the person who was trying to help ended up becoming a tormentor too. "Leon, *khalas*, enough. I don't want to and it's up to me. Now move so I can pass." She stamped her foot.

Leon stepped aside, shaking his head. "Fine, but I think you're wrong. I just want to help you, Tamar."

Tamar waved him away with her hand. She didn't want to talk to Leon any longer. There was nothing he could do anyway.

• • •

Ami was waiting for her at the gate when she arrived after her confrontation with Leon. He greeted her with a soft kiss.

"A hard practice?" he asked, pulling back and studying her.

"Yes, Ohad wouldn't let us leave until it was perfect and the more pressure he put on us, the more everyone kept screwing up." She forced a smile.

"So, when's your first gig?" he asked innocently.

"Next week, Hanukkah, at Hadassah Hospital." Tamar shook her head. "I hope we don't screw it up."

Ami was silent for a second, following her up Yoel Solomon Street towards the train stop.

"Is it open to the public?" he asked. "I mean, can anyone come?"

Tamar stopped and looked at Ami, a range of possibilities running through her mind. Did she want him there? It was a concert in honor of a Jewish holiday. Would he feel out of place? Would she feel out of place with him there? And what about Tal? Would it infuriate him? Would he start anything? She looked down at her boots, then up, straight into Ami's kind eyes.

"Yes, anyone can come. Will you?" She breathed.

"Of course!" He kissed her again and grabbed her hands. "I was waiting for you to invite me officially!"

"My mom is coming, and Aviv, too. You guys could come together." Tamar felt shy suddenly.

"Yeah, we could," he echoed and then fell silent. "What about your dad? Will he be there?"

"No. He's in America for work. Dori can't come either, but I only really care about you being there." Tamar squeezed his hand, and he responded in kind.

THE HOSPITAL

Working to set up their equipment on the makeshift stage, Tamar did her best to tune out Tal and Leon. She unfolded the metal stands for her and Noa, placing them neatly side by side at the front of the stage. Next, she connected microphones to the speakers and tested each one with a shaky 1, 2, 3. She could feel two sets of eyes on her, but each step on the floppy stage brought her closer to the moment she could start singing and escape. An excited crowd cheering her on, including Ami and Aviv—who texted to say they were on their way—gave her all the energy she needed to block out the bad vibes.

Thirty minutes until showtime. Tamar wandered over to the coffee shop, where the bitter scent of cappuccino filled her nostrils. As she grabbed a bottle of water from the fridge, she glanced outside the enormous windows and saw that the light was fading. People were already gathering in the atrium to watch the hanukkiah lighting, as two rabbis prepared candles and matches. Tamar breathed in deeply. Once all the candles were lit, The Jerusalemites would start their set. As she turned to pay for the water, she was conscious of someone beside her.

"I saw you." His breath tickled her ear. "With Ami. Is he your boyfriend now?"

Tamar's knees went weak as she handed over some coins. She refused to look at him and, keeping her lips tight, turned to head back to the stage.

"A Jewish girl and an Arab! Gross. What happened to you Tam?" Another hiss. "I hope for his sake that he doesn't show up here today."

Tamar felt her heart thump with fear. Maybe inviting Ami had been a mistake? But then she pictured his kind eyes, felt his strong arms around her and his soft lips brushing hers. She spun around to face Tal. "Why, Tal, I do so hope he is coming—he already texted to say he's on his way."

She glared into eyes of icy blue and steadied her voice: "What happened to *you*, Tal? Why so much hatred?"

Tal opened his mouth, but his words evaporated in the air between. He turned and stomped away.

Next to the band's backstage camp, Tamar saw Leon's face lined with concern, so she purposely stepped around the other side of the speakers to join Kobi and Gaya's small clique. When Ohad called out, "Okay, everyone gather round," Tamar let out a sigh of relief and moved in with the others for a pep talk. She kept her distance from Tal.

"Now, are we almost ready?" the teacher fixed each person. "I know you've been practicing really hard, but now you all need to relax and have some fun. Our goal here is to brighten up the lives of the sick and their worried families. Plus, it's the festival of lights, so this afternoon, we need to shine as bright as possible, Jerusalemites!"

A few minutes later, Tamar stood at the front of the stage, microphone in hand. Her voice was low and strong, and with each note she hammered down at the hostile exchange with Tal and the pitying looks from Leon. She let the growing tempo and the eclectic crowd—a perfect mix of everything Jerusalem—lift her and soon she was soaring, flying, above heads, above the atrium, above the mess in her life.

She searched for familiar faces—Ami, Aviv, and her mom—seeing the different threads in her life pulled together for one harmonious second. Music, she thought, really does bring people together. Arabs with their scarf-covered heads and long robes. Black-hatted ultra-Orthodox Jews, forbidden by some antiquated tradition from hearing a woman's voice. Secular Jews in jeans and sweaters. Those who knew the words sang along, while others tapped their feet or swayed, as Tamar belted out a song of hope.

• • •

"It seems to be healing nicely." Dr. Friedman peered over his computer monitor, regarding Nour with owl-like eyes. "That's the best thing about breaking bones when you're young. They heal fast. But, young lady, you still need to take it easy. No exercising, okay?" He drew his dark eyebrows together and then gave her a wide smile.

Nour forced herself to smile back. She was grateful Baba had decided not to tell him how she broke her arm. It would be awkward if Dr. Friedman, a tall, wiry man who sported a round knitted beanie, knew the truth—knew she'd hurt herself trying to confront Israelis. He understood she was initially treated at the hospital in Ramallah—Baba helped him read through the release papers, but all they revealed was that her fracture was from a fall.

After confirming the successful reunion of her splintered bones, Dr. Friedman took a pair of large black scissors and cut through the hard, fraying cast. "You should be much more comfortable without this." He peeled away the tattered tube-shaped carcass and set it down on his desk. "We'll put on a lighter bandage and a sling until I see you again in another few weeks."

The burst of cool air on Nour's skin felt weird and her arm was suddenly light and stick thin. She twisted her wrist gingerly, remembering her ride in the ambulance. Amazing how we forget pain, she thought. Then she held it up beside her other arm. Externally there appeared to be no difference between them but to Nour, her wrist felt free, released from the weight of the past three weeks, albeit much, much weaker.

"It will feel weird for a while," Dr. Friedman reassured her as she tested out the newly repaired limb. He knotted together some cloth and pulled a sling around her neck. "But you must keep on resting it until it gets stronger."

"When can she start physio, Alon?" Baba spoke from his perch by the door.

Nour noticed that he called all the doctors by their first names, and it made her happy that they answered him with fondness, too. Baba was so well-respected at the hospital, maybe that was the triumph over the way her people were treated, over the occupation, over how the soldiers had disrespected him the night Abdulrahman was arrested.

"Nour should probably get used to the feeling of having the cast off for a few days and then she can start doing some simple movements from the recommendation sheet." Dr. Friedman handed them a piece of paper. "In a week or so, you can take her to Shani. Do you know her? She's one of our best physiotherapists."

"Sure, I know her. I'll speak to her," Baba replied, scanning the paper. "Nour, it says you have to do these exercises three times a day."

"Do you want to keep this?" Dr. Friedman held up the removed cast, its side slit open like a scaled fish.

"No, I don't need it." Nour shook her head. She supposed some patients liked to hold on to such a keepsake, but she watched with satisfaction as he dunked hers into the large plastic garbage bin beside his desk.

Leaving Dr. Friedman's office, Nour and Baba made their way to the café beside the hospital's lobby. Baba had accompanied her to every check-up over the past few weeks, and they had a tradition of getting hot chocolate after each consultation. She hoped he had forgiven her now for going to the protest—she was working very hard to make it up to him.

Nour picked a table and sat down while Baba ordered their drinks at the counter. She noticed a musical band was preparing to perform on a low makeshift stage. Beside them was a huge eight-branched candelabra, which she knew the Jews used during their festival of Hanukkah. There was also colorful tinsel and shimmery lights decorating the ceiling, a reminder that it was soon Christmas.

While she waited, Nour watched as Jews and Arabs, Muslims and Christians, streamed past her. Some wore the denoting styles of their tribe, but the rest just blended together in an indiscernible mass. It looked harmonious enough, and she wondered why there was even such an emphasis on people's differences, when, underneath all the various guises, they were really all the same. Everyone got sick or broke bones.

Baba placed a large mug on the table before her and she brought her nose down close to the froth. Sweet chocolate filled her nostrils. "Baba, why do people keep on fighting each other?" She watched the rays of a late afternoon sun flicker off his honey eyes, making them an even deeper yellow.

He didn't look up, focusing instead on stirring away at the neatly drawn smiley face embedded in his frothy cappuccino. "Well," he began. "People really have very short memories. It's the human curse." He brought the white porcelain cup up to his mouth and then pulled it away, leaving a wisp of milk on his upper lip. "People forget pain and heartache very quickly. I suppose that's why women can have more than one baby, even though childbirth hurts very much, and that's why each generation goes out to fight, ignoring the mistakes of the previous ones."

Nour scrunched up her face and surveyed her arm. She knew about pain and about forgetting it quickly. "But the question is if there's a way for us..." She frowned again before pushing on. "I mean, as Palestinians... to live here with the Jews. I just wonder if we let go, give up on fighting, are we being smart or letting ourselves down?"

"Of course there's a way for all of us to live together, Nour, and we need to make changes from within, from inside our own people, but we must also never forget to call out those that rule us too, demand equal treatment and dignity. Not just for us personally, but for everyone," Baba spoke quietly. "We need to find our voices and we need to stay strong against extremists on all sides. It's not easy to find that voice or the courage."

Nour was about to add that maybe the trip to Jaffa she was organizing with Mrs. Rahman would provide some more answers, but just then, the sound of twangy guitars filled the air. She turned to watch the band now coming to life on the stage. They were a raggedy bunch of high school students, probably about her own age. "The Jerusalemities" read a logo printed on the front of the main bass drum.

. . .

Rivki floated along behind Ima as they made their way through the hospital to Dr. Jalal's office. It was like a dream that this was once her home. Of course, it was just as she remembered. The thick smell of bleach blowing up each nostril, the indecipherable chit-chat of human voices, the low hum of machines. Yet, everything now seemed to be operating on an altered frequency—like a well-worn shoe that suddenly gave you blisters.

On the children's floor, Rivki spied her old room, the door shut tightly. Who was living in there now? When she glanced inside her old classroom, a lump formed in her throat as she saw strange faces filling the same colorful chairs and beanbags that she once occupied with Ariel and Ayelet. Nothing good lasted, Rivki thought bitterly, folding into a chair beside Ima outside Dr. Jalal's office. Dreams, hopes slipped away so fast, like dying flowers.

"So, Rivka, how have you been feeling?" Dr. Jalal fixed her with a twinkling smile.

Rivki regarded his round genial face, foreign but intimate. She felt small under his gaze. He had seen inside her, fixed a hole inside her. How could she tell him that she was still broken? How could she tell him that she was trapped in a world that she could no longer relate to, a world where she no longer fit and that no longer fit her? Rivki shuffled in the hard chair. "*Baruch Ha-Shem*," she whispered like he was catching her in a lie. "Mostly fine, just little pains, sometimes."

"Well, I am very happy with your progress," he said, his tone celebratory. "Your vitals are within normal range, though you will need to start taking B-12 vitamins. Your blood work shows there are no more bacteria—that means the infection that caused the inflammation a few months ago is now gone." Dr. Jalal cleared his throat. "Moving forward, we'll need to do a colonoscopy, just to be sure the hole in your intestine is fully repaired and after that, you'll be in remission, back to normal."

Rivki knew she should welcome the diagnosis, but remission meant the barriers to returning to her old life were now lifted and the thought of going back to normal made her feel queasy. After everything that happened and was about to happen, was that even possible?

"You should be happy, Rivka," the doctor teased. "You won't have to see me again—at least not for a while. Of course, if there are any problems you must come back to me straight away and I will patch you up again."

"*Baruch Ha-Shem* doctor, thank you. We really appreciate everything," Ima cut through the thick silence before standing and scooping up her bag.

Rivki followed her mother back out through the familiar but now unfamiliar hallways. At the main doors leading into the atrium, Rivki felt her heart skip a beat. The usual hospital hum was disrupted by music. A song she intimately recognized. One that she would forever associate with sickness, with the hospital, and with Ariel and Ayelet. Romi Sofer's *Tikva*.

"*Tikva*, don't take that away from me now. *Tikva*, it's all that I have left now." Rivki mouthed the words, pulse pumping wildly. "Now you're gone.

Now you're gone. *Tikva* that I'll be able to carry on." Her spirits soared with each step towards the source of the music.

Then, suddenly, Ima stopped, turning on her heels. "You know... how do you know this song?"

Rivki blinked. Eyes darting from Ima to the low stage by the food court. Blinded by life. Deafened by low, harmonious voices.

"Rivki?" Her mother's face was thunderous.

Rivki remained quiet, euphoria slowly replaced by fear. *Don't be afraid. Tell her the truth.* She heard that voice in her head again.

"Ima, it's only a song. I heard it a few times in the hospital. What's the big deal?" She counted the dark, twisted lines on her mother's forehead.

It was Ima's turn to be silent now. Then, through gritted teeth, she muttered, "Be careful, Rivka, this is exactly how it all starts."

TAMAR

We r @ Burgers Bar u coming? The text message flashed across the screen as Tamar scooped up her books and a tattered pencil case from the graffiti-covered desk and shoved them into her backpack.

Course, she typed back, while simultaneously trying to zip up her loaded bag. After a protracted struggle, she gave up, leaving the bag partially open before swinging it onto her back. It was the first day back at school after the short Hanukkah break, and her bandmates wanted to celebrate the success of their first gig with greasy burgers.

As she shuffled to Burger's Bar, Tamar messaged Ami, reminding him that she was going to meet her music buddies today. *Would rather c u but have 2 do this.* She finished the text off with their usual purple heart. *Call u later x.*

"Burgers?" Aviv fell in line with Tamar as she wove through the school to the main gates that let out onto Hillel Street.

"Yes." Tamar tried to muster enthusiasm. "Not really into it, Aviv. I mean, they're my bandmates. I like them, but they're not really my friends." She thought about facing Tal, about stares from Leon.

"You like Leon," Aviv offered, reading Tamar's thoughts.

"He's alright," Tamar sounded shaky.

"You want me to come with you? Or you could ask Ami. I'm sure he'd be happy to have a burger. At least then, you'd have someone you like there." Aviv brushed her shoulder with a sympathetic hand.

"It's only for bandmates." Tamar swallowed. "It'll be okay. We'll just eat, chit-chat, and then I'll go."

"Fine..." said her friend, then added, "Tamar... you sure there's nothing you want to tell me?"

Tamar grimaced. "Listen, I'll text you later, okay?"

At the restaurant, Tamar hesitated before entering. Surely Tal wouldn't dare do or say anything with everyone else there, would he? The gang of guitarists, Ron, Kobi, and Gaya, were already snuggled in one of the much-coveted red-cushioned booths at the back. They waved her over, slapping a high five as she took up a place next to Ron.

Leon arrived a few minutes later with a shy hello. Instead of cramming into the already cramped booth, he pulled up a lone chair and seated himself at the tip of the table. Tamar kept her eyes down.

"Come on, bro, there's still plenty of room here." Kobi patted the space next to him.

"Nah, man, it's okay. I don't mind it on the chair." Leon held up both hands.

A few minutes later, Noa arrived, squashing into the booth next to Kobi. Good, no room left, Tamar breathed. Tal would have to sit in a chair like Leon. Or maybe he wouldn't even show. But then she spied him sauntering through the restaurant.

Even though there was clearly no more space in the booth, he shoved himself inside, a strong thigh overlapping with Tamar's even before there was time to protest.

Ron leaned in and grabbed everyone's attention. "First, let me just say, Tamar and Noa, you guys, you guys did a really great job! You really led us through all the songs."

"Aw... so sweet," Noa responded in her crisp voice, "but we couldn't have done it without you guys backing us up. It was a great gig—felt so good to be up there singing, right, Tamar?"

"Yeah, amazing," Tamar tried to keep her cool, ignoring the fact that Tal was practically sitting on her lap. She shuffled closer to Ron, but the more she shrank back, the more Tal seemed to spread himself out around her.

Tamar felt a trickle of sweat roll down her neck. She should have gone for a single chair, like Leon, but now there was no way out of there. If she tried to leave, she would have to ask him to move first and that would mean direct engagement, which would draw too much attention. She could already feel Leon watching.

She turned her face tautly away from his, trying to focus on the group's chatter. Everyone else was in such a good mood and they were complimenting her non-stop, but all she could think about was Tal's distinct aftershave permeating each nostril, making her dizzy.

"Great job on the drums, Tal," Ron talked over her head. "You really pounded out that last song,"

"Thanks, Ron, *achi*, my brother, you guys rocked it on the guitar too," Tal sounded fake, false. "But we all know who the real talent, the real heartthrob among us. We all saw the ladies going wild for ya... little Leon."

Tal ruffled the keyboard player's hair, giving him a wink. Others joined in and Leon smiled back weakly, giving Tamar a meaningful look.

"So, when's our next gig?" Noa asked from across the table.

"Purim probably," said Ron. "It'll come up soon enough. We'll need costumes and some new material. Kobi? That's your department."

"Oooh, how about we go dressed up as a famous band? KISS?" said Kobi enthusiastically.

Ron laughed. "I meant new material to sing, not sure we could pass as KISS, but we've got time to decide."

As the banter continued, Tamar heard a familiar hissing in her ear. "I saw him at the concert," Tal whispered. "It made my skin crawl. It's disgusting, Tamar. Why do you need to go out with an Arab when there are so many good Jewish boys around?" He paused a second before going on. "You know they hate us, right? You know he's only using you because all Arab guys think Jewish girls are easy? There's no future for a Jewish girl and an Arab boy, you know that too, don't you? You think your parents will be unhappy about you dating an Arab boy, but his parents will never tell him to stop, no.... they will tell him to go ahead and have sex with you just to get some experience for when he marries his cousin! You'll be nothing more than practice!"

Tamar felt fury spark inside her and was just about to respond to Tal's lecture when the server arrived.

"Finally! I'm starving," Gaya declared, as sizzling burgers, fries, and sparkling glasses of Coke were laid down carefully on the table.

"Me too!" Kobi threw a spiral chip into his mouth.

All Tamar wanted to do was puke right there on the table. Tal made her stomach churn. He made her insides burn. She curled her fists, barely able to contain her anger. She needed to get out of there, but how?

As she was considering her escape path, Tal's low voice was back in her ear. "Bet you haven't told your parents about your disgusting Arab boyfriend, have you? Have you let him do things to you? Touch you like this? Have you touched his dick? Ichs! Just makes me want to vomit. The thought of a dirty, fucking Arab doing that to you. You have to stop this now, Tamar, do you hear me? Stop!"

The word "stop," came out a bit too loud, and a few people turned to stare at them. In that instant, though, Tamar did not care. It was enough. "No! You stop, Tal. Just stop! I don't have to sit here and listen to this shit anymore." She couldn't sit next to him for a second longer. "You know nothing about me or my boyfriend. He's an Arab, that is true, but he's a good person. Better than you!"

Then it occurred to her that the only way to get out of there was to go down. Twisting and flailing like a hooked fish, Tamar wiggled between the couch and the table, pushing through a matrix of legs, and coming out right next to Leon. He put out a hand to steady her, but she flung it off.

"Tal," she spat. Everyone was looking at her now, everyone except Tal. "It's you who's a disgusting human being, not Ami! Do you hear me? It's you who should be ashamed of yourself! Now just leave me, leave *us*, alone."

Tal's face was dark now, but he did not reply and made no move toward her. Tamar didn't wait a second longer. Grabbing her bag, she walked as fast as she could out of the restaurant.

It was only when she reached the street that she realized Leon was with her. His voice was quiet but kind. "Tamar, wow, that was.... are you, are you okay?" He moved in closer to her, his stutter apparently cured. He was silent as Tamar tried to get hold of heavy gasps exiting her mouth. She bent forward, putting her hands on her knees. Then she burst into tears.

"Tamar, wha—" She felt an arm across her back and pulled back.

"I'm fine." Tamar put up a hand. "Thank you, Leon."

Then she turned and started walking. She needed to get away from there, as far away as possible from Tal. He was no doubt twisting things, as usual, probably telling them she was crazy, that he had no idea what her problem was. No doubt her band mates would be furious at her. Spoiling their rhythm, tearing them apart, just as everyone was getting along so well.

NOUR

"I really can't believe we pulled this off," said Nour, as she settled herself on the seat beside Yasmin and watched the minibus doors closing. "It's such an important trip, so important for Jews and Arabs to find a way to live together and soon we'll find out how, or at least one way."

They were finally on their way to Jaffa, twenty-six out of the forty or so girls who studied Hebrew in Nour's grade, a few parent chaperones, and some teachers, including Mrs. Rahman. Nour couldn't help feeling proud that she had succeeded in this difficult task. Of course, the letter Mrs. Rahman wrote with the principal explaining the importance of seeing different ways of life, helped propel the trip forward, but Nour was also sure that her own groundwork, including some fierce debates with her peers and even meeting with some of their parents, really helped get it all together. She was happy that Mama was there with them too, sitting across the narrow aisle beside Mrs. Rahman.

"I know about coexistence very well," Yasmin answered Nour in a low voice. "We even have it in my own family. My uncle is married to a Jewish woman. They live in Tamra, near Haifa. I don't know why people work so hard to highlight the differences. We're all human beings, really. Who cares if you are Jewish and I am Muslim or Christian? That's what my uncle said when he married Sarit. They loved each other, and that was that. My cousins are half-Jewish."

Nour looked at her friend incredulously. They had known each other since first grade, but this was the first time she heard her mention a Jewish aunt and cousins.

Yasmin shrugged. "You never know how people might react. It was hard for my family at first, but Aunt Sarit is so sweet. Everyone loves her now."

Nour wondered if there were others with similar family secrets that she didn't know about. Society only heard militant voices, only those who wanted to fight, because they were the loudest. Others, like Yasmin's uncle and aunt, just got on with the realities of living in this crazy place and kept a low profile.

· · ·

An hour later, Nour caught her first glimpse of the Mediterranean Sea. Sparkling blue in the late December sun, it stretched for miles before kissing the sky in a different shade of blue. Frothy white-tipped waves bounced playfully towards the shore, sending her spirits soaring.

"Look," she pointed it out excitedly to Yasmin. The two of them took out their phones at the same time and snapped a shot for Instagram. "It's beautiful," Nour purred, turning the camera around and taking a well-posed selfie.

The bus let them off in Jaffa's Old Port, where Palestinian fishermen once sat sorting fish, smoothing nets and greeting the world. A clatter of girls followed Mrs. Rahman into what looked like a discarded warehouse. Inside, instead of abandoned walls, they were greeted with bright, colorful paintings of doves, olive trees, and swirling rainbows. Each image was encircled with handwritten phrases and short poems.

Two women walked towards them from the far end of the room. One donned a colorful hijab; the other wore her hair cropped short and spiky. They introduced themselves as the project's founders and invited the girls to sit in a neat circle of chairs.

"Good afternoon, everyone, my name is Aisha," said the woman in the hijab. It was arranged in a way that made her look more like an artisan than a devout Muslim. Long gypsy earrings peeked out from below her scarf. She told the group how she was born in Jaffa and that her family lived here for many generations, even before Israel was created. Her great-grandfather was a fisherman, she said. She also talked about how she once resented Israel and Israelis.

"I supported the Intifada... at first," Aisha spoke softly, her hand on her heart. "I truly believed it would finally give us a state and help our people return to their homes here and elsewhere in Palestine." Nour looked around at her friends, who were listening with admiration and fascination.

"When the Israeli prime minister trampled our holy site, our beloved Al-Aqsa Mosque in Jerusalem, I and my friends were horrified and angry," Aisha continued. "We joined in with the protests against the Jews, but then something changed, at least for me."

Aisha took a deep breath now, turning her eyes upward to the ceiling. "My older brother was killed in a clash with the Israeli army. It was then that I realized the real price that we were paying. The human price was much too high."

Aisha's voice filled with sadness now and she waited, letting the tragedy sink in. Nour felt the silence in the room deepen even more. No one dared to shuffle their feet or even breathe. Everyone was now clinging to Aisha's heartbreaking words. Nour thought about the pain of losing a brother and was relieved that Abdulrahman was safe, albeit in jail, but at least alive.

"Burying Mtanes made me realize that if we wanted to make any real changes for our people, then we were going to have to first, better ourselves and second, find a way to work it out with the Jews. They aren't going anywhere and neither, of course, are we," Aisha sounded more polished now. "I was the same age you are now and after his death, my family joined a program for bereaved families. All bereaved families—Jewish and Arab. It was there I met Rotem."

"Right, Aisha was the only other person my age at the meetings," the spiky-haired woman joined in now, speaking in more rounded and flowing Hebrew than Aisha. "We were both still teenagers, and we both suffered from this conflict. My dad was also killed, not in clashes but in a suicide bombing. He was just sitting on a bus on his way back from the market."

Rotem looked down at the floor like she was remembering her father, then she faced the group. "We both suffered in this conflict and the Intifada was a terrible time. After many hours spent talking, we realized the only way we could change things was to work together. That's why we set up In Our House."

The goal, the women explained, was to forge partnerships between the two communities that lived side by side in Jaffa.

"We live here together, but there aren't many places or forums for us to meet, to interact, to get to know one another." Rotem ran a hand through the spikes on the top of her head. "We wanted to change that."

"Yes," Aisha interjected. "We wanted to find a constructive way to bring Arabs and Jews together, so we thought about working with women. Think of this place as a lab of ideas, women from both communities come here to hear inspirational speakers or take courses to improve their skills. We also offer practical assistance in the hope that it will encourage new ideas for businesses or projects."

The two women showed them a short film that showcased some of their past initiatives and then allowed time for questions. Mrs. Rahman stood first, calling on Nour to moderate the session.

"Why don't you get the ball rolling with the first question?" Mrs. Rahman urged her.

Nour hesitated before standing. So many questions ran through her mind, but she realized she needed to ask about the very concept of Arabs and Jews, Palestinians and Israelis, living and working together. She wondered if that meant negating Palestinian rights.

"Does collaborating like this, with Israelis, mean you've given up totally on the Palestinian cause and our right to our own sovereign state, and also our right to return to our lands?" Nour addressed her question to Aisha.

"Of course not! I am and always will be Palestinian," Aisha answered immediately. "I can't change that, but I also can't change the fact that we live here together and if that's our reality, then why not work together too? As for our people's right to return, I will always believe in that and I hope one day when there is peace, they—"

"But you are normalizing! You are giving up on our true struggle," Nidal interjected, eyes flashing and lips snapping after the word struggle.

"Nidal… let Aisha fini—" Nour glanced nervously at Mrs. Rahman.

"No. I don't think so." Aisha responded calmly. "We all need to improve our lives and create better futures for our children. Fighting just brings more fighting, more war, and more heartbreak."

"But you're making Palestinians look weak!" Nidal shot back, her hands waving wildly, reminding Nour of Fadwa. "Israelis already take us for granted and abuse our rights. They'll do it even more unless we fight back!"

"It's quite the opposite, actually." Aisha looked at her, unblinking. "We're definitely not allowing them to take us for granted. The truth is that we live in Israel while remaining proud Palestinians and we have to fight for our rights from within. Not by the sword, but by making our presence known, by matching them in education, politics, business. What you need to understand is that our people, both people actually, have lost so much. We've all suffered enough." Aisha reached over and grabbed Rotem's hand. "Friendships can be made across the divide. Rotem and I are proof of this."

The Israeli woman smiled back, and warmth rushed through Nour. She thought about how friendships came in all sorts of packages, cut through all sorts of boundaries. She hesitated a second, expecting Nidal to respond with something more militant, but she seemed satiated for now, and Nour let out a quiet sigh of relief.

Other tough questions followed, though framed slightly more politely than Nidal. Nour did her best to moderate, allowing everyone who wanted to ask a question. In the end, she thanked Aisha and Rotem for sharing their personal stories and telling them about the project.

"I don't know about everyone else, but I thought this was very informative and inspiring," Nour wrapped things up on a positive note. She looked over at her teacher, who gave her an encouraging smile. A few of the girls applauded.

As they shuffled out of the warehouse, Mama fell in step beside Nour and grabbed her hand. "That was such an interesting discussion, and you were amazing in there, Nour. I'm so proud of you for making this happen," she whispered in her ear, giving her a gentle kiss on the cheek. "You remind me so much of Baba."

RIVKI

Rivki's fingers tingled with cold as she stepped from the bus and made her way home through the now dark, narrow streets of Ma'alot Dafna. She marveled at how the winter chill succeeded in erasing any memories of the stifling summer heat. Why did it always seem when you were in the thick of a certain season that it lasted forever? Of course, at some point, the seasons ultimately changed. Winter always gave way to spring, summer always moved on to fall. She wondered if her own life could move on too from the dictates she'd known and accepted since she was small. Could she find a way to change that permanently?

She was still deep in thought when she slipped through the front door and was totally unprepared for the chaos that greeted her. Their tiny living room was packed, busier than Geula Street in the countdown to the Shabbos. The dressmaker, the caterer, the flower-arranger—all there to discuss last-minute details. There were also some distant relatives that Rivki vaguely recognized, a few neighbors, Ima's friends, and in the middle of it all sat Esti.

Her sister reveled in the attention. With each question or request or blessing, she scrunched and bunched her pretty face up as if life depended on giving the right answer.

In the bustle, no one appeared to notice Rivki's arrival, and she was hoping to make it anonymously to the safety of her bedroom when Mrs. Grumer, Ima's best friend, placed a hefty foot in her path, stepping out from the kitchen, balancing a tray of teas and coffees.

"Rivki!" she exclaimed as if shocked to see her in her own home.

"*Erev tov*, Mrs. Grumer," Rivki answered politely. "I just got home. There's a lot going on."

"Yes, well, please G-d by you, *motek*." She smiled at Rivki with barely a glance before attempting to maneuver herself and the tray through the mass of people.

"Thank you, Mrs. Grumer," Rivki mumbled after her.

In the solace of her room, Rivki sat down on her bed, thoughts thundering through her head like a thousand marching soldiers. She knew her mother's friend only meant well. Such phraseology was a required adage for such an event. Yet, she couldn't help but wonder if, in her case, what people really meant was, "Good luck to you, since there's no chance you'll be as lucky as your sister in netting such an incredible husband or marrying into such a wonderful family."

She knew what was expected of her as a good Haredi girl from a good family. She knew that soon a matchmaker, a neighbor, or a friend of her parents would begin inquiring into her character, her schoolwork, her interests, and then feelers would be cast to see if there was a good suitor for her. But with a chronic illness, who would want her now?

Rivki lay back on her bed, trying to block out the excited chatter wafting in from the living room. Her chest was tight as she pushed long breaths out through her mouth. The corners of her eyes stung, but she refused to cry. She would reject this life back. The chance of finding a soulmate evaporated for her and in its place were now new chances, new possibilities, a new dream. A dream of being free, like Ariel and Ayelet.

• • •

Rivki felt Esti sliding into bed next to her. She knew her sister had been at the *mikve* with Ima, to purify herself and prepare her body for what would come after the wedding ceremony, after the party, after all the guests and family left her at long last alone with Yaakov. Rivki shivered even though Esti's body next to hers was warm. She wanted to reach out to Esti, touch her, feel her for a final time, but her limbs were stuck, paralyzed. Even when her sister whispered her name, soft and caressing, Rivki's lips refused to move, words stayed stuck inside her dry, rough throat.

When she woke the following morning, Rivki could hear footsteps and voices, but Esti's spot beside her was already cold. The small electronic clock on the dresser told her it was 6:10 am. She tried to push herself up, find the energy to face the day, the day they'd talked about forever, the day her sister would be blessed by the rabbi, by their friends and relatives, the day her sister would be married, but her limbs felt like lead, as if someone had filled her body with a thousand rocks and replaced her heart with a giant boulder. Her head thundered too. Inside was gray, like the darkest days of winter. How would she make it through the next few hours?

Daring a foot outside the warmth of her bed, the rock in Rivki's heart grew even heavier as she eyed the bridesmaid's dresses hanging on the outside of the closet. There were two different sizes, matching in color and style. The larger one was for her, the smaller for Batsheva. Rivki curled her fists into tight, round balls at the thought of wearing the same dress as her little sister, not yet five years old.

"Ohhh, it goes so well with my dress," Esti cooed inside one of the wedding stores on Bar Ilan Street. "This is just perfect. One for you and one for Batsheva." She stroked the dress like it was made of gold.

Rivki detested it on sight. Everything, from the sickly cream color that paled her already paper-white skin to the ruffled neckline that looked like it might choke her, Rivki's stomach churned when the saleslady brought one out in her size.

Standing in the floor-length, three-tiered affair, Rivki couldn't stop her mouth from turning down into a scowl. But Esti, totally blind to her displeasure and her discomfort in a dress that bound her from head to toe, gushed with excitement, "It's perfect." She breathed and then repeated, like a mantra, how much she needed Rivki at her side.

Slipping into the stiff, unforgiving garment now, Rivki's skin itched inside, as well as out. She pictured herself dashing into her parent's bedroom, where she suspected the dressmaker was now working to perfect Esti's gown, grabbing the woman's massive metal scissors and cutting it to pieces.

You can do this another way, she heard that special voice enter her head.

"But how?" Rivki answered herself out loud. Suddenly, she thought: hair.

Esti would have hers coiffed and neatly sprayed into place by the hairdresser who was already turning their living room into an impromptu salon. Rivki couldn't really understand the point of Esti spending so much time and money on hairstyling, when it would be covered completely by a thick opaque veil. Only later, after the *chuppah* and the *brachot*, when she came to dance on the woman's side of the *mechitza*, could she even think about removing it. By then, it would be flattened and sweaty, any remnants of style totally destroyed.

Rivki pulled a hand mirror out of the dresser—she would take care of her own hair. Propping it up on the dresser, she swept her right hand through the frizz of blond and scooped up a length at the back. Twisting the handful, she worked the mess into a loose bun on top of her head and tied it together with an elastic band. She then wrapped a pale blue ribbon around the entire ensemble, pulling away rebellious strands to hang free around her face and neck. She would wear a messy bun just like Ayelet showed her when she was in the hospital.

Rivki eyed her reflection, shaking off the rocks and stones that dragged her body down. She was changing, she could feel it. Her journey was already in motion and there was nothing anyone could do to stop it. Returning the mirror to its place, Rivki opened the bedroom door and went to join the others in the living room.

"Rivi!" Esti exclaimed as soon as she walked in. "W-w-what did...? Your hair?" She was sitting majestically on her throne, the hairdresser pulling her head to and fro like she was a doll. There were only women in the house now—Abba and the boys were packed off to get ready at Mordechai's house—the hairdresser, the dressmaker, Ima, her friend Mrs. Grumer, Zehava, Yosef's wife, Ruthy. Chatter went silent as everyone turned to stare in judgment.

Rivki felt her cheeks flush. "I-I thought... wanted—"

"It's okay," Esti fixed her like a wise queen. "Chani will do your hair next, Rivi, so you can get rid of that funny ribbon." She scrunched her face before turning her attention back to a small book of psalms, lips moving rhythmically as if she was singing to herself.

"No. It's fine, Esti." Rivki cleared her throat. "I like it like this."

Esti's lips were still moving when she looked up, eyes wide. "Don't be ridiculous, you can't go to my wedding looking like that. What will people think?"

Rivki planted each foot firmly on the floor and held Esti's gaze. "I like it like this."

"But it's my wedding. I get to choose." Esti glared back at her.

"It's my hair, so I get to choose." The words flew out of Rivki's mouth fast, as though that voice in her head had suddenly turned real. From the corner of her eye, she noticed Zehava flapping her hands frantically, but it was too late to it take them back and Rivki wasn't sure she wanted to anyway. There was a fire in the pit of her stomach and she felt heat rising to the tip of her head. In that instant, she didn't care about codes or consequences. It was bad enough that Esti was taking over the entire house with her stupid wedding and now she was bossing everyone around, including her. She was so selfish. So self-absorbed. An image of when she was in the hospital filled Rivki's head, where even when Esti visited, all she did was talk about herself the whole time. Rivki forgave her sister then, but now it was all too much. She wanted her hair this way, and she didn't care if Esti didn't like it.

But then, Esti was standing right in front of her. Her face twisted. "What's your problem, Rivki? This is my wedding day, my special day. Why would you act like this? You're my sister, you're supposed to support me. You've been so selfish lately!" Esti's voice reached a tone Rivki no longer recognized, like one of the stray cats that howled at night in the yard downstairs. "Actually, now that I think about it, you've been acting strange ever since I announced I was getting married. You never seemed happy for me, from the start..."

"Me? Selfish?" Rivki snarled back. "That's not true! Esti! I listened to everything you told to me, every tiny detail about all your dates with Yaakov. It's you who's selfish, you who's been self-absorbed! Did you ever ask me how I feel? Ever? No! You only care about yourself, Esti... you're the selfish one. All I've heard for months is about you and your stupid wedding..."

The words were out now. Angry words. Forbidden words. Words that should never be spoken between sisters, but often are. Words that could never be retracted. And what was worse, they were said on a day that was meant to be magical. Rivki felt her eyes stinging just as loud shrieks burst forth from Esti's mouth and tears streamed down her face. She stomped from the living room, leaving Rivki trapped in the glare of incredulous eyes.

"Rivki Lefkovitz, what were you thinking? Upsetting your sister on her wedding day!" Ima was in front of her now. Rivki could smell freshly sprayed perfume mingled with Ima's familiar scent. She pushed back her own tears. Esti was wrong, and she didn't care if it was her wedding day. "I want to wear my hair like this!" Rivki thought she heard a gasp from her sister-in-law. "I don't want it any other way."

"For this," Ima spoke slowly, as if she was straining to keep calm. "For this silly matter, you upset your sister! The *kallah*! Sit. Now. Chani will do your hair exactly as Esti told her."

Rivki looked up at Ima. Despite her calm voice, her mother's eyes were narrow and cold. Rivki tried to catch Zehava's gaze, rally her support, but her sister-in-law just frowned and let out a deep breath.

What now? Rivki's heart pumped wildly. She thought she might stop breathing momentarily. She waited for the voice to guide her, but in that instant, it also seemed to have deserted her. Sullenly, she made her way over to the hairdresser's throne and watched with clenched fists as the blue ribbon was discarded and the messy bun cleaned up. The room was so quiet, she could hear her own breaths, loud and long, like bursts of dragon fire.

TAMAR

Tamar passed the familiar gates of her school and kept on walking. She reached the light rail stop and passed it by. She wasn't ready to go home yet. She needed to think. Tamar crossed over Jaffa Road, which split Jerusalem like a knife, and marched boldly into the ultra-Orthodox part of the city. She needed to get lost. She needed to get away from everyone, everything, from her life, from herself.

Tamar stomped on, passing men in heavy black overcoats, long scraggly beards reaching their chests and wispy, curling *payot* tumbling from beneath their black hats. She knew it was forbidden for them to even look at her. Even the women walking past paid her no mind, too busy chatting with each other or chasing after rowdy kids.

In her scraggly jeans and colorful sweater, Tamar certainly stood out, but she reveled in the fact that she was invisible here. It was like she was transported into another world. A world where she was an alien, an outsider. Tamar needed that anonymity; she needed space to get her head straight.

Was Tal right? She shuddered, thinking of his words, anger filling her again. There was some truth to the fact that they were worlds apart. She and Ami were like chalk and cheese, like a bird and a fish. An Arab and a Jew.

She was sure he wasn't using her for sex. There was no hint of that, but would they last the distance together? Probably not. They were from different cultures, different religions, different worlds that here, in Jerusalem, clashed.

Tamar didn't understand why their tribes hated one another. She thought about the concert in the hospital, people enjoying the music despite their differences. The chasm between them was fake, she thought, as she continued her march.

They were conjured up a long time ago by people who decided to divide the world based on certain beliefs and practices. Now she and Ami were paying the price. Was it her choice to be Jewish? Was it Ami's to be an Arab or Muslim? They were both born in Jerusalem—in the same hospital, in fact—and went to the same school. They had so much in common.

Tamar knew some people succeeded in breaking down these superficial barriers. In America and in England, friends of her parents were married to non-Jews. Could it happen in Jerusalem too? Could it happen between a Jew and a Muslim? Could it happen for her and Ami? Was she strong enough to do it? Strong enough to stand up to people like Tal? Tamar wasn't sure. She sighed and lifted her head, examining her surroundings. She had no idea where she was or how long she had been walking. She was in a totally unfamiliar part of the city. Laundry on the tiny balconies between densely packed buildings flapped in the wind. She could smell the detergent in the night air. She shivered, thankful she was wearing a sweater.

She sat down on a battered wooden bench, pulling her bag off her shoulders, and suddenly all she could think of was her dad. A lump rose in her throat. Was he still angry with her about Ami? He'd barely said two words to her before he left for his trip, but now Tamar wanted to speak to him so badly, more than anything else in the world. She wanted to make things right, make him understand, and confess to him all the things that had happened to her these past few weeks.

He was still in America, but even with the seven-hour time difference he should be awake, thought Tamar as she rummaged around in her bag for her cellphone. There were two messages from Ami, telling her to call him later when she was done with the *big burger celebration*. She also noticed messages from Gaya and Noa, both demanding she call them. They would all have to wait, though. Tamar needed to talk to her dad first. She needed to hear his smooth, soothing voice and make things right with him. She needed to make things right for her too.

"Dad?" Tamar breathed when she heard his familiar voice.

"Tamar! How are you? Is everything okay? Where are you? I just called home and Mom said you were out celebrating with your friends."

Tamar felt her lower lip tremble. She thought she had cried enough tears earlier, outside the restaurant, but hearing his voice made them start flowing again. "Dad, I really need to talk to you, to tell you some things," she sobbed.

"Are you crying? Honey? Tamar? What is it? What's wrong?"

Tamar heard his concern, and his warmth made the tears flow even more.

"Please, darling, stop crying for a second. I'm worried about you. Please, Tamar, tell me what's wrong," he pleaded. "It can't be that bad."

Tamar inhaled. "Okay, but you have to promise, promise to listen to me through to the end." She wiped away the wet from around her eyes and sniffed her sorrow back in. "There's so much to tell."

Tamar began with the restaurant. She told her dad about Tal, about her storming out, Leon, and crying. "They probably all hate me now." She suppressed a sob. "Everyone was so happy at how great our first gig was, and now I ruined it."

"Don't say that," he started. "Sounds like Leon understood, he—"

"Let me finish, okay, Dad? There's more." Tamar then told him about the man on the train, rough, coarse hands and the ugliness of his winking eye. It felt so long ago now. She told him how the man forced his hands down her pants, made her feel so dirty, and how she blamed herself for drawing his attention, and afterward, for not fighting back.

"Oh Tamar," he interjected again. "It wasn't your fault, you must—"

"I know that now…." Tamar's breath was returning to normal now. "But please, let me finish."

She moved on to the protest at the Knesset and then the attack in the gas station. "Remember how we heard them report it on the news on the way home?" Tamar reminded him. She told him how Tal had warned her not to tell anyone and how they were no longer friends. "I felt awful for leaving that man bleeding on the floor, for not helping him, and Tal didn't care at all. I don't think we'll ever be friends again." Tamar began feeling lighter now, like she was emptying the contents of a dark box that had weighed her down for weeks.

Now it was time to bring up Ami. "I know you're not happy about me and Ami." She felt the strength returning to her now. "But you really don't have to worry. He's a good guy, and it's not like we're going to get married or anything." She told her dad about the night at the mall and how he'd stepped in to help Gaya's boyfriend against the vigilantes. She also told him how Ami made her laugh and gave her support.

"I know we're from different worlds, but you always told me to be friends with good people, strong people, people willing to speak out for what's right." She waited for her dad's response now. "Look, Dad, I don't know if it will work. We're only sixteen, but I know he makes me feel good."

Tamar listened to her dad's breaths through the phone, and finally, he spoke. "I know, Tamar. It was just a shock, hearing that you had a boyfriend, that's all. You're still my baby. It's bad enough Dori is off living a hedonistic life in Tel Aviv, now I have to contend with my little Tamari becoming a woman too." He sighed. "As for the other stuff, we'll need to deal with each thing separately. I'm just really glad you told me everything. I can't believe you kept this all inside you for so long."

The line fell silent now, and Tamar could almost hear her dad thinking. Then he said, "Listen, I'll try to book a flight to get back tomorrow so we can unpack it all and work through everything together. In the meantime, you need to go home. I don't even know where you are. You need to find Mom, tell her all you just told me. She'll understand, she'll know what to do. Promise me you'll go home now?"

The line crackled and Tamar remembered sadly that he was millions of miles away. She wanted him to be closer, beside her, so she could snuggle into his strong arms and all the bad things would go away.

"Don't worry, Dad," she reassured him. "I'll find my way home. I can put on the map's app."

"I'll text you my flight details as soon as I know them, okay? Now, go home. It must be getting dark there."

Before Tamar could hang up, the line went dead. Her phone was out of battery. There went her plan to use the maps app to get home. She would have to find her own way out of this weird parallel universe.

Oddly, the idea that she was lost didn't feel like a big deal. She wasn't even bothered about not listening to music while she walked. It was good to connect with the world again. After telling her dad everything and knowing that he still loved her, things didn't seem so bad. She was pure again, her slate wiped clean. Her dad said they would work through it all together, that it would be fine. She believed it would.

NOUR

The week after their trip to Jaffa and visiting the In Our House project, Mrs. Rahman pulled Nour aside at the end of class.

"Something has come to my attention, and I thought it might interest you," Mrs. Rahman began, allowing Nour to settle into the chair opposite her desk. She sounded strained and Nour began to panic that something bad had happened. Maybe she was angry about letting Nidal ask such tough questions? Or did Mrs. Rahman get into trouble for taking them to Jaffa? Nour had heard some of the girls complaining afterwards that it was propaganda. One even said she wasn't sure whether Aisha was really Palestinian. Perhaps Mrs. Rahman was finally going to confront her about going to the protest, or about Abdulrahman. Nour was sure she'd heard what happened by now and while Mrs. Rahman had never mentioned it before, there was always a first time.

Then her Hebrew teacher surprised her. "Now, Nour, I know how much you love fashion, clothes, designers, well an opportunity has come to my attention, and I thought perhaps you might like to try out for it. It's a scholarship, at the prestigious Shenkar College in Tel Aviv. You still need to apply, but I thought you would be an excellent candidate. They have many courses there relating to the fields that interest you, and your grades, your Hebrew are all good enough."

Nour was stunned. A scholarship? At a fashion school? In Tel Aviv? She couldn't breathe. Could she try out for it? Could she study fashion in Tel Aviv? It was one thing, going to Hebrew University, also an Israeli institution, but that at least was in Jerusalem, close to home. Many Palestinians studied there these days, unlike when Baba went in the eighties and was a minority. Then she remembered Baba, and her heart sank. He would never agree. Nour could tell Mrs. Rahman was waiting for her to say something.

"Shenkar? In Tel Aviv." Nour blinked, wondering how far she could go. If she got it, got a place, then her father couldn't really say no. "They accept Arab students? Is that allowed?"

"Of course, actually, they put out a call specifically for Arabs. They want to boost the number of minority students they have at the school; they believe it will bring a different and fresh perspective to the field," Mrs. Rahman said brightly. "I think it would too, and I think you would be perfect. Do you think you would like to apply? I could help you."

A million thoughts raced through her mind about the proposal Mrs. Rahman had just laid before her. She imagined herself, the only Arab student in a sea of Jewish students, and wondered if she would cope. It made her furious when Jewish people stared at her, moved away from her on the light rail, suspected her of being a terrorist.

And what would her peers, her brother, Fadwa, think? They would criticize her for bowing to the occupation, for studying among the enemy. Nour frowned slightly and looked up again at Mrs. Rahman.

"Of course, if it would complicate things at home with your parents, I'm happy to talk to them," Mrs. Rahman offered, as if reading Nour's thoughts. "If it's an issue of social pressure, though, I think you've proven you're strong enough to stand up to that."

Social pressure? Nour hadn't even thought about that, but Mrs. Rahman was right. There would be pressure. A day visit to Jaffa was one thing, but studying full time in Tel Aviv, in Hebrew, in the heart of the occupation, people might see her as a traitor like Aisha.

But she wanted to be a fashion designer more than anything and the option of studying in more conservative places like Jerusalem or Ramallah, even Amman, Jordan, where many of her friends would go to school, was less appealing. In a way, it had to be Tel Aviv. The vibrant Israeli city with its trendy boutiques and newly opened fashion mall was the gateway to the world's fashion capitals in London, New York, Paris.

"I, I'd like to try." New energy surged through Nour. "It's what I've always wanted to do, but what..."

"Listen, Nour, sometimes you need to follow your dreams despite all the barriers. I saw how you were when we went to Jaffa. There was resistance from every corner, but you managed to convince so many people to come along. I think you're a leader, a trailblazer." Mrs. Rahman patted her shoulder. "I'll print off the application papers and we can at least look them over tomorrow."

. . .

There was only one place Nour felt like going after leaving Mrs. Rahman's class—Mamilla. It was weeks since she'd visited the mall. Her broken arm made trying on clothes uncomfortable and after the cast came off, she got busy studying for the end-of-semester exams and arranging the Jaffa trip. But now, she needed a place to think, a place to consider Mrs. Rahman's suggestion. Could she really win a scholarship to Shenkar? Did she have to tell Baba? Would he let her go if she was successful?

Mamilla was busier than usual when Nour arrived. The Jewish festival of lights was passed, but Christmas was in a few days and Christian tourists flooded the holy city. The fairy lights strung across the street came to life as the dusky evening quickly turned into a cool winter night. Nour felt the chill on her cheeks as she made her way along the bustling boulevard, studying the festive displays in the store windows and thinking about all the possibilities studying in a prestigious fashion school could bring her.

Passing one of the small cafes, its tables and chairs spilling out onto the uneven paving stones, Nour was drawn by a sweet smell. Without too much thought, she ordered herself something the menu described as marshmallow hot chocolate and sat down with the warm frothy drink beneath one of the street heaters. Basking in the warmth, Nour watched the throng of shoppers streaming in and out of the stores. She enjoyed seeing their contented faces as they walked out with plumped-up shopping bags and wondered if she might be more than an observer in the fashion world at some point. Could she become a real contributor, an inspirer, a creator?

She noticed how Mamilla served as a conduit for the city, her city, which was so divided in so many ways. She liked how it brought together the old and the new, the Jews, both secular and religious, the Arabs, some Muslim and some Christian, not to mention tourists from all over the world, too. This was why she loved fashion, clothes, shopping so much. It blurred the superficial differences and was something everyone could be a part of.

Warmed inside from the hot chocolate, Nour decided to have a quick browse in the shops. She loved the collections this time of year, the rich, deep colors—maroons, dark greens, blues, browns—and the heavy fabrics of winter.

Inside one store, she let her fingers rest on a crushed velvet jacket. She relished its softness, and the cuff embroidered with a neat green, blue, and white Celtic pattern. She imagined her own work, inspired by the black and red threads of Setty's gowns, but modernized to reflect Jerusalem's diversity. She would give her designs depth. She would say something about the world. Baba was wrong. Fashion was powerful, not shallow.

It was in another of her favorite stores that Nour fell fully in love. She spied the boots from the outside. Shiny and black, they were displayed in the window. She went inside for a closer look. To her delight, they were reduced to half price.

"There's only one pair left in a small size," the saleswoman, clumpy mascara clinging to her eyelashes, informed her nonchalantly.

"That's good." Nour's heart lit up. "I'm a small size, 35. Will they fit me?"

The saleswoman shrugged a cool 'I don't know, let's try,' before turning to fetch them from the storeroom. Nour sat on the cushioned bench, unlacing her boots in preparation for trying the new pair. She pulled her phone out of her bag to make sure no one was looking for her and put it back inside when the saleswoman returned with a battered box. She placed the dream boots at Nour's feet without a word and Nour slipped her toes easily inside. They felt like they were always meant to be hers. Like she was always meant to be a fashion designer. Like she was meant to have a scholarship— or at least apply for one.

Nour stood up to test drive the new boots, pacing this way and that in front of the mirror. There were still so many hurdles to pass, even just to apply, and who knew if she would actually win a place? Nour eyed herself in the mirror where the black boots shone in the store spotlights. Her heart bulged at the smoothness of their shape, and she knew then it was worth a try—with or without Baba's support.

Nour paid for the boots and watched the saleslady bag them up for her. "I don't need the box away," she told the saleswoman joyfully.

As she walked to the light rail stop, Nour formulated the words she might use to convince Baba that this was her dream, that he had to let her at least try. She would need to get him to drop the idea of her becoming a pharmacist and convince him to let her study in Tel Aviv, not in Jerusalem.

"You told me that the most important thing in life was to try," she announced to the air, suddenly not scared if people around her were listening too. "Mrs. Rahman wants me to try out for a scholarship—yes, a full scholarship, which will cover all my tuition fees for college—but it's not for Hebrew University and it's not to study pharmacy. It's for Shenkar College. Shenkar? You haven't heard of it? It's only the most prestigious fashion school. Oh, it's in Tel Aviv."

Nour wondered what her father's answer might be. Should she mention Mrs. Rahman? She didn't want Baba to think that her Jewish teacher was manipulating her. Surely, he wouldn't. Mama could help with that. She and Mrs. Rahman seemed to get along well on the school trip.

As for Fadwa, Abdulrahman, the rest of her family, and her friends, she would worry about them later. She wasn't sure there was much she could say to convince them to support such a plan, but if Baba was on board, that was all that mattered.

RIVKI

When they arrived at the wedding hall, Rivki was ushered along with the other women through the entrance on the right-hand side. The men, dressed in smart suits or silky robes, went left.

Esti was still not speaking to her since stomping from the living room, and Rivki hung back watching as her sister entered the hall. Carefully, she was eased into a large wicker chair. A combination of her oversized frock and fasting made her movements drawn and labored. Rivki knew Esti would only be permitted food after the marriage contract was signed. Despite her weakness, Esti greeted each female guest with a delicate kiss, while holding in her hands a crumpled sheet of paper listing the names of the sick or misfortunate—those unable to conceive, those who had lost loved ones and were now alone. As a *kallah*, she was required to pray for them all, using her special wedding day powers to connect with G-d.

Rivki wondered if Esti even gave her a thought—said any prayers for her? Did her sister even know how much *her* words burned her? How much all this hurt *her*? Why couldn't her sister see her? Why couldn't anyone here see her? Feeling more invisible than ever, Rivki watched as her future brother-in-law, the *chatan*, appeared from behind a large white partition that ran down the center of the hall.

The chanting grew louder as Yaakov, surrounded by an entourage of men including the rabbi, Abba, and his own father, crossed the *mechitza* divide and headed towards Esti, head bent low in hypnotic prayer. It was time for the *bedeken*.

When Yaakov finally reached Esti, he pulled back the heavy material shielding her face, and Rivki noticed her light up immediately when their eyes locked. Maybe she did really love him? Rivki thought bitterly. Could she blame Esti for wanting to marry a *tzadik*? For wanting to build a life and start a family according to His commandments? That was what they were all brought up to believe they wanted. That was what they were always told G-d wanted for them, expected from them.

Yaakov recited the ancient blessing given to Rebecca, Rivki's namesake from the Bible, just before she married Isaac. "Our sister, be thou the mother of thousands of ten thousands," he muttered. Other blessings followed, first from Ima, and then Abba placed his hands on Esti's head, offering her a special benediction.

Hearing her father's voice, Rivki took an automatic step towards Esti but, as if blocked by a magical force field, she stopped. Angry words from earlier filled her head and she stayed inside the crowd as Esti followed Yaakov and the men toward the *chuppah*. Bright, colorful lights shone down on the procession. Flowing, joyous voices permeated the air, but all Rivki could see was gray.

Ima, Abba, Mordechai, Yosef, Dovi, Shimshon, and even Batsheva gathered in and around the wedding canopy. Esti's new family, Yaakov, his parents, and his brothers, stood there too. Only Rivki was lost. Floating in a dream, a thick sea of bodies separated her from those she loved.

She didn't belong here anymore. This world rejected her and now she wanted to reject it. She knew she would never find the same happiness as Esti or any of her friends, who would soon stand beneath the same gold and white embroidered canopy where her sister stood right now. There was no choice but to turn her back on it. Even if that meant leaving it all—her family, her community, everything she knew. It was black and white; she knew that. There was no in-between.

Slowly, Rivki backed up through the crowd as if guided by a sixth sense. Near the main doors, she felt the cool evening air willing her outside, and she knew no one would notice her absence. Esti was busy being a bride. Ima was busy being the mother of the bride. The guests, her family, and her friends were busy celebrating.

Stepping outside, she turned around and faced the street. Each step away from the wedding hall made her feel more certain this was the right thing to do. She had no clue where she was going or where she would end up, but at least she was free.

THE ATTACK

The clouds in her mind were now cleared and Tamar, for the first time, was able to notice the curved crescent of the moon in the night sky. A tiny silver star winked brightly at its lower tail. She hoped it was a good sign as she walked down the maze of narrow streets, feeling infinitely lighter. Even though she had no clue where she was and had no phone, Tamar was emboldened. She would find her way out the old-fashioned way—ask people, like her parents did.

Her footsteps tapped a gentle beat on the lonely street as she searched for someone who might be able to help her. Up ahead, she made out the silhouette of square shoulders emerging from one of the apartment buildings and marched forward in her mission. Coming closer, however, she froze when she saw the rounded outline of a yeshiva hat. A memory of that day at the protest with Aviv flooded back, and Tamar hesitated. Could she walk up to him, talk to him, ask him for help? Would he answer her? She held her breath as the figure got closer, but she had no phone, no navigation app, and no choice.

"Erm, excuse me, do you know how I can reach the nearest stop for the light rail?" Tamar asked. Her muscles flexed, ready to run.

Her potential savior stopped right beside her, coming up close. "Yes, of course, you need to turn right at the next opportunity, then you'll find a small alleyway that will take you onto a main street, take a left there, and then the first right. Just follow along for... oh... mmm, like a few hundred meters, then you should see Jaffa Road. From there, you'll find the light rail line," he said, regarding her for a second. "Are you okay?"

"Yes, fine. Just a bit lost." Tamar gulped. "T–thank you." She peered at him again. Was she mistaken? Maybe he wasn't Haredi? But all the signs—the jacket, the hat, the curly sidelocks, the facial hair—told her he was. Perhaps they weren't all bad, she mused.

"Okay, then. Goodnight." He tipped his hat at her and walked away.

Tamar followed his directions as best she could remember them, winding along streets lined with apartment blocks that seemed to stretch for miles. Wide windows faced the road. Warm lights inside offered a glimpse into the lives within this cloistered community. Families milled about living rooms, sitting down to dinner like anywhere else.

Entering a narrow alleyway as per the directions, Tamar found herself caught up in the midst of a burgeoning ultra-Orthodox family. The parents were conversing in a rough, guttural tongue that sounded like German. Tamar guessed it was Yiddish. Like being in another country, she marveled. Then she saw the father turn, his wide coat swishing in the night and berate one of about a dozen kids. She could not understand his words, but she recognized their meaning. After all, some actions were universal.

Suddenly, Tamar realized that beneath all the external make-up, clothes, and hats, people were all the same, really. Even here, in a place that was so insular, so impenetrable, there was still a human side. Haredim were just like any of the other Jerusalem tribes. Jewish or Muslim. Israeli or Palestinian. Religious or secular. Each person was born more or less the same. It was what happened to them afterward, who their parents were, where they lived, where they grew up, what they were taught about life, culture, religion, that made them different—like the strokes of a paintbrush on a white canvas.

Tamar wondered whether such superficial differences could be bridged and how. People were influenced in so many ways, but could they change? It wasn't easy; she knew that. People didn't like to be challenged, and they clearly preferred to stick within their own tribes. But there were some who were brave enough to break through the force fields of each group.

Eventually, Tamar found herself back on Jaffa Road and made her way to her usual stop. It was hours since she'd stormed out on her bandmates in Burgers Bar, and telling her dad had brought calm. She'd traveled in a full circle and for the first time in months, she was at peace.

The train was mostly empty when it finally arrived. Just a tired, elderly couple surrounded by bulging shopping bags and an ultra-Orthodox girl about Tamar's own age. She sat down opposite the girl, immediately struck by her odd ensemble. She was dressed for a wedding, her own perhaps? Tamar couldn't decide. Stiff cream folds puffed out in all directions like it was about to swallow her bony frame.

The girl looked up suddenly and Tamar dropped her gaze, catching only a quick glimpse of eyes that were liquid blue. The girl looked totally distraught. What problems did ultra-Orthodox girls have? Tamar thought gently and glanced back up. "Are you okay?" She smiled.

The girl responded with what could have been a return smile or a frown, and Tamar understood instinctively that her life was just as fraught and as complicated as her own.

• • •

Nour was still engrossed in an imaginary conversation with Baba when the light rail finally arrived. She moved ghost-like into the brightly lit carriage, choosing a spot near two other girls about her own age. She dumped the new boots and her school bag on a seat and was just about to settle herself into another, when out of nowhere, a man shoved past her, pushing her down into the seat with an awkward slump. She let out a loud, combative sigh, but her assailant appeared oblivious, just striding on and settling himself further down the carriage, near an older couple surrounded by a slew of bulging shopping bags.

People were so rude, Nour huffed. She adjusted her body into a normal sitting position, regarding her assailant with narrow eyes—just his hunched shoulders and shabby jacket were annoying. Probably a laborer, Palestinian, from one of the villages outside Jerusalem. Not smart. She shook her head, puckering in her lips. Bad manners were not confined to a particular religion or culture.

The train started up on its clickety-clack journey, easing away Nour's irritation. What could she do about it anyway? There were bigger things to worry about. She closed her eyes, repeating the words she would say to Baba.

"I promise you," she whispered. "You will not regret this. I will make you proud. I promise."

Satisfied with her monologue, Nour opened her eyes and pulled herself up straighter, noticing the two girls sitting beside her. The girl closest to her had wild, curly hair framing a round, pleasant face that emanated calm. On closer inspection, though, Nour noticed rough puffy shadows around her deep green eyes.

The other girl was a different story. Obvious sadness spilled out all around her, like the odd cream gown that puffed and flowed onto the seats beside her. Her head was bent, wisps of blonde poked out in all directions. Suddenly, the girl looked up and Nour caught sight of two glassy blue eyes bathed in anguish. She wondered what problems Jewish girls might have and if they were the same as hers. Did their fathers also try to control their dreams, stymie their ambitions? Did they also worry about their future and the future of their people here in this land? Then, she realized that everyone—Muslim, Arab, Jewish, Israeli—were all stars of their own dramas.

Nour followed the ultra-Orthodox girl's gaze down the carriage and a flare of anger returned as she noticed the scruffy-looking guy again. What was his story? Why was he in such a rush? He hadn't even stopped to apologize. She shook her head, catching, in that instant, a stone-like expression and lips moving manically, like he was begging for divine intervention.

. . .

Rivki kept her shoulders stiff, and head bent to the floor. She could feel eyes on her, drawn in by the stupid meringue dress, like a milk dish in a pile of meaty ones. The two girls sitting nearby were clearly staring at her. She could hear their questions, feel their pity, but there was also no way she could have stayed at Esti's wedding. Not even for one more second.

She tried for weeks, for days, for hours to be happy for her sister. She wanted to be there for her, but how could she force something that was not meant to be? How could she hold a feeling that didn't exist? Her life was going in a different direction. She could feel the powerful pull of a magnet. Where it was taking her, she did not know yet.

Rivki frowned, squirming to make herself more comfortable in the bed of frills and lace, but each movement sent a thousand ants scurrying across her body. She longed to take it off and never look at it again, burn it even, but for now, it was her only possession. She didn't even have any money. Sliding onto the train without even buying a ticket, she prayed no inspector would turn up. She hoped just this once that He would be on her side.

Where was she going? What was she going to do now? Rivki didn't know. All she knew was that she needed to get on Facebook to send Ayelet and Ariel a message in hopes that they would help her. She remembered the story about Ayelet's Haredi friend, who had become secular.

"She went to an organization, a center in Jerusalem that helps people, you know, people like you, those who grow up Haredi, but who want to be secular." Ayelet had spoken like it happened every day. Maybe it did. Rivki didn't know.

"They have all sorts of programs there to teach ex-religious people how to cope in the secular world and with being away from their families," Ayelet had told her.

Rivki had been shocked. How could anyone leave their family, reject their own way of life, the only way they'd ever known? But now it made sense to her, and she wished she had paid more attention, collected the details. At least if she had an address or even just the name of the place, she could check if it was really true.

But she didn't have a name, or a phone number, or even a phone. She didn't even know if she could really up and leave her family, her siblings, her friends, everything she'd known her entire life. Rivki slunk down further into the puff of her dress, eyes still trained on the floor, heart low. She wasn't sure about anything, but she knew she couldn't just go home, either. Not now. Esti despised her and Ima was angry at her for upsetting Esti. Abba and everyone else would be furious that she'd walked out of her own sister's wedding.

Unsure of what to do, Rivki thought it best just stay on the train for now. It was warm and seemed safe. She just wished, with G-d no longer guiding her, there was someone else to talk to. Ariel and Ayelet returned to her mind. She really needed to get on Facebook. She needed a phone. Rivki glanced up at the girl sitting opposite her, the one who had asked her if she was okay, and took her chance.

"Excuse me," her voice was thin and high. It took great effort to push out the rest of her words. "C-c-could I... is it possible I could use your phone? I need to send a message—on Facebook."

"It's dead," the girl answered in a voice flatter than Rivki's.

Rivki shrank back. Maybe she'd misjudged the girl's kindness.

"I have a phone," said the other girl. She had the thickest, blackest, shiniest hair Rivki had ever seen. She held out the flat metal screen. "Oh, wait... just a sec... let me log off my Facebook, and then you can log onto yours." She tapped the phone with red painted nails and handed it to Rivki.

"Thank you," Rivki took it from her, mustering all the muscles in her cheeks to smile.

• • •

The cry of "*Allah Hu Akbar*" came first, followed by a blood-curdling scream that bounced off the train's curved ceiling, touching the velvet-covered chairs before reaching every corner of the carriage. It was so loud, it sounded supernatural, superhuman, animalistic, even. Before Tamar even had time to turn, the pumping in her heart told her it was bad. Very bad.

The Arab girl with the thick black hair was already on her feet, screaming something in Arabic. Her voice was strong and commanding and although Tamar could not decipher what she was saying, she understood it was a plea and a warning rolled into one.

The Haredi girl, despite the heavy ensemble, was already moving, dragging thick skirts through the narrow carriage. Her blue eyes were now burning with an almost feral glare, prompting Tamar to spin around so fast she almost lost her footing.

The howl came again, this time deeper, sharper. It sent spikes down Tamar's spine. Before she could calculate the horror of what was unfolding, she was also moving, following the other two girls charging at the man.

On the floor, Tamar saw the crumpled shape of the old guy, the handle of a large kitchen knife protruding from his chest. Spurts of red flowed outwards in uneven circles. His wife still sat on the cushioned seat, her eyes as wide as coins, and the screams emanating from her open mouth mixed with the throaty yells of the black-haired girl. The Arab man shuffled swiftly backward, spilling shopping bags stuffed with fruits and vegetables in all directions.

Tamar pushed past the still-shouting Arab girl and pulled up beside the terrorist, just as a flash of cream and lace flashed past her, with wide-open jaws that clamped down on the terrorist's left arm. Another howl was now added to the cacophony and Tamar stopped for half a second, watching in horror as he swung the other girl like a loose rag doll and bent down with the other hand to grab the knife from the old guy's chest.

Instinctively, she jumped at him, slamming into him with her body, but he stood there like a wall of steel, sending her flying backward instead. Winded and dizzy, Tamar still managed to get on her feet again and, climbing onto the closest seat, grabbed onto a thick clump of the man's hair with both hands. She yanked as hard as she could.

Then the girl with the shiny hair was beside her, something big and black in her hands that she brought down on the same head in a series of heavy blows. Tamar felt the stabber's whole frame shake and gripped onto the coarse, sweaty, matted mess even tighter.

The onslaught made him flail wildly; a wounded animal caught by a ferocious pack. From her vantage point, Tamar did not notice that he had succeeded in freeing his knife. Blood dripped off the blade as it swished through the air and there was another cry of *"Allah Hu Akbar."* Tamar saw it then, plunging into the ensconcing folds of her co-conspirator's dress, sending a stream of red flowing onto the cream.

Then she felt herself land with a thud onto something soft and realized the train was no longer in motion. Silence filled the air like dust and Tamar wondered who was beneath her.

· · ·

Nour was still studying the scruffy man when she saw his mouth opening wide and cry out, "*Allah Hu Akbar*." Was this part of the prayer? Why was he exalting God? On the light rail? Why now? It wasn't prayer time. Then she saw the knife gleaming in the carriage's fluorescent lights seconds before he plunged it into the old Jewish man's chest.

The howl as the knife came down sent Nour to her feet. All she could think was "wrong" and she started screaming, "Stop, stop! Allah shows no mercy to murderers."

But the stabber didn't even look up until the Jewish girls were on him. First came the one in the fluffy dress, flying through the air like a swan, baring sharp teeth that she sank right into his left hand. Then the other girl—the one with the curly hair—slammed into him with her whole body before jumping onto the seat and grabbing his hair, yanking his head back as far as it would go.

Nour knew she needed to act, too. She needed to stop him before he killed the old man or someone else, or worse. "Boots," another word flashed into her head. She fished around the plastic bag for her precious purchase. Pulling out one of the new boots, she also clambered onto the seat, bringing a clumpy heel down hard on his head.

Whack, whack, whack. She didn't even think about it. The boot was heavy and her arm, only recently healed, was a jackhammer. She needed to stop him. Stop this madness. Didn't he know this was bad for him? For all of them, not only the Jews? It stained their religion too. It did nothing to further the Palestinian cause. Grievances needed to be solved through discussion, dialogue, debate, and hearing the other side.

Nour saw him pull the knife free from the old man's chest. She saw him swing the bloody blade around, bringing it dangerously close to the other girl and even closer to her, but she didn't stop. She saw it plunge into the mass of dress enveloping the Haredi girl. She heard him use that phrase again. Words she knew so well, as if what he was doing was holy.

It was only after the light rail came to a halt suddenly that Nour noticed blood on her own shirt. At first, she didn't think it belonged to her, but she watched as the stain spread across her middle and she lifted her shirt. Everything went black.

· · ·

When the old man started screaming, Rivki's first reaction was to run. Escape like she did from Esti's wedding, like she was doing from her problems, from her life and everything she knew. She heard about *piguim*. Her parents discussed them in hushed tones late at night when they thought everyone was asleep. There were so many lately and not far from Ma'alot Dafna. It was impossible to avoid seeing them or hearing about them— Arabs stabbing Jews, driving over them with cars, shooting people with guns.

The rabbis talked about them too, warning their followers to stay away from Arabs. The *goyim*, the non-Jews. They said they wanted to wipe out the Jewish people, drive them from this land, the land G-d gave to them. Some said it was a punishment from G-d for an unjust and unholy society. They called on the pious and humble to pray to G-d for forgiveness and for strength.

On the light rail, as the bloody scene unfolded, Rivki prayed to Him for strength and felt a power overtake her. Forgiveness would come later and running away again was no longer an option, she decided. It would not solve her problems now. It would not stop the attack unfolding before her very eyes. She needed to confront her fears head-on.

In a split second, Rivki decided to fight. She was gripped by a feeling of freedom like never before. Something feral, something wild, took over her body, and baring her teeth, she shot towards the terrorist, plunging her jaws into his hand. She sank in hard, tasting blood as she broke through his skin. She heard his howls coming as if from a distance and clamped down tighter as he tried to shake her off with a powerful fling.

The more he attempted to push her off, the more fire Rivki felt rising in her, like a phoenix in one of Dovi's cartoon books. When the other two girls joined her, she was spurred by their power.

From the corner of her eye, she spied the curly-haired girl grabbing onto his hair, pulling his head back as far as his neck would allow. Above her, she felt heavy thuds as the girl with black hair hit him with something hard. She felt his body struggling, but getting stronger and stronger the more they fought with him. She wondered if their united power could hold him, stop him. Then she knew with G-d's help they could. She believed.

As he pulled the knife free from the old man's chest, Rivki felt a splat of liquid hit her face, but still refused to let go with her teeth. But then he spun around, and she felt something sharp sting deep in her leg. She opened her mouth to scream, slackening her jaw and spitting out his hand like it was poison. Pain screamed through her leg, worse than the ripping of her stomach when her Crohn's flared. Was this *Ha-Shem*'s punishment for her or was this His way of teaching her? Suddenly, her thoughts of running away, leaving her family forever, becoming secular, were now replaced by images of Esti. Ima. Abba. She needed those she loved the most.

Spluttering for breath and clutching onto the heavy folds of her dress, Rivki felt her body falling heavy, landing on the floor at exactly the same time the light rail came to a screeching halt.

THE HOSPITAL II

Tamar felt a gentle hand on her shoulder and forced open her eyes.

"This one's conscious," a burly policeman, metallic badges twinkling in the bright lights, was crouched beside her. With strong arms, he lifted her and carried her like fragile glass into the crisp night air. A thousand flashing lights—red, white, blue—whirled in the darkness.

"Alive, are they alive?" Tamar tried to make herself heard.

"Shhh, young lady. No need for questions. No need to worry about that. Let's get you to the ambulance," he spoke as if he was addressing a tiny child. "The medics need to look at you, make sure you're not hurt. You seem to be whole, but you never know."

The policeman delivered her to a waiting medical team, crisp white coats glowing in the dark, but all Tamar could think about was the old guy lying slumped on the floor, blood spurting like red fireworks from his chest. Was he alive? And the Haredi girl. Did the knife make it through the armor of her puffy dress? She'd seen blood there, too.

"Alive? Is he, are they alive?" Tamar tried to get her words out as the medics ushered her onto the gurney and set to work checking her vitals. She pushed back, pulling herself up, but the effort hit her head like a baseball bat. The world started spinning, and she fought back the urge to vomit.

"It's okay, miss. Lie down, you're safe now. Let me take your pulse," said a young woman, the ends of her spiraling jet black hair touching her neat white coat. "Where do you feel pain?"

"I'm just dizzy," Tamar answered, her voice floating. "But please, I need to know about the others... what happened to the old man, the two girls who were with me? Are they okay? Is he alive?" A wave of sickness hit her again as the medic lifted one eyelid and then another, shining a bright beam directly on her pupils. She wrapped a thick rubbery band around the top of Tamar's arm and pumped it with air until it squeezed out all the energy left in her.

"Let's focus on you for now," the medic finally replied. "Does it hurt anywhere?" Tamar's whole body hurt.

"Now, tell me, what's your name?"

"T—it's Tamar but—" she protested.

"And, Tamar, how old are you?"

"Sixteen."

"Okay, Tamar, that's good. Now, we need to get your heart rate back to normal, so I need you to be calm. Think calm," she ordered.

Tamar didn't think she would ever calm down again. She wanted to scream for answers. Scream until she knew if they were all alive. She was about to make another appeal for information when she felt a sting on her forehead. She gasped.

"Sorry, Tamar, but there's a deep gash here. You'll definitely need a few stitches," the medic continued, dabbing at her hairline. "And probably a CT scan to rule out any internal injuries. Your heart rate's high too, though that's probably from the shock. We need to get you to the hospital as soon as possible. Sorry, I know it hurts, but you really need to take some deep breaths. Please, for me."

Tamar opened her mouth wide and felt air rush inside. She tried doing what the medic told her, but her mind was still racing. One minute, they were sitting on the light rail, the next, screaming, a guy with a knife, an old man on the floor, blood, and fruit everywhere. Then red on cream.

"Please, I need to know." Tamar could feel the panic rising in her chest. She couldn't stay silent. Not this time. She'd been quiet for too long, about so many other things. Now it was time to speak up.

"I'll try to find out for you, but let's call your parents first, okay?" The medic's voice was gentle now and Tamar felt the tight wrap of a bandage around her head. "Tell them where you're going so they can meet you at the hospital."

Her parents. She wanted them too. But her phone. It was in her bag, and she had no idea where that was. It must still be on the train. Tamar thought about her dad. He was probably flying somewhere over the Atlantic. She would have to call Mom. She hoped she wouldn't freak out.

Searching her memory, she managed to relay the digits of her mom's cell phone number to the medic just as the ambulance's engine surged into motion. Accompanied by a siren, a faceless driver navigated them through bumpy, narrow streets to the hospital. Above the din, Tamar heard her mom's panic as the medic told her what happened.

"Meet us at Hadassah Hospital... yes... Mt. Scopus...." She instructed her in a steady voice. "Yes, yes, you'll probably get there before us, you're much closer. Just wait at the entrance... yes... to the emergency room."

Tamar knew they'd reached their destination because the screaming siren was suddenly silent. A rush of cold air brushed her face as the back doors of the ambulance were pulled open, waking her to the reality of her situation. Her body was rigid as a harried medical team pulled out her gurney and rushed it toward the hospital's bright lights.

The click, click of cameras greeted them as they entered the wide doors, a row of photographers vying for a shot of the victims in Jerusalem's latest terrorist attack. Tamar wondered if the others were here yet—her two accomplices and the old couple. She was desperate to know what happened to them and was about to ask again when the silence was suddenly filled with the wail of more sirens. She considered jumping off the moving gurney and rushing back to see who it was, check what state they were in, but suddenly she was in a tangle of warm, tight arms.

"Tamar, Tamari, my baby, are you okay?" her mom cried. "Oh my god! I was so worried. I tried reaching Dad, but he's already in the air. Dori will get him from the airport and bring him here as soon as he lands. Please, my darling, speak! I need to know that you're okay."

Tamar felt a rush of unconditional love and marveled at her mom's composure. She wasn't angry at all. There was no reprimand for disappearing for hours, for not being in touch, for being out so late, for doing something stupidly dangerous. "I'm fine, Mom, really, I am. It's just a cut... on my head, but I'm okay."

The orderly rushed her past a row of curtained cubicles surrounding the triage area and into one of the empty spaces. A tall, slender doctor in a long white jacket and crowned with a crop of messy curls was beside her, flipping through several sheets of paper stuck to a clipboard.

"Er... Tamar." He looked up at her now. 'I'm Dr. Sarid... How are you feeling?"

"I'm okay, I guess." She reached up to touch the thick bandages now weighing down her head.

"Yes, we'll get those off in a second and examine that cut, but we'll also want to do some more tests, make sure there's no internal damage." Dr. Sarid moved in closer now, long thin fingers shining a flashlight into her eyes.

Slipping the flashlight into his top pocket, the doctor then gently peeled away the white cloth on Tamar's forehead. The small gasp from her mom's mouth told her that the gash was deep, but her head was as numb as a rock, like it wasn't even part of her at all.

"Oh, Tamar." She heard her mom again and was just about to reassure her when a coldness, a wetness on her forehead, sent a searing pain reverberating into her brain.

"Ah! Ouch!" Tamar put up a hand to defend from further assault.

"Mmm, it's quite wide." Dr. Sarid moved his face in close to Tamar's. "We'll need to get this cleaned and sewed up as quickly as possible. Then we'll see about the other tests."

"What tests will she need, doctor?" Her mom was more composed now.

Dr. Sarid ran a hand through his scraggly hair and reached for the clipboard he'd laid down earlier at the end of Tamar's bed. "Definitely a CT scan, and then we will see. Hopefully, it will be clear, and with a few stitches, you'll be as good as new." He began to scribble on the pages with a blue pen. "Can we give you something for the pain?"

Tamar nodded as a thud, thud, thud pounded through her head. Dr. Sarid moved out of the cubicle and returned a second later with a nurse carrying a small plastic cup. She handed Tamar a white pill.

"We'll give you something stronger soon, a localized anesthetic, so we can do the stitches," Dr. Sarid assured her before turning to her mom. "You know, Mrs. Rubin, your daughter is a very brave young woman. The police tell me that she and her friends saved a life...."

"Who? What? The old man? He's alive?" Tamar's words tumbled out of her mouth.

"He is, thanks to you and your friends." Dr. Sarid nodded.

"And the others? Where are they?" Tamar didn't correct him about the other two girls not really being her friends.

"The couple went to Ein Kerem hospital. I believe the man is in stable condition and your friends are here." He motioned behind him. "But looks like you came off the best. Now hold still, this will only hurt a little."

Tamar saw the syringe coming towards her. A fierce prick just above her eye sent a rush of liquid into her skull. She held her breath and closed her eyes, fighting to manage the discomfort. What did he mean, she'd come off best?

"Just a few more seconds. You're doing great, Tamar." Dr. Sarid breathed deeply. "And.... we're done. Thirteen in total. You still need a scan, but hopefully they'll call you soon." Tamar felt the whoosh of his jacket as he stood.

When she opened her eyes, her mom was watching her. "So, you're a hero?" She spoke softly. "You saved a life... but you know, you could have been killed."

Tamar watched her mom's chest puff in and out. "I know, Mom, it just didn't cross my mind. All I could think about was what needed to be done." The screams filled her ears again. Then silence. "Listen, Mom, I need to tell you a few things and then you'll understand better why I did what I did." Tamar began slowly, relaying to her mom the same details she'd shared with her father a few hours earlier. She knew some of it would be hard for her mom to hear, but she needed to tell the truth.

"Oh, Tamar!" Her mom put a hand over her mouth as Tamar told her about the morning on the light rail when the man shoved his hands down her jean shorts. "Why didn't you say anything? We could have gone to the police!"

"Please, Mom, let me go on. There's more," Tamar willed her.

She told her about the gas station, the beating and Tal pressuring her to stay quiet, and then about events that afternoon in the restaurant. Since her mom already knew about Ami, she swiftly moved on to what had just happened on the train.

"Well, it was a risky thing to do, but it paid off, I guess..." Her mom picked up her hand and squeezed it. "I wish you had told us about all the other things. Poor dear, you shouldn't have to shoulder such things alone."

"I know, I know." Tamar squeezed her mom's hand back. "I just didn't know how to... then it all got out of control... I didn't even know where to begin... but I'm glad now that you and Dad know everything."

"And I'm glad you've told me now, too." Her mom leaned in, placing a kiss close to where the doctor had sewn her up. Tamar smelled fresh lemon. "Listen, whatever happens now, we'll face it together. That's what family is for. And Tamar, I'm really proud of you."

• • •

When Nour came to, she was in the hospital. The first thing she saw was Mama's wild eyes. The first thing she heard was Mama's wild voice: "Samir! She's awake."

Then came Baba's chalky one: "Nour, my baby, Nouri, we're here. It's okay. You're in the hospital, you're safe, and the doctors say you'll be fine. The knife only grazed you; it caused no internal damage. Thank God."

It took Nour a few seconds to remember what he was talking about, then it all flooded back—the light rail, the scruffy laborer, the knife. But how did she get here, to the hospital? And what happened to the Jewish man? There was so much blood. Was he alive? And what of the other girls? Where were they? One of them was badly hurt. Red spots on taffeta.

Nour tried to get the questions out through her mouth, but Baba placed a finger on her lips. "Shhh," he whispered. "No need to talk. You've been through a traumatic experience—stabbed with a knife, a blow to your head, a heavy object fell on top of you. You really need to relax; your blood pressure is still high."

But she couldn't relax. When she closed her eyes, all she could see were stormy eyes, frantic lips. The face of insanity. Perhaps if she'd acted faster, she might have been able to stop him? Talk him out of it? Or at least warn the others to get away. She shivered still hearing his cry, the exaltation of one so revered, the veneration of one so powerful, but used for harming innocents. She felt Mama pulling the blankets up around her chin, tucking them beneath her body, but the chills still rattled inside her.

Nour felt her eyes fill with tears. Why did people inflict such pain on each other? She turned to Baba and spoke, her voice coming out stronger and clearer than even she expected. "How does someone get filled with so much hatred that they want to kill someone they don't even know?"

Baba stayed silent for a long second, then let out a deep sigh. "Nour, this is a tense place, you know that. You went to Ramallah with Fadwa, you saw the protests there. People are angry. They are desperate. They've been living under occupation for fifty years and they're still traumatized by the *Nakba* before that. Our people have been humiliated, kicked off their lands, lost their homes, seen relatives murdered unjustly. They want dignity and freedom. The violence is an expression of this. I'm not saying it's right, but that's just how it is."

He paused before going on. "I truly understand them. I think you do too, Nour, but I'm also proud of those of us who advocate for our rights peacefully." Baba put out a thick hand to brush her cheek. "Today, you showed you don't believe in violence either, and that makes me proud to call you my daughter. All this violence, from both sides, has kept us stuck in this conflict for too long."

Baba leaned in and kissed her just below the hairline. "We must rise above the hatred on both sides, judge people for their actions, not for their religious beliefs or because they happened to be born into a Muslim family or a Jewish family. It's so important. I can't tell you why that man acted the way he did, why he decided to pull out a knife and stab someone else, someone Jewish in particular, but what I can tell you is that I am so proud of you for standing up to him, for trying to stop him. It means that you know what's wrong and what's right. It means I taught you well, and you listened."

Nour felt a glow inside her. She also saw a chance. Maybe now, he would listen to her when she told him she wanted to study fashion, not pharmaceuticals. She was about to say something when a doctor entered the room.

"You're a very lucky young lady." The doctor, a young Arab woman not much older than Nour, stepped up to the bed. "I know there was a lot of blood. You probably fainted from the shock of seeing it seeping through your clothes, but the knife only really grazed your skin. It did not go any deeper."

• • •

Only half-conscious, Rivki barely heard the electronic doors slide open. She barely felt the cool air tickling her face. She tried to move, roll from where she'd fallen on the carriage floor, but the lower part of her body was a dead weight. Lifting her head, she let out a small cry when she saw her legs pinned beneath the bulky frame of the terrorist. He wasn't moving. She wondered if he was dead.

She gasped again as she spied other bodies around her. They were not moving either. Were they alive? She closed her eyes again, not daring to think of a massacre, and was woken abruptly by the sudden shrill of ambulances followed by heavy booted footsteps.

"Can you move?"

Rivki felt a hand on her and flinched. She tried to open her eyes and managed a flittered image of a darkly dressed man.

"What hurts? What's your name?" Came the voice again.

"R-rivki," her voice sounded distant, as if it did not even belong to her.

"Okay, Rivki. Stay still, I just need to..." But the rest of his words were drowned out by more sirens and shouts. She heard everything and nothing, but she could feel. First, a tight, burning ring around her leg, a pressing, a pinning. She knew pain from inside her stomach, but this was different. This was sharp, this was a sear and a scream that made yellow dots dance in the corners of her eyes.

"Ahhhhhh," Rivki released the valve that held everything inside her until now. She felt the anger, frustration, fear fly out in grunts and shouts. Then she was crying, her whole body convulsing, sobbing, screaming, louder and louder. Louder than she'd ever screamed before.

"Rivki, it's okay. Rivki, it's okay," came the voice that hovered over her. "I know it hurts, but the worst is over now. It's over."

She knew he was only trying to help her, soothe her, but she kept on screaming, a genie unleashed from a bottle. She felt herself being lifted up, moved, and carried out into the cool night air. Still, she screamed, her cries blending with the screaming of the night. She was in an ambulance now, but she barely heard the woman telling her to hold still. She barely felt the needle prick her skin or the rush of fluids flowing into her veins, mixing with her blood.

"Rivki." The voice was strong, like Ima's when she was angry at someone. She knew it wasn't Ima, but it made her stop screaming. She was silent now and heard the question. "We need to call your parents—do you know the number?"

Rivki tried to form her words. What could she say? They were all at a wedding, Esti's wedding, her sister's wedding. A wedding she was also supposed to be at, but wasn't.

"No," Rivki's breath was rapid. Her mind was a blurry fuzz of watercolors, lavender on blue, turquoise on green, red on cream. Her body felt numb. She tried to pull herself under control before speaking again. "They're all at a wedding." She spoke slower, rejoining the world, filling with misery as she imagined Esti, Yaakov, her parents still together, still celebrating. "There are no cell phones," she whispered. "But it's at the Jerusalem Gate Hotel."

This was G-d's way of punishing her, she thought as a river of pain raced determinedly up and down her leg. Suddenly, Rivki wanted to go back in time. She wanted to erase the fight with Esti and embrace each member of her family. Show them she loved them, say sorry for not being like them anymore.

• • •

Tamar saw the curtain ruffle as a burly police officer entered her cubicle.

"Tamar Rubin?" He cleared his throat. "Erm, we need to ask you some questions.... er... about tonight's events."

"Okay." Tamar nodded, glancing quickly at her mom. Ignoring the aches in her legs and between her shoulder blades, she did her best to answer the officer's questions, describing what happened from the moment she entered the light rail until she was carried out to safety.

"So... er.... you didn't know them, the other two girls, before?" He flicked swiftly through his notebook. "You didn't, er, know, er, Rivki Lefkovitz and Nour Asa'ad before today?"

"No, no, I told you. The Haredi girl, Rivki, I guess, asked to use my phone, but I never met her before. The other girl, Nour? She just happened to be there, too. She was about to let Rivki use her phone because mine was dead." Frustration filled Tamar's stomach.

"So, you... didn't plan what you were going to do then, to stop him? The terrorist? Discuss it in advance, or something?" He eyed her dubiously.

"No, no, there was no time. We all just did what we needed to do. No words. I guess it was just instinct, stars aligned or something, or maybe just luck we were all in the same place at the same time," Tamar tried to explain and then added, more to herself than to the officer, "It's like we were all meant to be there together to stop him."

The policeman raised a cynical eyebrow. "Well, whatever it was, young lady, you and the other two girls are real heroes. If you hadn't been there and acted the way you did, then Mr. Isaac would most certainly have been killed." He snapped his notebook shut and placed his pen in the upper breast pocket of his uniform.

"W-where are they? The others?" Tamar was again gripped by curiosity.

"Mr. Isaac was taken to the other Hadassah Hospital. The terrorist, his name's not been released yet, is at Shaare Zedek hospital. His injuries aren't too bad, considering... not that you needed to know that...." He coughed. "As for your two friends, they're just down the hall. My colleagues are talking to them now. Would you like to see them?"

He looked over at Tamar's mom as if seeking approval.

"Yes. Yes, I would," Tamar answered without hesitation. "Mom, will you help me up?"

Once she was seated in a low wheelchair, the police officer pulled back the curtains.

"Rivki's over here." He guided them across the vinyl floor, then whispered, "We're still trying to reach her parents. Maybe you and your mom could keep her company."

He pulled back the curtain to reveal a small shape lying beneath a pile of blankets. She was already hooked up to an IV, and a machine monitored her heart with a gentle beep.

"Oh my, Mom, push me inside," Tamar commanded. "*Shalom*, I'm Tamar," she said gently. "We were on the light rail together, remember?"

The girl turned her head slightly and whispered, "Yes."

"How are you? Rivki, right?" Tamar tried to sound cheery but immediately felt foolish. Obviously, she wasn't doing so great at all.

"My leg," Rivki's voice was cracked, weak. "He stabbed it."

"Yes, I saw." Tamar felt pity wash over her. How had this tiny, frail creature turned so ferocious? She motioned to her mom to push her closer and then fished beneath the blankets for Rivki's hand. "It's okay, they'll fix you up, you'll see. They already sewed me up, look." She pointed to her forehead.

Rivki turned the corners of her lips upwards into what looked more like a grimace than a smile. "They're looking for my parents." Her voice was edged with misery. "They can't... do anything for me until they get here and they're all at a wedding.... I should be...." she breathed deeply and turned her face away from Tamar.

Tamar looked up at her mom, who shrugged silently.

"Listen, I'm sure they'll find them soon." Tamar squeezed Rivki's hand. "And when they get here, they'll be so proud of you and what you did. Biting him like that, wow! It was incredible. You're a real hero."

When Rivki didn't respond, Tamar looked up at her mom again.

"Perhaps Rivki should rest." Tamar's mom put a gentle hand on her shoulder. "Shall we go and meet Nour?"

Tamar was filled with sadness as she withdrew her hand from beneath the blankets. She wished she knew more about her new friend. Why was her whole family at a wedding and Rivki was not? She obviously had been at the event, why else would she be wearing such a fancy dress? Why had she left? Tamar frowned, then turned to her mom. "Okay, let's go and find Nour."

At the nurse's station, they were directed to an actual room, not a cubicle. Her injuries must be bad, Tamar shivered. Her head felt heavy as she wondered if Nour spoke Hebrew. The thought of hearing Arabic again sent a jolt of cold coursing into her bones, but then she thought about Ami. Not all Arabs were bad. She usually spoke to Ami after each terrorist attack. They checked in to make sure the other was safe, expressing the same indignation over such horrific, violent acts. He was probably looking for her now, worried because she was not answering, but her bag, her phone and all, had yet to resurface.

As soon as she entered Nour's room, Tamar heard a jaunty "shalom" from the bed. Despite the lack of color on her face, she immediately recognized the Arab girl from a few hours earlier. Tamar also knew immediately that the woman standing beside the bed was her mother. She and Nour were mirror images.

"My partner, my hero," said Nour in Hebrew scented with a slight Arabic accent. "You were so strong, you inspired me."

She opened her arms, beckoning Tamar over for a hug. With her mom's help, Tamar stood up, almost falling into Nour's arms. It felt like the right thing to do. They were forever bonded now. Like her and Rivki.

"Tamar, right?" Nour asked her. "These are my parents. My father works at the hospital. That's why I'm in here."

Tamar pulled herself up and placed herself back in the wheelchair. "This is my mother." She gestured behind her, then turned back to Nour. "But it's you who's the hero. You were the one who confronted him first. I don't know what you said to him, but I'm pretty sure it was a warning and then you knocked him out! What was it you used? I couldn't see–"

"One of my new boots," Nour choked. "I'd just bought them. I hope I get them back, too."

"A boot?" Tamar looked at her in shock. "What made you think of using that?"

Nour shrugged. "I didn't really think, I just acted. I think it was the old guy's screams that got me going...." She looked at Tamar, her face cracking into a smile, and then burst out laughing. Tamar joined in and soon the two girls created a ruckus rare for a hospital emergency room.

"Nour, really! I don't think it's all that funny," Nour's mother sobered their chuckles. "You could have been killed!"

"My thoughts exactly," Tamar's mom concurred.

The two older women stood there shaking their heads as their daughters laughed.

. . .

As soon as she saw the girl with the wild, curly hair, a thick white bandage now decorating her forehead, Nour's heart pulsed wildly. Without hesitating, without thinking, she opened her arms and was delighted when the girl, the sparky smell of medicinal alcohol clinging to her, practically fell into her embrace.

Nour knew that if it hadn't been for Tamar's quick actions, she would not have been inspired to take out her boot. Then who knows what else might have happened to them on the light rail?

"My partner, my hero," she whispered in Tamar's ear.

She was surprised when Tamar suddenly pulled back and exclaimed, "No! It's the other way around. You were the one who confronted him first. I didn't understand what you were saying to him, but I sensed you were warning him and then you knocked him out! What was it you used? I couldn't see—"

"My new boots... Well, one boot actually," Nour frowned, wondering where her dream boots might be now, and then looked back at Tamar before bursting into laughter, her lungs filling with dizzy happiness. She really couldn't remember the last time she'd let herself go like that, and with a Jewish girl, no less. What would Fadwa think? Or her brother? But then, her mother let them both know what she thought.

Nour was about to respond when a nurse put her head around the door. "Is Tamar Rubin here? I was told she was." The nurse looked from one girl to the other.

"That's me," said Tamar, giving Nour a conspiring grin.

"It's time for your CT. Please follow me."

After Tamar left, Nour reflected on her new friend's words. She pondered the meaning of the word 'hero' and why they both saw the other that way. In school, her friends had called her a hero after the protest in Ramallah, but there she knew her actions were not brave.

Was being a hero doing something that everyone else was doing, even if you knew it was wrong? Or was being a hero doing something that ran against the grain, something no one else expected you to do because it was the right thing to do? Nour hoped it was the latter.

"I want to meet the other girl, the religious one," she told Baba. She watched him nod slowly, stand to bring a wheelchair over to her bed. He helped her up and then pushed her gently through the emergency room to a tiny cubicle at the other end.

Mama, whose face was much calmer than earlier, pulled back the curtain and led the way cautiously inside. Even with covers pulled up to her chin, Nour recognized the girl's narrow face and prominent cheekbones. Her skin was as pale as the folds of her cream-colored dress, which peeped out from among the blankets. She knew her name was Rivki.

"Rivki," Nour whispered, afraid of waking her but anxious to meet her too. "Are you awake?" She noticed a slight movement and continued in a gentle voice. "I came to say thank you."

Rivki's eyes fluttered open, pools of glassy blue.

"You saved my life and Mr. Isaac's." Nour motioned for Baba to push her closer to the bed. She waited for a response, but suddenly the silence was destroyed by a burst of noise from behind them.

"Rivi! Rivki! Rivkale!"

Light from the ward flooded the cubicle as the curtain swished back to reveal a portly matron. "*Baruch Ha-Shem*! Shmuel! She's over here." The woman was closely followed by a broad Haredi man in a flowing silk robe over a bright white shirt. Nour felt her wheelchair moving, Baba dragging her aside to allow the people—who were obviously Rivki's parents—into the small space.

"Rivkale! My Rivkale, are you okay? What's going on? What happened? What were you doing on the light rail? It doesn't make sense; we don't understand it! How did you get to the light rail? When did you leave the wedding?" The girl's mother moved frantically up to the bed.

Baba pulled Nour out of the cubicle and they watched as a stream of ultra-Orthodox Jews, the last one wearing a wedding dress, no less, vied for space beside Rivki.

Then Tamar was beside her, upright now and looking much stronger, watching the reunion between Rivki and her family.

"You were with Rivki? When it happened?" the older woman, the matron, confronted the two of them. Nour reached out and grabbed Tamar's hand.

"Yes, we were both there." Tamar spoke clearly.

"Your daughter saved our lives…" Nour swallowed her final words as the imposing woman, sparkling rubies dangling from her ears, watched them sternly.

"Rivki's a real hero," Tamar continued. "So brave…"

"Yeah, a really special person. You must be very proud of her. If it wasn't for her, I would have been killed too," Nour found her voice. If people were people, then why shouldn't she be able to talk to an ultra-Orthodox Jew?

Back in her room, Mama announced she was going home to take care of Adam and Khalil. Nour knew it was now or never if she was going to confront Baba, tell him about the dreams and plans before things took a crazy turn.

"Baba," she breathed in deeply, totally forgetting her practiced monologue. "I want to study fashion, not pharmaceuticals." She didn't wait for him to answer, but went on, feeling strong. "I want to go to Shenkar College in Tel Aviv. I know it's not what you had in mind for me, but it's what I want. It's important to me. Mrs. Rahman says I can try for a scholarship. Please, will you let me try?"

She searched her father's face, hoping not to find disappointment, praying he might respect her more now that she'd shown that she was a strong person.

For a while he didn't answer, his silence making her squirm, but she knew better than to rush him.

Then, to her surprise, he said, "I understand."

• • •

Rivki felt like she was watching one of the grainy old films her teachers sometimes projected onto the wall in her classroom. She caught only snippets of scenes—sparkles in the night sky, glowing lights, figures in white, in blue, and in green. Each time she opened her eyes, something else was happening around her or someone else was talking to her. She'd managed to give them her name and her ID number and the place where they could find Ima, Abba, and the rest of the family. She'd even managed to tell them about her Crohn's, but this time it was her leg. Her leg was on fire.

In a small cubicle, curtains closed around her, Rivki heard a throat clear and felt cold hands prodding her stomach. "Anything hurt here?" came a brusque voice. Rivki's eyelids fluttered open to see thick, dusty gray eyebrows resting above intense dark eyes. She shook her head, trying not to think about the pain further down her body. "You're Dr. Jalal's patient?" Another question. Another nod of the head. "I'm Dr. Shimron. I've called Dr. Jalal and told him you're here, but it might be awhile until he arrives. It's good there is no stomach pain. Sometimes stressful situations can cause a flare-up. Now, let's look at this leg." Dr. Shimron cleared his throat again, chalk stuck in a tunnel.

Rivki followed his movements as he stepped to the end of the bed and willed him not to touch the source of her agony. The sharp scraping burns were less now, replaced by a low hammering on her bones. She closed her eyes again, wishing she could leave her body and her life. She didn't see Dr. Shimron touch her leg, but she felt it.

"Ahhhh, hurts," came out as an exasperated sigh.

"Yep," was Dr. Shimron's reply. "We need to treat this as soon as possible. The knife may have penetrated the rectus femoris. I hope your parents get here soon." Rivki didn't see him frown, but she felt it. "We really need their permission to continue. We can give you something stronger for the pain though and give your parents... and Dr. Jalal... a little longer."

Rivki opened her eyes again, as a nurse—short, middle-aged, clad in the hat of a modern-Orthodox religious Jew—arrived with a small white plastic cup. "Drink this, *motek*," she urged Rivki. "It'll help with the pain until we know what to do with you."

Rivki obliged her, using all her strength to stop her teeth from chattering and her body from shaking. She was strong, but didn't know how much more she could take. She wished this medicine would take all the pain away.

"Now, why don't you try to sleep a little until your parents arrive? I'm sure they'll be here any minute." The nurse grabbed a pile of blankets from a nearby pile and covered Rivki up to her neck. She slid a pillow under her head and brushed the hair from her forehead. "Now close your eyes."

The next time Rivki opened her eyes, it took her a second or two to place the face before her. Then she remembered, it was the curly-haired girl from the light rail. She was in a wheelchair, eyes at Rivki's level, hair pushed back by a thick white bandage. She was with a woman, clearly her mother—they looked so much alike. Rivki's heart sank. Did her own mother even know she was here? Was she really on her way? What about the others? She felt misery mixing with the pain in her leg. Tears rushed forward, stinging her eyeballs. Then she felt the fleshy warmth of another hand touching hers.

She felt Tamar squeezing her hand, her words floated and hovered around above her head, but she couldn't hold on to any of them long enough to form a reply. Did she call her a hero? That couldn't be right. How could she be a hero after the way she treated Esti? Abandoning her own sister on her wedding day. Could a person be both good and bad? Rivki struggled to see the gray between the black and the white, between the right and the wrong. All she wanted now was to see Esti—and Ima and Abba and the rest of her family—ask them for their forgiveness, for their understanding, to make it all right. Rivki closed her eyes and prayed to G-d for a second chance.

The next time she woke, Rivki saw an ashen face framed by long, dark hair. The girl who tried to lend her the phone. The Arab girl. She heard her name and tried to focus, but the fire in her leg was back, sending a scorching heat that made everything jumbled. She thought she heard her say that she,

Rivki, had saved her life. She also thought she heard a burst of familiar voices calling her name. "Rivi, Rivki, Rivkale."

It was only when Ima's face, deep, dark lines etched across her forehead, that she realized it was really her. "*Baruch Ha-Shem*! Shmuel! She's over here." Rivki's hope turned to fear at her mother's voice.

"Thank *Ha-Shem* she's alive, Shmuel," she heard Ima say. "We're just glad you're here, safe, alive." She felt warm, fleshy lips on her forehead and the quiet sting of tears in her eyes again.

"I love you too, Ima," was all Rivki could whisper.

Their words lingered for less than a second, quickly stolen by the ruckus of her other, older, siblings. Yosef and Ruthy, followed by Mordechai and Zehava, filed into the crowded cubicle. Then came Esti, her flowing gown taking up the space of three people. Yaakov stood shyly, next to her. Both faces lined with fear.

Rivki felt her pain, her guilt, her anguish replaced with a rush of love. Esti—and her new husband—they had deserted their own wedding, their own *simcha*, to see if she, Rivki, was okay.

She knew there would be questions later. A lot of them, and hard ones too. She knew she owed them all an explanation, especially Esti, but in that instant, Rivki relished the fact they were all there for her.

Maybe she wouldn't need to leave her family, her community, and everything she had ever known after all? She still believed in G-d; she was sure of that. He'd punished her, but He'd also saved her—and the others—on the light rail. That was the only way to explain how they'd overpowered a terrorist with a knife.

Esti was at her side then, face close to hers. "Rivki." She sobbed. "I was so worried about you! I thought you were killed! All we heard was a terrorist attack, nothing made sense, but *Baruch Ha-Shem*, in the name of G-d, you are here and alive, thank G-d."

Rivki was just about to answer, explain, beg forgiveness when the nurse in the hat reappeared. "We need to take you now... to the operating theater. I need everyone to stand aside." She clicked the break under the bed and wheeled Rivki out of the cubicle, past her family, past the two girls who'd saved her life, and down the brightly lit hallway.

THE REUNION

March 2016

The stinging chill whipped at Tamar's bare legs, and she shivered stepping up to the security booth outside the president's house. She was wearing her favorite dress, topped with a cool denim jacket and a pair of shiny white sneakers.

"You should have dressed a bit warmer," her mom chided. "And maybe something a little nicer than a jean jacket."

Tamar rolled her eyes. "Mom! It's called fashion. Why do you always have to focus on practicalities. Can't you see the bigger picture? We're at the president's house and I'm about to get an award. Who cares what I'm wearing?"

"Yeah, Mom." Dori pushed her way between them. She was also wearing jeans. "Tamar's about to be honored for her bravery. We should be proud."

"Of course, we're proud of her." Her dad joined in, flinging an arm around each of his daughters and smiling at his wife. "Eve, it doesn't matter what she's wearing, right?"

"Well, it's an important event." Her mom's mouth turned upwards into a smile. "But, yes, of course I'm proud. I'm just being a mom. That's my job." She moved in towards them too, putting out her own arms for a family embrace.

Tamar stood, her face close to Dori's like when they were younger, and she breathed in the mix of her mom's lemony scent and her dad's powdery cologne. She felt lucky to be alive, to be here, and to be together with them.

Inside the President's Residence, they watched their bags, jackets, and phones slide through the security machine before they stepped through a metal detector. A security guard checked their IDs and handed them each a visitor badge, which Tamar hung around her neck. A woman in a smart navy suit led them through a pretty garden plush with pink and red rosebushes, and past a row of bronzed busts showing all of Israel's previous presidents. They entered a large, airy hall lined with chairs facing a low podium, white and blue Israeli flags lined up behind it. Television cameras on spindly tripods stood poised to capture the ceremony and Tamar felt dizzy, thinking that her face would soon be broadcast into every living room in the country.

"The ceremony will take place in the hall, but you and your family can relax in here until we're ready to start." The navy-suited woman guided them into a side room with beige-colored couches and fake plants in oversized vases. "There's some tea and coffee for you while you wait."

"Wow, this is fancy!" Dori plopped down on one of the couches. "I just can't believe it! My little sister, only sixteen, but already a household name." She gave Tamar a wide grin and patted the seat next to her.

Tamar fell onto the couch beside her with a matching grin. "I'm just happy you're here to celebrate with me." She lay her head on Dori's shoulder, a thousand butterflies fluffing up her stomach. "I know we're supposed to be celebrating my bravery, but honestly, I'm a bit nervous."

So much had happened in the last three months and Tamar was still trying to make sense of it all. The cut on her head was just a tiny scar now. The doctor said it should disappear eventually, but there were deeper scars after everything that had happened since October.

Talking to her therapist, was helpful, but Tamar still saw the terrorist's face sometimes when she closed her eyes, still saw his knife plunging into her instead of Mr. Isaac, scraping her stomach, not Nour's, or penetrating her leg, rather than Rivki's. She knew he was locked up in jail, but each time he appeared in a dream, it took her a few seconds to realize she was unhurt and safe.

Tamar also talked to her therapist about the assault on the train, the gas station, and Tal. She struggled with disappointment, mostly at herself, for not fighting back or speaking out in each case. Together, they agreed that hard situations were always part of life and it was what you learned from them about yourself and about others that mattered most. Tamar learned that keeping things locked inside made the world a much darker place.

Sharing problems and being honest, even if it was difficult, was what was most important.

Her next challenge was telling Ami when he came to visit her at home a few days after the terrorist attack.

"I got mixed up with the wrong people," Tamar's voice came out croaky, patchy like she had a cold or something. "I regret it." She could not look him in the eye.

Ami was quiet for what seemed like hours and Tamar wondered if he could ever see her in the same light again. When he did eventually speak, Tamar heard no judgment or disappointment, only flat, practical reality.

"Listen, Tamar, there are so many ugly things going on in this city, it's easy for any of us to get duped into being part of it. But maybe it was because you witnessed such an awful thing that you found your way to me." She felt a soft hand on her cheek and looked up into his warm chestnut eyes, soft lips brushing on hers for a few seconds, sending a surge of hope through her body.

When she returned to school a few days later, Ami was at her side—a bodyguard if things got complicated with Tal or anyone else from The Jerusalemities. She made it clear to her bandmates that it was either her or Tal. She would not continue making music with a raging racist. To her surprise, they rallied around her, and it did not take them too long to replace Tal. She also made peace with Leon, who she knew was only trying to be kind—even if he was annoying about it sometimes.

At her dad's urging, Tamar gave the police all the information about the attack at the gas station. Two officers were at her house again, collecting more information about the terrorist attack on the light rail, when her dad said, "I think Tamar has information about another attack." He was sitting next to her on the couch and gave her leg a squeeze of encouragement. "It happened a few months back. In a gas station, an Arab shopkeeper was beaten up."

The officer who was taking notes in a flimsy notebook raised an eyebrow and looked at Tamar. She gave him the date and all the details she could remember. "I was so scared; I didn't know what to do. My friend and I were outside, and we ran away afterward." Tamar's heart thumped as she mumbled through the last few words.

"I see," said the officer still scribbling with his pen. "Any names you can give us?"

"The only one I know is..." Tamar swallowed. "Hezi. He's my friend... er, my ex-friend.... Tal's cousin." She studied her toes, prickles of heat on her neck.

"Officer, is it possible for you to keep Tamar's testimony on this anonymous?" her dad asked, as if he could read her mind.

"Yes, well, I'll check, though it's not my department." The police officer coughed. "It's a different unit that's responsible for Jewish hate crimes. They'll probably be in touch, if the case is still open."

The letter from the president came a few weeks later. It informed Tamar that she was the recipient of the Tribe of Humanity Award—a new honor, "designed to heal Israel's fragmented society and shine a spotlight on those who challenged the dictates of their own people and strived for the good of humanity."

"It will be bestowed to you, Tamar Rubin, and two others, whose actions stopped evil in its tracks and who should serve as an inspiration for everyone."

The letter was accompanied by an invitation to a ceremony taking place on March 20, 2016, at the President's Residence, in Jerusalem.

. . .

"Tamar! *Habibti*," Nour called the minute she spotted her new friend sitting on a beige-colored couch beside a girl with almost identical frizzy hair. She rushed over, leaning in for a hug and almost losing her balance.

"Ah, I'm so sorry." She steadied herself, smoothing down the lapels on her pin-striped jacket. "I'm just so happy to see you, my friend. Let me take a look at you... mmmm... a lot better than last time we met."

"It's so good to see you too." Tamar pulled herself up to stand beside Nour. "You look a lot better than the last time I saw you, too. Although I've seen your posts on Instagram. You're such a fashion guru. Did you finish the application to Shenkar?"

Since the attack, Nour and Tamar remained in touch, but they had still not managed to meet in person. Partly it was the practicalities of an Arab and a Jew meeting up in their deeply divided city, but it was also Nour's crazy schedule, taken up mostly by her application to the fashion school.

"I'm nearly done, just a few more pages to go. You've been such a help, thank you." Nour threw her arms around Tamar again and Tamar blushed. "Come, I want you to meet my family."

Nour led Tamar to where the Asa'ad family stood shyly at the refreshments table. They looked a little out of place here, she thought, but then shrugged. This was her city too, and the president invited them. Mama looked beautiful, mystical, her favorite dark pink scarf pinned up stylishly around her head, and Baba proudly donned a newly purchased suit. Adam and Khalil were oblivious to any etiquettes, helping themselves to handfuls of cookies laid out on a small table.

"You remember my parents; you met them in the hospital." Nour put an arm around Tamar's waist. "And these brats are my little brothers— Adam and Khalil, come say hello to Tamar."

Nour purposely didn't mention Abdulrahman. Baba and Mama thought it best just to keep quiet about him. People wouldn't understand, Baba said. Her brother's time in jail was nearly done, and Nour felt a small drop of optimism during their last visit to the jail.

"Wow, *akhuti*." Abdulrahman exclaimed when he heard about her actions that night. "That was a really.... really stupid thing to do. You could have been killed."

Nour was surprised. She had worried that he would be disappointed with her, think her actions unpatriotic, but when she looked into his eyes, she saw admiration and understood that this experience changed him. She decided, however, not to tell Abdulrahman about the president's award— that might be pushing things a little too far.

Plus, she was determined not to let anything or anyone spoil her excitement. She was honored to be meeting the president, who she learned was forthright about people showing each other respect, especially towards

Arabs who live under the Israeli occupation. She was also proud to be the first recipient, along with Tamar and Rivki, of The Tribe of Humanity Award.

Mama and Baba were proud of her too, though they refrained from bragging about it too much. Not everyone they knew was impressed. Mama had told Aunt Heba, who told Fadwa, who made her feelings known in the form of a curt text. "Collecting a prize from the Zionist president? Ashamed to call you my cousin!" She wrote to Nour. The protest in Ramallah and her subsequent banishment had done little to dilute Fadwa's hard stance toward Israel.

Nour did not take it personally though. Thanks to her father, she now understood the complexity of the situation. It was emotional, divisive, and everyone was entitled to his or her own views. Still, she was filled with frustration every time events from the train replayed in her mind.

She struggled to fathom what drove a person to such desperation that he or she wanted to kill another human being. Propelled by curiosity, Nour discovered the stabber's name was Ashraf Abu Jamal. He was from one of the Palestinian villages on the outskirts of Jerusalem. His brother, Muhammad, had been murdered a few weeks earlier by Israeli forces. The Israeli authorities said Muhammad had carried out a terrorist attack using his car. He killed three people and was shot dead at the scene. Because of that, Nour learned, the family's house was destroyed by the army. Reports in the Arabic media told her too that Abu Jamal's wife left him the morning of the attack and that he was destitute. She almost felt sorry for him and was relieved he was still alive, even if he was behind bars. Maybe he would feel remorse like Abdulrahman now did.

"I understand things are not good here," she questioned Baba one day. "Israel stole our ancestral lands, controls our people's lives, and humiliates us, but I don't see how attacking a random person, an old man at that, helps strengthen our nation or bring us closer to having our own state."

Baba nodded in agreement and Nour's heart went out to him for being the only person who seemed to understand her.

"The way I see it," she went on. "Israel is here to stay. It might not be the country of my people, but I still think we need to make the most of what we have, strive to improve ourselves, through education and advocacy, while at the same time viewing the other people who live here as human beings."

Baba fixed her with his wise eyes. "Nour, I can't think of anyone else more deserving of the president's award. Before anything else, we are all human beings."

· · ·

Rivki spied Nour and Tamar as soon as she entered the reception area. She no longer needed crutches, even though her leg was still weak.

"We should have brought the wheelchair," she heard Ima mutter as she hobbled slowly across the room like an old lady.

"It's fine, Ima," Rivki called back, shame spreading across her ever-pale face. Why did her family have to draw so much attention all the time? She considered how out of place they must look right now. Dark clothes in a bright room, in the plush residence of Israel's president. Stuffy bodies surrounded by relaxed, secular people. She understood the president welcomed everyone, all the country's citizens—he'd written it in the letter she received explaining the award.

"Humanity is more than the differences between people," he'd said. "That is why you have been selected to receive the Tribe of Humanity Award."

"Rivki," the other two girls called to her in unison. Their greeting spurred her on and she dismissed thoughts of any objections her family might have to her newfound friendships. She hoped this would make them see humanity, and make them more open and accepting from now on.

Tamar and Nour were at her side now. Tamar slipped an arm around her waist and Nour took her arm, guiding her into a large armchair. She huffed as she sat.

"So good to see you walking now! Doesn't it still hurt?" Tamar scanned the folds of her long skirt for signs of a bandage.

"*Baruch Ha-Shem*, I can walk now, just a little, not too far, but the bandages came off last week. It still feels weird." Rivki stroked her thigh.

"Oh yes, I remember when they removed the bandage after I broke my arm. I felt so exposed." Nour laughed.

"Oh, you broke your arm?" Rivki glanced nervously at Ima, but she was busy examining the refreshments.

"Yes, a few months ago..." Nour wavered. "It's a long story."

Rivki looked up at her again, taking in her impressive black hair and stylish suit. "Well, I'm just so happy to see both of you," she said speaking from her heart. "I don't know if I ever thanked you enough for what you did."

"You saved *us*!" Nour and Tamar exclaimed in unison again and all three girls started laughing.

When Rivki looked up again, she noticed Abba studying them. She gave him a curious smile, and he smiled back, encouragingly. Her body relaxed now, as she chatted with her two new friends like it was the most natural thing in the world.

The days immediately following the attack, Rivki's family tiptoed around her as if she might break. She stayed in the hospital for nearly a week but, unlike last time, Ima made sure someone was always with her. Abba, Esti, or Zehava sat willingly at her bedside, entertaining her with stories from the family or from the neighborhood. They wanted to understand what had happened, why she'd bolted from Esti's wedding, and why she'd flown at a terrorist who was holding a knife. They'd all heard about her biting his hand, though no one confronted her then about her actions.

Then Dr. Jalal gave her the all-clear to go home. He was pleased that her intestinal surgery was holding up and the Crohn's was still in check. "You're very lucky, young lady," he told her, signing the release papers.

As soon as they were home, however, the inquisition began. Rivki tried, but it was hard to find the words to explain the doubts she had about her life, her community, her family, and her place in it. How could she tell those who loved her that she rejected the path laid out for her? It was too big to shrink into a few words.

Then, one night when it was just her and her parents left in the living room—her younger siblings asleep and Esti across town in her new home with Yaakov—she found the courage and the words.

"I remember feeling like that at your age," Abba surprised her. "It's natural to question life, Rivkale, to have doubts, especially after everything you've been through with the Crohn's and now the *pigua*."

Ima sat quietly at his side, and Rivki again traced the weathered lines across her face. Sadness filled her, and she truly hoped that she would not have to choose again between family and life.

"No, it's not surprising you feel like this," Abba continued, "but you need to trust in *Ha-Shem*—"

"I do trust Him." Rivki flicked her eyes at Ima. "I just don't know if this lifestyle is for me. I don't want the same things as Esti. I want... to study, have a real job where I can help people."

"Well, you're just nervous about getting married. That's also normal," Ima's voice was so low, Rivki wasn't sure she was speaking.

Rivki shook her head. "No, Ima. I don't even want to get married. At least not like this, and certainly not yet. If that means I have to choose between being here or leaving then I—"

"You don't need to leave, Rivki," Abba spoke clearly. "We will love you no matter what you choose. You will always be our daughter."

Silence descended between them, and Rivki thought she heard the crack of Ima's heart, but then her mother spoke. Louder this time. "We will always love you, Rivka. *Ha-Shem* will help you find your way."

Rivki hoped her mother was right. She prayed every night that He would show her a sign, guide her to the right path, and help fill the hole that still burned inside her, even though Dr. Jalal had fixed the one in her intestine.

She still believed in *Ha-Shem* and she wanted to stay with her family, her friends, her community, but it stifled her. She could no longer blindly follow the path laid out for her. Watching Esti now build her life with Yaakov made her realize more than ever before that she wanted something different. She told her sister as much when she came over to visit a few days after her conversation with Ima and Abba.

"I blame myself." Esti slid into her old bed like it was still her spot. "I didn't mean to desert you, Rivi, didn't mean to forget about you. I just got swept up in wedding fever. I'm so sorry, Rivi, but I guess you'll understand what it's like when it's your turn."

"Esti, I love you, you know that, but I just don't want it, I don't want any of it. I want to work, to help people. That's more important to me than finding a husband." Rivki's voice was sharp now. She was determined to make her sister listen this time.

Esti blinked at her. Rivki couldn't tell if she was shocked or impressed. Then she just nodded and said, "You're right, marriage is hard."

Now it was Rivki's turn to be surprised. She regarded Esti. She still looked the same on the outside, her dark-haired *sheitel* closely mirrored her hair. Was she unhappy in her new home, in her new life? Rivki was so busy with her own misery she hadn't considered what Esti might be going through, moving in with a stranger and doing whatever it was husbands and wives did. She shuddered and hugged her sister.

"I'm here if you need me," she whispered in her sister's ear. She felt Esti stiffen, but she remained silent, strengthening Rivki's resolve that an arranged marriage would never be an option for her.

The letter that came from the president, informing that she was the recipient of the Tribe of Humanity Award, served only to strengthen her views. She hoped it would also show her family there was more to life than getting married and raising a family. She was delighted when they all agreed to attend the ceremony.

TAMAR, NOUR, RIVKI

"You're all invited to take your seats in the main hall," announced the woman in the navy suit.

Tamar followed as she ushered the three families, representatives of three distinct Jerusalem tribes, into the auditorium. It was filled now, mostly with official-looking people. Suits and fancy dresses. She wondered who exactly turned out to witness three sixteen-year-old girls—one secular Jewish, one Haredi, and one Arab—receive an award for fighting a terrorist.

She searched the crowd for the familiar faces of two people who meant so much to her. They'd promised to be there for her. A few rows back, beyond the spaces reserved for family members and dignitaries, Tamar spied Aviv and Ami.

"Hi!" she mouthed across the hall, waving excitedly.

Aviv bounced in her chair and returned the wave in the same manic way. Ami crinkled his entire face into a broad smile that made Tamar blush.

Floating behind Nour and Rivki to their designated seats in the front row, Tamar recognized the old couple from the train. Mr. Isaac and his wife. They were dressed smartly, looking a whole lot better than the horrendous night on the light rail. She bent down to kiss Mr. Isaac on the cheek, and he encompassed her hand with his large one. "Thank you," he rasped.

Tamar smiled and took up her seat. She turned her attention now to the president, who was now standing behind the lectern.

"A few years ago, I identified a very real threat in our society, and particularly in Jerusalem, our capital. We have been going through a dynamic change, one that has not been obvious, but which threatens the very fabric of our existence.

"In the State of Israel today, the basic systems that form people's consciousness are tribal and separate, broken down into distinct tribes. In light of that fragmentation, I issued a wake-up call for people to come together and rekindle the hope of mankind, the hope of humanity, the Israeli hope.

"I have called to shed a spotlight on partnerships between the various sectors and for people who are bold and willing to go against the grain of their own group and to stand up for what is right.

"Today, I have before me the first of those people. Three young women, one from each of the tribes, who took it upon themselves to fight for justice and humanity. In the process, they saved precious lives.

"These three women are courageous and should serve as a clear example to others of what can happen when a person looks beyond their tribe and sees the other, sees the humanity."

The president motioned first to Rivki, who stood up shakily from her seat. Slowly, but sure-footed, she headed to the podium. She was followed by Nour and finally by Tamar.

"Rivki, Nour, and Tamar," the president addressed them with kind eyes. "You have proven that the superficial disguises of your communities are inconsequential, that cooperation can bridge all divides, and that Jerusalem's tribes can find a way to work together. I now name you all as the first members of a new Jerusalem tribe. One that is not defined by a single group, one that does not exclude anyone. It is a tribe that belongs to everyone and is for everyone. It is all-inclusive. It is the tribe of humanity."

Looking out at the sea of faces, Tamar realized that her stomach was free from the tickle of butterflies. She was filled with a new power that spread out all around her. Grabbing first Rivki's hand and then Nour's, she raised both her arms high in the air. It was a victory, a moment to be proud of, a moment, she hoped, that would show others the importance of unity.

ACKNOWLEDGEMENTS

I don't really remember how my obsession with words, books, and stories started but it probably had something to do with my parents and my grandparents, especially Grandma Vi, who encouraged me to do what I loved and always let me believe that anything was possible. No dream is foolish or too big. Grandma Vi also loved to tell and hear a good story. She was often my sounding board for ideas and the first person I would read my stories to as a child. I know that she and Grandpa Sid, who was a big reader, would have been so proud of my achievements in journalism and now in literature.

I also could not have written *Parallel Lines* without the incredible and constant support of my husband, Michael. Mike is my rock, my base, my foundation. Without his ability to sponge up my frustrations or withstand my rage when my writing goes sour, I would not have been able to complete this work.

I must also say a big thank you to my children, Ben, Gefen, and Ela. Now young adults, you put up with a work-obsessed, writing-obsessed mother who sometimes refused to do anything but sit in front of her computer and throw words at the page. Thank you, darlings. Your experiences as adolescents growing up in Israel gave me so many ideas and examples for this book. Thank you for listening to my ideas. I really hope that the publication of *Parallel Lines* makes you realize, too, that anything is possible. Dreams are achievable. And thank you to my parents, Norma and Eli, who worked hard so I could chase those dreams.

And now to those who provided me with the framework and expertise that allowed this project to come together. I will start with my former boss, *Washington Post*'s Jerusalem Bureau Chief William Booth, who taught me how to write a news story and gave me the opportunity to better understand and experience the Israeli-Palestinian conflict up close.

Kathie Giorgio, you were a great writing coach who taught me about discipline and style. Melissa Weiss, my editor at *Jewish Insider*, thank you for reading over the final draft and finding my mistakes. Steve Linde, my former editor from *The Jerusalem Post* and lifetime friend, for also giving *Parallel Lines* a thorough edit. Michael Milshtein, I am forever impressed that you speak Hebrew, Arabic, English, and even Yiddish fluently. And to editor Cate Perry, who also gave the final work a thorough readover, thank you.

My good friends Gaynor Mann, Ada Harvard and Alon Velan, thanks for being early readers of *Parallel Lines* and encouraging me with kind words, and cousin Leah Corper, who was my first relative to read my first novel.

I would also like to thank Gefen Eglash and her friends, Shira, Noga, Inbar, and Yamin for providing the inspiration for Tamar and her story. To prolific journalist Tzippy Yarom and her daughters for helping me to build the character of Rivki, as well as Tali Chasson, my faithful hairdresser, who made me look pretty while giving me loads of details about the ultra-Orthodox community, and to Malkie Mann who patiently answered endless questions about life as a Haredi woman. Bayan, Sarah, Tamara, and Maram, intelligent and impressive young Palestinian women, thank you for sharing with me your experiences of growing up Palestinian, Arab, and Muslim in Jerusalem. I hope you all stay strong.

GLOSSARY

Abba—Father (Hebrew)

abaya—cloak or robe-like dress for men (Arabic)

achi—my brother (Hebrew)

akhuti—my sister (Arabic)

aleph—the first letter of the Hebrew alphabet

Allah—God (Arabic)

Allah Hu Akbar—Allah or God is Great (Arabic)

Am Yisrael Chai—the nation of Israel lives (Hebrew)

Ani beseder—I am fine (Hebrew)

Aravia—Arab female (Hebrew)

Asur—forbidden (Hebrew)

Ayawa—yes in spoken language (Arabic)

Baba—father in spoken language (Arabic)

Bagrut—matriculation exams (Israel)

balaboste—Yiddish expression describing a good homemaker

Baruch Ha-Shem—Thank God or God is blessed (Hebrew)

bashert —a person's soulmate, especially when considered as an ideal or predestined marriage partner (Yiddish)

Bais Ya'akov—elementary and secondary schools for ultra-Orthodox Jewish girls

bedeken—the ceremony where the groom veils the bride in a Jewish wedding

ben ha-cham—a wise or learned son (Yiddish)

beseder—fine (Hebrew)

bet—second letter of the alphabet (Hebrew)

bevakasha—please (Hebrew)

binti—my daughter (Arabic)

B'ezrat Ha-Shem—please God (Hebrew)

bli neder—God willing (Hebrew)

brachot—blessings (Hebrew)

chatan—groom (Hebrew)

Cheshvan—second month of the Jewish calendar, usually around October

chuppah—Jewish wedding canopy

chutzim—matriculation exams for ultra-Orthodox Jewish schools in Israel

cookoo—ponytail

dati—religious (Hebrew)

dosim—ultra-Orthodox (Hebrew slang)

Eid—Muslim holiday marking the end of the month-long Ramadan fast

erev tov—good evening (Hebrew)

finjan—small pan for making coffee (Arabic)

freiers—suckers (Yiddish/Hebrew)

goy/goyim—non-Jew or non-Jews (Yiddish)

habibi/habibti—habibi (m), *habibti* (f) my love (Arabic)

Ha-Cham—wise (Hebrew)

Halacha—Jewish religious law

hamsa—a five-fingered hand considered a good luck charm (Hebrew, Arabic)

Haredim—ultra-Orthodox Jews characterized by their strict adherence to Jewish law and traditions.

Ha-Shem—Jewish name for G-d (Hebrew)

hefetz hashud—suspicious package that could be a bomb (Hebrew)

hijab—Islamic head covering, usually a scarf (Arabic)

Ima—mother (Hebrew)

Intifada—violent Palestinian uprising against the Israel (Arabic/Hebrew)

istishhadi—someone intentionally seeking martyrdom by Terror operation (Arabic)

kallah—bride (Hebrew)

kapara—I love you so much, you are the atonement of my sins. (Hebrew slang)

khalas—that's enough (Hebrew slang, Arabic)

keffiyehs—traditional Arab headscarf

keta—a fling (Hebrew slang)

khubez—bread (Arabic)

kippot—yarmulkas (Hebrew)

kita yud—10th grade (Hebrew)

Kollel—an educational institute for the full-time, advanced study of the Talmud and rabbinic literature

laffa—large flatbread (Hebrew/Arabic)

layla tov—Goodnight (Hebrew)

lechaim—a celebratory toast meaning 'to life' (Hebrew)

ma kara lach?—what happened to you (Hebrew)

manhig—leader (Hebrew)

mashallah—Arabic phrase that is used to express a feeling of awe or beauty

matsav—the situation, a Hebrew phrase often used to refer to the situation or conflict between Israelis and Palestinians.

maqluba—a traditional Palestinian dish of meat, rice, and fried vegetables placed in a pot and then flipped upside down when served. Literal translation is "upside-down." (Arabic)

mazboot—correct or exactly (Arabic)

mechitza—wall set up to divide genders at an event (Hebrew)

meideleh—unmarried girl (Yiddish)

mehabel/mehabelet—terrorist (m.f.) (Hebrew)

metzuyan—excellent (Hebrew)

mikve—Jewish ritual bath (Hebrew)

mitzvoth—commandment or good deed (Hebrew)

motek—sweety or cutey (Hebrew)

mumtaz—excellent (Arabic)

musakhan—Palestinian dish composed of roasted chicken baked with onions, sumac, allspice, saffron, and fried pine nuts served on flat bread. Often considered the national dish of Palestine.

muqawama—resistance, used by Palestinians to describe the military or any other means of struggle to overthrow Israeli control over aspects of Palestinian life (Arabic)

Nakba—catastrophe (Arabic) usually referring to the events of 1948, when many Palestinians were displaced from their homeland by the creation of the new state of Israel

nekama—revenge (Hebrew)

pashkavilim—notices to keep the ultra-Orthodox Jewish public informed (Yiddish)

payot—side locks worn by ultra-Orthodox Jews (Hebrew/Yiddish)

Peleg Yerushalmi—an ultra-Orthodox Jewish sect.

pigua/piguim—terrorist attack/attacks (Hebrew)

prutza—immodest woman (Yiddish)

sababa—great (Hebrew slang)

Savta—grandmother (Hebrew)

Samet hat—top hat worn by ultra-Orthodox Jewish men

Salam—hello or peace (Arabic)

Setty—grandmother (Arabic)

Shabbat—Jewish sabbath (Hebrew)

Shabbos—Jewish sabbath (Yiddish)

shadchanit—matchmaker (Hebrew/Yiddish)

shalom—hello or peace (Hebrew)

sharmuta—whore (Arabic/Hebrew slang)

sheitel—wig worn by ultra-Orthodox Jewish women (Hebrew/Yiddish)

sheshbesh—backgammon (Hebrew)

shiduchim/ shidduch—match between a man and a woman (Hebrew/Yiddish)

shinshin/shnat sherut—post-high school, pre-army voluntary program (Hebrew)

shiksa—non-Jewish woman (Yiddish/Hebrew)

shish taouk—marinated chunks of chicken (Arabic)

shuk—market (Hebrew)

shukran—thank you (Arabic)

shu ismekk?—what is your name? (f) (Arabic)

shvi—sit (f) (Hebrew)

simcha—celebratory event (Hebrew)

suq—market (Arabic)

tatreez—Palestinian embroidery stitch (Arabic)

tehillim—psalms (Hebrew)

tinokot shenishbu—babies that were held captive by non-Jews and therefore could not have a Torah education (Hebrew/Yiddish) *toda*—thank you (Hebrew)

Torah—Jewish bible (Hebrew)

Tawjihi—Palestinian matriculation exams

thobe—robe or dress worn by an Arab man

Tikva—hope (Hebrew)

traif—non-kosher food (Hebrew/Yiddish)

tzadik—righteous man (Hebrew/Yiddish)

tzav rishon—*initial* interview with the army literally meaning 'first call up' (Hebrew)

vort—Jewish engagement party (Yiddish)

walla—*an expression* of surprise (Hebrew slang)

yallah—let's get going (Arabic/Hebrew slang)

yofi—beautiful/wonderful (Hebrew)

Yamim Tovim—good days, referring to the Jewish high holidays (Yiddish)

zona—whore (Hebrew)

PLACES

Damascus Gate (English)—one of the main entrances to the Old City of Jerusalem. In Hebrew it's called *Sha'ar Shechem*; in Arabic it's called *Bab el-Amud*

French Hill—largely secular Jewish neighborhood in Jerusalem where Tamar lives.

Hadassah Hospital—There are two Hadassah Hospitals in Jerusalem, one on Mt. Scopus, the other in Ein Kerem.

Jaffa Gate (English)—one of the main entrances to the Old City of Jerusalem. In Hebrew it's called *Sha'ar Yafo*; in Arabic it's called *Bab el-Khalil*.

Jerusalem—In Arabic, *al-Quds*; In Hebrew *Yerushalayim*.

Knesset—Israel's parliament.

Mamilla—an outdoor shopping mall that is attached to the Old City.

Ma'alot Dafna—largely ultra-Orthodox neighborhood of Jerusalem where Rivki lives.

Mea Shearim—ultra-Orthodox neighborhood of Jerusalem.

Pisgat Zeev—a northern, eastern suburb of Jerusalem.

Qalandia Crossing—an Israeli military checkpoint between Jerusalem and the Palestinian city of Ramallah

Ramallah—de facto capital of the Palestinian territories/Palestinian authority

Shuafat—Palestinian neighborhood and adjacent Refugee camp in Jerusalem where Nour lives. (Residents there largely identify as Palestinians and most are not citizens of Israel but can access Israel for work and healthcare)

Tachana Merkazit—Central Bus Station (serving west Jerusalem)

ABOUT THE AUTHOR

Ruth Marks Eglash is an award-winning veteran journalist based in Israel. She currently writes for an array of media outlets such as *Jewish Insider* and *Fox News*. She spent eight years as the Jerusalem correspondent for *The Washington Post*, and 13 years as senior editor and beat reporter at *The Jerusalem Post*. In 2010, Ruth won the United Nations Alliance of Civilization Journalism Award.

Born and raised in the U.K. to a British mother and an immigrant Israeli father, Ruth studied media communications at the University of Leeds and immigrated to Israel in the mid-1990s. After short stints in New York and in Milwaukee, Wis., she now lives just outside Jerusalem with her husband, three young adult children, and a Shih-Tzu named Kylie.

NOTE FROM THE AUTHOR

Word-of-mouth is crucial for any author to succeed. If you enjoyed *Parallel Lines*, please leave a review online—anywhere you are able. Even if it's just a sentence or two. It would make all the difference and would be very much appreciated.

Thanks!
Ruth Marks Eglash

We hope you enjoyed reading this title from:

BLACK❧ROSE
writing™

www.blackrosewriting.com

Subscribe to our mailing list – *The Rosevine* – and receive **FREE** books, daily deals, and stay current with news about upcoming releases and our hottest authors.
Scan the QR code below to sign up.

Already a subscriber? Please accept a sincere thank you for being a fan of Black Rose Writing authors.

View other Black Rose Writing titles at
www.blackrosewriting.com/books and use promo code
PRINT to receive a **20% discount** when purchasing.